TOO MUCH LIKE LOVE

SWEET LIFE IN SEATTLE
BOOK 5

ANDREA SIMONNE

Too Much Like Love

By Andrea Simonne

Copyright © 2021 Andrea Simonne

All rights reserved. Published by Liebe Publishing

First Print Edition, December 15, 2021

ISBN: 978-1-945968-04-4

Edited by Hot Tree Editing: www.hotreeediting.com

Cover Design by: LBC Graphics

No part of this book may be reproduced in any form or by any means, electronic or mechanical, including photocopying, recording, or by any information storage and retrieval system, without the express written permission of the author.

Publisher's Note: This is a work of fiction. Names, characters, places, and incidents either are the product of the author's imagination or are used fictitiously. Any resemblance to actual persons, living or dead, business establishments, events, or locales is entirely coincidental.

CHAPTER ONE

"Life & The Art of Automobile Maintenance
By Brody Austin

"Brace yourself. You never know what's going to roll into the shop."

"Can you at least look at me when I'm talking to you?"

Brody is lying on his back under a Toyota Tacoma with a small flashlight in his hand, examining the undercarriage. The owner, a regular customer, had taken it off-road over the weekend and said there was a rattle afterward.

"I need my car *now*. For God's sake, are you even listening to me?" the angry female voice goes on. "Are you hearing a word I'm saying under there?"

Even though Brody has three other mechanics working for him, he somehow knows this angry female is talking to him. He sighs and pushes himself out from under the truck.

First thing he sees is a pair of black stiletto pumps with heels like ice picks. Shoes you could lobotomize someone with.

"Finally!"

Attached to those ice picks are long tan legs and a black skirt that stops above the knee. The bottom half of a power suit. Blonde hair falls around her shoulders, and even with the scowl on her face, he can tell she's good-looking.

"Can I help you with something?" he asks.

She throws her hands in the air. "Yes, you can help me! Why do you think I'm standing here? It's not for my health!"

Brody doesn't bother responding or even getting up. She appears to be having a tantrum, and he figures it's best to let her ride it out.

"Is my car ready yet? Why is it sitting in the same spot as it was this morning?" she rants. "What kind of lousy place is this?"

Unfortunately, when you own a garage, rude customers are part of the package.

Slowly, he stands up, slips the mini flashlight back into his pocket, then pushes the creeper he was lying on aside.

Glancing around with annoyance, he realizes he's the only one out here working. Must be lunchtime. Brody grabs a cloth to wipe his hands. The woman in front of him is still having her tantrum.

"You guys called me with an estimate that was basically price gouging! I assume it's done by now, at least."

"Is that your Audi?" he asks, nodding toward the silver Audi parked off to the side. It was brought in this morning with a tow. He'd been in the back office working on payroll, but Chavez told him about it.

"Of course it's mine." She rolls her eyes. "Is it finished yet? Can I drive it?"

"Nope." He continues wiping his hands. Chavez told him the car was having ignition trouble, stalled out at a stop sign. Luckily, it was an easy fix, and they were just waiting on some spark plugs to be delivered from a local auto supply. "It's not running yet. We'll call you when it's done."

"*Call* me? I don't want a phone call! I've been waiting all morning. I took an Uber to get here. I want my car!"

"Well, it's not ready."

"Maybe I should tow it to a different garage. One that knows what they're doing!"

"That's your prerogative." Brody studies her. She's a little older than he is, probably in her late thirties. Watching her, he can tell she's having a bad day. The power suit is rumpled, her hair's sticking out like a banshee, and her eyes are red like she's been crying. He's seen this before. For some reason, car trouble and bad days go hand in hand. Despite her rudeness, he feels a little sorry for her. "Look, it's an easy fix," he says. "Go have lunch somewhere and relax. There are plenty of restaurants nearby. We'll have it ready for you in a couple hours."

"Relax?" Her red eyes stare at him as if he suggested she go jump off a cliff. "I don't need some jerk telling me to *relax*. Got it?"

His eyes narrow. He's dealt with plenty of rude customers, but apparently she's going for a gold medal.

But then he shrugs to himself. Screw it. Over the years, he's learned that not everybody wants to be helped. You can throw someone a lifeline, but that doesn't mean they'll catch it. Some people would rather drown.

"Actually, where is your manager?" she asks in a snotty tone. "I'd like to speak to him. Better yet, let me speak to the owner. I'm sure he'd like to hear all about your insolence."

Brody tries not to smirk. He tosses the cloth he was wiping his hands with onto a nearby tool cart. "You're looking at him."

"What do you mean?"

He stands up to his full height of six feet and crosses his arms. "I'm the owner."

"You've *got* to be kidding me."

"Nope."

She doesn't seem to know what to do with this. "How *old* are you?"

"Old enough."

She shakes her head. "This is unbelievable. I shouldn't let you idiots touch my car with a ten-foot pole. Who knows what you'll do to it."

He's getting irritated by her rudeness. Calling him names is one thing, but insulting his skills as a mechanic is another. "Look, you want to have your car towed to another garage? Be my guest. But decide soon. I need to get back to work."

Brody drags the creeper over with his foot and lies down on it again. He pulls the mini flashlight from his pocket and slides himself back under the Tacoma.

To hell with this unreasonable woman.

He stares at the truck's undercarriage and waits. He figures she's either going to call for another tow or leave.

"*Fine,*" she says, exasperated. "I'll be back in two hours, and my car better be ready. If not, I'll be leaving a nasty review online."

Brody rolls his eyes. He hates social media. Hates the way any idiot with an internet connection can post smack about his business.

Eventually he hears her ice pick shoes walking away. He rolls out from under the truck and sits up, watching her head toward the busy street, lingering on the determined way she walks. He watches until she rounds the corner and disappears from sight.

Then he gets up and goes into the break room, where he finds all three of his employees lounging around the table, watching the baseball game on the small flat-screen television that he never should have set up in the first place.

"What the hell is going on in here? What did I say about everybody taking lunch at the same time? I don't want the garage left empty."

"It's not empty. *You* were out there," Trevor says, holding a burger in one hand while shoveling fries into his mouth with the other, his brown eyes glued to the screen.

"There should be two of us out there at all times."

"Sorry." Anka smiles at Brody sheepishly. "I'll go back out. I'm done eating anyway." She gets up and puts her lunch bag in the fridge. Anka is his newest employee, and the only female he's ever hired. He knows she's been trying to fit in, and it hasn't been easy.

"Thanks. I appreciate it."

"Yeah, we *really* appreciate it," Trevor says in a smart-ass voice. "That way I can watch more of the game."

After she leaves, Brody smacks him in the head.

"Hey, *ow*. That hurt! What was that for?"

"Knock that shit off." Trevor is his twenty-two-year-old cousin, which is the only reason he hired him three months ago. A decision he's been regretting more every day. "Stop giving her such a hard time."

"I'm just helping her learn her place." He smirks. "The little woman."

Brody smacks him again.

"*Ow!* What the hell, dude?" He rubs the side of his head. "Are you trying to give me a concussion?"

"I'm trying to knock some sense into you. I'm serious. Leave her alone."

"I don't know why you hired her in the first place," Trevor grumbles. "Since when do women know jack shit about cars?"

"I hired her because she's an excellent mechanic," Brody says. "And if you want to keep working here, you'll treat her with respect or you'll be looking for a new job."

"Sheesh." Trevor rubs his head some more and sticks another fry in his mouth. "Touchy, touchy."

Brody frowns. He's known Trevor his whole life. As a favor to his aunt Jeanie, Brody gave him a job when he finished his mechanic's training, but he wasn't expecting so much attitude and entitlement.

Chavez laughs. "Trevor's jealous because Anka figured out that hybrid's electrical problem while the genius here was still sucking his thumb and looking confused."

"Screw you," Trevor says. "I would have figured it out if she hadn't stuck her nose in where it wasn't wanted."

"Sure you would have."

Brody looks over. "Chavez, I need you to run by the auto supply and pick up the spark plugs for that Audi."

"What?" He glances over at Brody. "Why? They said they'd deliver it. I still got that engine rebuild I'm working on."

"I know, but do it anyway. I need that Audi ready to go in two hours."

Chavez shakes his head. "Let me guess, that crazy lady called and had another meltdown about her car."

"What do you mean?"

"She's loco, dude. She was ranting and raving when the tow truck brought it in. Kept telling me all men are scumbags, and that I was a scumbag too. I nearly asked the tow truck driver to take her car someplace else."

Brody wishes he had. "Just get it done so we don't have to deal with her anymore."

Chavez nods. "Fine."

Brody's eyes flicker to the game on-screen. "What's the score?"

"Three-two, Giants."

He nods. *Hopefully the Giants win.*

Brody goes back out to check over the truck again and finally finds the cause of the rattle—a 10mm bolt on the skid plate got knocked loose.

When Chavez shows up with the spark plugs, he tells him to go back to the engine rebuild and that he'll fix the Audi himself.

Once he's got the car running perfectly, he heads over to the front desk and brings up the invoice on the computer. The owner's name is Nina Ellis. He leaves her a voice mail and also sends a text to let her know her car's finished and ready to be picked up.

The afternoon gets busy, and Brody doesn't think much more

about the Audi, except when it gets near closing, and he notices her car is still sitting there. Brody calls and texts her again, snorting to himself. Apparently it wasn't as urgent as she made it out to be.

"I can't believe that lady still hasn't picked up her car," Chavez says, coming over to where Brody's finished replacing the brakes on a 1971 Camaro he did a rebuild on a few years ago. "It figures, doesn't it?"

Brody shrugs. "I hope she shows up soon, because I have to leave by seven." He already told his cousin Tori he'd stop by for a visit. She gave birth to a baby boy named Oliver a couple of months ago. Her sister-in-law, Blair, also had a baby back in April. A little girl named Ava. He was happy for them both but had to admit it was weird that everyone around him seemed to be having babies all of a sudden. It definitely wasn't anything he could relate to.

"What do you want to bet the loco lady doesn't show up until tomorrow?" Chavez says. "She'll make a big stink about how she never got any messages from us and will want her invoice reduced."

Brody nods. They've both seen that sort of thing before, people trying to work an angle. Fixing cars, you pretty much saw everything.

He knows mechanics in general have a bad reputation, but he takes pride in the fact that his shop is 100 percent aboveboard. His crew does excellent work, and his prices are fair. He never rips anyone off or tries to upsell his customers. It's the reason they're so damn busy all the time. He's grown a solid business the last five years and even has a waiting list of classic car owners.

By quarter to seven everyone's left for the day, and Brody is going through the receipts. The Audi is still sitting there. He empties the till and locks up all the cash and paperwork in the office safe until he can make it to the bank tomorrow.

Once he's done, the clock says it's five after seven. He's still in the back office when he hears the front door chimes open.

"Hellooo?"

The voice is female. He gets up and goes out front.

"There you are," she purrs. "I was hoping it'd be... you."

He raises a brow. It's the Audi's owner, finally come to collect her car—except something's not right.

She's leaning against the counter. Her clothes and hair look like she's been through a windstorm, and she's holding those ice pick heels in one hand, swinging them back and forth.

She smiles at him, though her eyes are bloodshot. Her blouse is opened low enough to show a white bra and smooth cleavage. Despite being barefoot, she seems unsteady on her feet. As he moves closer, a cloud of perfume and alcohol envelopes him.

"I'm here for my...." She licks her lips and seems to have trouble getting her tongue back in her mouth. "My car. I need my car."

Shit. She's plastered.

Brody studies her, trying to decide the best way to handle this. He's had drunk customers before, and it's never pleasant.

"Is there anyone I can call for you?" he asks. "To pick you up."

"What do you mean? Give me my... car."

"Maybe a husband or a boyfriend?"

Her face twists into anger. "I don't need... a man. Men are all cog suggers." Her voice slurs as she leans against the counter.

He glances down at her left hand. No wedding ring.

"What about a family member?" he asks. "Or a friend?"

She stares at him bleary-eyed with a mixture of confusion and anger. "What the hell? Give me my car keys."

"I'm sorry," he says, "but I can't do that. You're obviously intoxicated."

"I'm not intogzi... fated."

Brody almost smiles. "I can't allow you to drive, so let's call a friend or family member to come get you, okay? I know you're having a bad day. It happens to all of us." He keeps his voice calm and reasonable. Unfortunately, he's dealt with drunks in his life on a personal level.

She blows her breath out. "I'm fine."

He glances over at the clock on the wall. It's already a quarter after seven. He's going to be late getting to Tori's. "Your name's Nina, right?" He leans closer to her on the counter. "Listen, Nina, let's give your best friend a call. What do you say?"

She stares at him with those bloodshot eyes and yells, "*What's your problem? I'm not drunk!*"

He pulls back and changes tactics. "All right, well, I can't give you the car until you pay." He figures he'll get her address and then call her an Uber.

"Fine." She stands up and reaches for the purse on her shoulder, struggling to unzip it. He waits patiently as she finally opens it, tries to pull her wallet out, but flings her purse and all its contents onto the floor instead. "Oh shit."

Sighing to himself, he walks around the counter to where she's now sitting on the floor, clumsily trying to pick up all her stuff. Pens, loose change, lip gloss tubes, lipstick, tampons, antacids, her phone...

Immediately he kneels down and grabs the phone, trying to open it so he can call someone to come get her. The phone is dead though or turned off. It's probably locked, but maybe he can get her to open it once it's turned on.

"Hey, give that back to me!" Nina reaches for her phone.

He holds it away from her, but without warning, she tackles him, knocking him off balance.

"What the hell!" he yells right before pain shoots through his shoulder from hitting the hard floor. "Get off me."

Meanwhile, Nina doesn't appear to be going anywhere. The smell of alcohol coming off her is ten times stronger up close. She's squirming on him like an octopus, all hands and legs, trying to reach for the phone, which he's holding at arm's length. There's a crazed look in her blue eyes. "*Don't turn it on!*"

If the situation were different and she weren't drunk and acting nuts, he might have found this amusing, possibly even arousing, but instead he's getting pissed. "You need to get off me right now."

She bites her lip, wiggling upward, still reaching for the phone.

The scent of feminine sweat, perfume, and booze surrounds him. He doesn't want to hurt her, but he needs to take control.

And then, before he knows it, she manages to snatch the phone from his hand. She sits up and hurls it across the room so hard it smashes against the wall, clattering as the case flies off.

He stares at her in disbelief. "You just broke your own phone."

"Good."

This situation has gotten so strange that Brody's not even sure what to do anymore.

He glances down at her body. She's straddling his waist, her black skirt hiked up around her thighs. He catches a glimpse of white lace panties. Her blouse is missing a button and hanging open to reveal an eyeful of cleavage along with that lacy white bra. He's trying not to stare, but he can't seem to look away.

This is too weird.

She must have noticed where his gaze was pointed, because she's smiling at him. "You're really... hot. Do you know that?" She licks her lips. "Do you want to have sex?"

Brody chuckles. This is turning into a bizarre porno. Except he's not interested in having sex with a woman who's blind drunk.

"Come on...." She moves her body against him. "Let's have sex."

"I don't think so."

Nina smiles. "Kiss me. You know you want to." She leans closer and then, without warning, belches loudly. It sounds like a foghorn.

"*Jesus Christ*." Brody turns his head away and waves a hand in front of his nose. "Damn, woman. Let me guess, onion rings?"

"Oops." She giggles, bringing her hand in front of her mouth as she sits up again, swaying on top of him.

He uses the opportunity to put his hands around her waist and lifts her off of him.

"Hey, wait," she says, giving him a loopy drunken smile. "Come back."

He puts her on the floor and then sits next to her. "You need help, Nina. Serious help."

She sucks in her breath at his words and glares at him, straightening her shoulders. He gets an intuitive flash that in her normal life she's probably damn formidable.

"I don't need *anyone*." She's still glaring at him, but then her shoulders slump and her eyes drift shut.

He picks up the fancy striped leather wallet on the floor. It's lined with credit cards, most of them to high-end department stores.

He holds the wallet closer to study her driver's license. Nina Anne Ellis. It shows an address downtown. Out of curiosity, he checks her age. Forty. But then he does a double take on the date.

It's today.

Holy shit.

"Happy birthday, Nina."

She rouses slightly and gives him the stink eye. "Fugg you."

He chuckles at her feistiness. "One hell of a way to spend your fortieth birthday."

Brody studies the ID some more, especially the photo. The long shiny blonde hair and big blue eyes. An all-American girl if he ever saw one. The kind who's probably had everything in life served to her on a silver platter.

But then how the hell did she wind up like this?

She must be having the worst day of her life.

He puts the wallet down and weighs his options. He figures he can call an Uber or he can call the police. Neither sounds appealing. He wouldn't feel right sticking her in a car with a stranger when she's nearly passed out drunk. Calling the police isn't an option he much cared for either.

What the hell am I supposed to do?

It's not like I can leave her here alone in the garage all night.

He sighs to himself. There's one more option. He doesn't like it, but he doesn't see any way around it.

He'd have to bring her home with him.

CHAPTER TWO

> ## Life & The Art of Automobile Maintenance
> ### By Brody Austin
>
>
>
> *"If your engine gets too hot, be sure to let your mechanic cool it down."*

Nina dreams of water. Luscious water cascading over her in a swirling pool, cool and clear, except none of it's going into her mouth. And she's so thirsty, like she's been eating sand.

She opens her eyes and immediately shuts them against the bright light piercing her skull.

"Oh my God," she croaks.

Slowly, she opens them again. The light is terrible, and the pain is a knife stabbing her.

What happened? Where am I?

Her pulse skyrockets.

She attempts to sit up but immediately flops back down on the bed as the room spins like a merry-go-round. Her throat is drier than dust. She tries to swallow but can't get enough saliva.

Somehow, she manages to sit up and take stock of her surroundings. She's in a strange bedroom. Looking down, she still has all her clothes on.

Thank God.

Yesterday comes flooding back. The awfulness of it.

Standing in Noel's office at eight in the morning, and instead of talking about the plans for her birthday or their trip to Aspen, he confessed he was having an affair with Emily—his twenty-four-year-old intern.

In a crazy rage, she threw her hot latte at him. And then she threw everything else within reach, both of them shouting.

It didn't take long for company security to come rushing through the door, for someone to take Noel to the ER with first-degree burns from the coffee and a bleeding forehead from the stapler she'd chucked at him.

Bastard.

He deserved it.

Six years of her life. That's what she gave him. He told her they'd get married once his youngest was out of high school.

But then what does he do instead?

He starts having sex with Emily, who looks like she's in high school herself.

Nina wonders how she could be so stupid. She loved him. And look what that got her.

After they took Noel to the ER, she left. As head of marketing, she had a full schedule, but instead she drove aimlessly through Seattle, half out of her mind, until her car broke down at a stop sign. A tow truck brought her to the nearest garage.

All day people kept texting and calling her—not that she answered. Too many people. Her phone never stopped buzzing. A cacophony of noise. Some of them wishing her a happy birthday, though most of them were from work. Where was she? What about the meeting with Google? Her admin, Davis, said everyone had arrived and was waiting for her in the conference room. More frantic messages. Rochelle and Mark called to see if she was okay and to let her know Google was pissed that she no-showed.

Finally, she turned her phone off.

Except how did I wind up here? And where is "here"?

Judging by the plain decor and the clothes she can see hanging in the open closet, it's some guy's bedroom. The only things of interest are a couple of prints on the wall that look like tribal art.

Nina tries to swallow again, but her throat's too dry. Her head feels like it's stuffed with dirty gym socks. She notices an open door that leads into what appears to be a bathroom, so she forces herself to get up.

The bathroom's small, just a sink, toilet, and shower. It isn't gross, but it could use a good scrubbing. There's a big bottle of hand soap and a few different nail brushes next to the sink, which is a little unusual.

The sink's faucet is all she can focus on though. She blasts it and drinks handful after handful of chlorine-scented water straight from the tap. A far cry from the bottles of Evian she's used to.

Except it tastes like bliss.

She drinks until her stomach cramps with nausea. Finally, Nina turns the tap off and lifts the toilet seat lid to use the bathroom, staring at the dust bunnies in the corner. It occurs to her that she's still drunk.

Amazing how in one day your whole life can be ruined.

Eventually, she gets up. When she sees her reflection in the mirror, she groans in horror. What a mess. She looks every single day of her forty years.

I might as well be eighty.

There's a tube of toothpaste in a cup near the sink, and she grabs it, brushes her teeth with her finger, then splashes cold water on her face.

The towel hanging nearby smells clean at least.

Nina wonders what time it is. She's due at work by eight but has no intention of going in today. At this rate, she wonders if she'll ever go in again.

How can I?

Is she really supposed to sit in meetings with Noel and Emily?

She saw Emily right after they took Noel to the ER. The two of them glared at each other, but then Emily's expression changed until she was looking at Nina with pity. It was unbearable.

Nina finds a hairbrush on the bathroom shelf and uses it to tame her hair. She tries to smooth down her suit, though it's hopelessly wrinkled.

The room spins for a minute, and she grabs the edge of the sink, closing her eyes and taking a deep breath.

All she can see are images of Noel with his intern. The way she always seemed so attentive toward him. The way he always acted so fatherly toward her, or at least that's how Nina saw it.

Turns out she'd been seeing it all wrong though, hadn't she?

Nina wonders how Claudia will view all this. Noel's ex-wife, the one he still has a close relationship with, the one Nina has spent years being jealous of. Nina was even jealous of their kids. All the family vacations they still took. All the holidays they still spent together. Sometimes Nina felt like she was dating a married man.

But Noel was just being a good dad, right? How could Nina fault him for that? She'd felt such agonizing guilt over her jealousy, certain it made her an evil witch. Especially since Claudia had a boyfriend too—Michael, the heart surgeon—and he seemed to handle everything fine. He never demanded more time like greedy Nina did.

She snorts loudly.

To hell with all of them.

She marches into the strange bedroom. She needs to find her shoes and purse, and then she needs to get out of here.

Except neither is in sight. She searches the floor first, but all she finds under the bed are more dust bunnies. She glances over at the nightstand. There's an empty iPhone charger and a lamp. Not much else. Out of curiosity, she opens the drawer. There are condoms. Loose change. Various nuts and bolts. A couple pens and a few scraps of paper with meaningless numbers written on them.

Nina notices some sort of laminated ID. She picks it up. It shows a photo of a handsome young guy with shoulder-length black hair. He appears to be part Native American or maybe Latino. She studies the picture. He looks familiar. The name on the ID says Brody Austin.

And that's when it hits her.

It's the guy from the garage yesterday! The owner, though he had looked too young to be the owner.

Oh no.

She remembers how obnoxious she was toward him. She'd been horrible.

Nina swallows and tries to remember how she got here into what must be his bedroom. Obviously they didn't sleep together. She remembers going to have lunch at a restaurant near the garage and then treating herself to a glass of wine. One became two until finally she switched to martinis.

Things became hazy after that. At some point she left the restaurant and wandered into a local bar, where she kept drinking. There was a jukebox, and she danced with a couple guys. One of them was very persistent, but she gave him the slip by claiming she had to go to the bathroom and leaving out the back.

Nina rubs her forehead. Somehow she must have found her way to the garage again, but she doesn't remember how.

It's not like her to drink so much, but it had felt good to be intoxicated, like an escape. A way to stop thinking.

She shoves the ID back into the drawer and stands up. It's time to get out of here, to go home and take a hot shower and sober up. But first, she needs to find her purse, shoes, and phone.

Quietly, she leaves the bedroom and steps into a dim hallway, the hardwood floor cool beneath her feet. It opens up into a living room and dining room combination. The first thing she notices sitting on the dining room table is her purse.

Hallelujah.

She smiles with relief as she goes over to grab it, then searches inside for her phone. Except when she pulls the phone out, there's something wrong with it. The case is missing, and the screen's cracked. She tries to turn it on, but nothing happens.

Just great.

She slips it back into her purse and then slides the purse onto her shoulder.

When she turns, she glances around the house. The walls have a few more prints—all of them pictures of old-fashioned cars. A huge flat-screen television dominates another wall. There's a case of motor oil being used as an end table next to a couple of black leather couches that look straight out of the nineties.

Sleeping on one of them is the guy from the garage—Brody Austin.

Nina's breath stops.

He's lying on his back with one arm thrown overhead. There's some kind of colorful crocheted blanket covering his legs.

She remains still, not sure what to do. Eventually she walks toward him, stepping lightly, trying to make as little noise as possible. Any second, she expects him to wake up, but he doesn't.

When she's right beside him, she stands there for a long moment, watching him sleep. She's not even sure why she's doing it. She knows it's weird, but there's something about him.

He's beautiful really.

Younger than her. If she had to guess, he's probably only in his late twenties or early thirties. His hair is longer than in the ID photo and goes past his shoulders. He has a black goatee, and his bone structure is so clean and strong that she's almost certain he's Native American.

She studies the arm above his head. The hollow of his armpit with dark hair peeking out from beneath his white T-shirt. There's some kind of black swirling tattoo on his forearm. Her eyes drift lower. He's a big guy. Muscular and long-limbed. One bare foot sticks out from the crocheted blanket with a dusting of dark hair on his calf.

Nina studies the blanket covering him and wonders what he looks like beneath it.

To her surprise, as she's standing there, he wakes up. His brown eyes open and the two of them study each other though neither of them speaks.

Before she can question her actions, she sets her purse on the wooden coffee table.

She thinks about the last man she was with, the only man she's been with in six years—Noel. The one who was supposed to be the love of her life.

Nina turns back to Brody and senses his eyes following her movements as she reaches for the blanket covering him. She figures she must still be drunk. Surely there's no way she'd be doing this if she were sober, coming on to some guy she doesn't know.

Brody watches her with interest as she lifts the blanket away and places it on the armrest. He's wearing forest green boxer briefs with a black band on top.

She can't resist looking him over. He's well-made with just the right amount of bulk.

He still doesn't say anything, and that's when she notices something else. There's an erection currently filling his boxers.

Nina stares at it.

Noel often woke up with a hard-on. He was in his midforties but definitely had no trouble getting it up. She remembers all the early morning sex they used to have on the nights he stayed over. He liked to bring them both to a slow climax in the mornings. Afterward, they'd curl up together. He'd kiss her lips and then trace his finger lightly over her nose and cheek. "So beautiful," he'd whisper. "My golden girl." He told her how waking up beside her was the best way to start the day, how he couldn't wait until they woke up beside each other every day.

Hot tears threaten to spill from Nina's eyes, but she blinks them away.

I guess now he's curling up with Emily.

She wonders what pet name he calls her.

Nina senses Brody's eyes still on her as she shrugs out of her suit jacket and places it on the coffee table next to her purse. She moves closer and then kneels next to him on the couch. She lets her gaze wander, enjoying the look of him. Noel was in good shape and had a nice body, but he's got nothing on this guy.

When she reaches out to touch him, sliding her hand over his T-shirt, Brody grips her wrist. "What are you doing?" he asks, his voice rough as it breaks the silence.

She can feel his hard-on pressing against her forearm through the boxer briefs

"Would you like me to give you a blow job?"

He studies her, still holding her arm. "Why?"

"Because I think we'd both enjoy it."

Brody blinks at this, but then he lets her wrist go. Nina moves her hand lower and slips her fingers beneath the waistband of his shorts, stroking his cock. He's hot and hard. If she's correct, he's larger than Noel. Wider, at the very least.

She smirks to herself. *See that, Noel? You're inferior.*

Nina tugs his boxers down, and Brody lifts his body to help her shove them lower.

Now that his cock is right there, she bends over and takes him in her mouth. She sucks him deep into her throat. Somewhere in the back of her mind, she knows this is wildly unlike her. Giving some strange guy a blow job? Has she lost her mind?

She glances at his face, at the way he's observing her, his skin flushed.

For a brief moment, there's something unusual in his gaze. A flash of something wounded. It's gone so quickly that maybe she imagined it. She pulls her mouth away.

He reaches up and touches her hair. "Don't stop," he whispers.

Brody's eyes fall shut. He'd been dreaming of Kiera before he woke up. Missing her like always and dreaming that she was still here with him, that nothing had changed.

But, of course, that's not true.

Instead, he was surprised to find it was the crazy drunk woman from the garage. The Audi's owner—Nina. She was standing in front of him wearing a strange and needy expression.

He had a hell of a time getting her to his house last night. She passed out cold at the garage, so he had to carry her out to his truck like a sack of potatoes. He laid her down on the back seat, trying not to bump her head, and could only imagine how he would have explained it to the cops if he'd been pulled over with a near lifeless woman sprawled in back.

Thankfully, that didn't happen. Except when he got home, she was still passed out, so he brought her into the house, praying none of his neighbors saw him carrying a limp female body through the front door like a serial killer.

He didn't relax until he finally had her lying in bed, rolled onto her side, with pillows tucked behind her like he did with Thunder.

She didn't stir once, though he was relieved to hear her breathing and snorting occasionally, mumbling nonsense.

He called Tori on the way home and explained that something came up, and he couldn't make it to dinner after all. She said it was fine, that they'd do it another time. He was irritated as hell with the situation. Tori's husband, Liam, had become one of his best friends, and he hated to disappoint either of them.

And now here I am letting the crazy drunk woman give me a blow job.

What the hell am I doing?

Except when he closes his eyes, he discovers it's easy to pretend it's Kiera's warm mouth on him instead.

"Why would you want to fix something that isn't broken?" he asked her before she left. Hell, he fixed broken things for a living. If anyone knew how dumb it was to interfere with an engine that ran perfectly, it was him.

"It's not about fixing something," Kiera said. "Getting married is about making something good even better."

Except he didn't believe that was true. Marriage would change things between them, and he didn't want things to change. They were already a perfect engine.

But apparently Kiera didn't agree, because she moved out. Took a job in Arizona, and here he was almost two years later still hung up on her.

A warm tongue swirls around the head of his cock and then sucks him deep into an even warmer mouth.

Damn. He lets out a moan. It feels good.

He moves his hips in a mindless way as his balls tighten, his climax approaching. He's still thinking about Kiera, remembering her voluptuous body, how much he loved the feel of her breasts and ass, all the sweet sounds she made when they were together. But then the warm mouth pulls away. It's gone. His dick is left stiff in the cool air.

Brody's eyes open. "What...?"

Almost like a car crash, he's brought back to reality. It's not Kiera he's with but the crazy woman.

Shit. He'd almost forgotten.

She's standing next to him, stripping off her panties.

Still fully clothed otherwise, she climbs on top of him.

He knows what she's doing, and he wants it. It's been too long. His breath trembles as she sinks down onto his erection.

"Jesus," he mutters as she takes him into her tight, warm body. It's incredible. So good he's surprised by it.

Brody grabs her hips as she moves on top of him. Her perfume surrounds him with the scent of jasmine flowers. It smells expensive. He didn't think much of it last night, but now it's getting him hot.

He pulls her skirt up and kneads her ass.

She moans and grabs his shoulders, yanks his shirt up, and then digs her nails into his chest.

"Take your top off," he says, barely catching his breath. "Let me see your body."

She does as he says, pulling her blouse off and then her white lace bra. A pair of pretty breasts falls into his hands. He cups them, then pinches her nipples while she gasps. Her long hair is all over the place, kind of wild, brushing against him, and that's getting him hot too.

When she leans over, still riding him, he can tell she's trying to come, so he slips his fingers between her legs, feels where they're joined, then rubs her all over, not just her clit but her vulva too. Rubbing and squeezing her.

It lights her up like a stick of dynamite, and she moans, grinding into him, giving it everything. He tries to hold back, except his balls have gone tight. When she gets louder and goes over the edge, he can't stop himself and, with a groan, goes over it with her.

"Holy shit," he gasps after she collapses on top of him.

She laughs lightly against his neck. "I'm glad you enjoyed that."

"Hell of a way to start the day." He caresses her back. She feels different in his arms than Kiera. Smaller and wiry.

She goes quiet at this.

"Did I say something wrong?"

She shakes her head and sits up with him still inside her. She lifts off his dick, grimacing slightly. "It's fine." She glances down at herself. "Oh no, we should have used a condom."

Brody's eyes widen, and he looks down at where they were joined only a moment ago. "Damn, you're right." He has a whole drawer full of them in his bedroom. Not that they get much use.

The two of them study each other. The sex had been surprisingly good, but in truth, he's already regretting it and wonders if she is too.

"I'm on birth control," she tells him. "So no worries there."

He nods, relieved. "Glad to hear it. I'm definitely safe. What about you?" He wonders if she's promiscuous.

She hesitates, and he doesn't like that. There's something high-class about her. Expensive. But that doesn't mean she doesn't sleep around.

Shit. I'm probably going to have to get tested.

She bites her lip. "Normally I'm fine too, but...." She swallows and looks away. "Things have changed. The man I was with... my boyfriend... it turns out he's been unfaithful."

Brody takes this in. So that's what caused her bad day yesterday. "I'm sorry."

She nods and takes a shaky breath.

"Come here." He pulls her down so she's lying on top of him again. He pushes her hair aside and strokes her back. It's always been hard for him to see a creature in pain, and something about Nina reminds him of a lost bird.

She stays there on him but doesn't say anything more.

His eyes fall shut as he listens to the quiet of his house. Everything calm. The clock in his kitchen ticks the seconds by, and he wonders what time it is. It feels early. At least Chavez is opening the garage today.

He continues to caress her back. Nina's skin is silky. She seems fragile. He can feel the notches of her spine sticking out like small tree knots.

After a while, she lifts up and looks at him.

The two of them study each in the morning light. He has to admit she's pretty. There are lines on her face, around her eyes and mouth, but they don't detract. If anything, he likes them.

He decides her eyes are especially pretty. A clear blue. Sky eyes, his grandma would have said.

"How did I get here?" Nina asks, studying him. "I don't remember it."

"That's because you were passed out drunk."

Her eyes widen at this. "Passed out?"

He nods. And then he describes the whole thing to her, figuring she'd want to know. She seems shocked. He's known people who drank too much and then acted surprised by their actions, but Nina seems legitimately horrified. He's guessing this isn't a regular thing for her.

"Thank you," she whispers, shaking her head. "I hate to think what could have happened to me."

"I wouldn't recommend doing that again."

"You're a good person, aren't you? A real gentleman."

He raises his brows. He's never been called that before. "I guess so."

When she smiles at him, her mouth shows a lot of teeth, all of them white and straight. He imagines the time and money that went into a mouth like that. She could model for dental ads.

"Can I ask you a question?" She strokes his facial hair. "How old are you?"

"Thirty-two. How old are you?"

Nina hesitates, and he watches her closely. She licks her lips and then glances to the side before coming back to him. "Thirty-six."

She's lying. Lying straight to his face even, except she's terrible at it, which means she probably doesn't do it a lot.

Still though. He doesn't like it. It's not a good sign.

They study each other for a moment longer, but then Nina seems to grow uncomfortable. She looks over at her purse on the coffee table. "I should get going." She sits up all the way and then climbs off him, tugging her skirt down.

Brody pulls his boxers back up, tucking himself inside.

"Do you mind if I use your bathroom?"

"Go right ahead."

She disappears, and it sounds like she's going into his bedroom. He reaches for his jeans on the end of the couch and slides into them. His phone is on the makeshift end table, and he checks the time. Quarter to nine. He doesn't have to be at the garage until ten.

He gets up and puts the phone in his pocket, then heads into the other bathroom down the hall. He takes a piss and wishes he could take a shower. Instead, he goes into his bedroom to grab some clean clothes and underwear. He tosses his dirty clothes in the hamper and is naked when Nina emerges from the bathroom.

"Oh, sorry," she says, looking away as if she hadn't just screwed his brains out ten minutes ago.

Brody smiles to himself as she slides awkwardly by him.

He goes into the bathroom and, after soaping up his dick and underarms, brushes his teeth. He throws on clean clothes and emerges to find Nina sitting in one of the tall chairs at his kitchen counter, drinking a glass of water and studying her dead phone.

"I'll need to come with you to the garage to pick up my car," she informs him in a voice that sounds managerial.

"Sure, of course."

"I helped myself to some water."

He notices she's found her shoes by the front door and is now wearing those ice pick heels again. "Do you want coffee?" He fires up the Keurig and gets down one of his travel mugs, setting the whole thing up like he does every morning.

She's still studying her busted phone. "Do you know what happened to my phone, why it's all smashed up?"

He smirks. "You threw it against the wall last night."

She pauses and then stares at him. "I did?"

"Yep."

When the coffee's done, he pulls a packet of stevia from a box on the kitchen counter. Kiera's the one who got him into using this stuff. Before her, he always drank it black, but then he discovered he liked a little sweetness.

"Why did I throw my phone against the wall?"

He swallows a sip of hot coffee and can already feel it energizing him. "I don't know. I think it's because you didn't want me to call anyone to come get you."

"That must be it." Except there's a funny expression on her face, and he suspects there's more to it.

"Are you sure I can't make you some coffee?"

Nina eyes his Keurig and then shakes her head dismissively. "No, thank you. I'll get an espresso later."

"How about some food? It'll probably help with your hangover."

She shakes her head. "I'm fine."

"Are you ready to go?"

She nods and appears to be taking one last look around his house. "Ready as I'll ever be."

CHAPTER THREE

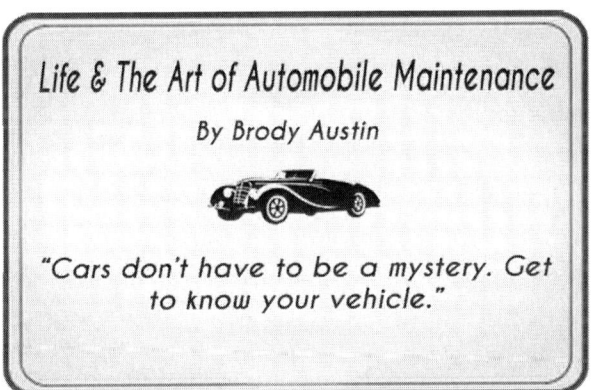

Life & The Art of Automobile Maintenance

By Brody Austin

"Cars don't have to be a mystery. Get to know your vehicle."

They arrive at the garage a little before ten. Brody sees Chavez's eyes pop out of his head when Nina, of all people, steps down from his truck. He chuckles to himself, knowing Chavez is going to have a field day with this as soon as she leaves.

Nina follows Brody inside, where he pulls out her invoice. After she pays and is putting her credit card away, he grabs her car keys from the office. "Here you go."

"Thank you for everything. I mean it." She takes the keys from him. "I think you may have saved my life last night. I also want to apologize for my abhorrent behavior yesterday morning. I know I acted terrible toward you and your other employee. It's amazing you were still kind enough to take care of me after that."

"It's true, you were pretty damn rude." He strokes his beard and smiles a little. "Not the worst ever, but probably in the top ten."

There's a pained expression on her face. "I'm really sorry. There's no excuse for it."

He shrugs, then grins at her. "Don't worry about it. Come on, I'll walk you to your car."

They head out to where her Audi is still parked in the same spot as yesterday. She walks briskly. He stands by her driver's side door, and just before getting inside, she turns to him. "Thank you again, Brody." She reaches for his hand and squeezes it. "I hope you have a wonderful life."

"You too, Nina."

She's acting really thankful and grateful toward him, but he can tell she's dying to get the hell out of here. Not that he can blame her. In her shoes, he's pretty sure he'd feel the same way.

He's ready to wave goodbye and is thinking about the workday ahead when he hears a clicking noise coming from inside the Audi. The engine isn't turning over.

He stares at the car in disbelief.

Nina gets out and doesn't look happy. She puts her hands on her hips with obvious annoyance. "My car's not starting. I thought you said you fixed it."

"I *did* fix it."

"Well, what's going on then? Why doesn't it work?"

He shakes his head. "I have no idea."

He tells her to pop the hood, and as soon as he's under it, he sees the problem.

Somebody ripped out the spark plugs he put in yesterday.

What the hell? Is this a joke?

He turns toward the garage. Chavez is still working on that engine rebuild. Anka's replacing the brakes on a Subaru SUV. There's no sign of Trevor.

Nina tries to talk to him, but he tells her to give him a minute and heads over to Chavez. "Where's Trevor?"

"He went home sick."

"He was here this morning?"

Chavez nods. "He said he wasn't feeling good." He glances at him and then at Nina standing over by her car. "What's going on between you and loco lady?"

Brody explains how her car is missing its spark plugs.

"You think Trevor did it?"

Brody is furious. "Yeah, I do." In fact, he knows his cousin did it. It's exactly the kind of bullshit stunt he used to pull as a kid. It was obviously payback for yesterday.

"Dude, you should fire his ass."

"He's my cousin."

"I know, but damn. That's too much. He's testing you."

Brody heads back over to where Nina is still standing next to her car, obviously perturbed. He explains how he'll have to get another set of spark plugs and fix the car for her again.

"I'll need to use your phone to get an Uber or a taxi," she says impatiently. "I don't have time to hang around here. I'll come back later when it's done."

"Don't worry about it. I'll take you home."

"I live downtown. I don't want to put you out any more than I already have."

"It's not a problem." Not only is he embarrassed that her car isn't running, he figures after everything that happened, he might as well see this business with Nina through to the end—make sure she gets home safe and sound.

The ride in his truck is mostly silent. After all her gushing and gratitude about saving her life, Nina doesn't seem to know what to say to him. Apparently she's decided to go with formal politeness, making small talk about his garage, though he can tell she's not interested.

As he drives, Brody's mind wanders back to the sex they had. He kind of wishes they hadn't done it, but at the same time, there was something compelling about it. He knows she was using him to get back at this other guy for cheating on her, but still, he finds himself lingering over it.

"So what do you do for a living?" he asks, figuring two of them can play the small talk game. He's always been good at shooting the breeze with customers.

She hesitates for a long moment, and he wonders if she doesn't want to tell him where she works. "I'm director of West Coast marketing for Tolland," she finally says.

He raises his brows. Tolland is a big Seattle software company. Not quite Google or Microsoft, but big enough that he's heard of them.

Following a hunch, he asks, "Does your boyfriend work there too?"

"*Ex*-boyfriend." She frowns and glares out the window. "Yes, he's the CEO."

"Damn. It sounds like that's going to be uncomfortable."

She snorts and then sits up straight with her back pressed against the seat. "Actually, I don't know if I'll be going back there."

"You're going to quit?"

"I'm considering it."

He takes this in. "So, who was he cheating with?"

"I don't want to talk about it. I barely even know you."

"We had sex two hours ago." Not to mention she was passed out in his bed all night.

She remains silent.

"All right, it's true. We're basically strangers." He glances at her. "I doubt we'll ever see each other again after this, so what does it matter?"

She's still staring out the window, watching as he takes the exit to get off the freeway. "He cheated with his intern. Her name's Emily. She's twenty-four."

"Damn, that's harsh. How long were you two together?" Brody's not sure why he's being so nosy. It isn't like him at all.

"Six years." She tells him how she's always been career focused and was happy with that, but she'd finally met someone she wanted to spend her life with. "He said he wanted to wait to get married until his children were out of school." Her voice shakes with fury. "I loved him and believed in him, and this is how I'm treated? Do you know how many Christmases I spent alone? How many excuses I had to give family and friends for Noel over the years because something came up with his ex-wife or one of their kids?"

"The guy's name is Noel?"

She nods. "Yes, why?"

He makes a face. "Because if you ask me, that's a real pansy-ass name."

Nina blinks at him and then laughs out loud. "It is, isn't it? *Very* pansy-ass. The worst ever. I'm going to tell him you said that."

Brody decides she has a good laugh. "With a name like *Noel*, you probably should have expected the worst to begin with."

"Probably." She's still smiling, and he senses her watching him. "So what's your story? I'm assuming you're not married and don't have a girlfriend."

He shakes his head. "Not married. No girlfriend."

"I'm kind of surprised."

"Oh yeah? Why's that?"

"Because you're hot, Brody. I'm sure you're aware of it."

He chuckles. Women have occasionally told him he's good-looking, but he never took it too seriously. It's not like it's ever opened any doors.

"Or maybe you're a player and don't want to settle for just one woman. Is that it?"

"I'm not a player." The thought of dealing with an endless stream of women sounded exhausting. He could never be into that.

"Then I'm curious. What *is* your story?"

"I was in a long-term relationship that ended."

"Ah, that explains it." She goes quiet. "I'm sorry. I hope there wasn't cheating involved."

"No, it wasn't anything like that."

"What was it, then?"

He shrugs. "We just wanted different things is all."

"How long ago did you two break up?"

"Almost two years."

He can feel Nina's eyes on him, studying him. "Are you still in love with her?"

He takes a deep breath and wonders if he should tell her the truth. Most people assume he's over Kiera, and he never says anything to dissuade them of that notion. "Yeah," he admits, his eyes steady on the road in front of him. "I'm still in love with her."

"I'm sorry. That sucks, Brody. You two can't work it out?"

"She moved to Arizona and is with another guy."

"I see. And how long were you together?"

"Four years."

Her brows go up and she nods, glancing out the passenger window. "That is a while."

Brody's driving down Second Avenue toward Belltown into thicker traffic. "So, am I getting close to where you live?"

"We're almost there."

Nina gives him instructions for where to turn. Apparently she lives in one of the high-rise condos facing the water.

"It's that building right there," she says, pointing toward a giant tower made of metal and glass with balconies running up each side. "You can just let me out in front of the lobby." She picks up her purse from the floor and turns to him. "Thank you again for everything."

"I'm going to park and walk you inside."

She waves her hand dismissively. "That's not necessary. I've got it from here. Just drop me off."

"I need to see this thing through to the end, to make sure you're home safe, so I'll walk you inside." He glances at her. "That's the way I roll."

She studies him, but there's a little smile on her face. "All right. If you insist."

He drives around the block a few times looking for a parking spot, but of course, this is Seattle, so there isn't any.

"Actually, why don't you drive into the building's underground parking? You can use my spot."

He sighs to himself, wishing she'd said something sooner. He lets her guide him to her private parking spot.

They get out, and he follows Nina toward some elevators. Once inside, she pushes the lobby button.

"How far will you need to chaperone me to feel like you've followed it through to the end?" she asks.

"To the lobby should do it."

She smiles. "You're such a gentleman."

Brody raises a brow. There's that word again. In truth, he's never liked loose ends. "Do a job right or don't do it all" has always been his motto.

The elevator opens into a spacious lobby with marble floors and a chandelier hanging from the tall ceiling. It looks like a hotel. There are mailboxes off to one side and a large desk with some uniformed guy sitting behind it.

Jesus, what is this place?

"Nina!"

Brody turns as some woman with a ponytail and colorful jeans rushes up to them.

"Where have you been?" The woman hugs Nina. "We've all been worried sick. Why didn't you answer your phone?"

"Suzy?" Nina seems surprised. "What are you doing here?"

"Are you kidding? I've been searching for *you*! You never showed up for dinner last night or responded to your birthday messages. I couldn't get a hold of Noel, and when I called your work, they said you left yesterday and haven't been heard from since! I was ready to call the police."

"Well, I'm... fine." Nina glances over at Brody, who's watching them.

Suzy looks at him expectantly. "And who's this?"

"Um...." Nina's face flushes a light shade of pink. She doesn't seem to know how to answer. "He's a... friend?"

Brody sticks his hand out. "Hi, I'm Brody. Nina's mechanic."

Suzy's eyes widen as she shakes it. "You're her *mechanic?*" She glances at Nina in confusion. "Why is your mechanic here?"

"She had some car trouble, so I'm helping out."

"Car trouble?" Suzy still seems confused, though she's eyeing him up and down with a smile of approval on her face. "Hmm, I think I understand. Or at least I hope I do. I'm Suzy, Nina's younger sister."

Brody nods. "It's nice to meet you." When he glances over at Nina, he can tell she's uncomfortable, so he spares her any further embarrassment. "Well, I'll be off now. Your car should be ready in a few hours."

"Wow!" Suzy says as soon as the two of them are in the elevator headed up to her condo. "Who was that tall drink of water?"

"Like he said, he's my mechanic." Nina leans against the elevator wall, feeling sick to her stomach again. She probably should have eaten something at Brody's when he offered. Her headache is back with a vengeance too.

"Well, he can tune me up anytime he wants."

Nina rolls her eyes. "Don't be vulgar."

Suzy just laughs. "How old is he? He looks kind of young. Did you sleep with him?"

Nina looks down at the floor, trying to quell her nausea. "Of course not. What do you take me for?"

Her baby sister's watching her closely. "Oh, wow, you did, didn't you? I don't believe it. What happened last night? Did you finally get sick of Noel and all his bullshit?"

Suzy's never been fond of Noel. They just never hit it off, though Nina always thought her sister could have tried a little harder. Suzy said she thought Noel was using her, and that he treated his ex-wife like they were still married. "Noel and I broke up."

The elevator dings open on her floor.

"Wait, *what?*" Her sister gawks. "Seriously?"

They both exit, and Suzy follows her down the long hallway toward her condo. There are windows on one side looking out onto the city, and it smells like glue from the new carpet laid down last month.

Nina already has her keys out when they get to her door. Her sister's right behind her, practically bouncing on her heels.

It's easy enough for Suzy to criticize Noel when she's married to the perfect man and has two perfect children. Nina shakes her head. *What am I doing? I need to stop defending that bastard.*

Once she steps inside her home, Nina finally feels like she can breathe again. She drops her keys in the crystal bowl by the door and kicks her shoes off. When she reaches the living room, she collapses onto the large white couch.

Home sweet home.

"Are you okay?" her sister asks. "Tell me what's going on."

Nina gazes out at the view of the city and Elliott Bay from the floor-to-ceiling windows in her living room. "If you want to know the truth, I'm not okay. I also have a terrible hangover." She then tells her sister everything—the whole story with Noel and then everything Brody told her happened too.

"Oh my God." Suzy comes over and sits next to her on the couch, taking her hand. "I'm so glad that mechanic helped you. You could be lying dead in a ditch somewhere."

Nina shudders to think of it.

"It's nice to know there are still good people in the world," Suzy continues. "So at what point did you have sex with him?"

"I didn't have sex with him."

Suzy rolls her eyes. "I know you did, so just spill it."

Nina sighs. She's never been a good liar. Plus, her sister can usually read her like a book. "This morning."

"Did he come on to you?"

Nina snorts. "Hardly." Then she explains the rest of it, leaving out details that were too personal.

"So you did it to get back at Noel?"

She shrugs. "More or less." Although what's strange is she didn't think about Noel even once while she was having sex with Brody. It had felt weird being with a stranger, earthier than what she was used to, but also surprisingly good.

"Are you going to see him again?"

"I have to pick up my car later today. Though I kind of hope he's not there."

"Why?"

She rolls her eyes. "Come on. It was a one-time thing. It's not like I'm going to have a relationship with the guy."

Suzy leans back on the couch and sighs. "So, what are you going to do about Noel? I can't believe he dumped you on your birthday."

Nina shakes her head. "What can I do?" Her heart feels heavy. Part of her still doesn't believe any of this is real. It's like she's taken a left turn and wound up in a different universe.

"Well, I say good riddance. For once the trash took itself out."

Nina glances at her sister. "I don't know why you never liked him."

"You know why. He treated you like his mistress."

"It wasn't like that. He's a good guy who puts his kids first. How could I fault him for that?" But then Nina stops herself. She's so used to championing Noel that it's become her default mode.

"Except he puts his ex-wife first too." Suzy pauses. "I wonder what she's going to think of all this. Of Emily the intern."

Nina has to admit she's curious too. Despite Nina's ongoing jealousy of Claudia, the two of them had a cordial relationship. Nina can't imagine Claudia being too thrilled about Noel dating a girl who's only a few years older than their oldest daughter.

"You look pale," Suzy says. "Why don't you rest, and I'll make you something to eat."

"What time do you have to pick up Grace from school?" Nina's niece just started kindergarten, while her nephew, Henry, is in the second grade. She chose a career over having kids, so instead she's become an involved aunt.

"I've still got a couple hours before I have to be there."

Nina closes her eyes as she's hit by a wave of exhaustion. "I need to sleep some more, though I should probably email work first." Her admin, Davis, can get her a new phone delivered.

"I'm going to make you some toast," Suzy says, getting up. "You need food to help with a hangover. And more liquids."

Instead of going into her office, Nina lies back on the couch and gazes out at the magnificent view. Her condo cost a mint, but in the two years since she bought it, she hasn't had a single regret. She and Noel shopped for it together. They'd looked at a number of high-rises downtown, treating it like their future home. He even considered going in on it with her, but in the end decided against it since he was still paying on his house in Medina.

Thank goodness for that. This place is all hers, and if she had to give it up because of him, she'd be even more crushed.

Nina must doze off, because the next thing she knows, her sister is offering her buttered toast. It's on her favorite whole wheat bread she buys from a bakery in Pike Place Market.

"Thanks," Nina says, sitting up. She eats a few bites and realizes it is settling her stomach. Not to mention the butter is delicious. She can't remember the last time she had butter. She only keeps it around for Noel.

They sit and talk some more. Suzy tells her about the latest with her husband, Luke, how he might travel to London for work next year, and they're hoping to turn it into a family vacation. "I was thinking Mom and Dad can fly out from Portugal, and if there's time, we'll stop in Dublin to visit Lauren and Paul. Kate and Declan are planning to be there too."

"Sounds great." Nina finishes the first piece of toast and drinks half the bottle of Evian water her sister brought out for her. Kate and Lauren are two of Suzy's best friends who somehow wound up married to Irish cousins. Ironically, Nina briefly dated Declan before he married Kate.

By the time Suzy has to leave to pick up Grace from kindergarten, Nina is almost feeling human again.

"Are you sure you don't want me to come back and take you to pick up your car?" Suzy asks.

"That's okay. I'll get a taxi." Nina figures she'll have Elliot, her building's doorman, call one for her.

After her sister leaves, Nina takes a long hot shower, then slips into a cozy sweater and leggings. Perfect for a late-September day.

Just as she's sitting down in front of her computer to email work, there's a knock on her front door.

She wonders who it could be and is shocked to find Noel standing there. Her heart stutters in her chest. He looks handsome and slightly windblown. His cheeks are flushed from being outside. The scent of his spicy cologne, the one she's always loved so much, drifts over the threshold.

She hates that she still feels the same draw toward him, the same flip in her stomach, after what he's done.

There's a bandage on his forehead from where she hit him with the stapler yesterday. Guilt flashes through her, but she brushes it away.

"What are you doing? I don't want you here," she says, her voice shaking. She should have told Elliot not to allow him up anymore. It hadn't occurred to her.

Noel appears incredulous. "Are you seriously asking me that? Where have you been?" He's studying her with concern. "Are you okay?"

"Of course I'm okay. Why wouldn't I be?"

"Because you haven't been answering your phone. No one's heard from you since yesterday morning."

"Well, as you can see, I'm perfectly fine."

He takes a deep breath. "We need to talk, Nina."

She glares at him.

"Are you going to let me in?"

Nina doesn't want to, but she also doesn't want to have this conversation in the hallway. "Fine. Come inside."

He follows her into the living room, where she sits on the couch. Unfortunately, her headache from earlier has come back.

Noel walks over and gazes at the view for a moment before turning toward her. "I'm sorry for the way things came out with Emily. It wasn't my intention to be so careless with your feelings, especially on your birthday."

Nina studies him. The way the autumn sunlight shines on him from the large windows. She's still in love with him. Of course she is. You don't fall out of love with someone in one day, no matter how bad it is.

Noel comes over and sits next to her on the couch. "Is this safe?" He smiles. "You're not going to start throwing things at me again, are you?"

Nina knows she should apologize, but she doesn't have it in her. She'll never understand how they wound up here. She gave him everything he ever wanted. Nina has never been so accommodating toward a man, and she did it because she thought he was the love of her life.

"I know I screwed up," he says. "And I know you won't believe this, but I still love you. I'll always love you, Nina."

Tears flood her eyes, and she quickly brushes them away. "Does that mean you're not staying with Emily?"

He gazes out toward the water again. "Emily has been a tremendous surprise to me in every way. I never expected it. But I can't deny my feelings for her either."

Nina's heart sinks in her chest. A part of her still hoped he'd say

Emily was the biggest mistake of his life and then fall to his knees, begging her forgiveness.

It's odd. She never thought of herself as the kind of woman who'd take a man back after he cheated on her, after he broke her trust so thoroughly, but apparently she's been wrong about herself all these years.

Noel rakes a hand through his hair like he always does when he's frustrated. "This thing with Emily... it just happened. It was right before the new release last month. We were working late in my office one night. I offered her a tumbler of scotch after we finished going over the material for the promotional packages, and the next thing I knew, we were kissing." He studies his hands. "The whole thing was an accident."

She feels nauseous. She wants him to stop talking, to shut the hell up, except there's a perverse part of her that wants to hear every detail. Like ripping off a Band-Aid. It's the one thing she hopes might help her fall out of love with him.

"Afterward, we both decided it was a mistake, you know? I told her I loved *you*."

She stares at him.

"But then it happened again." His hazel eyes fill with compassion. "We didn't mean it to be this way, but somehow we've fallen in love with each other."

"She's a child."

He shakes his head. "I know she's young, but she's not a child. She's a grown woman."

"So you were sleeping with both of us? Does she know you stayed the night here only a few days ago?"

"She knows. I told her I needed that closure with you."

Nina has a sudden urge to throw something at him again. "Have you told Claudia or your kids about her yet?"

Noel's face changes. "Not yet. Obviously I will, but I don't see the rush."

Nina snorts. So now it's Emily's turn to deal with Claudia. In a way, Nina almost feels sorry for her. Almost.

"Listen, this isn't the only reason I came here to talk to you." He faces her, his expression solemn. Then he leans forward and clasps his hands together in a pose she's seen him use when addressing their shareholders. "You're fired, Nina."

"What?" Her eyes widen and her mouth falls open as she sits up straight. "Did you just tell me I'm *fired?*"

He nods. "I have to let you go. I don't have a choice."

She jumps off the couch. "So you cheated on me, and now you're firing me? *What the hell, Noel?*"

"I have to. You attacked me at the office yesterday. The company wants to take out a restraining order against you. They even talked about pressing charges. You're lucky I talked them out of it."

She blinks at him, the edges of her vision turning red with fury. "I can't believe this. After all my years of working there. Maybe *I* should be the one pressing charges, calling my lawyer and suing for wrongful termination."

"You can try, but you won't get very far. You signed the same papers as I did."

Nina goes quiet. Right after they started seeing each other, they had a meeting with HR. The company was strict about romantic relationships between employees. She and Noel both signed an interoffice relationship agreement stating that neither of them would sue the other or Tolland should they break up.

"So now you've ruined my life in every way. You couldn't have fought for me a little harder?"

He shakes his head. "Don't be like that, Nina. I know this is terrible, and you probably hate me right now. But I want you to know how much you've meant to me the past six years. I might not be *in* love with you anymore, but I'll always love you. You're my golden girl." He gives her a gentle smile. "And you always will be."

"Go screw yourself, Noel."

CHAPTER FOUR

Life & The Art of Automobile Maintenance
By Brody Austin

"Cars are unpredictable. You may find yourself questioning what's under the hood."

Brody stands outside talking with one of his regular customers, an older Hungarian guy who collects antique cars and bought a 1953 Buick Skylark convertible at an auction last year. He hired Brody to help him restore it to its former glory. They'd recently installed a brand-new V8 with 188 horsepower under the hood and were going to start work on the transmission next.

"What do you think about burgundy for the outside?" Sándor asks. "I kind of like it with the white seats."

Brody nods, studying the body. There are a number of rust spots they'd have to either sand down or fill. "I think that would be slick. And it would be true to the time she was made." He lightly strokes the hood. This car is a real beauty.

Speaking of beauty, he looks over in time to see Chavez handing Nina the keys to her Audi. He hadn't even seen her arrive. Brody debates whether he should go talk to her. This whole situation between them is kind of weird.

But then their eyes meet across the garage.

"Excuse me," he says to Sándor. "I'll be back in a minute."

He heads over to Nina, who waits for him when she sees him coming toward her. As soon as he draws closer, he notices her eyes are puffy, like she's been crying.

"You okay?" he asks. She's got the lost bird look again.

She nods. "I'm fine." Then she pauses. "Noel showed up at my condo earlier."

"The pansy ass?"

She smiles a little. "It turns out I've been fired. Can you believe that?" Her jaw tightens as she shakes her head.

"I thought you were planning to quit anyway."

"It's one thing to quit and another thing to be fired!"

He nods and strokes his goatee. "True enough."

She sighs. "I don't know why I'm even telling you all this. You must think I'm completely crazy."

Brody shrugs and smiles. "People tell their mechanic all sorts of things. We're kind of like shrinks."

Her blue eyes study his with a wisp of humor. "Is that right?"

"You'd be surprised."

She strides toward her car, and he follows along. He can't resist checking her out. She's changed clothes from earlier. The suit is gone, and instead she's wearing a long white sweater, leggings, and black boots. He likes her dressed like this—though the power suit wasn't bad either.

When they arrive at her car, she opens the door.

"Do you want to get coffee sometime?" Brody asks impulsively before she gets inside. He doesn't do a lot of things impulsively and has surprised himself with the suggestion.

She turns, and he can see she's surprised too. "Um... that's nice of you to ask, but I don't think it's a great idea."

"Why not?"

He watches her and can tell she's trying to come up with a good reason for turning him down that won't hurt his feelings. "We're just too different. I doubt we have much in common."

"Did you and Noel have a lot in common?"

She nods. "Practically everything. We went to the same college, had the same taste in food and music. We even read the same books...."

He doesn't say anything, just lets her draw her own conclusions from that.

Nina's expression changes, and he can tell she doesn't like what he's implying. "Look, I appreciate everything you've done for me. Truly I do. But we just aren't suited." She licks her lips. "This morning was... nice, but it was a one-time thing. A lark."

"Sure." He stuffs his hands into the pockets of his coveralls. "I get it."

"I don't mean to hurt your feelings, but we come from different worlds."

He nods.

"I'm also a few years older than you."

He glances back at Sándor and is regretting his impulsive invitation. "It's fine," he says. "It's just coffee. I wasn't asking for your hand in marriage."

She laughs lightly and then rolls her eyes. "I know. I'm kind of messed up right now."

He decides he's more than ready to end this conversation. "Well, you take it easy, Nina."

"Thanks, you too."

She gets inside her car. This time the engine turns over perfectly, roaring to life exactly as it should.

Brody puts his hand up to wave goodbye, then turns and walks back toward the garage.

Later, after he closes up for the night, he drives over to the apartment where Trevor lives. He knocks on the door, and as soon as Trevor sees him, Brody can tell he's nervous but trying to hide it.

"Hey, cuz. What brings you over? You should have brought some beer."

Brody scowls, then follows his cousin into the living room, where he's playing some kind of video game. The place is a mess, with bags of junk food and empty soda cans everywhere. The whole room smells like stale body odor. Brody glances around, but there's no sign of Kevin, Trevor's housemate.

His cousin plops down on the couch and grins. "I hope you guys didn't miss me too much at work today."

Brody crosses his arms and stands there silently staring at him.

Trevor shifts uncomfortably. "Damn, Brody. You seem kind of pissed off. Is everything okay?"

"No, everything is not okay. And you know damn well why I'm pissed off."

At least Trevor has the good sense to seem embarrassed. He doesn't say anything at first, then takes a deep breath. "It was just a joke, all right? Chavez told me that lady was acting rude, so I figured she got what she deserved."

"Is that so?"

Trevor nods. "Plus, you shouldn't have smacked me in the head yesterday." He gets a pompous expression on his face. "What can I say? You mess with the bull, you get the horns."

Brody stares at him. He has a good mind to smack him again. "What the hell am I supposed to do with you, Trevor? Tell me."

"I don't know." He smiles. "Give me a big fat raise and a nice long vacation?"

"And why would I do that?"

"Because I'm your cousin, and I'm an outstanding mechanic."

Brody snorts. "You're a huge pain in my ass is what you are." The irony is that Trevor *is* a decent mechanic, or at least he could be if he got out of his own way. "If you were anybody else, I'd fire your ass for that stunt you pulled today. And if it happens again, I *will* fire you. Got it?"

Trevor meets Brody's angry gaze, then looks away and shrugs. "Fine. Maybe I did go overboard."

"You think?"

He turns back to him. "What happened when that lady tried to drive her car and it wouldn't start?" He chuckles. "I'll bet that was funny."

Brody massages his forehead. Aunt Jeanie was always good to him as a kid. He'd go on the rez to visit Thunder, and after his grandma died, if things went south, he always knew Jeanie would help. As a result, he didn't want to let her down. When she asked him three months ago if he'd give Trevor his first job after getting his mechanic's certificate, he was happy to do it.

"No, it wasn't funny," Brody says, trying to get through to him. "I'm the owner, and I stand by our work. If I tell someone their car is fixed and ready to drive, that's exactly what it should be."

Trevor nods like he understands, though Brody suspects he's just humoring him.

His young cousin stretches his long, lanky legs out in front of himself. He's wearing jeans with the knees torn through. His dark hair is cut into layers.

Brody shakes his head. Trevor has talent, and he could do well in life, but he needs to smarten up.

Brody moves an old pizza box out of the way and sits down. "So what's happening with you? Are you actually sick?"

Trevor nods and points at himself. "I had a tickle in my throat."

"A tickle?"

He nods and gives a fake-sounding cough. "See?"

Brody stares at him.

Trevor gives another fake cough and then lies back on the couch like he's dying. "I might be contagious. You probably don't want to be around me too much." He glances over. "I hope I don't have the black lung."

Brody chuckles despite himself. "I don't know what to do with you, Trevor."

For the first time since she was a teenager, Nina finds herself unemployed and with nothing but time on her hands.

She decides her immediate goal is to put together a fantastic résumé, contact the best headhunter in the city, and find a new job that's ten times better than the one she was just fired from.

That'll show them. I'll go work for the competition!

Except that's not what happens.

Instead, every day she wakes up and tells herself she's going to get started on that résumé. She's going to take charge of her life. And every day she falls into the same old pattern.

She sleeps all morning and then lounges around all afternoon in her pajamas, watching trashy talk shows and courtroom dramas. They've become her addiction. She especially loves the talk shows where there's a cheating spouse or an illicit love affair. *"Bobby Tom is screwing around on Betty Sue with a skanky whore named Mary Ellen"*—though in Nina's mind, all skanky whores are named Emily. Nina revels in the righteous indignation she feels on Betty Sue's behalf. The hurt and the anger. These are her people. Who knew?

And then, of course, there are all the ads running all day that are geared toward senior citizens. She gets sucked into those too. All the safety devices and hearing aids. All the pharmaceuticals with a litany of frightening side effects listed in a quick dismissive manner.

Is this where I'm at? Turning forty and ready for orthopedic shoes? Ready for medication where a possible side effect is death?

She's already bought a device that opens jars more easily and is thinking about getting some special reading glasses with a light attached.

After almost two weeks into this odyssey of self-pity, Nina gets a call on her condo's intercom. She debates even answering it, but whoever is calling from downstairs is persistent.

"Yes?" She pushes the intercom button in her kitchen with annoyance. She dislikes being pulled away from her shows. Obviously, she needs to get a new phone, but she hasn't gotten around to that yet either.

"It's Davis. I'm here with your stuff."

"Already?"

"I emailed you last week. I told you we'd bring everything over today."

She pauses. *That was last week?* "All right." She sighs. "Come on up."

In a flurry, Nina runs into the bedroom and changes out of her pajamas and into yoga pants and a T-shirt. She pulls her hair back into a messy bun, hoping it hides the fact that it hasn't been washed in days.

"Ahoy, Captain," Davis says with a smile when she answers the door. A joke they used to share after Nina once told him that leading the West Coast marketing department at Tolland was like being the captain of a large ship. There's a guy standing next to him she doesn't recognize, and the two men are standing there behind carts stacked high with boxes.

Her brows go up. "Is that all my stuff?" She steps out of the way to let them in.

"There's more downstairs in the van too. I didn't pack it though, so don't blame me if it's a mess." Davis and the other guy bring everything inside. "Where do you want it?"

Nina considers this. It's all the stuff from her office at Tolland. Six years of memories, awards, and accomplishments.

She's tempted to tell them to take it all to the dump.

"I guess you can put it in my home office." She leads the way for them and has them stack all the boxes against the wall.

"Do you want us to bring all the furniture in here too?"

Nina had nearly forgotten about her office furniture from work. "Yes, that's fine." She'll have to figure out later what to do with it.

It takes two more trips, but Davis and the other guy, a temp named Skip, have finally stuffed everything into her home office. There's not a lot of space, so things are piled on top of each other. It's basically a maze now to reach her desk and computer.

Nina offers the two men Evian water or ginger ale, and they each accept a ginger ale.

"Thank you for bringing everything here," she tells Davis. "It was nice of you to do it yourself."

"I wanted to. Plus, I wanted to see you." Davis glances at Skip, then tells him he can wait for him in the van, that he'll be down shortly. As soon as he's gone, he eyes Nina with interest. "So how's it going? Things have been crazy since Noel fired you. Everyone's still in shock over it."

"I'm not surprised. What are they saying?"

"That you jumped Noel and security had to pull you off him." He chuckles. "Is that true?"

"*What?*" Nina gawks. "Of course that's not true!"

Davis leans against the kitchen counter with his bottle of ginger ale. "Then what did happen?"

Nina hesitates but then tells him anyway. She realizes throwing a latte and then a stapler at Noel's head doesn't sound a whole lot better.

Davis studies her. "What none of us can figure out is why you attacked him to begin with."

"I guess you don't know about Noel's affair with Emily." "*What?*" Davis nearly chokes on his ginger ale. "Noel and *Emily?*"

Nina nods, feeling somewhat gleeful that she's let the cat out of the bag.

Davis shakes his head. "Wow, I can't believe it. She's so young."

"Tell me about it."

"How old are his kids?"

"His youngest is still in high school, and his two older kids are in college. I think his daughter's graduating soon."

Davis makes a face. "So Emily's only a few years older than his daughter? That's gross. What's he, like, in his forties?"

"Forty-five."

"Damn." He takes another swig from his bottle of soda. "Unbelievable."

"Who have they given my job to?" Nina asks out of curiosity. She tried emailing a few of her colleagues right after she got fired, but no one responded. Apparently she's become a pariah. Davis is the only one she's ever heard back from. "Or have they replaced me yet?"

"Rochelle. They announced it yesterday."

Nina takes a deep breath. She mentored Rochelle for two years, so she's not surprised they chose her. And Rochelle was definitely ambitious. "What about you?"

Davis rolls his eyes. "They've put me on with Mark."

"That's not so bad. He's okay, isn't he?"

"He's all right, but I prefer to be your first mate."

Nina smiles. "Thank you for saying that. I appreciate it."

"Have you started looking for a new job yet? I'll bet you'll be snatched up quickly."

"Of course," she lies. "I've already gotten several tempting offers. I want to take my time deciding. I don't want to rush into anything."

Davis nods. "That makes sense, and if you need a new assistant, keep me in mind." He finishes the last of his ginger ale and puts the bottle on the counter. "Well, I should probably head out now. It was really good seeing you, Nina."

"You too, Davis."

She walks him out and gives him a hug before saying goodbye. Then she closes the door and turns back to the silence of her empty apartment.

"I've decided to join a spinning class," Nina tells her sister on the phone the next day. "I think it'll be good for me."

After Davis came by yesterday, Nina realized it was time to quit hiding from the world and get out there again. The first step was getting a new phone, so after he left, instead of going back to her daytime shows, she took a long hot shower, got dressed, and drove to the nearest Apple store.

"Have you started looking for a new job yet?" Suzy asks.

"Not yet. I'm working up to it. I mean, I figure, what's the rush? For the first time in two decades, I don't have to be anywhere. In fact, I've decided to take a sabbatical." Nina likes the sound of that word. She's always thought people and their self-important "sabbaticals" were ridiculous, but now she doesn't know why she ever felt that way. "I might even do some traveling."

"I don't know. Can you afford that?"

"For now." The truth is, she has a nice nest egg. It's not as big as it would have been if she hadn't bought her condo, but she's lucky enough that she doesn't need to find a job right away.

"Well, that's great then. Good for you. I'm glad to hear you're at least getting out of the apartment. I get that you needed to wallow for a while, but that can be unhealthy too."

Suzy stopped by last week, and Nina had answered the door unbathed, hair in tangles, and still in her pajamas. Since Suzy was her sister, the doorman had let her up without calling first, so Nina had no warning. It was embarrassing. As the older sibling, Nina has always felt like she should set a good example and be a sensible role model for Suzy.

"That was just a phase," Nina says, referring to the pajama episode. "I'm past that now."

"You should come over this weekend. I know Grace and Henry would love to see you."

"I'd love to see them too."

They hang up, and Nina, who's been having all her food delivered, decides it's time to go grocery shopping. It's a crisp October day. Fall is one of her favorite seasons in Seattle.

She goes to the Whole Foods near her condo, but as soon as she enters the store, she realizes her mistake. Noel loves Whole Foods, and this was their main store. They used to come here shopping together on the Sundays when he didn't have to be with his kids.

I can do this, she tells herself. *It's just groceries, for God's sake, and I have to eat.*

She pushes her small cart down each aisle, pretending not to notice all of Noel's favorite foods. He's a picky eater and extremely loyal to certain brands, most of them expensive.

Nina sees the aged cheeses and picks up a chunk of the imported Grana Padano they used to buy. Noel made the most wonderful shell pasta dish with it, cooking up a storm while he spoke in the worst fake Italian accent of all time. "All you have to do is add a *vowela* to the end of every *nouna* and *booma*, you're speaking *Italiano*," he used to joke.

It was so silly. Such utter nonsense, but it always made her laugh. Tears sting her eyes, and she throws the Grana Padano back into the dairy case like she's pitching a baseball into hell.

Nina quickly heads down a different aisle and randomly takes items off the shelf, tossing them into her cart. She also grabs six large bottles of Evian water. There's an odd hysteria rising within her, but she tries to keep it at bay as she continues.

When she hits the pet food aisle, she thinks she's finally safe. No memories here. But then she sees the bags of dog food.

For years, she and Noel had talked about getting a dog. A little Scottish terrier they planned to name Sherlock.

Sherlock.

Isn't that the sweetest dog name ever? Can't you just see it?

When she was growing up, her parents never wanted pets. And then, as an adult, Nina worked so many hours that it didn't seem feasible, but having a dog has always been one of her dreams.

By the time she reaches the front register, her nose is running, and tears are streaming down her face. She's basically a hot mess. Nina knows she should abandon her cart, should leave the store immediately—she barely knows what she's buying anyway—but inexplicably soldiers on.

"Everything okay?" the checker asks as he starts ringing up her groceries.

"Oh, I'm fine." She sniffs and tries to laugh it off. "It's just allergies. I'm allergic to everything right now."

The guy nods but eyes her with concern.

She senses the people in line behind her, all of them watching her like she's a freak.

"What are you looking at?" she snarls at the woman directly behind her, who seems stunned. "You've never seen anyone with allergies before?"

The woman opens her mouth.

"Sorry," Nina says quickly and tries to smile, though her skin feels tight, like the Joker from *Batman*. "I'm just kidding. I hope you have a nice day."

Somehow she makes it to her car and tosses the bags of groceries in back, desperate to leave.

Once she makes it home, it takes two trips to bring everything upstairs to her condo. *Why did I buy so much?*

Finally, she collapses on the couch as if she's just returned from fighting a war. She stares out at her view of the water, letting it calm her. It occurs to her that this *is* like fighting a war. A war against every happy memory of Noel she's ever had.

How am I supposed to get over him?

She calls Suzy. Her sister's the only one she can talk to about this. What happened to all her girlfriends? All the work colleagues she used to consider friends? Apparently they weren't her friends after all.

"It feels like I have no one anymore," she tells Suzy over the phone. "Everyone's abandoned me."

"I'm coming over there right now," her sister says. "You don't sound good."

"Don't do that. I'm fine. It's just so hard. I can't believe I'm in this situation."

"I know." Suzy's voice softens. "You've never had your heart broken before, have you?"

Nina shakes her head and starts to cry again. "No." She gulps. "I haven't."

For years, she focused solely on her career. She dated here and there but wasn't interested in any man who wanted her to settle down and get married, who wanted her to give up the thing she'd worked so hard for. None of them seemed to understand her. It always felt like they wanted to hold her back, but then she met Noel. And he rocked her world. Because he understood her. Better than anyone.

"I can't believe I'm freaking out over a guy," she tells Suzy. The ironic thing about Noel was that, for the first time in her life, she'd met a man who *did* make her want all those things she hadn't wanted before. Marriage and a life with someone. Settling down. "Do you know he told me he loved me three times when he came over here to fire me? Who does that?"

"I'm sorry, Nina. He's an asshole."

She continues to cry. "I guess I should have listened to you all along."

"Hey, it's not like I saw this coming. If anything, I worried he might go back to Claudia."

Nina snorts. "And to think I was jealous of Claudia all those years. Little did I know it was a twenty-four-year-old twit I needed to be concerned about."

"It takes time," Suzy says. "I know you don't believe it now, but eventually he'll be a memory to you and that's all."

"I hope you're right." Nina reaches for the box of tissue she's kept close by lately and blows her nose. "I can't wait to feel normal again."

CHAPTER FIVE

Life & The Art of Automobile Maintenance
By Brody Austin

"We've all had that one car that cost us more than it's worth."

"Are you trying to set me up with Danica?" Brody asks Tori when he finds himself alone with her in her kitchen at this small gathering.

"Um... maybe?" Tori smiles. "What do you think of her? She's great, isn't she?"

Brody sighs. This is the third time his cousin has tried to set him up. His mom has also tried to set him up twice. It's too much. "I can meet women on my own. You know that, right?"

"Are you sure?" She's putting crackers on a tray with some kind of vegetarian pâté on them. "Because I talked to your mom, and neither of us has seen you with anyone since Kiera."

Brody doesn't reply. Even though he's never admitted it out loud, he suspects Tori and his mom both know he's still hung up on his ex.

"Maybe you should ask Danica out for lunch or dinner. What do you think?"

"She's nice, but I'm not interested."

Tori studies him with sympathy. "At least give her a chance. You might *get* interested."

A baby squeals, and she immediately turns toward the sound.

It feels like the whole house is full of babies, though there are only two: Tori and Liam's son, Oliver, along with Blair and Road's daughter, Ava.

Everyone's gathered in the living room, so Brody heads back out there to join them. And even though he has no problem with babies or toddlers, and in fact even kind of likes them—their cute little faces and exaggerated expressions—being around Oliver and Ava makes him uncomfortable. Mostly because it reminds him how everything's changed. It's all so different now. He can barely keep up.

"I heard Summer's moving back," Tori says to him as she takes Oliver from Liam and sits down. "She sent me an email recently."

Brody nods and takes a sip from his beer. "Yeah, she sent me one too." Summer is one of his younger sisters—twins named Summer and Autumn. Technically they're his half sisters, since they have a different dad. They both moved to Oregon for college a while ago. Autumn dropped out and is now touring the country with her boyfriend's band, while Summer went to midwifery school.

"Do you know where she's going to stay?"

He shrugs. "Probably at my parents' house."

Oliver fusses in Tori's arms, and she turns to Liam. "I should probably go feed him someplace quiet. I think he's hungry."

"Do you need anything?" Liam asks her.

"Oh, I'm fine."

Brody watches how the two of them gaze at each other before Tori gets up. They're obviously deeply in love and thrilled about their new son. He takes another swig of beer and thinks about how strange it is to feel lonely in a room full of people.

Liam takes Tori's abandoned chair, reaches for one of the pâté crackers, and asks him who his favorite teams are for the World Series, which starts next week.

Brody lets out a quiet sigh of relief. *Thank God for baseball.* At least that never changes—not in any way that's significant. Liam is an FBI agent but played professional ball for a few years as a catcher until knee injuries forced him to give it up, so Brody always enjoys hearing his opinions about the game.

The two of them discuss the merits of the various teams and players this year, mostly agreeing on their favorites.

At some point, Road comes over to join them. His cousin's an enthusiastic baseball fan as well. He brings Ava, holding her in his arms as the little girl with a head of auburn curls falls asleep against his shoulder.

Eventually it's time to leave, and Danica comes over to Brody as he puts his shoes on. "Is it all right if I give you my number?" she asks. She smiles, and Brody feels bad that he's mostly been ignoring her all evening, especially since Tori invited her over specifically to meet him.

She seems nice and attractive, and he doesn't want to hurt her feelings. "Sure," he says, getting his phone out and thumbing in her digits as she recites them. She asks for his number, and he gives it to her as well.

"Maybe we could get lunch or coffee sometime?"

"Let's play it by ear," he says, letting her know he's busy at work lately, not wanting to give the wrong impression.

When he finally gets home, it's barely after eight. He heads out to the garage where he keeps his secret project—though it's not an actual secret, and he only calls it that for fun.

Not long after Kiera left, a customer told him about a woman who was selling an old Lincoln that belonged to her late husband. Brody spoke to the woman over the phone, but she wasn't sure what model Lincoln the car was, just that it was very old. So he took a chance and drove out there. The woman, Ruth, led him to a barn that was half rotted away, and when Brody pulled the moth-eaten cover off the car, he could barely believe his eyes.

It was a 1941 Lincoln Zephyr Convertible Coupe—one of the most beautiful cars ever made. There were fewer than a thousand produced that year.

Granted, the Zephyr didn't look beautiful anymore. The interior was a mess, and rats or some other rodents had chewed up the seats. The body wasn't much better, though you could still see patches of the original paint—dark jade green. To most people's eyes, Brody knew it looked like something that should have been hauled off to the dump ages ago, but he saw the Art Deco beauty that was still there.

He paid Ruth what he considered a fair price and then had the car towed to his home, where it's become his passion project.

Since then, he's done a lot of work on the exterior. The body's been restored, and he's recently started on the interior and the engine.

Brody props open the hood and hangs a light on it to get a better look at the new engine. He recently bought a 125-horsepower 292ci L-head V12 and has been working on getting it running.

The truth is he spends a lot of time out here. Working on this car for the past two years is probably what's kept him sane.

He's feeling cheerful as he reaches for the tool he needs. There's something meditative about coming out here to work on the Zephyr. When his phone rings, he almost ignores it, until he sees the caller ID.

Surprise and then apprehension swarm through him as he answers. "Hey, what's up, Kiera? Everything okay?"

"Hi, Brody. Everything's fine. How are you doing?"

"I'm good." It feels strange hearing her voice. He wonders why she's calling. They've spoken a couple times since she left, but it's been mostly radio silence.

She asks after his family, and he tells her the latest news about Summer moving back. To be polite, he asks about her family too.

The whole time they're talking, he can feel his heart pounding. His upbeat mood is gone, and he's filled with a sense of foreboding. She sounds like her normal self, like his Kiera, and the part that misses her, that wishes he'd done things differently, is recording every detail of this conversation so he can play it back in his head later.

"I'm calling because I have some news," she says. "I wanted you to hear it from me first and not someone else."

"News?"

"Yes." There's a soft intake of breath and what sounds like her licking her lips. He tries to picture her in his mind, and it's so easy. "I've gotten engaged. Scott and I have decided to get married."

Brody feels like he's been punched in the gut. Or maybe the face. "Shit... *wow*." His voice sounds rusty, and he clears his throat. "Congratulations."

"Thank you. Like I said, I didn't want you to be blindsided hearing this from anyone else, so that's why I'm calling."

"Yeah, thanks." He takes a deep breath and wonders if he's going to throw up. "I appreciate that."

"You're still someone I care about, Brody. I hope you know that. I'll always care about you."

"Me too. I mean, I understand. The caring part. You're someone I care about too." *Jesus*. He rolls his eyes and rubs his forehead. He sounds like a dumbass. "I hope this guy makes you happy. Seriously."

"Thank you. He does. Very happy. I hope you're doing well and are finding happiness too."

"Um... yeah. I am." Sort of. *Not*. "Well, thanks for the phone call." He needs to get the hell away from her.

"No problem. Take care, Brody."

"You too."

He puts the phone down and tries to catch his breath. His

hands are shaking. His throat feels like it's closing up, like he's being strangled. He stares at the car in front of him for a long moment, then gets up and closes the hood before leaving the garage altogether.

Once he's inside the house, he can't decide what to do. Should he get drunk? Destroy something? Or maybe he should curl up into a ball and cry like a baby.

In the end, Brody sits on the couch for a long time, staring at the wall, doing nothing at all.

This is more like it, Nina thinks. She's finally gotten a good routine down. It's been almost a month since Noel announced he was cheating, and she's starting to feel normal again. Or sort of normal.

She has her dark thoughts. It's true. Mostly at night when she's alone in bed, imagining all the ways Noel might suffer and die. But during the day, she's too busy to have dark thoughts. She has her spinning class, her Swedish class, and her soapmaking class. All in all, a very full schedule, though she's thinking of adding a class on bagpiping. She's always loved the sound of bagpipes.

"Do you think that's too weird?" she asks Suzy. They're meeting for coffee at La Dolce Vita—one of her favorite bakeries in the city. "Learning to play the bagpipes?"

"It's kind of weird. What about looking for a job?"

Nina huffs. "I'm on sabbatical, remember?"

"I know, and I'm happy you're on sabbatical. But I have to wonder...."

"What?" Nina takes a sip of her usual latte, but it doesn't taste right. In fact, she's noticed some foods she normally loves have been tasting strange lately. Of course, she blames it on Noel. He's become her scapegoat for everything.

"You seem very intense about these classes. It's almost like you're on a mission. Are you actually having fun?"

"Of course I am." Nina rolls her eyes. "You know how I get. I always have to be the overachiever."

"Maybe this would be a good time to slow down a little. To really figure things out."

Nina shrugs. "What's there to figure out?" She finishes the last bite of her croissant and takes a sip of water instead of the coffee. "I'm forty years old. I think I know myself by now."

"Have you thought about dating again?"

Nina scowls. "Why would I do that? I just got out of a long-term relationship. The last thing I need is another one."

Suzy picks up her iced mocha. "I'm talking just for fun. It could be good to widen your circle of friends. It might help you stop obsessing over Noel."

"I'm not obsessing over Noel."

"You called me at two in the morning because you had a nightmare that he grew bat wings and flew in through your bedroom window like a vampire."

Nina cringes with embarrassment. "I know. Sorry, it seemed significant at the time." She dabs her finger into the crumbs on her plate and licks them off. "I think it means he's a bloodsucker."

Suzy laughs. "I won't argue with that. Though being a vampire is way too cool for that jerk." She tilts her head. "I just worry that you're alone too much. It might be good for you to make some new friends."

"I suppose." Nina has been trying to widen her circle of friends. She's met people in her classes but hasn't clicked with any of them. She suspects it's because she's coming on too strong. Normally she had great instincts and was good with people, but not anymore. Another thing to blame on Noel.

"What about the mechanic who helped you that night?" Suzy eats the last bite of her cupcake. "Didn't you say he asked you out for coffee?"

"Brody?" She sits back in her chair. "He's far too young for me. Plus, I sort of lied to him about my age."

"You did? Why would you do that?"

Nina shrugs. "I'd just had sex with the guy, and he tells me he's only thirty-two. When he asked me how old I was, I panicked."

"You know...." Suzy picks up her drink and swirls the straw around. "I looked him up online."

Nina's brows go up. "You did? Why would you do that?"

She shrugs. "I was curious about him. When I mentioned the name of his garage to Luke, he said he'd heard of it. Apparently he has a friend at work who takes his classic car there. I guess Brody's been helping him restore it."

"Really? Small world." Though Nina is slightly horrified. The last thing she needs is any connection to her night of blackout drinking. She hasn't touched a drop of alcohol since. Even the thought of a glass of wine makes her nauseous.

"From what I can tell, he's successful," Suzy says. "His garage has made a name for itself locally."

"Well, good for him. But I prefer to put that whole incident behind me, and that includes Brody."

Her sister nods and takes a sip from her coffee, then puts it down and glances around the bakery. "I should go pee before I pick up Grace. Do you remember where the bathroom is?"

Nina points to an area behind the main pastry case. "It's just past the bread area over there. You'll see it."

Suzy gets up and leaves while Nina takes another sip from her water. She glances down at her empty plate. She's been inordinately hungry lately and is tempted to get a second croissant.

Instead, she picks up her phone. Out of curiosity, she types the name "Brody" along with "Seattle Motor Works" into her browser's search bar. A number of entries pop up. To her surprise, the first one is an article in the *Seattle Times*.

She clicks on it, and it shows a picture of the garage where her car was towed along with Brody and his employees. There's a second photo that shows Brody alone standing in front of an old-fashioned car that's been rebuilt.

Her eyes linger on him. He's absurdly handsome. Instead of being pulled back into a ponytail, his dark hair hangs over his shoulders. She's never been into long-haired men but has to admit he's sexy. His broad shoulders and muscular arms are crossed, and even though he's smiling, there's something serious about him.

Flashes of that morning when they were intimate come back to her. It's not the first time she's thought of it. She wasn't exactly in the right state of mind when she came on to him, still drunk, and mostly wanting to get back at Noel.

The chemistry they had was surprising. And he was kind to her afterward—it's hard to forget that.

She starts to read the article and learns he's part Native American from one of the local tribes. He bought the garage five years ago from its former owner and had worked there as an employee before that. Apparently he's made the Seattle Top Ten three years in a row for best mechanic and is well known for his expertise on restoring classic cars.

The article continues, but Nina's interrupted when Suzy reappears.

"I should probably head out now to pick up Grace. Are you going to stay here longer?"

Nina puts her phone away in her purse. "I'm leaving too, though I think I'm going to get another croissant for later."

"Wow, did I just hear you correctly? You're buying pastries for home consumption? That doesn't sound like you."

"I know, but I have a craving."

Suzy laughs and rolls her eyes. "Me too. I always have a craving for sweets. Come to think of it, I should get some to take home for Luke and the kids."

They get in line near the pastry case, both of them ordering items to go. Nina gets a couple more croissants, some cookies, and then throws in a loaf of French bread as well.

Suzy eyes her bag of goodies. Nina tells her there's a bookstore down the street she wants to stop in at and gives her a sister a quick hug goodbye.

"At least there's one good thing that's come out of you and Noel breaking up," Suzy says.

"What's that?"

"We get to see each other a lot more."

Nina smiles in agreement. "Definitely a silver lining."

The two of them walk in opposite directions as Nina heads down to the bookstore on University Avenue. It's a sunny fall day, and everything's bright and colorful. The "Ave," as everyone calls it, is bustling with hippies, hipsters, and students from the University of Washington. Nina's always loved this time of year, and being here reminds her of her own college days. She got her undergraduate degree at Yale, and getting into such a prestigious school has always been one of the highlights of her life.

Noel, of course, also attended Yale. He was there a few years before her, and it was one of the many things they had in common and that drew them to each other. They'd both been liberal arts majors, she there for art history while he studied economics.

She gets a pang of longing as she remembers them traveling to New York on a business trip last year. After their meetings were done, they rented a car, drove up to New Haven, and spent a whole day visiting their shared alma mater.

Nina scowls at the happy memory and wishes she could erase it like everything else. Erase it like a hard drive on a computer. Then it occurs to her that she doesn't feel that upset. She doesn't even feel close to crying.

Maybe I'm finally getting over him.

She looks around at the beautiful day and takes a deep breath, enjoying the crisp air. All the stores have Halloween displays or fall themes, and she window-shops as she heads toward the bookstore.

For the first time in a long time, Nina isn't in a hurry. She has nowhere to go and nothing to do. She doesn't have any classes again until tomorrow, so she takes her time strolling down the Ave.

She sees a flower shop with bundles of colorful flowers for sale and is considering buying one for herself when she notices a couple walking on the other side of the street. The guy's wearing sunglasses and a gray peacoat similar to one she bought Noel a few years ago. He's holding hands with an attractive young woman with long curly dark hair.

Adrenaline skyrockets through her.

It's Noel and Emily.

Nina blinks rapidly. *Is it really them?* They were walking in a crowd and have already disappeared from sight. Her heart pounds. *It can't be them.* What would Noel be doing on the Ave in the middle of the afternoon? Surely he'd be at work.

Unless he's taken the day off. Noel was a firm believer in mental health days or "playing hooky," as he liked to call it. Once a month, he cleared his schedule and took a day for himself. Usually he went hiking, but sometimes he hung around the city.

Waves of nausea swim through her as she takes deep gulps of air, trying to calm herself. She's never seen them together as a romantic couple. Nina tries to cross the street, but there are too many cars, so she walks quickly up toward the crosswalk.

She accidentally bumps into a young woman with a backpack. "Hey, watch it."

"Sorry," Nina mutters.

She gets a glimpse of the guy with the woman across the street again, and now she's certain it's Noel. It's that coat. The one *she* bought him in Venice four years ago. *That bastard. How dare he still wear it?* She has a good mind to rip it off his back.

Finally the light changes, and she's able to dart across the street. She's still carrying the bag of pastries, which are getting jostled around so much they're probably nothing but crumbs.

She weaves her way up the sidewalk. Just when she thinks she's lost them, she sees them again. They've stopped walking and are standing in front of an Indian restaurant studying the menu on a sandwich board.

Nina strides over, not even sure what she plans to say. Her heart is in her throat when she notices how comfortable they are with each other.

"I hope you two are *happy* with yourselves!" she rages at them. "Because I think you're both *assholes!*"

Noel turns toward her, and she expects anger or indignation, but he looks confused.

And that's when she realizes her mistake.

"Excuse me? Do I know you?"

Oh my God.

All the blood rushes from her head.

It isn't Noel at all. It's just some random guy. Nina glances over at the woman, who clearly isn't Emily.

I could die.

The two of them stare at her like she's nuts.

"I'm so... so sorry," she stammers. There's a roaring noise in her ears. "I thought you were someone else."

And then she turns and runs away as fast as she can, letting the crowd of pedestrians swallow her. Her heart hammers against her rib cage, and her skin feels hot all over, like she's burning up.

Did I hallucinate them? What's wrong with me?

She doesn't even know where she's going or what she's doing. Finally, she turns into an alleyway and stops for a moment, leaning against the wall. She closes her eyes and tries to catch her breath.

"You okay, lady? You need help?"

Nina startles and turns to the homeless man speaking to her.

"I'm fine. Thank you," she says.

He stares at her with watery red eyes. "You sure? I get the jitters sometimes too. It ain't no fun."

She doesn't know what to say to this. "I'm quite all right. Thank you for asking." She pulls away from the wall and leaves.

Forgetting the bookstore altogether, she hurries up the street, frantically searching for her car. Once inside, she locks the door and leans back in the seat.

Get a grip, Nina.

Up close, the guy with the gray peacoat looked nothing like Noel. His hair was too dark, and his features were all wrong. The girl she thought was Emily looked nothing like her either.

She just made a fool of herself with a couple of perfect strangers.

And what if it *had* been Noel and Emily? What then? She still would have made a fool of herself.

As she grips the steering wheel, she's tempted to call Suzy but knows she shouldn't. Her sister has her own busy life with a husband and two young children, and Nina needs to stop leaning on her so hard.

She shakes her head and swallows.

When will this nightmare end?

CHAPTER SIX

Life & The Art of Automobile Maintenance
By Brody Austin

"Your mechanic's advice may not always be what you're expecting."

After the incident on the street with what Nina now calls "the fake Noel and Emily," she slides back from all the progress she made. She skips her classes for the rest of the week and goes back to watching daytime television.

It's just for a little while, she tells herself. *Just so I can center myself.*

She orders groceries delivered online and doesn't leave the

building at all. She even sneaks down at night to get her mail so she doesn't have to risk talking to any of her neighbors.

Somewhere amid her downward spiral, she remembers that *Seattle Times* article about Brody. She brings it up on her phone to finish reading it, but mostly she stares at the pictures of him.

How did he do it? How did he continue to not only function after his breakup but thrive?

She remembers how he admitted he was still in love with his old girlfriend, but obviously it hasn't broken him.

When Suzy calls and asks how things are going, Nina doesn't tell her about the fake Noel and Emily or about the way she's gone back to watching television all day. It's too embarrassing.

I'm the big sister. I'm the one who should be helping her, not the other way around.

"You sound strange," Suzy says. "Are you sure everything is okay?"

"Of course it is. I'm fine."

"Do you want me to come over with the kids?"

Normally, Nina loved seeing her niece and nephew, but she wasn't up for a visit right now. "Let's do it another time. I have my soap-making class soon."

"I thought that was earlier today?"

"They had to reschedule it." Nina feels bad lying, but if she tells the truth, Suzy will only start worrying again.

They talk for a little more, and after they hang up, Nina goes back to watching her shows and all the commercials for seniors, wondering what bizarre gadget she'll get suckered into buying next.

Her mind keeps drifting back to Brody. It occurs to her that if anyone would understand her current predicament, it might be him.

An idea comes to her, but she dismisses it. Instead, she watches a trashy talk show with yet another cheating couple—though this time there's a twist, and the woman is the cheater.

"It turns out Betty Sue is cheating on Bobby Tom with his best friend, Billy Bob. Bobby Tom is yelling at Betty Sue, telling her she's a

despicable whore, that she broke his heart into a million pieces, and he hopes she rots in hell."

"You tell her, Bobby Tom," she says, cheering him on.

When the weekend arrives, Nina switches to Netflix. She watches thrillers—ones where the bad guy—who hopefully resembles Noel, meets a brutal and untimely death.

As she's watching television, it occurs to her that at some point, it's likely she'll run into the real Noel and Emily. And what will she do then? Fall to pieces like she did with the fake ones?

Maybe I need therapy. Though she hates the idea of going into therapy to get over Noel. It's like somehow she's letting him win. *I mean, it's not like he's in therapy getting over me, is he?*

But she's desperate to talk about this with someone who might be able to offer her solid advice. And that's when she makes a decision.

Nina turns the television off and gets up. It's already dark out, but she doesn't want to wait, afraid she'll lose her nerve. She takes a shower and puts on black leggings and a sweater.

She hopes he doesn't turn her away or think she's insane. At this point, what does it matter though? He's already seen her at her worst.

Nina eats a quick meal as she sits on the couch, gazing out at her view of the water and the city lights. Canned soup and salad with the last piece of that French bread she bought at the bakery. She even butters the bread. She can't help herself. She's been so hungry lately. Of course, that's Noel's fault too.

Heartbreak apparently burns a lot of calories.

By the time she's done eating, it's already seven o'clock. It occurs to her that Brody might not be home, or he might have company. Female company. It is Saturday night, after all. What will she do then?

Traffic headed north on I-5 moves quickly. Luckily she's always had a good sense of direction and remembers the route from when he drove her back to the garage. Except when she drives by his house, there are a number of vehicles parked in front.

Is he having a party?

Maybe I should go home and forget the whole thing.

No. Screw it. I'm doing this. Even if he thinks I'm crazy. Even if he tells me to get lost. Which, let's face it, he has every right to do.

Nina cringes, remembering how rude she was to him the day her car was towed to his garage, and even when he asked her out for coffee. She's certain she didn't handle that well, either.

She drives around Brody's neighborhood and then parks a little way up the street so she can see his house. Eventually, his company will leave, and then she'll talk to him.

Brody stretches his arms out. *Damn, it's been a good day. Nothing like watching the World Series with a group of your closest buddies.* The game ended over an hour ago, but they've been hanging out, analyzing some of the finer plays, comparing them to previous years.

"I should probably head home," Liam says with a yawn. "I told Tori I'd try to get back before ten, and it's almost that now."

"Same here." Road reaches over for his can of soda and swigs the rest down. "Ava's been up teething most nights lately. It's been rough."

"I hear that. Oliver is still not sleeping through the night."

Road nods. "Neither is Ava, and she'll be six months soon. I've heard it can take some kids up to a year."

"Is that right?" Liam asks.

"It's true," Chavez says, joining the conversation. "My little nephew didn't sleep through the night until he was almost two. Just about drove my sister crazy." Chavez's little sister had lived with him for a while after she had her baby a few years ago.

Brody tries to listen to everyone, but his mind keeps drifting back to that phone call from Kiera last week. He's been trying not to think about it, but it's been hard.

Eventually everyone gets up and helps put the snacks away, but Brody tells them to stop. "Just leave it. I'll take care of it. You guys get home to your families."

He walks everyone outside to tell them goodbye and tells Chavez he'll see him on Monday. Standing at the end of his driveway, he waves as everyone drives off. He's about to go back into the house when he notices a car parked up the street.

It's an Audi. He might be imagining things, but it looks familiar. What's weird is it almost looks like someone's sitting in the driver's seat, though it's too dark to be sure.

That can't be Nina's car. What would she be doing here?

When he gets close enough, he's surprised to discover it *is* her. She's sitting in her car with her eyes closed, asleep.

Definitely weird.

He knocks on the driver's side window. "Nina?"

Immediately her eyes pop open, and she jumps, startled. She seems confused by her surroundings. She turns toward him in a fright, looking more like a lost bird than ever.

"You okay?" he asks. He motions for her to lower her window.

She blinks at him a few times but then rolls it down.

"I thought that was you," he says once they're face-to-face. "What are you doing out here?"

She appears indignant. "I came here to talk to you. What else?"

"How long you been sitting here?"

"I don't know." She glances at her dashboard. "I must have fallen asleep."

Her nose and cheeks are red, and she appears chilled.

"You look like you're freezing to death. Do you want to come inside the house?"

She studies him. Finally, she nods. "Okay. That would be good."

He stands back and waits for her as she gets out of the car.

"It's not a great idea to sleep in your car when it's this cold out," he tells her as they walk toward his house.

"I didn't intend to fall asleep," she says, sounding annoyed. "I was waiting for all your guests to leave so I could talk to you alone."

He takes this in and then chuckles. "So you want to get me alone again, huh?"

She flashes him a look of exasperation. "That's *not* why I came here."

"I thought you might want to get wild like the last time you were here." Brody doesn't know why he's flirting with her. It's been ages since he's flirted with a woman. He's surprised he remembers how.

"Don't get any funny ideas. I just need to talk."

"As I recall, *you* were the one with the funny ideas."

They walk up the steps to his front door and he opens it, leading them both into the house. The warm air feels good after being outside.

"Should I take my boots off?" she asks.

He glances at her knee-high black boots and has to admit they're kind of sexy. "Do whatever is comfortable for you."

She reaches down and unzips them. For a moment, he stands there watching her. She's wearing black leggings and a fitted sweater with a puffy black vest over it. Her pale hair is long and straight, and he remembers how messy and erotic it looked that morning when they were together.

"Can I get you anything?" he asks. "Something to warm you up? I have coffee, or I might have some herbal tea."

"Tea sounds good."

He goes into the kitchen and roots around in the cabinet until he finally finds a box of tea left over from Kiera. It's orange spice flavor.

Nina joins him in the kitchen, her eyes roaming over all the bags of chips and dip that he hasn't put away yet.

"Does this work for you?" He holds up the tea box.

She nods. "Perfect. Actually, that's one of my favorites."

The box feels light, and when he opens it, he discovers there's only one bag left. "Well, you're lucky enough to get the last one."

He gets a clean mug out and sets up the Keurig for hot water. The two of them stand there silently as the mug fills.

"Do you want honey or stevia?"

She shakes her head. "Just plain is fine."

Brody hands her the hot mug, and the two of them head into the living room.

He takes a seat on one end of the couch while Nina sits on the other. She takes a couple sips and then places the mug of tea on the coffee table next to some plates and glasses left there from earlier.

"So what's so important?" he asks. He has to admit he's curious. After taking her home last time, he was pretty sure he'd never see her again.

Nina opens her mouth and then closes it, glancing around the room at the various prints he has on the wall. "I saw an article in the *Seattle Times* about you and your garage."

Brody studies her. He knows the article she's talking about. It came out last year and has been great for business.

"I wanted to ask your advice on something," she says.

"Is it car-related?"

She shakes her head. "It's about my ex-boyfriend, Noel." She reaches for her tea and takes another sip in what appears to be an attempt to fortify herself. "I'm having a really difficult time with our breakup."

He's still confused.

She seems to be choosing her words carefully. "You told me you were still in love with your ex-girlfriend the last time I saw you."

"Did I?" He's embarrassed that he admitted that to her, since he hasn't admitted it to anyone else.

She nods, then purses her lips. "After I read that article, I wondered how you managed it."

"I don't understand. Managed what?"

"How you've managed to get over your ex. Or at least live with it, since you seem to be doing very well."

He's stunned and then laughs out loud when he realizes she's coming to him for relationship advice on dealing with her breakup.

"What's so funny?" she asks.

"You're coming to me for advice on how to get over your ex? Nina, I hate to tell you this, but I'm the last person whose advice you want."

"But you seem to be managing just fine. You're thriving even."

He chuckles some more. "Honestly? You should probably go see a shrink. Hell, I should go see one too."

Her mouth falls open, but then she sits up straight. "There's no way in hell I'm going into therapy to get over Noel. Forget it."

"Then I'm sorry to tell you this, but you've come to the wrong place. I don't know shit about how to get over someone. Hell, I just found out last week that Kiera's getting married, and it's completely messed me up."

Her eyes fill with sympathy. "I'm sorry to hear that."

He snorts. "Yeah, me too."

"Maybe you could just tell me how you got through the first few months, at least. I seem to be... struggling. I keep having weird dreams about Noel, and I even thought I saw him and Emily together." She tells him how she went off on a couple of perfect strangers because she thought it was her ex and his new girlfriend.

Brody nods. "About six months after Kiera left, I thought I saw her in a Costco parking lot with some other dude. I nearly lost it before I realized it wasn't her at all." He thinks back to the incident with embarrassment. The way two strangers had looked at him like he was crazy as he babbled to some random woman about what a mistake he'd made and how much he missed her.

"You did? Really?" She laughs with what appears to be amazement. "I'm glad I'm not the only one."

"The dreams are the worst," he says. "I still dream about her like we're together, and then I wake up feeling like shit all over again. It's bad."

"I dreamed Noel was a vampire the other night."

He chuckles. "Really? That's strange."

"I've had other dreams too. Ones where we're still together. And then I just get so angry at what he did to me. I want him to suffer. It's so hard knowing he's out there enjoying life when he's left me here like this."

Brody listens and then takes a deep breath. "The only person I get angry at is myself for screwing up the best relationship I ever had."

"How did you screw it up?"

He glances to the side and then shakes his head. "It's pretty simple really. She wanted to get married, and I didn't."

Her brows go up. "That's it?"

"Basically, yeah. Stupid, huh?"

"I'm sorry to say this, but yes. That is stupid. If it was the best relationship you ever had, and you loved her, why didn't you want to get married?"

"I don't know." He gazes over at one of the prints on his wall that he got at a classic car show in Las Vegas a few years ago. "I thought it would change things between us. We were so good together. What's the point of fixing something when it's already working perfectly?"

She smiles. "You sound like such a guy. What happened when you finally realized your mistake? She didn't want you anymore?"

"I never told her. She'd already left and moved away by then, built a new life for herself with some other guy."

"Are you serious? You never told her?"

"I didn't see the point."

"Wow, you *are* stupid."

He laughs. "Gee, thanks. Guess you're done asking for my advice, huh?"

"I guess so." And then she laughs too.

He watches her, still smiling. It occurs to him that it's kind of relaxing sitting here talking. He's surprised he's being so honest. He hasn't told anyone what happened between him and Kiera.

"I'm worried now how I'll react if I ever see the real Noel and Emily together," she says, reaching for her mug. "That I'll lose it again."

He strokes his goatee. "Maybe you should try some kind of visualization to prepare yourself."

"Like what athletes do?"

"Sure, why not?"

The two of them study each other, and he can't help but think how pretty she looks sitting there. She's taken her puffy vest off and has her legs curled up under herself like a cat as she sips her tea.

She puts the mug down. "How *did* you get through the first few months after Kiera left? Was it hard? I just need some advice on how to get my life back."

Brody lets out his breath. "It *was* hard. I mostly threw myself into work."

"Well, I don't have that option. I got fired, remember?"

"I'm surprised you haven't started looking for another job yet."

She reaches up to smooth her hair down. "I'm currently on sabbatical."

"What for?"

"What do you mean, what for? Because I *am*."

"I thought sabbaticals have a purpose. Like climbing a mountain or living in a monastery. Trying to find yourself."

She picks some hair off her sweater. "Well, I might do some traveling. I haven't decided yet."

"Also, aren't sabbaticals when someone takes a break from their job and then goes back to it?"

She gets a condescending expression. "Technically, yes, but I believe what I'm doing still qualifies. I'm just taking a sabbatical between jobs."

"I see. So you're really just unemployed."

"If you want to call it that."

He chuckles and crosses his arms. "That's definitely what I'd call it."

Nina seems annoyed, but Brody prefers to see things for what they are instead of giving it a fancy name and pretending it's something it's not.

She sighs and glances around. "Well, I've probably taken up enough of your time. I should get going. It's late."

"All right."

He gets up and walks her to the door, where she puts her boots back on. When she's almost ready to leave, she turns to him. She seems kind of nervous. "Do you remember when you asked me out for coffee?"

"Yeah."

"Is the invitation still open?"

He considers her for a long moment. "Sure, it's still open." Brody hopes he isn't making a mistake. She seems kind of high maintenance, even for a friendship.

She pulls out her phone. "Could I get your number?"

He gives it to her, watching her face. He senses there's something vulnerable about her wanting his number and softens toward her.

"Don't you want mine?" she asks.

He gets his phone from the kitchen and thumbs it in. Then he shoves his feet into his sneakers. "Come on, I'll walk you to your car."

"You don't have to do that."

He grins. "Sure I do. Don't you remember? I'm a gentleman."

Well, that was mostly a waste of time, Nina thinks as she drives back home. Though it had been nice talking to someone who understands what she's going through, how it's not easy falling out of love. She feels stupid and angry with herself for still having feelings for Noel after what he did to her, but obviously Brody's still struggling to get over his ex too.

Nina thinks back to the two of them sitting on the couch. He's certainly easy on the eyes. She had to make a conscious effort not to stare at him too much. He was wearing jeans and a T-shirt, but he wore them well.

I can't believe another woman hasn't come along and snatched him up. He must really be keeping them at arm's length.

She was embarrassed when he found her sleeping in her car. *He probably thinks there's something wrong with me.* It's hard to believe she fell asleep like that. It must be the emotional stress making her more tired than normal.

Nina decided on one thing tonight at least. She's going back to her classes next week. Maybe they're all frivolous, but who cares? Brody's right. Keeping busy helps.

She pulls into her building's underground parking and, on the way upstairs, stops in the lobby to get her mail. Once she's in the elevator, she flips through the various ads and junk mail, noticing an elegant white envelope addressed to her.

When she opens it, Nina discovers it's a "save the date" for a wedding. It's from Rochelle, who she used to mentor and who now has her job. They'd become friendly during the time Nina mentored her. She, along with Noel, had even gone out for drinks with Rochelle and her fiancé, Guy, a couple times.

The wedding is in February. Still four months away.

Her first thought was that she couldn't possibly go. Too many people from Tolland would be there. It would be humiliating.

On the other hand, wouldn't it also be humiliating if she didn't go?

Nina ruminates on this as she lets herself into her apartment. She's so tired of every little thing throwing her off-balance. Sometimes it's hard to believe only a month ago she was managing director for a large marketing department, when now a simple "save the date" has her questioning her self-worth.

This is, of course, all Noel's fault like everything else.

She changes into her pajamas and then gets herself a bowl of fruit, even though she doesn't normally like to eat late. Curling up in bed, she brings up Netflix, searching for a good thriller—one where the bad guy gets justice handed to him in the most torturous way possible.

CHAPTER SEVEN

Life & The Art of Automobile Maintenance

By Brody Austin

"Keep an eye on your dashboard. Those warning lights are there for a reason."

"Hey, big brother!" Summer throws her arms around Brody. "It's been ages."

He hugs his little sister in return. "I agree, it's been too long. I'm glad to see you're back home."

His mom's in the kitchen, and his dad's just come in through the patio door, probably from working in the yard. "Are you staying for dinner?" he asks Brody. "Your mom will probably make you stay even if you say no."

He laughs. "Yeah, I'd love to stay for dinner."

Summer smiles at him. She looks like her name. Blonde and cheerful and a bit of a hippie. She's also smart, kind, and down-to-earth—qualities he's always appreciated about her.

Dinner turns out to be one of his favorite meals—tacos with all the fixings. He douses each one with hot sauce as they all listen to Summer describe her experiences at midwife school down in Oregon.

"You're now all looking at a certified professional midwife. I've already accepted a job with a birth center here in Seattle."

Their mom smiles. "I'm so proud of you. I can't believe I have a daughter who's an actual midwife. It's amazing what you're doing."

Summer smiles. "Thank you."

"Me too," their dad says. "Don't forget. I'm proud too."

"And I haven't forgotten the way you both have helped me. I plan to pay you back as soon as I can."

Their dad waves her offer away while Brody listens to her insist that she'll pay them back. Dad also helped him buy the garage from Howard five years ago, and Brody paid him back too, even though he didn't want to accept it at first. Kurt was actually his stepdad, but to Brody, he's as real as it gets.

"So you're an actual midwife now," Brody says, drowning another taco in hot sauce. "That sounds intense."

"It is intense, but I love it. I can't imagine doing anything else. It's such an honor and a privilege to help mothers and babies."

Brody nods. Being a midwife fits his sister perfectly. She's always wanted to help people.

"And what's new with you?" she asks him. "I still can't believe you broke up with Kiera and that I'm only now hearing about it. Mom said she assumed I already knew."

He swallows a bite of food. "Yeah, that's been over for a while. In fact, I just heard that Kiera's getting married."

His mom's eyes widen as she picks up her glass of ice water. "She is? How do you know that?"

"She called and told me."

"I'm surprised Brenda hasn't said anything to me." His mom is still friendly with Kiera's mom. "When is the wedding?"

He shrugs. "No idea."

"I can't believe you guys broke up," Summer says. "You seemed so perfect for each other."

"Guess we weren't after all. So, what have you heard from Autumn?" He pops the final bite of taco in his mouth, hoping to change the subject. The last thing he wants to do is talk about Kiera and how perfect they were together.

"You know, I have a friend I think you might like," Summer says with a sly grin. "Maybe I should set you up."

Brody vigorously shakes his head, still chewing a mouthful of food.

"She's someone I went to midwife school with and is also moving back to Seattle."

"No," he says when he finally swallows. "Do *not* set me up."

Summer laughs. "Are you sure? Maybe I should invite her to the party this weekend." His mom is throwing Summer a welcome home party and has invited a bunch of family and friends. "I think you guys would really hit it off."

He was beyond tired of all these setups. First Tori and now Summer, not to mention his mom. Between all three of them, he realizes it's only going to get worse.

He glances over at his dad, who just smiles at him with sympathy.

Mom turns toward Summer. "That's a great idea. Though if that doesn't work out, a friend from my book club has a daughter who might be a good match."

"Actually, I'm kind of seeing someone," Brody says, interrupting as the two of them plot out his love life, "so you guys can stop setting me up." He has no idea how that came out of his mouth and is stunned at himself. *What the hell?*

"You *are?*" Both Summer and his mom latch on to this with excitement.

"Who is she?" Mom asks. "You never told me that."

"Well, it's kind of... new." *Shit.* He doesn't know what's possessed him. It's not like him to make stuff up. "There's not much to talk about."

"I'm so glad to hear that. I've been so worried about you lately," Mom says.

"Really? Why?"

"Oh, you know." She glances over at his dad, and he gets the impression he's been the subject of conversation between them. "I've been worried that you're still pining away over Kiera."

Brody scoffs like that's ridiculous. "Of course not."

"Well, I'm glad to hear you're seeing someone. Do you want to invite her to the party on Saturday?"

"Nah, I don't think so." He reaches for his glass of ice water. "It's still pretty casual between us."

"Well, if it's that casual, maybe you'd like to meet my friend," Summer interjects with hope in her voice. "I'm going to call and invite her."

"No, don't do that," Brody says. "Please."

"What's your new girlfriend's name?" Mom asks. "How did you meet her?"

Damn. Brody isn't sure how to get out of this hole he's dug for himself. It's like he's caught in a bear trap. "Her name's... um... Nina." It was the first name that popped into his head since he saw her last night. "She's a customer from the garage."

"Well, I think you should definitely invite Nina over on Saturday," his mom says, while his sister nods enthusiastically. "We'd all love to meet her, and we're really glad to hear that you've moved on from Kiera. It's about time."

"Yeah, sure," he says with an inward groan. "I'll ask her."

∽

"Hej, her mår du?" Nina says in Swedish, trying to pronounce each word precisely. "Jag heter Nina." *Hello, how are you? My name is Nina.*

Her great-grandparents are probably turning in their graves at the way she's mangling each word. On the other hand, hopefully they'd be happy that she's trying to learn the language of her heritage. She took French all through high school and college and speaks it well, but she's always thought it would be fun to learn Swedish.

She starts the video again and continues. "Talar du engelska?" she says slowly. *Do you speak English?* "Är delta rätt buss till flygplatsen?" *Is this the right bus for the airport?*

Nina pauses. *That seems kind of random. Why should I be worried about a bus to the airport when I can barely remember how to say hello and thank you?*

She went to her Swedish class and was dismayed to discover she's behind everyone because she skipped last week. She's not used to being behind in anything and will have to study extra hard to catch up.

As she goes through the rest of the video, trying to concentrate, her phone keeps buzzing. She ignores it for a while, then finally checks it to discover a flurry of text messages. They're all from Claudia.

What is going on between you and Noel?
Did you break up with him?
Is he really dating his intern, Emily?
Let's meet for lunch tomorrow.

Nina studies all the messages. Claudia sounds panicked, or maybe that's just Nina's imagination. It occurs to her that not having to deal with Noel's controlling ex-wife anymore is the one silver lining in this whole mess.

She debates whether she should meet with her at all, then decides she's too curious and replies.

Where do you want to meet for lunch?

Claudia messages right away with the name of an Italian restaurant in Pioneer Square. It's probably near the gallery where Claudia works. Ironically, Claudia has what was once Nina's dream job—managing an art gallery. That path never worked out for her though, and she wound up going to grad school at Harvard for her MBA instead.

Of course, the first thing she does after agreeing to lunch with Claudia is call Suzy and tell her about it.

"Wow, I wonder what she wants?" her sister says.

"I guess she finally heard about Noel and Emily. I can't believe it took this long. He must have kept it secret from her this whole time."

"Maybe she wants to be friends, to keep the relationship going between you two. She might be supportive."

Nina considers this. "I doubt it. I wouldn't exactly call us friends. Noel was the only thing we really had in common." Nina had occasionally tried to discuss art with Claudia, since she did have an art history degree, but it always felt like Claudia was humoring her.

The next day, Nina takes her time deciding what to wear. Few people ever intimidate her, but Claudia has come awfully close to succeeding. She's gorgeous and stylish and spends most days hobnobbing with artists and wealthy collectors.

In the end, Nina wears flattering jeans, a T-shirt, her black boots, and a funky scarf she bought on that trip to Venice a few years ago.

She's going for relaxed chic. She wants to look like she doesn't have a care in the world, that this whole business with Noel is already in the past.

When she heads into the Italian restaurant, she finds Claudia is already there. And, of course, she looks stunning.

"Nina!" Claudia waves her over.

They give each other a quick hug and sit down. Claudia's perfume is smoky and expensive. She's wearing a black turtleneck, cropped emerald slacks, and gold pointy-toed mules that curl up at the tip, like the kind a genie would wear. They should look silly, but they don't. Instead, they look cool and on the cutting edge of fashion.

Nina feels like a frump, but then Claudia always makes her feel that way.

"I'm so glad you could come today," Claudia says. "I wasn't sure when I texted, but then I thought, 'What else could she be doing?'"

"What do you mean?"

She leans closer. "I heard you were fired."

Nina stares at her. "Yes, Noel fired me right after he told me he was having sex with his intern."

Claudia sucks in her breath. "That's what I wanted to talk to you about. Is Noel having a nervous breakdown?"

Nina considers the possibility as a waiter brings her a glass of water. "I don't think so. A midlife crisis, maybe, but certainly not a breakdown."

"I just can't believe any of this. What happened between the two of you? I thought things were going so well. Did you have an affair too?"

Nina stares at Claudia with her long black hair, gorgeous face, and immaculate makeup. She's always wondered how Noel could have gone from a dark, sophisticated beauty like his first wife to someone blonde like her. They looked nothing alike. The irony is that both she and Claudia had done some modeling when they were younger. Nina did catalog work—mostly clothes, nightgowns, and occasionally underwear. She used the money to help pay for her expenses at Yale. Claudia, of course, did runway work in New York. As a result, she dismissed Nina's catalog work as if she were modeling tractor-wear for farmers in Nebraska. "Of course not. Are you seriously asking me that?"

"I'm just trying to figure out what drove Noel to Emily. Something must have done it."

The server comes over to take their orders, but they both tell him they're not ready yet.

"And you think it was *me*? That I drove him away?"

"What else could it be? Happy men don't have affairs."

"This is unbelievable. You're seriously suggesting that Noel's affair is my fault." Nina stares at Claudia, not bothering to hide her anger. "He cheated on me with someone half his age."

"I'm sure we can fix this. There's no reason to get testy."

Nina shakes her head. She should have guessed this is how Claudia would see it, that she's blaming Noel's affair with Emily on her.

Claudia leans closer. "In fact, I already have a plan to set this right. First, you'll need to call and ask him over for dinner. Make sure you put yourself together." She glances down at what Nina's wearing. "Let me know if you need my advice on that. Once you have him there at your apartment, you can seduce him, then apologize for whatever's happened between you two."

Nina stares at her.

"Don't worry. I'm sure he still loves you," Claudia says, leaning back in her chair. "It shouldn't be too hard to patch things up. And then we can all go back to our normal lives."

"Our normal lives?"

Claudia nods as she peruses the menu. "I think I'm going to have the puttanesca. It's delicious here. I highly recommend it."

"I'm not calling Noel. I don't plan on calling him ever again."

Claudia rolls her eyes. "Don't be silly. You're not really taking this thing with Emily seriously, are you? I'm sure whatever drove him to her can be managed."

"You're actually blaming me for Noel's affair." Nina still can't wrap her head around it. Unfortunately, a tiny bit of worry has started growing inside her that maybe Claudia is right. *Did I do something to drive Noel away?*

"Not really. I'm not blaming anyone. Relationships have their ups and downs, but what you two had was working."

"For you."

"For all of us."

Nina feels like she's living in the twilight zone. "I can't believe I put up with you all these years," she says. "But I always felt like I didn't have a choice."

Claudia's eyebrows shoot up. "Excuse me?"

"All you're concerned about is that nothing disrupts your perfect life, isn't that right?"

"Well, I want you to be happy too."

"I'm sure somewhere in that selfish brain of yours you actually believe that."

"Selfish?" Claudia scoffs. "I'm trying to help you."

"You're helping yourself, that's all. You couldn't care less about me." Nina stands up. She feels shaky from anger, but she's hungry too. Not to mention she has to pee. "I'm done. I've put up with this situation long enough. I hope you and Noel and Emily are blissfully happy together."

She left Claudia's stunned face behind and heads for the door. The restaurant is stifling, and the cool air outside feels like a relief.

On the way to her car, she stops in an artsy coffee shop and uses the bathroom in back. After coming out, she feels light-headed, so she orders herself an herbal tea and a croissant to go.

Once she's back in her car, she tries to calm herself, but she's still angry and upset. She eats her croissant quickly and then wishes she'd ordered two. *If I'm not careful, I'm going to get fat.* In fact, she thinks she may have already put on weight.

Does Claudia really blame me for Noel's affair?

And is there possibly any truth to it?

Nina feels sick to her stomach. She tries to call Suzy, except it goes to voice mail. She's so upset she's shaking.

Finally, she starts her car and drives. She heads home but then drives past her building. It isn't until she gets on the interstate that she realizes she's driving toward Seattle Motor Works.

Nina parks on the street near the garage and walks toward it. She can already see Brody. He's standing in front of a car talking to one of the other guys who works there.

As she approaches, she wonders what she's even doing here. She showed up unannounced at his house a few days ago, and now she's doing the same thing at his work.

When Brody notices her, he leaves the guy he's talking to and walks toward her. Despite how upset she is over what happened with Claudia, she can't help admiring Brody. He's gorgeous. His long dark hair is pulled back into a ponytail that emphasizes his cheekbones. Even wearing gray mechanic overalls, he's hot.

"I apologize," she says as soon as he gets closer. "I didn't have anywhere else to go. Not really." It sounds pathetic, but it's basically the truth.

His eyes roam over her face. "What's wrong?"

She shakes her head. "I needed to talk to someone. Is that okay?"

"Come into the office." He touches her arm. "We can talk there."

He leads her up to the garage, and she can feel all the other mechanics watching her. She smiles and nods at the guy who helped her with her tow that first day, and he nods back. There are two more mechanics who she's never noticed before. A tall lanky guy, who's probably only in his early twenties, and a young woman with pale skin and dark curly hair pulled off her face.

"I know how inappropriate this is," she says to Brody after he leads her into some kind of small office. "If you want me to go, I will."

"Just sit down for now." He motions to a worn leather couch next to a metal filing cabinet that looks straight out of the seventies. The office smells faintly of coffee and motor oil.

She takes a seat on the couch and puts her purse on the floor. Instantly, she's overcome with a terrible wave of nausea. "Oh no." She puts her hand up in front of her mouth. "I think I'm going to be sick."

Brody's eyes widen, and he quickly grabs the wastepaper basket and shoves it toward her. "Here, use this if you have to."

Nina closes her eyes as another wave of nausea hits her. She opens her mouth and takes deep breaths, waiting for it go away, praying she doesn't actually throw up.

"I'll be right back," he says, leaving the room.

When Brody returns a few seconds later, he's holding a bottle of cold water. She takes it gratefully. "Thank you." Her wave of nausea appears to be subsiding.

"You look pale. Why don't you lie down for a minute?"

She nods. "I think I will." Nina lies on the leather couch, still clutching the cold water bottle.

Brody comes over beside her and places the back of his hand against her forehead and then her cheek. His touch is nice. "You don't feel warm."

She nods and closes her eyes. Amazingly, she feels cozy with him in this little office.

"Maybe you ate something that disagreed with you," he suggests.

"All I had was a croissant and tea."

"It could be a bug. Let's hope not though."

She opens her eyes to discover he's watching her with concern. They linger on each other, but neither of them speaks.

"I think I'm feeling better." Nina sits up and discovers the nausea has passed completely. "It's gone. I feel totally fine now. Weird."

"That's good."

She stares down at the water bottle in her hand. "You don't have Evian by chance, do you?"

"What's that?"

"It's a brand of water... never mind." She cracks open the bottle and takes a sip. Surprisingly, it tastes fine.

He pulls one of the chairs in front of the desk closer and sits down. "So what brought you here today?"

She takes a deep breath. "I had lunch... or almost had lunch with Noel's ex-wife Claudia."

"Really? Is she a friend of yours?"

"No." Nina licks her lips. "It turns out she blames the whole thing on me. She says I'm the reason he's having an affair with Emily."

Brody crosses his arms. "That's nuts."

"Is it? Maybe I did something that chased him away. Maybe it *is* my fault. But what did I do? I'm not perfect, but I tried to make him happy."

"Don't even go there, Nina. That's bullshit. That pansy ass could have broken up with you any time before he started sleeping with Emily, but he chose not to."

She nods. "Noel said the first time they had sex, it was an accident."

He snorts. "An accident?"

"I know." Nina rolls her eyes. "It's absurd. Who has sex accidentally?"

"Stubbing your toe is an accident, or burning your mouth on hot coffee. Not banging someone."

She can't help but laugh. It's all so ridiculous. She takes another drink of water and then stares at the bottle, scraping her nail over the generic label. "I have to move on from all this. I know I do, but I don't know how."

"I'd start by not having lunch with his ex-wife anymore."

"That would be a good start, wouldn't it?" She smiles at him. "Thank you for being nice to me. I can't even imagine how crazy I must seem. If you'd met me six weeks ago, you'd never believe how different I am now. How much this has affected me."

"I believe it. I'll bet you're formidable as hell."

She smiles. "I ruled my team at work with a combination of discipline and reward. Mostly discipline."

He chuckles. "I'm not surprised." Then his voice softens. "Getting over a broken heart isn't easy."

She meets his brown eyes. They're toasty and warm, and Nina has this sudden wish that she could gaze into them for hours.

"I'd better let you get back to work." She starts to get up, but he stops her.

"Actually, I wanted to ask you something. In fact, I was going to call you, so it's kind of lucky you stopped by."

She sits down again. "What's that?"

He takes a deep breath. "There's this party happening at my mom's house this Saturday. It's a welcome home for my little sister. Would you like to come?"

She blinks in surprise. "As your date?"

"Yeah, sort of." He scratches his chest and tells her how his mom, sister, and cousin keep trying to fix him up with all these women. To stop it, he finally told them he was seeing someone. There's a pained expression on his face. "I had to give them a name, and yours popped out."

"Mine?" She's surprisingly flattered, and then an idea occurs to her. "Actually, I'd be happy to come to the party and pretend to be your girlfriend, on one condition."

"What's that?"

"You come to a wedding with me at the end of February. I know it's four months away."

"A wedding?" His brows go up as he leans back in his chair. "You mean I'd have to wear a suit and everything?"

She nods.

He strokes his goatee, thinking it over. "Well, shit, I'd say one wedding is worth at least four family parties. The holidays are coming up, and my family *loves* to throw parties."

"Two parties, and I'll even pretend that I'm interested in cars."

"Three, at the very least. And I won't tell everyone that you lied to me about your age."

Nina's jaw drops open. "*What?* Why do you think I lied to you about my age?"

"Because you did."

She shifts uncomfortably. Her face grows warm with humiliation. "I'm thirty-six."

"No, you're not. You're forty." He holds up his hand. "You can stop bullshitting me. I saw your driver's license when you were drunk that night."

"You saw my driver's license?" She feels outraged, which is better than humiliation, so she goes with it. "What were you doing? Snooping through my wallet?"

"I was trying to figure out where you live so I could send you home in an Uber, but then I changed my mind after you passed out."

"Oh." *And we're back to humiliation.* She runs her fingers along the couch, then takes a deep breath. "Yes, it's true. I'm forty."

"Why the hell did you lie?"

"Because I'm a lot older than you. And we'd just had sex."

"Eight years." He shrugs. "It's not that much. Besides, who gives a shit?"

"That's easy for you to say. You're not a woman, and you're not forty."

He nods. "True enough. But you lied right to my face while we were lying there naked together."

"You're right. I'm sorry. I should have told you the truth."

"You're damn right you should have." His eyes meet hers. "Don't lie to me again, Nina. That's a deal breaker for me."

"I understand."

They study each other some more. Finally, he smiles. "So, what did we agree on again? Four family parties in exchange for one wedding?"

She scoffs. "Hardly. Three parties, and I get to tell everyone I think cars are boring."

"All right, three it is." He considers her for a long moment. "Do you really think cars are boring?"

"Extremely boring."

He smirks. "I might have to change your mind about that. Oh, and also I should mention one more thing about the party on Saturday."

"What's that?"

"Since it's Halloween, it's a costume party."

CHAPTER EIGHT

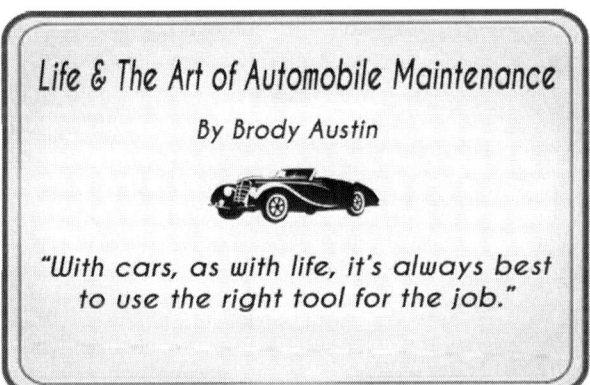

Life & The Art of Automobile Maintenance
By Brody Austin

"With cars, as with life, it's always best to use the right tool for the job."

"What is this?" Suzy asks, holding a misshapen orange ball in her hand.

"A gift for you. It's some of the soap I made in my class recently," Nina says. "Smell it."

Suzy brings the object to her nose, and her eyes widen. "Mmm... that smells good. Is it pumpkin pie?" She examines the soap again, turning it over. "Why is it shaped so weird? And why is it glaring at me?"

Nina laughs. "I took it out of the mold too soon. I should have waited longer. That's why the pumpkin's face is all messed up. It's supposed to be a jack-o'-lantern smiling." She shrugs. "I guess being patient is all part of the learning process though."

Suzy gives her a look. "Who are you, and what have you done with my Type A, overachieving, control freak sister?"

"I know. I nearly threw all the soap in the garbage when I saw how awful it looked, but then I talked myself down from that ledge."

Suzy puts the soap to her nose. "It really does smell good. I'm sure the kids will love it too."

"Hopefully my Christmas soaps won't look quite as bad as these."

"How are all your classes going, anyway?"

"Klasserna är bra," Nina says. "Tack för att du frågar."

Suzy laughs with delight. "Wow, that's pretty great. What did you just say?"

"I said, 'The classes are good. Thank you for asking.'" Nina grins. "Or at least I hope that's what I said."

Suzy nods. "Very cool. I wonder if I should try learning Swedish."

"You should, because then we could practice with each other. Actually, as part of my sabbatical, I'm thinking of taking a trip to Sweden." Nina's been there once, but it was many years ago.

"You are? That's exciting. When?"

"Well, I want to learn more of the language first, but maybe next spring or summer."

"Wow. Is your sabbatical going to last that long?"

Nina shrugs. "Maybe... we'll see." She's not sure why she's still putting off looking for a job. The longer you wait, the harder it is, but she can't seem to get motivated. The thought of going back to work and playing the same old political games, jumping through the same old hoops sounds meaningless. She's always been ambitious, so where has that gone?

"You're not worried about running out of money?" Suzy asks with worry. "The mortgage on your condo can't be cheap."

"I'm fine for now."

"Is this all because of Noel still? You should go to therapy and send that bastard the bill."

Nina shakes her head. They're sitting in Suzy's comfortable but messy living room. It's filled with kids' toys and IKEA furniture. Her sister only works part-time and yet her house is always a mess. Nina secretly used to think Suzy's house should be cleaner. I mean, what was she doing all day? But now that Nina's not working and had to let her weekly cleaning lady go, her place is even messier than Suzy's. She's come to realize that her former attitude may have been a bit high-handed.

"I still can't believe Claudia had the nerve to blame his hooking up with a near teenager on you!" Suzy says. "She's a piece of work, isn't she? Well, at least you never have to see her again."

"True."

Her sister leans closer. "I want to hear more details about Brody and this date you're going on with him."

"It's not really a date. We're basically helping each other out."

"I hope you guys help each other out in *lots* of ways." Suzy gives her a sly smile. "And have lots of fun doing it too."

"It's not like that."

"Not *yet*."

Nina rolls her eyes. "Is your mind always in the gutter?"

Suzy laughs and takes a sip from her glass of ice water. "Usually."

"He's too young for me."

"I don't think that's true, and besides, who cares?"

"That's the same thing he said."

Suzy leans back on the couch. "Well, it's true. At some point, you have to live life for yourself, don't you? Stop worrying about other people's opinions."

"My goodness, when did you get so wise?"

Suzy shrugs. "I've always been wise." She looks up and smiles. "I'm not saying you have to marry the guy. Just have some fun."

"I'll think about it, but first I have to go to the bathroom." Nina gets up and is immediately hit with a wave of nausea. "Oh no, not this again."

"What is it?"

She sits down and takes deep breaths. "I've been feeling nauseous lately."

"That's weird. Maybe you should see a doctor."

Nina shakes her head, continuing to breathe slowly and deeply. "I'm sure it's nothing. Probably all the stress I've been under." She describes what happened to her when she was in the office at Brody's garage the other day, and how she nearly threw up in the trash can.

Suzy nods, but then her eyes grow wide. "I just had a thought. You don't think... you're not pregnant, are you?"

"*Pregnant?*" The nausea is almost gone already. "That would be something. I'm on the birth control shot, remember?"

"When's the last time you had it?"

"Back in July. Although I'm off it now. I was due for it again right after Noel and I split up, but I canceled the appointment." She figured, what was the point? Instead, she had to get tested for STDs. Nina frowns at the memory. Thankfully, everything came back in the clear.

Suzy nods. "When was your last period?"

This gives Nina pause. When *was* her last period? "Last month, I think. I'd have to check my calendar."

"So it's possible."

"No way." She waves her sister off with a laugh. "Like I said, I stopped the shots, but it would have still been in effect. My period is late, but stress can delay it. In fact, I've been having cramps lately. I'm sure I'll be getting it any day now."

Suzy nods. "That's how I felt with both my kids. Maybe you should get a pregnancy test to be sure."

Nina gets up to go use the bathroom, grateful the nausea is gone. She chuckles. "I'm sure that's not necessary. I'm probably too old to get pregnant anyway."

"I can't believe you're taking the loco lady to your sister's party tomorrow," Chavez says. "Are you two actually a couple now?"

Brody's taking a short break in the back room at work, reading a baseball article on his phone. "I don't know what we are—friends, I guess."

"How old is she?"

"Forty."

Chavez's brows go up. "She's good-looking for forty." He pauses. "Is she... nice? She seems to have a lot of personal problems."

"She's all right." Chavez doesn't know he had sex with Nina that one time. All he said when Chavez saw him and Nina arriving together that morning was that she'd been too drunk to drive, so he'd let her sleep it off at his house.

"I hope you know what you're doing with the loco lady. She seems... I don't know, kind of high maintenance, if you ask me."

Brody frowns. "Don't call her that anymore. Her name's Nina."

Chavez shrugs. "Whatever you say. She still seems high maintenance."

Brody doesn't admit it out loud, but Nina probably is too high maintenance for him. For some reason, he's been thinking about her lately. He even looked her up online last night and found various articles about her, mostly in business publications. There were photos too, a number of them taken at charity events and fundraisers full of rich people. He saw pictures of the pansy-ass Noel too. A distinguished-looking older dude with short wavy brown hair. He and Nina were smiling together in a lot of the photos.

He sighs to himself and hopes inviting her to the party tomorrow at his mom's wasn't a mistake.

As he's thinking about this, Anka comes into the back room. "Can I talk to you about something?" she asks Brody.

"Sure, what is it?"

Her eyes flash over to Chavez, who takes the hint. "All right, I'm leaving. I need to get back to work anyway."

After he's gone, Brody realizes Anka is upset about something. He puts his phone down. "What's going on?"

She sits at the table and appears to be gathering her thoughts. "I've worked in a couple garages now," she says, "and I've usually had to put up with guys giving me a hard time about being a woman. I hate it, but what can I do? Usually I just ignore it until it goes away, because all I really want to do is work."

Brody listens and doesn't like where he thinks this conversation is headed.

"I'm not a rat," she says. "And I don't go running to the manager or owner over every insult."

"I know you don't." In fact, she hasn't complained once since she's been working here, even though he suspects Trevor's been giving her a hard time.

Anka takes a deep breath, and it's obvious she's trying to calm herself. "But I can't be expected to do my job if somebody keeps hiding my tools or throwing them away."

"What do you mean?"

She snorts. "Just that. *Somebody*"—she gives him a pointed look, since they both know who that somebody is—"keeps hiding my tools. I either find them later in another part of the garage, or I never find them. I've already had to buy replacements for a couple pliers and some sockets. After I used the bathroom earlier, I couldn't find the impact wrench I needed, even though I'd been using it five minutes before."

"Maybe somebody else borrowed it?"

She shakes her head. "I wish that were the case, but no. I finally found it buried in a drawer under some rags."

Brody shakes his head with fury. "Goddammit," he mutters. He tries to control his anger. Like all mechanics, Anka owns her own set of tools. "I'm sorry this has been happening to you."

"I asked Trevor where the wrench went, but he pretended not to know what I was talking about."

Brody massages his forehead. He really hoped the talk he had with Trevor had straightened him out. Apparently not. "How long's this been going on?"

"I didn't want to say anything. I was hoping he'd get bored with his little game and stop, you know?" She pauses. "It's been happening for a few weeks now."

He nods. "Thanks for coming to me with this. I'll take care of it. Also, let me know how much the pliers and sockets you had to replace cost, and I'll refund you the money."

Anka nods and stands up to leave. "I appreciate it." She walks toward the door, but then she stops and turns back to him. "Are you going to fire him?"

"I'm going to handle it."

She shifts uncomfortably. "Don't fire him."

Brody watches her with surprise. "Why not?"

"I don't want to be responsible for him losing his job."

"You're not. He's responsible for behaving like an idiot."

"I know, but could you just talk to him instead? I don't want him to get fired."

He sighs to himself. "We'll see. I'll think about it." *Shit.* What he'd like to do is go out there and wring Trevor's skinny neck.

She leaves the room, and a little later, Brody goes out to where Trevor's working on a transmission. "I need you to come see me before you leave work tonight. There's something I have to talk to you about."

Trevor eyes him suspiciously. "What is it? I was planning to clock out a little early."

"I'll talk to you about it at quarter to six tonight."

"No can do."

"What do you mean?"

"It's Friday. I got plans."

Brody stares at him, amazed at his sense of entitlement. "Your plans are going to include the unemployment line if you're not here at quarter to six."

"Fine," Trevor grumbles. "But I hope this isn't some bullshit."

Brody takes a deep breath and has to restrain himself from firing him right now. "You know, if this job inconveniences you so much, maybe you'd like to find someplace else to work."

Trevor grins. "Damn, cuz, calm down. Can't you take a joke?"

"Not everything is a joke."

He rolls his eyes. "Sheesh, fine, I'll stay until six."

Brody walks away, not trusting himself to continue this conversation.

At least the rest of the day goes smoothly. During the afternoon, one of his regular customers, who owns a maroon '93 Honda Accord LX, comes in, and everyone gathers around to admire it.

Brody wipes his hands on a rag. "What's the mileage up to now?" he asks Steve, the owner.

Steve grins. "Just turned over four hundred thousand."

"Damn," Chavez nods with approval. "They sure don't make them like this anymore."

Anka walks around the outside of the car, shaking her head with amazement. "It looks like it just rolled off the assembly line. How's that possible?"

"He keeps it garaged," Brody says. "Plus he takes damn good care of it."

"The right quarter panel had some rust," Chavez tells her. "We repaired it a couple years ago. Other than that, everything is stock."

"Amazing." She nods. "My aunt had an Accord and got it past 300K before she finally had to junk it. It didn't look as good as this though."

Trevor comes over to see what all the fuss is about. He laughs when he sees the car. "Holy shit. My grandma on the rez had one of these. I've seen pictures of it." He considers the car. "I don't know. It's minty but kind of dowdy."

Brody gets annoyed. "*Our* grandma had a Corolla, not an Accord.

Hell, it would probably still be running if one of her kids hadn't wrapped it around a tree."

Chavez nods. "Corollas, Camrys, and Accords—when the world ends, that's what people will still be driving. Those cars just don't die."

Steve hands the keys over, and Brody says he'll call him when the car's ready. He grabs a bottle of water and gets back to work.

When it's near six, he goes into the front office and prepares to close up for the night. Anka waves goodbye when she leaves, and he waves back. Chavez already left a half hour ago.

He's not looking forward to the discussion with Trevor. At this point, he's not even sure what to say anymore. Part of him wants to fire him, but the other part still wants to help him smarten up somehow.

Brody locks the cash and the printed receipts into the safe, then takes a seat in the office chair, checking the sports scores on his phone as he waits for Trevor.

He glances at the time. It's already ten to six.

What the hell's taking that kid so long? I just saw him in the garage.

Finally, at five to the hour, he gets up and goes out there to get him. *He's probably on his phone texting his homies.*

Except when he walks out to the garage, he discovers it's empty.

"Trevor?" he calls out, even though there's obviously no one there. Brody goes to check the break room and then the bathroom. Completely empty.

"I don't believe this."

He's been ghosted.

"A Halloween costume party," Nina says out loud as she studies her reflection in the mirror. Noel usually spent Halloween with his kids and Claudia, even when they got older and didn't trick-or-treat anymore. She thought it was odd, but he said it was tradition that he went over and helped hand out candy.

Nina studies the witch costume she's wearing. She went to a couple different stores but felt so overwhelmed that she finally decided to be a witch. Simple. Easy. And hopefully still appropriate at her age.

Ugh. That's been one of the hardest things about turning forty—deciding if her clothes are too young or not.

The witch costume is a long black dress with white lace and green satin. When she lifts her arms, it has draped sleeves. The best part is the hat. It's tall and pointy, with feathers, dried flowers, and mesh.

She bought the costume because of the hat, which is amazing. She wears her blonde hair straight and long.

Nina takes a deep breath.

All right. Let's do this.

This is her first date since she and Noel broke up. She knows it's not a real date, but close enough.

Brody asked if she wanted him to come pick her up, but she said she'd meet him at his house. It would be easier, as his mom lives up in Shoreline.

Nina spritzes herself with her favorite jasmine perfume, then gathers her purse and phone, and heads out the door.

She puts the radio on a pop music station on the way to Brody's, trying to get herself into a socializing mood. The hat sits next to her in the passenger seat. She has to admit, she's curious about Brody's family. He hasn't said much about them.

When she arrives, she positions her hat on her head and checks herself in the rearview mirror, then grabs the bags she brought with her, and heads up the walkway to his door, ringing the bell.

"Wow," he says when he answers, looking different somehow. "You look great. I've always liked Stevie Nicks."

"I'm a witch," she says with annoyance. "Not Stevie Nicks."

"Oh, really? Well, whatever, you look cool."

"Thank you." She steps into the house and then suddenly realizes why he looks so different. "You shaved your goatee!"

He laughs and strokes his smooth jaw. "Yeah, being clean-shaven works better with my Halloween costume."

"What are you exactly?"

Brody grins. His hair is slicked back into a low ponytail. He's wearing all black, including a long black coat that flares out at the bottom. Tall and broad shouldered, he's almost intimidatingly hot.

"You'll see. It will all become clear with one addition." He puts on a pair of small dark oval sunglasses.

"Um... I'm still not sure what you are. It does look sort of familiar."

"I'm Neo from *The Matrix*."

She nods. "That explains it. I've never seen *The Matrix*."

"What?" Brody's mouth drops open. "Seriously? That's one of the most badass movies ever."

She shrugs. "I'm not really into science fiction. Here, I brought you something." She hands him one of the bags she's carrying. She also brought a bottle of wine for Brody's mom.

He takes the bag and looks inside. "What is it?"

"Soap. I made it in one of my classes."

"Huh, thanks." Brody puts it on a side table. "So, are you ready to go?"

"Actually, could I use your restroom?"

"Sure. Go for it."

Nina heads toward his bedroom before realizing it probably isn't appropriate to use that one again. Instead, she finds another bathroom at the end of the hall.

After peeing, she inspects the toilet paper for any signs of menstrual blood. Ever since Suzy suggested she might be pregnant the other day, Nina's been anxiously waiting for her period to start. The notion that she could be pregnant is absurd, but still.

"Nothing," she murmurs, still staring at the toilet paper. Surely it'll arrive this weekend. She checked her calendar and her period is kind of late, which is unusual for her. On the other hand, breaking up with a man who she thought was the love her life but turned out to be a lying, cheating scumbag is also unusual.

When she leaves the bathroom, she finds Brody sitting on the couch, examining a piece of her soap.

"These are freaky," he says. "They're like angry deformed pumpkins. Were you in a pissed off mood when you made them?"

"You'd think, but I just took them out of the mold too soon."

He turns one of them in his hand. "Figured maybe you were thinking about your ex."

She snorts. "I assure you, they'd look a lot worse if that had been the case."

When they walk outside, she assumes they'll be taking his black truck, but Brody goes over to a different vehicle that's under a carport and covered with a tarp.

"What's this?" she asks. "We're not taking your truck?"

"Nah." He grins. "I figured we'd drive there in style." Then he pulls the cover off what looks like some kind of muscle car.

"Wow, it's gorgeous," she says, and means it. The car is an older shiny sapphire convertible with a black top. "What kind of car is this?"

"A 1969 Mercury Cougar XR7." He looks over at her and winks. "What can I say? I've always had a thing for cougars."

Nina rolls her eyes. "How long have you been waiting to use that line?"

He chuckles. "Since I bought the damn car, if you really want to know."

She laughs. "I guess I should be glad to fulfill a long-held desire of yours then."

He smiles and then comes over to open the door for her. "Allow me... to be a gentleman."

She takes her hat off and climbs inside the car's black interior, which smells like vanilla air freshener. He closes the door, and she holds the witch hat in her lap, puts her purse and wine on the floor, and then reaches around, fumbling a bit with the seat belt.

Brody slides into the driver's seat like the car was made for him. The engine starts with a roar.

She sits up straight in her seat as they head out of his neighborhood. Nina is surprised to discover excitement vibrating through her. Riding in a muscle car with some hot young guy. This experience is so far from anything in her former life that it feels like she's a different person. Someone less uptight. Someone who isn't hung up on her ex but who embraces life with a sense of adventure.

She looks over at Brody's handsome profile. "This car really suits you. Do you know that?"

"Thanks. I bought it a while ago. Took some time to restore it."

"It's exceptional." Her eyes roam the interior. "I really like it. I dare say I feel glamorous."

"And you said cars were boring."

"Well, most cars *are* boring." She watches him shift gears as they approach a stop sign. "But this one's kind of sexy."

He smirks. "I fully agree. Cars like this are a part of history too. I always like to think about the people who drove it before me. The conversations they've had in it." He glances at her with a sly grin. "And, of course, *other* things too."

She raises her brows but doesn't comment.

"So what's with the soap-making class?" he asks. "Is that something you're into?"

She shrugs. "I know it sounds frivolous, but it's one of those things I've always thought would be fun to learn." She pauses. "I'm also taking a Swedish class, and I'm thinking of learning to play the bagpipes."

He chuckles. "I don't think it's frivolous. People need soap. I take it this is all part of your sabbatical?"

"It is." She looks out the window. "There are so many things I always said I'd do someday but never have because I've been too busy with work. I decided I might as well do them now. Plus, I figured it would help take my mind off of Noel."

Brody nods. "I get that." He points up ahead. "That's my mom and dad's house."

Nina sees all the cars lined up in front of what appears to be a gray rambler in a very normal middle-class neighborhood. She takes a deep breath and hopes she doesn't make a fool of herself.

She's usually good socially and is great at making small talk, but ever since her life's been turned upside down, she hasn't been her normal self.

There's music coming from the house as they walk toward it. She recognizes Deep Purple's "Smoke on the Water."

"I have to warn you, my dad's a huge fan of classic rock."

"That's all right. I like classic rock."

He glances at her. "Do you?"

She doesn't get a chance to answer because the front door is opened by a young woman wearing a pink bathrobe, pink lipstick, with her hair in a pink towel.

"Wow, Neo. I love it. You even shaved the goatee. You look just like him." She gives him a hug and then turns toward her. "And you must be Nina." She puts her hand out, and Nina takes it. "It's so nice to meet you. I'm Brody's sister, Summer. Oh, and great costume. I love Stevie Nicks." She grins. "I'm a spa girl, if it isn't obvious."

Nina tries to tell her she's a witch and not Stevie Nicks, but before she knows it, the two of them are whisked into the house, and Nina's introduced to a dozen people in various costumes, from the Mad Hatter to some guy dressed as a yellow banana. Everyone seems surprised when they meet her, though most of them try to hide it. Nina suspects it has something to do with her age. People keep complimenting her on Stevie Nicks.

There's a cooler with beer and sodas, and at her request, Brody pulls out a soda for her.

An attractive middle-aged blonde wearing tight jeans and a pair of high-heeled hip boots comes up to them, and Brody gives her a hug. "This is my mom," he says, introducing them.

"It's nice to meet you." Nina offers her hand.

"I'm Lisa," the woman says, and Nina can tell she's surprised though she tries to hide it too. "Oh, and I just love Stevie Nicks. What a clever costume."

Nina opens her mouth to correct her but then decides, *Why bother?* "Thank you."

"If you can't tell, I'm a rock star groupie." She grins and then poses with pouty lips. "My husband, Kurt, over there is the rock star."

Nina sees a middle-aged guy wearing a long blond wig with a bandana tied around his head.

"He's going for a Bret Michaels vibe."

Nina nods, though she has no idea who that is.

"That's pretty funny," Brody says with a laugh. "I haven't seen dad with hair since I was a kid."

"I brought wine." Nina holds up her bag. "It's a dry Riesling. I wasn't sure what would be appropriate."

Lisa takes it from her. "Thank you. That's sweet of you."

Nina can't help noticing that Brody doesn't look much like either of his parents or his sister. She wonders if he's adopted, but then when Lisa smiles at her again, she realizes Brody has his mom's smile.

"So, how did you two meet?" Lisa asks, glancing between the two of them.

Nina freezes. This is not exactly a story she wants to share.

"I thought I told you," Brody says. "Nina's one of our customers at the garage. Her Audi came in as a tow. I guess you could say it was pure luck we met." His eyes linger on Nina's.

"It was definitely luck," she murmurs.

The three of them chat some more. It turns out Brody's mom is a hairdresser who owns her own salon. "It's small, just four chairs, but we like it. We've been there for almost twenty years now."

"That sounds like a real accomplishment," Nina says.

Some guy comes over to Brody and tells him he's got to come check out Gunner's new ride.

"Do you mind?" He turns to her. "I've got to see this car."

"Of course not," Nina says. "You don't need to stay by my side all night."

"Oh, honey, would you mind putting the wine on the table with all the other bottles?" Lisa hands the Riesling to Brody.

"Sure." He takes the bottle and leaves, and Nina's left alone with Lisa.

"So, do you have any kids?" Lisa asks.

Nina shakes her head. "No kids."

"Really? I guess you've been focused on your career, huh?"

"You could certainly say that." If she had to guess, Lisa is dying to know her age but is too polite to come right out and ask it.

"Have you ever been married?"

"No, I haven't."

Lisa nods. She asks what Nina does for a living, and Nina explains she used to work for Tolland as their head of West Coast marketing but is currently on sabbatical. She hopes she doesn't sound pretentious or self-important but suspects she does.

There are more probing questions from Lisa. Nina doesn't hold it against her though, since she's obviously being protective of Brody. Instead, she thinks about how strange it is to be grilled by the mother of a man she's supposedly dating who's not that much older than she is. But then she thinks about Noel and how he's most likely the same age and possibly even older than Emily's parents.

It occurs to her that she should tell Lisa her age and get it over with, but a stubborn part of her holds back. Why do men get to date younger women and nobody cares, but if a woman does it, suddenly it's all anyone can focus on?

Eventually Lisa excuses herself to go tend to some more of her party guests, and Nina finds herself standing alone in a crowded living room full of strangers. Some kind of Southern rock is playing that she doesn't recognize.

She thinks about the last party she attended. It was a $500-a-plate fundraiser for the art museum downtown. Noel was by her side.

They danced to big band music, ate canapés, and drank champagne. Afterwards, he stayed the night at her place.

Nina sips her root beer. It's then she notices her purse buzzing. The purse is a small black clutch, and she can feel it vibrating under her arm.

When she pulls it out to see who's calling, her pulse jumps.

Think of the devil and he appears.

CHAPTER NINE

N ina stares at her buzzing phone with Noel's name on the caller ID. She frowns, then swipes to decline the call and puts the phone back in her purse.

She wonders why he's calling but figures it can't be anything good.

It's hard to believe there was a time when she used to smile every time she saw his name on the caller ID.

Now she wants to smash her phone with a hammer.

Taking the last swallow of root beer, she puts the empty bottle down and wanders around the party. Brody is still nowhere in sight, and she figures he must still be out front, looking at Gunner's car. Whoever Gunner is—probably another cousin. He seems to have an inordinate number of cousins.

Her family isn't anywhere near as close as Brody's. She has two cousins who both live on the East Coast, who she hasn't seen in years. Noel's family is basically the same way, which was one more thing they had in common. It's also why he insisted on being so close with Claudia and the kids.

Suzy is the only family she sees regularly. Her parents don't even live in the States anymore. After her dad retired, they moved to a beautiful area in Porto, Portugal, and seem quite happy there. Nina and Noel have visited them a couple times and were planning a trip next year.

Her heart aches. Her parents, of course, love Noel. He fit in perfectly with them, and her mom said he's exactly the kind of man she's always imagined for Nina. She hasn't told them they've broken up yet, knowing how disappointed they'll be.

"Hey, you okay?" Brody appears in front of her.

"I'm fine." Glancing around, she realizes she's wandered outside to the back patio, where a couple outdoor heaters are set up.

"You look kind of upset. Are you really okay? No one's said anything rude to you, have they?"

Nina shakes her head. "I was just thinking about things I shouldn't be, that's all."

To her surprise, Brody takes her hand. "I understand. More than I care to admit."

They study each other, and it's strangely calming to realize that he really does understand. He gets it.

"Are you having a nice time? I know it's weird being at a party where you don't know anyone."

She smiles at him. He's wearing the dark sunglasses on top of his head and is achingly handsome. "I think everyone is wondering how old I am, but they're all too polite to come out and ask me."

"Polite?" He chuckles. "That doesn't sound like my family. I guess they don't have enough alcohol in them yet."

He's still holding her hand, and Nina has to admit his touch feels good. He's lightly rubbing his thumb over hers. It's making her insides flutter.

Her purse buzzes. She's tempted to ignore it but checks her phone anyway. Of course, it's Noel again.

Brody must notice the scowl on her face. "Who is it?"

"Noel. I have no idea why he's calling. I haven't heard from him since he fired me." *Fired. That's right.* She likes to remind herself of that because it makes her angry, and feeling angry is far better than humiliated and rejected. "Whatever." She tosses the phone back in her purse.

"Brody, there you are!" A gorgeous woman with long curly auburn hair and dressed like either a princess or a fairy godmother comes up to him. "Nathan's been looking for you. We just got here."

"Hey, Blair. I was wondering if you guys were going to make it tonight."

"Well, we had to find a sitter. Luckily my parents said they could do it."

"Are Tori and Liam coming?"

"I think so. Liam's sister agreed to watch Oliver, though I think Tori is freaking out." She turns to Nina. "It's my sister-in-law. She has a two-month-old, and it's her first time leaving him with someone."

Nina nods. "I see."

Blair glances down at the way Brody's still holding Nina's hand. "I'm Blair, by the way. My husband, Nathan, is Brody's cousin."

"Oh, sorry," Brody says and lets go of Nina's hand. "Blair, this is my friend Nina."

"It's nice to meet you," Blair says with a smile. She smacks Brody on the shoulder. "You sly dog. I heard you were bringing someone. I'm glad we finally get to meet her."

Blair's still grinning and, as far as Nina can tell, doesn't seem surprised by their age difference, though it's possible she's better at hiding it. Nina has a good feeling about her.

"I love your witch costume," Blair says. "What a gorgeous hat."

"Thank you. Everyone seems to think I'm Stevie Nicks."

Blair laughs. "Well, I can see that. I think it's your hair that makes you look like her with that costume."

"Are you a princess or a fairy godmother?" Nina asks, admiring her long blue dress and the tiara on her head. "You look great."

"Thank you. I'm a princess. It's sort of an inside joke with my husband because he always calls me that."

Nina's phone buzzes again. She tries to ignore it, then wonders if something bad has happened. She pulls it out of her purse.

"It's Noel again," she says.

"Who's Noel?" Blair asks.

"My ex."

Blair's brows go up.

"You might as well answer it," Brody says. "He'll probably just keep calling otherwise."

"I'm sure you're right." Nina sighs and takes the call. "Hello?"

"Finally!" It's Noel's familiar voice. "I've called three times already. Why aren't you answering your phone?"

"What do you want?"

"What do I *want*?" He sounds angry. "Did you really think you could treat Claudia that way and not hear from me?"

"I don't know what you're talking about."

"I'm talking about the way you mistreated Claudia the other day after she invited you for a friendly lunch."

Nina blinks in shock. "Are you serious?"

"Just because you're unhappy with me doesn't give you the right to take it out on her. She was really upset, and frankly, so am I."

"I mistreated *her*?"

"Yes, that's right. She told me how she asked you out for lunch as a kind gesture and that you were extremely rude and insulting."

Nina's face grows hot. "She's the one who insulted *me*, not the other way around." She can feel Blair and Brody watching her. "In any case, I have to go. I'm at a party right now."

"A party? What party?"

"A friend invited me. I don't want to speak to you."

"You're out partying?" He scoffs. "Well, I'm happy you've moved on so quickly. And to think I actually felt bad about what happened between us. But being angry with me doesn't give you the right to insult Claudia. After all these years, she was only trying to be a friend to you."

"I didn't say anything to Claudia that she didn't deserve." Nina's stomach is in knots, and she wishes he wasn't upsetting her so much. "Just leave me alone. I want nothing more to do with either of you, so stop calling me!"

Brody steps closer to her. She can still hear Noel ranting about manners and civility. Civility! As if he'd know the first thing about it.

"Give me the phone," Brody says to her, putting his hand out. "Let me talk to him."

"I guess you aren't hearing Nina," Brody says to the guy on the other end of the line, "so I'm going to see if I can clear things up for you. Nina wants you to leave her alone. Got it?"

"Who the hell is this?" Noel rages. "I don't know who the hell you are!"

"This is Nina's date."

"Her *date*? She's on a *date*?" The guy keeps repeating himself like an idiot.

Brody's glad he looked up Nina online the other night, because now he can put a face to this asshole.

"So you heard me. Good. Glad you're finally paying attention. Yep, that's right. I'm her date."

"This is absurd. I'm not talking to you. Put Nina back on the phone this instant!"

"Dude, you're embarrassing yourself. Nina's already told you to get lost, so now I'm going to tell you. She doesn't want you in her life anymore. So piss off."

"I don't know who the hell you think you are, but I—"

Brody pushes the End Call button and hangs up on him. Nina and Blair are staring at him with their mouths hanging open.

"What?" he asks, handing the phone back to Nina.

"That was *awesome*," Blair says, grinning. "Wow, I don't even know what's going on here, but damn."

Nina, to his surprise, throws herself at him. She wraps her arms around his neck, and he's surrounded by that jasmine perfume of hers.

"Thank you. You were magnificent," she says. "That was really nice of you."

"Sure, no problem." Brody hugs her back. He's amazed that Nina and Blair seem to think what he did was so great. "I just told that guy the truth. It sounded like he was having trouble with it."

Nina smiles up at him. "I appreciate it more than you know."

"Hopefully you won't hear from that asshole again."

Blair is watching the two of them with interest. "Is somebody going to tell me what that was all about?"

Brody doesn't say anything. He figures it's up to Nina if she wants to share something that personal.

She turns to Blair. "It's a long story, but basically after dating for six years, he cheated on me with his intern. Then after that, he fired me from my job."

"It sounds like he really is an asshole."

"Of course, I may have thrown my hot latte and a stapler at his head."

Blair laughs. "It sounds like he deserved it."

As the two women begin a discussion about how Nina's been trying to move on and has been taking all these classes, Brody notices a tall skinny guy from the back who looks a lot like his cousin Trevor. He's standing near the patio doors talking to someone.

"Is that Trevor?" Brody asks.

Blair glances over. "It might be. I think so."

He shakes his head in amazement. "That kid's got some balls." He turns to the two women. "Excuse me."

Brody heads over and, when he's a couple feet away, calls out, "Hey, Trevor."

Trevor turns with a smile on his face, but when he sees Brody, it turns to comical horror. Brody would laugh if he weren't so angry.

"Hey, cuz," Trevor says, trying to smile again, though it looks more like a grimace.

Brody crosses his arms and glares at him but doesn't speak.

"Sorry about yesterday." He licks his lips, obviously nervous. "I kind of forgot. No big deal, right? We can talk Monday. I'll stay as late as you want."

Brody still doesn't say anything, just continues his death glare.

"That's a... uh... really awesome costume, dude. You look just like him. For real." Trevor chuckles. "Should I take the blue pill or the red pill? I think for me it's going to be the blue one all the way."

Brody watches Trevor as he continues babbling nonsense. He's so done with this shit. "You're fired."

Trevor's eyes pop out of his head, and his mouth drops open. "*Fired?* Cuz, you can't be serious! Just because I missed a meeting?"

"No, you're fired because you've been harassing one of your coworkers."

"Oh, is that what she said? You know she's lying."

Brody has to force himself not to go off on this young idiot. "And how do you know exactly which coworker I'm talking about?"

Trevor smirks. "Who else could it be? She's jealous of me. I'm not surprised she wants me fired."

"Actually, Anka specifically asked me *not* to fire you."

"She *did?*" Trevor appears shocked. "Then why the hell are you firing me?"

"Because I'm sick of dealing with your bullshit. If you weren't my cousin, I would have fired you months ago."

"Come on, cuz. We're blood, man. Tribal blood. You're not really doing this, are you?"

"You've given me no choice. No matter how many chances I give, you never listen." In truth, Brody is pained that he has to fire Trevor. He had high hopes for him when he first gave him the job.

"One more chance," Trevor says, pleading with him. "Just one more. I swear I'll listen and do whatever you say. I won't even talk to Anka. I promise."

Brody shakes his head, vaguely aware that they're causing a scene, and that everyone's watching. "You have to learn there are consequences for your actions."

"And I've learned it, I swear. Please, cuz—"

"I want you to come in on Monday and get your tools. I'll give you a good reference, but that's it. At this point you're lucky to be getting that from me."

"*Fine! I'm out of here!*" Trevor yells. "Screw you and your shitty garage. I don't want to work there anyway!" And then he stomps off in a huff.

"Very nice attitude," Brody mutters under his breath. He glances around and sees most people are grinning at the theatrics and some are frowning at them.

"What on earth is going on?" Summer comes up to him. "Did you really just fire Trevor? Why would you do that?"

Brody rolls his eyes. "It's a long story." He glances at his sister. "What's he even doing here?"

She seems surprised and then shrugs. "What do you mean? I ran into him at the store the other day and invited him. He's family."

"My family. Not yours."

She gives him a look. "Well, I don't differentiate between the two."

Brody feels tired all of a sudden. Exhausted. "I'm going to head home now."

"Don't go."

"Sorry, but I need to leave."

He searches around for Nina and sees her still standing with Blair. His cousin Road is there too. Brody walks over. It's obvious the three of them saw the whole thing, judging by their stunned expressions.

Road shakes his head. "Don't think I even want to know what that was about."

"Are you okay?" Nina asks him with concern.

Brody sighs. "That kid has been nothing but trouble since the day he came to work for me." He turns to Nina. "I'm ready to go home now. Is that all right with you?"

She nods. "Of course."

"Come on, Brody," Blair says. "Are you sure you don't want to stay longer? We just got here. Tori and Liam haven't even arrived yet."

"Sorry. I know this sucks, but I'm not in much of a partying mood anymore."

Road nods sympathetically. Brody's told him enough about Trevor to understand why he fired him. "I'll see you next week. We're still hitting the batting cages with Liam on Thursday, right?"

"Yeah, I'll see you then."

He and Nina walk through the house and say their goodbyes to everyone. Nina thanks his mom and sister for inviting her. Brody feels a kind of gloom settling over everything, though he knows it's just him.

By the time they get back out to the Cougar, he's feeling even more like shit for firing Trevor. *But what else can I do?* It's chilly enough outside that he turns the heat on in the car as soon as they get in.

They don't talk much on the way back. He keeps thinking about Aunt Jeanie and what he's going to say to her. She's going to be upset when she finds out that he fired her son. He may have to go up to the rez and tell her in person. It's just as well, since he hasn't been up there to see Thunder in a while.

Once they arrive at the house, he carefully drives the Cougar back under the carport, then turns to Nina. "Sorry for the way this whole evening has gone down. I wasn't expecting any of that to happen."

"I recognized that guy from the garage," she says. "I didn't know he was your cousin—though I probably should have guessed it."

Brody chews his lower lip. "I didn't want to fire him like that, and definitely not at a party in front of a bunch of people. Shit." He massages his forehead. "I should have waited until Monday. I screwed up."

Nina shakes her head. "I agree, it's not ideal, but firing someone is never easy, no matter where you do it."

He glances at her. "You've had to fire people?"

She nods. "I ran a department with over fifty employees, so I've definitely fired people." She takes a deep breath and then smiles without humor. "Half the men, and a quarter of the women, usually called me a bitch afterwards."

He's not sure why, but he enjoys the idea of her taking names and kicking ass. "So how did you usually go about it?"

Nina shrugs. "A lot like you did, actually. I always told them straight out, though I didn't use the word 'fired.' I usually said we were 'letting them go.'" She turns to him. "Why did you fire your cousin?"

He studies her. The car is cooling down, and the tip of her nose and her cheeks have turned pink. He likes it—likes *her*, though he's not even sure why. He senses she's very different from anyone he's ever been with.

"Do you want to come inside?"

Her eyes widen, and he knows what she's thinking. Because he's thinking it too.

"Just to talk is all," he clarifies. "Nothing more." Unless, of course, she wants more, but he doubts that's a good idea anyway.

She seems to consider his offer. "Okay, we can talk some more. I wouldn't mind that."

They get out of the car. He was planning to go around and open the door for her, but she's got it herself. Instead Brody grabs the all-weather cover he uses and throws it back over the Cougar to keep it protected.

"Why don't you just park it in the garage?" Nina asks. "Wouldn't that be easier?"

"There's no room. I've got my secret project in there."

Her brows go up. "Your secret project? What are you building, a Batmobile?"

He chuckles. "Something like that. If you're nice to me, I might even show it to you."

Once they're inside the house, Nina slips her shoes off. She's still holding the elaborate hat. "Where should I put this?"

"Anywhere you want is fine." He shrugs out of the long black coat he was wearing, then takes the sunglasses off his head and puts them in the coat's pocket. Next, he kicks off his shoes. "Can I get you anything to eat or drink?"

She puts the hat and her purse on his dining room table. "I'll take some more of that orange spice tea if you have it."

He goes into the kitchen and pulls out a new box he bought during his recent grocery run, then grabs a mug from the drying rack next to the sink to put under the Keurig.

Nina comes into the kitchen and leans against the counter, watching him. "Do you drink that tea as well?"

"I bought it for you."

"You did? How did you know I'd be back?"

He shrugs and then grins. "I guess I'm an optimist."

Their eyes meet, and he senses the heat between them, that spark of something. They had it when they were together before, and it's definitely still there.

She bites her lip but doesn't say anything.

When the tea's ready, he hands her the mug, then makes himself a cup of decaf, emptying in his usual packet of stevia.

"Come on, let's sit on the couch," he says.

She follows him into the living room, and they both sit at opposite ends like before. It occurs to him that she's the first woman who he's sat and hung out with like this since Kiera.

"So, you never told me why you fired your cousin," Nina says before blowing on her tea. He watches her mouth. Her lips have a sensual shape to them. "What did he do?"

Brody takes a sip of coffee and then places his mug on the table. He tells her about all the stuff he's been dealing with since he hired Trevor.

"*He's* the one who broke my car the second time?" she says, outraged. "It's amazing you didn't fire him then."

"Believe me, I almost did. Instead, I talked to him and tried to straighten him out. He seemed to understand, but then I found out he'd still been giving Anka a hard time."

Nina nods. "I don't know if this helps or not, but you did the right thing. If Anka were litigiously minded, and you did nothing about Trevor, she might have grounds to sue your garage for harassment."

Brody shakes his head. "What a mess. I still feel bad for firing him. He's my cousin, for God's sake." That stuff Trevor said about tribal blood was true, and it made him feel even worse. "His parents are going to be upset with me. Aunt Jeanie...." He looks over at the fireplace that he rarely uses. "I hate to let her down."

"Nepotism often leads to incompetency. That's not your fault."

"I'm the one who's going to get blamed."

Nina takes another sip of her tea. "So how many people asked you how old I am tonight?"

Brody smiles at the change of subject. He picks up his mug of decaf and pretends to be perplexed. "What makes you think anybody asked me that?"

She gives him a look. "Because I could tell that's what they were all thinking."

He shrugs and tells her the truth. "My mom's the only one who asked me outright. Though I heard a few cougar jokes, which I ignored."

"I'm not surprised about your mom. I don't think she approves of me. You might have been better off giving them a different woman's name when you told them you were seeing someone."

"She didn't say anything against you." His mom did seem a little skeptical of the relationship, but she didn't openly discourage it.

"If I had to guess, I'm quite different from Kiera."

He chuckles. "Yeah, you're different." He thinks about how easily Kiera always fit in with his family, how easily she fit into his life. "You know, it's going to be the same all over again when we go to your friend's wedding. People are going to talk."

Nina grins over her cup of tea. "That's okay." She shrugs. "You'll be my boy toy. I might have to dress you up in something skimpy and parade you around."

He scoffs. "Screw that. I'm nobody's boy toy."

She laughs at his indignation.

Brody puts his mug down and then leans back on the couch, stretching his legs out in front of himself. "I don't care if people talk. I've dealt with that shit my whole life. I never let it stop me from doing what I want."

"What do you mean?"

He turns to her. "I'm guessing you noticed I don't look like anyone else in my family, except for Trevor, of course."

She nods. "I noticed. Though you do have your mom's smile."

He grins a little at that. "You're right, I do. But I look mostly like my dad's family. They're from one of the tribes up north."

"So the dad I met tonight is your stepdad?"

"Yeah, but I consider him my *dad*, if you know what I mean. He's a good guy. He's the one who raised me. My real dad, Thunder, split with my mom when I was a baby. She met Kurt not long after that."

"Your real dad's name is Thunder?"

He chuckles. "No, his real name is Ray, but everybody calls him Thunder."

"Is that some kind of tribal thing? Like a... spirit name?"

Brody shakes his head. "It's just a nickname. I guess he had a temper as a kid, so my grandma used to joke and say, 'Here comes Thunder.'"

Nina smiles at this. "I had a feeling you were part Native American that morning when I saw you sleeping out here."

He turns his head to look at her. "You were watching me sleep?"

"Of course not." But she seems embarrassed, so embarrassed that he wonders if she *was* watching him. She takes a deep breath. "I should probably clear the air about that. When I approached you that morning... I was still kind of drunk from the night before."

"Ah, so that's the excuse you're going with," he teases. "You were drunk and didn't know what you were doing."

They're both smiling at each other, but then the smiles fade and he's very aware that it's just the two of them. The room has gone quiet, and Brody can hear the seconds on the kitchen clock ticking by.

"Come over here," he says to her softly.

"Why?"

"Because I want you to."

Nina moves closer, so they're nearly up against each other. Brody's pulse kicks up a notch. The scent of her jasmine perfume is going straight to his head.

"This probably isn't smart," she whispers, except he can tell she's feeling the chemistry between them too. "I should go."

"Don't go." And then, because he really doesn't want her to, Brody moves in even closer. He touches her cheek and then brings his face up to hers, inhaling the orange spice on her breath, and finally he leans in and kisses her.

CHAPTER TEN

> **Life & The Art of Automobile Maintenance**
>
> By Brody Austin
>
>
>
> "The first look under the hood of your new car can be an enlightening experience."

Nina's eyes fall shut. It's a bad idea to be kissing anyone, much less Brody, but he feels so good, and she wants to feel good. She wants to pretend that all her problems are far away.

Her arms slip around his neck as he pulls her in tight against him, deepening the kiss. Everything about him is different than Noel. He kisses different than Noel. Smells and tastes different.

Nina ends the kiss but doesn't move away. Instead, she strokes Brody's jaw. "What are we doing here? Tell me."

"Does it really matter?"

"You don't want to get involved with me, Brody. I'm a mess."

"I know. So am I, remember?"

She caresses his face some more. So handsome. And too young for her. Nina knows she should get up and leave, but her body seems to have other ideas.

"I don't think we have to put a label on it," he says. "Let's just hang out. Would that be so bad?"

She can't help her smile. "Does hanging out include having sex?"

"I don't know." But then he grins. "Probably. Unless you don't want to."

Nina thinks it over. And then she thinks about all the classes she's taking, all the ways she's been occupying her time, trying new things. Maybe that's what Brody is—another new experience. Another way to help her move past Noel.

"All right, let's hang out. Maybe it'll be good for both of us."

"And what about the sex?" He moves his mouth close to her ear and whispers, "I hope that's not off the table."

Nina sucks in her breath, amazed that she's so aroused by him, can still feel this way while her heart's broken over someone else.

He nibbles her ear and then moves down to her neck, and she can barely catch her breath. She grips his shoulder as desire slides through her like honey in a jar.

Brody pulls away and gazes at her. Then he takes her hand and pulls her up from the couch with him, leading her toward his bedroom.

Her eyes wander to his broad shoulders, to the way the muscles move beneath his shirt. Once they're in his room, he moves behind her to unzip her witch costume. It's dark, but there's enough ambient light to still see each other. Underneath her dress, she's wearing black tights and a black bra and panties. She steps out of the dress and then pushes down the tights herself, using his arm to lean against for support.

Then he's kissing her again, and she reaches behind him to pull the band from his hair so it comes tumbling loose.

The only sound in the room is their hot breath. They move onto the bed, and Brody tells her to lie on top of him. Nina enjoys the feel of his firm body, but there's something strange starting inside her, a tightness developing in her chest.

When he rolls her over so he's on top, the tightness moves to her throat. They're still kissing, but a wave of terrible sadness sweeps over her, and without warning, she pushes Brody's shoulders away.

"Are you okay, Nina?"

She shakes her head and realizes she's on the verge of crying. "I'm sorry. I don't think I can do this."

He moves off her completely and lies next to her instead. He strokes her hair. "Did I do something wrong? Tell me."

Nina shakes her head. "It isn't you." She licks her lips and tries to steady herself. "Apparently I'm not ready."

Brody nods. "Okay." He takes a deep breath. "I understand."

She sits up and brings her knees in close. "I'm sorry." She glances back at him and tries to smile. "I warned you, I'm a mess." The tightness in her chest and throat are still there as she tries to stop herself from crying. A few tears escape, but she brushes them away.

"It's all right, Nina. Really."

She shakes her head. "I should go home." She doesn't move though, because the thought of going back to her condo and being alone all night with her thoughts is depressing.

Brody strokes her back. "You don't have to go. Stay here with me."

"I don't think I can have sex tonight."

He sits up now too, so he's right beside her. "That's okay. We don't have to do anything. Just stay. We'll sleep, and that's all."

She turns to him, wiping away more tears. "Really? You don't mind?"

"Of course not."

She studies him. In the dark, his eyes seem deeper and larger, and she wonders if he's lonely too. She tries to breathe. "Okay, I'll stay."

"Good." He lies back down on the bed and puts his arms out. "Come here. Lie down with me."

She turns and then snuggles next to him, resting her head on his shoulder. He strokes her hair as she tries to relax. She's comforted by how solid he is beside her. They lie that way for a long while until Nina gets chilled in only her bra and underwear.

"Do you have something I can change into? Like a shirt maybe?"

"What?" He seems startled out of his thoughts. "Ah, yeah. Sure, let me get you something."

Brody gets up and goes over to the dresser drawers, pulling out a black T-shirt for her. "Hopefully that works."

"Thanks. I'm going to go change in the bathroom." She gets out of bed and then goes into his small bathroom, flicking the lights on. It looks the same as the last time she was here.

She pees and checks for any sign of her period. Still nothing. She doesn't let herself dwell on it. The odds of her being pregnant are miniscule.

She takes her bra off and slips the black T-shirt over her head. It's long and comes to the tops of her thighs. In the mirror, she can see it's an advertisement for Seattle Motor Works. The letters are silver and done in the same bold font she recognizes from his garage.

When she leaves the bathroom, she finds Brody sitting up in bed, studying his phone. The lamp on the nightstand is on, casting a warm glow over the room.

He looks up at her. "That shirt looks good on you."

She smiles. "I feel like one of your employees now. Maybe you should put me to work."

"Sure, might as well. I've got an opening."

Nina grimaces. "Sorry, I forgot. I didn't mean to remind you of all that."

"It's okay." He shrugs. "It is what it is."

She pulls the duvet back and slips beneath it. Brody puts his phone down and heads into the bathroom. As he's in there getting ready for bed, she lies there studying the various objects in his room—the tribal prints on the wall, the clutter on his dresser, a laundry hamper filled with clothes—and thinks about how strange it is that she's staying here.

When Brody emerges from the bathroom in nothing but a pair of dark blue boxer briefs, her breath stops. *Holy shit.* She tries not to gawk and stare, but he's even hotter than she remembers. Miles of smooth hard muscle that culminate in a set of washboard abs. *My God.*

He glances over at her. "I hope this is all right. I could put a shirt on if you want. This is what I usually sleep in though."

She nods, remembering it from that morning on the couch. "It's fine." She pretends to act indifferent, though it feels like her whole body just woke up.

Did I really turn down having sex with this beautiful man?

She sighs in annoyance. One more thing to blame on Noel.

The bed dips when Brody gets in and slips under the covers. Without warning, he reaches over and turns off the bedside lamp so they're plunged into darkness.

They both shift around a little, trying to get comfortable. Brody's on his stomach, while she's on her side facing him. Despite how strange this all is, Nina has to admit it's nice too. There's something comforting about being with Brody. He seems capable, the kind of man you want around if things go wrong.

"Can I ask you something?" she says. "It's personal."

He pauses for a second. "Sure. What is it?"

"How long did you wait after Kiera left before you dated or slept with another woman?"

He snorts. "That's easy to answer. Too long."

"What do you mean?"

"Months."

"Really?" It's not what she expected him to say. She knows how guys are, and she figured he was out there picking up women right away. "I'm surprised. I assumed you wouldn't have waited long at all."

He rolls onto his side and props his head up. "This is going to sound arrogant as hell, but after she left, I didn't think it was permanent. I figured it wouldn't last long. That she'd be back."

"You thought she wasn't serious when she left?"

He thinks it over. "I knew she was serious. But I assumed when enough time had passed, she'd realize the giant mistake she made and come home. We were so good together. I couldn't believe she was willing to give that up."

"So what finally made you realize she wasn't coming back?"

He chuckles a little. "You mean, when did my delusion end?"

"I guess so."

"It finally ended when I found out she had a boyfriend."

"What did you do then?"

He takes a deep breath and appears to be choosing his words. "I went out to this tavern that's near the garage. Chavez and I sometimes go there for a beer after work. One of the barmaids was always coming on to me, so I went and sat at the bar alone one night. I had a few drinks, and then I let her take me home."

"Did you ever see her again after that?"

He nods. "A few times. We dated, if you want to call it that, for about a week or so. Until it lost its luster."

"What was her name?"

"Mindy."

"Why did it lose its luster?"

He shrugs. "I don't know. The sex wasn't that great, and then when we weren't having sex, there was nothing to talk about."

"Did you miss Kiera?"

He nods. "Yeah. That didn't help either."

Nina tucks her arm beneath her head. "Do you still miss her as much as you ever did? Has it gotten any better at all?" She wonders if this is how she'll be with Noel. Still getting over him two years later.

"It's not quite the same." He licks his lips. "Sometimes it's better, and I don't think about her for a few days. I tell myself that I'm over her, but then I'll have a dream or I'll remember something, and it pulls me back in. The hardest part is living with the regret that I ever let her go in the first place."

"Not to rub it in, but I can't believe you didn't go after her when she left."

He swallows. "Believe me, I've thought about it a million times. I hope I never make a mistake like that again." He focuses on her. "What is all this about, anyway? Are you worried you'll never get over Noel?"

She nods. "I *so* want to be done with him. Except it's not easy. Even though he broke my heart, I still love him. I don't know what to do. It's like I both love and hate him at the same time." Tears burn her eyes. "He *wounded* me. And then I think, how could he do that to me? I really thought he was *it*."

Brody lightly strokes her arm. "It sucks what he did—no doubt there. But you're tough, Nina. Don't forget that."

"I don't feel tough. Not anymore. I feel dumb and used. To think I gave him my trust so completely and for so long, and this is how he treats me?"

"That's on him, not you. You were sincere and honest. You gave him your best, but he didn't deserve it."

She nods in response, not trusting herself to speak without crying

He watches her for a few moments and then takes a deep breath. "All right, now I need to ask you a question that's very personal, and I want you to answer honestly."

"What?"

"I hope it's not *too* personal."

"What is it?" She eyes him with trepidation.

His expression, even in the dark, appears grim. "How is it possible that, after all these years, you've never seen *The Matrix*?"

She cracks up laughing, rolling onto her back. "I don't know, Brody. That *is* personal." She wipes the wetness from her cheeks. "Next thing I know you'll be asking me to watch it with you."

"Oh, you're *definitely* watching it with me. In fact, the next time you come over, we're having a *Matrix* marathon."

"What do you mean?"

"We're watching all three movies."

"There are three of them?" She hesitates. "I don't know. I'm not really into science fiction. Although...." She thinks about all the thrillers she's been watching recently.

"What?"

She tells him about the downward spiral she's been on, watching daytime television and thrillers on Netflix. It feels weird confessing her odyssey of self-pity to anyone. She hasn't even told Suzy. "I never used to like thrillers, but now I love them."

"See? And you're going to love these too. Trust me. It's happening. You can add it to your list of things you've always wanted to do."

She laughs. "But that's silly. I've never wanted to see *The Matrix*."

"Sure you do. You just didn't know it."

Nina smiles. "Okay, fine. I'll watch them with you on one condition."

"What's that?"

"You tell me something that's on *your* list. Something you've always wanted to do but haven't made time for."

His brows go up, and he seems surprised by her question. "Hell, I don't know. I'd have to think about it."

"There must be something. And it can't be about cars. It has to be completely non car-related. And not baseball either." She's noticed he's really into baseball as well.

He chuckles. "Damn, you just made it ten times harder."

"Something that's totally off the wall, like me learning how to make soap."

Brody rolls onto his back and tucks his arm behind his head, staring up at the ceiling. A few minutes go by as he appears to be thinking it over. "All right." He licks his lips. "I think I've got one. I've always thought it would be cool to do something musical, like learn to play an instrument. The problem is, I have zero musical talent."

"Well, you can't let that stop you. I mean, you've seen my soap."

He glances at her. "I like your freaky soap."

"So what instrument do you want to learn to play?" She sits up, getting excited. "You're not interested in the bagpipes by chance, are you?"

Brody laughs out loud. "Sorry, I don't think so." He considers it some more. "A friend of mine in high school had a guitar. Occasionally, I used to pick it up and pretend to play, but I had no idea what I was doing. Sometimes I've thought it might be cool to play one for real though."

Nina bounces on the bed. "That's it, then. You'll have to learn how to play guitar."

"I don't know." Brody seems skeptical. "How am I going to make time for that? I'm busy as hell at work, and now I'm down a man."

"That's the whole point. You do it anyway. I mean, think of all the brooding you've done over Kiera. Maybe this will give you something new to focus on."

He shrugs. "Maybe. I'll think about it." He looks over at her. "Let's do our *Matrix* marathon next Saturday. Unless you've already got plans."

"No, I don't have any plans." She smiles at him, and there's something aglow within her at the thought of them hanging out together some more. She remembers all the awkwardness and struggles she's had meeting new people lately. "We've become friends, haven't we?"

Brody pauses. "Yeah," he says softly and reaches for her hand, stroking his thumb over her fingers. "It looks that way."

Nina wakes up the next morning confused where she's at for a few seconds, but then she remembers. *That's right, I'm at Brody's.* She glances over, but she's in bed alone. He's already gotten up.

She stretches and rolls over onto her back, gazing toward the hazy day outside the window blinds. She feels astonishingly well-rested, like the best sleep she's had in weeks.

After getting up and using the bathroom—*still no sign of a period*—she washes her face and then brushes her teeth with her finger again. Afterward, she gets dressed in her witch costume from yesterday, since it's the only thing she has to wear.

Venturing outside the bedroom, she smells coffee, which turns her stomach, and she takes a few deep breaths to push away the nausea. She wanders out to the living room and kitchen, expecting to find Brody, except there's no sign of him, so she heads back down the hall again, opening doors. It feels like she's snooping, but she keeps going nonetheless.

One door opens to a closet stuffed with towels and other junk. The next is a room with a weightlifting bench and free weights stacked nearby. The third door, which she can barely get open, appears to be a junk room filled with boxes and old furniture.

"Have you found what you're looking for yet?" Brody asks, startling her. He's standing right behind her.

"My God, you scared me. This room is a mess. You need to get rid of all that stuff."

He reaches past her for the handle and closes the door. "Are you always this nosy?"

His scent surrounds her. Clean like fresh laundry. He must have taken a shower while she was still asleep. He looks good too, but she tries not to focus on that so much.

"I was searching for *you*. I didn't see you anywhere in the house."

He heads back toward the living room, and she follows him. "I was just working in the garage," he says. "Can I get you anything? I'm not much of a cook, but I can make eggs or a bowl of cereal."

"I can make breakfast, if you like."

He turns to her with surprise. "You can?"

She laughs. "Yes, Brody. I can cook. I'm not a chef, but my repertoire is larger than eggs and cereal. Of course, that depends on what you have at home."

"You don't mind?"

"I don't mind at all."

He grins. "Okay, have at it. I'm going back out in the garage for a while."

Nina wanders into the kitchen in her bare feet, since she didn't bother putting the black tights on. He hasn't mentioned her going home yet, and since she's not in any big hurry to leave, she might as well make breakfast.

She goes through his fridge and cupboards, which are a jumbled mess. There's a box of pancake mix that's two years expired. Lots of expired canned vegetables. She tosses them all in the trash. There's sugar and some baking supplies, which she suspects are left over from when Kiera lived here. The fridge could use a good scrubbing, but at least it has fresh food. She figures Brody went grocery shopping recently.

In the end, she makes stuffed French toast. Easy and tasty. Her mom used to make it regularly when she and Suzy were growing up.

"I don't think I've ever had stuffed French toast," Brody says after they both sit down in front of their plates. He shovels a large bite in his mouth. "It's damn good though."

"I usually use cream cheese, but you didn't have any, so I used jam instead."

He chews and then swallows. "I don't normally eat cheese, or any dairy, really. It doesn't agree with me."

"You're lactose intolerant?"

He nods, cutting off another piece of French toast.

She considers this and seems to remember reading once that a lot of Native Americans are lactose intolerant.

"Aren't you having any?" he asks, motioning to her plate, which she's barely touched.

"I'm feeling a little nauseous again. Actually, I think it's the smell of your coffee."

His brows shoot up. "You don't like the smell of coffee?"

"I normally love it, but it's bothering me lately."

As she's telling him all this, an alarm bell sounds deep within her. She remembers her sister complaining about certain smells when she was pregnant. *Can it possibly be?* She doesn't want to start imagining scenarios that aren't true. It's hard enough dealing with reality right now.

"You want me to put the coffee in a travel mug with a lid? Or I can just dump it. I don't have to drink it right now."

"A travel mug would be good," she says. "Thank you."

He gets up and goes into the kitchen while she takes another bite of French toast.

When they're done with breakfast, she heads back into the bedroom and puts her tights on, deciding it's time to leave.

She ventures out from the door in the kitchen to the garage and finds Brody out there. "Hey, I think I'm going to head home now."

He's leaning over the engine of an old-fashioned car. "You are?" He seems surprised.

She takes in the car, and she has to admit, it's kind of amazing. It looks like something a movie star would have driven around in during the golden days of film. "What kind of car is this?"

"A 1941 Lincoln Zephyr Convertible Coupe."

"It's impressive."

"Not quite yet, but it will be."

She walks around and can see how the inside of the car has been almost completely gutted. "Where are the seats?"

"I had to toss them. They'd become a nest for a family of rodents."

Nina makes a face. "Gross. So this is your secret project?"

He nods and then motions to a book that looks like a photo album on the back table. "If you want, you can see the progress. I like to take photos and then print them up as a record."

She picks it up and then stands there flipping through the album with stunned amazement. "*This* is what it looked like when you first started?" The car had obviously been abandoned for years and should have been junked. "I can't believe you did all this. Did it cost a lot?"

He snorts. "Let's just say it ain't cheap restoring a car like this."

"Are you planning to sell it?"

"Hell no. This is one of my favorite cars of all time. This Art Deco beauty is mine forever."

She puts the book back down. "It is quite impressive. It looks like something you'd imagine Rita Hayworth riding around in."

He chuckles. "As a matter of fact, Rita Hayworth *did* own one of these, though I'm not sure what year hers was. There were only 725 of them produced in 1941."

Brody's still leaning over the engine, and Nina tries very hard not to stare at his ass. He's wearing jeans that are snug in all the right places. In fact, she'd be happy to start her own photo album with nothing but pictures of this.

"Well, thanks for having me over last night," she says. "I had a nice time."

He stands up from under the hood and turns toward her, leaning against the car. With the back of his hand, he pushes some stray hair off his forehead. "Yeah, me too. Sorry for having to leave the party early."

"Don't worry about that."

They study each other, and Nina's stomach turns fluttery. She's not sure what this is with Brody, but she knows one thing: she likes it.

Nina takes a deep breath. "All right, then, I should get going."

He reaches for a rag and wipes his fingers. "Let me walk you out."

"You don't have to keep doing that."

Of course, he does it anyway. They go out through the front door, and he walks her down to her car. It's a brisk day, and everything's wet from the rain last night. She opens the passenger side and sets her hat and purse on the seat. Before she heads over to the driver's side, he grabs her hand and pulls her in close.

"What are you doing?" she asks.

"I'm saying goodbye."

There's something happening between them, and though she's not sure how to put it into words, the thoughtful expression on his face says it all. It reminds her of how he looked when they were up talking most of last night.

Without thinking about it, she wraps her arms around Brody and hugs him close. His arms encircle her, and they stay that way for a long moment. When she pulls back, he reaches for her hand again.

"Take care of yourself, Nina banana."

Her brows go up. "Nina banana?"

He's smiling now. "It just came to me. Has anyone ever called you that?"

"No, I can't say they have." She can't even imagine anyone giving her such a silly nickname. Oddly though, she kind of likes it.

He squeezes her hand. "Then let me be the first."

CHAPTER ELEVEN

Life & The Art of Automobile Maintenance
By Brody Austin

"If there's a warning light on, don't wait for an emergency to see your mechanic."

Brody rubs his eyes and takes another sip of coffee as he studies the schedule Monday morning. It's always difficult being down one employee. Last winter, Chavez had the flu and was out for a full week. Brody wound up calling a temp agency and hiring a mechanic who worked as a contractor to fill in, which is exactly what he did when he arrived this morning to get a replacement for Trevor.

Unfortunately, the agency said they couldn't send anyone over until tomorrow.

Both Chavez and Anka didn't seem that surprised when he told them he'd let Trevor go.

"Dude, you *had* to," Chavez says to him later when he's in the back office. "You weren't doing that kid any favors keeping him on and letting him get away with that shit."

"Did you know he was giving Anka such a hard time?" Brody asks.

Chavez shrugs. "I had a feeling something was going on, but I didn't know he was hiding her tools or throwing them away. That's messed up."

Brody opens a can of soda and takes a swig. He had trouble sleeping last night and could use the hit of caffeine and sugar.

As the day goes by, he waits with dread for Trevor to come pick up his stuff and for Aunt Jeanie to call him. He's certain she's going to ask him to hire Trevor back again, to give him another chance, and what's he supposed to say then?

The three of them work late into the evening, and by the time the day's finished, they're all exhausted. Eventually he sends Chavez and Anka home before finally handing the last customer of the day their car keys. Trevor never showed up at all.

Brody goes ahead and packs up all Trevor's tools himself, loads everything into the back of his truck, and then drives over to his cousin's apartment. He knocks on the door and rings the bell, but no one answers.

Great. Now what?

He heads home and then lugs everything inside to store it in his garage. Hopefully he'll hear from his cousin soon. Maybe things will get better for Trevor if he works for someone else. It'll force him to take things more seriously and smarten up. Or at least that's what Brody's hoping.

The next few days go by without any problems. Jackson, the guy the temp agency sent, is a good worker and a decent mechanic. He's from Australia and has a thick accent, along with an entertaining sense of humor. There's still no word from either Trevor or his aunt, and he can't decide if he should be relieved or worried. He knows he's going to have to deal with the fallout from this eventually, and he'd rather just get it over with already.

Brody's been thinking a lot about Nina lately. He's looking forward to seeing her again on Saturday. It was relaxing hanging out with her last weekend. Cathartic even. It's a relief to discuss the Kiera situation so openly. In a weird way, the two of them are kind of in the same boat.

Obviously sex with Nina is off the table, at least for a while, but he likes being close to her. He misses that part of being with a woman.

He's not sure how you'd define their relationship, but who cares? Who needs labels anyway? He's dealt with people labeling him his whole damn life.

Nina nearly faints when she sees the two pink lines on the second pregnancy test.

Oh my God! Is that real?

It certainly looks real. Very real.

She keeps staring at the back of the box and then comparing it to both tests. She's staring so hard, she's starting to see spots instead of lines.

It definitely looks positive.

She's grateful she bought two tests or she never would have believed it.

Is it possible they're both faulty? What are the odds of that?

Nina sits on the toilet seat, her heart racing, and looks it up on her phone. She discovers the odds of them being false are infinitesimally small.

Okay. So that's it. I'm pregnant. I guess I'm not too old after all.

She stands up and stares at herself in the mirror. Her blue eyes appear huge and uncertain, blinking back at her with shock. This is not a possibility that she ever saw for herself.

What do I do now?

Anxiety floods through her, but there's also a kind of giddy excitement. "You're going to have a baby," she tells the freaked-out person in the mirror. "You're going to be a *mom*."

She places a hand on her abdomen. *To think there's someone developing in there.*

Nina stares down at the pregnancy tests again. It doesn't feel real.

And then she has another thought that knocks the wind out of her completely. She flops back down on the toilet seat lid, trying to catch her breath.

Whose baby is it?

She has no idea.

It could be Noel's or Brody's. Either is a possibility.

She lifts a shaky hand to her forehead. This is crazy. Of all the ways she pictured her future, this was never in any of her wildest imaginings. Being pregnant and not even certain who the father is?

Then she bursts out laughing, covering her mouth. "Wow, I'm such a slut."

She's played it safe her whole life. Focused on school. Then focused on her career. Always careful. Always coloring within the lines.

And now here she is forty years old, knocked up, unemployed, and with no idea who her baby daddy is.

She thinks about all the scandalous daytime talk shows she's been watching this past month with all those people screaming at each other. *Apparently I really am one of them.*

The first person she calls is Suzy. It's eleven at night, and she hopes her sister isn't already asleep.

As soon as Suzy answers, Nina blurts out her news.

"What did you just say?" a groggy-sounding Suzy mumbles into the phone.

"I'm pregnant."

"Oh my God!"

Nina laughs. In the past, before Suzy was married with kids, her little sister was the one always doing scandalous things.

I guess it's my turn now.

"Are you sure?" Suzy asks.

"I took two home pregnancy tests."

"Well, that explains the nausea."

"I know. It explains why I've been feeling so weird in general."

She hears Suzy moving around, like she's getting out of bed, then hears Luke in the background asking what's going on. Suzy tells him, "My sister's pregnant," and then Luke says, "Whoa."

"All right," Suzy says to her. "I'm going to the other room so we can talk. Do you need me? Do you want to come over here, or should I go over there?"

Nina smiles in appreciation for her sister. "Thanks, but I'm fine right now. I don't need a babysitter. I just needed to tell someone."

"Mom and Dad are going to flip out. You haven't even told them about breaking up with Noel yet or being fired, have you?"

Nina sighs. "No, I haven't." Her parents are definitely going to freak out.

"Is Noel the father?" Suzy asks. "Or, oh my God, is it *Brody*?"

"I have absolutely no idea. It could be either."

Suzy sucks in her breath. "Damn, you're a little hussy, aren't you?"

Nina laughs despite herself. "Is this really the time for jokes?"

"I think it *is*, actually. Humor is our friend right now."

Nina wanders into her living room and flops down on the couch, gazing out at the city lights and the inkiness of the water. "I can't believe I'm in this situation."

"Frankly, I can't either. You were always the perfect one. The golden daughter."

"Apparently I'm not so golden anymore."

"What are you going to do? You know Luke and I will help in any way we can."

"Thank you. I appreciate that, but you have your own family. I don't want to be a burden to anyone."

"You're my sister, not a burden. And you *are* family."

Nina sighs. "I better make a doctor's appointment this week and have it officially confirmed."

"I can give you my midwife's number too." Nina was there with Suzy when Grace was born at the birth center. "There's a lot of stuff to think about. When are you going to tell Noel and Brody?"

Nina picks at a loose thread on her sofa. "Soon. I'll have to get a paternity test. They'll both need to submit DNA." The thought of telling either of them makes her queasy again.

"How does that work?" Suzy jokes. "Will they have to jerk off into a cup?"

Nina laughs. "I'm fairly certain that's not how they determine paternity. I imagine they'll each have to give a blood sample. In any case, I'll find out."

~

After a fitful night without much sleep, and obsessing over this new reality, Nina calls her doctor's office first thing in the morning to schedule an appointment. As luck would have it, they had a cancellation and can see her late that afternoon.

She goes to her spinning class in the morning, then her Swedish language class in Ballard. Afterward she walks around the area a bit, window-shopping. Some of the stores have kids and baby clothes on display. *So sweet. Everything's so tiny.* She stares at it, trying to wrap her head around the fact that she'll be having a baby. She's even tempted to buy something but doesn't feel quite ready for that yet.

A music store catches her eye, and she walks inside. They don't sell bagpipes, but they do sell guitars. Some very nice-looking ones. On impulse, Nina decides to buy one for Brody. Mainly because she suspects he'd never buy one for himself. She gets him a very nice

Fender acoustic guitar—a brand even she's heard of—that comes with its own case.

She lugs the guitar back to her car, then drives over to her doctor's appointment, drumming her fingers on the steering wheel, trying to calm her nerves.

By the time she's sitting at her appointment, chewing her cuticles, she's basically a nervous wreck.

"Well, congratulations," her doctor says, coming back into the room after her exam. "You're definitely pregnant."

Nina takes a deep breath. "So there's no mistake."

She smiles. "Definitely no mistake. Judging by the timing of your last period, I'd say you're about six weeks along."

"Really?" Nina takes this in. "Six weeks."

"That gives you a due date of June 10th. Let's schedule you for an ultrasound in a couple weeks and have you do some labs today."

"I, ah... actually...." She takes another deep breath and tries to figure out how to ask about paternity tests without sounding like she's sleeping with every guy in her building. "There are two men who could be the father. I'll need to find out about getting a paternity test."

To her doctor's credit, she doesn't bat an eye, and Nina figures she's not the first pregnant woman who doesn't know which guy knocked her up. Her doctor explains that there's a simple blood test that can determine paternity and how the men will need to give a DNA sample, typically a cheek swab.

"You'll need to wait until you're eight weeks along for the test. I can give you the name of a lab we use to make the appointment."

On the way home from the doctor's office, she calls Suzy.

"So, how did it go?" her sister asks.

"My due date is June 10th."

"Wow. How are you doing? Are you still freaking out?"

Nina navigates her car into traffic. This is the worst time of day to be out in Seattle, and she probably should have avoided it altogether. "Kind of. I mean, I'm unemployed, single, and pregnant. At least I still have health insurance." When Tolland fired her, they gave her a severance package that included twelve months of insurance.

"It'll be okay. We'll figure this out."

"I'm going to have to tell Noel. I wish I didn't, but he deserves to know." For all her hatred of Noel, she has to admit he's a good father. "I'm going to see Brody this weekend, so I'll tell him then."

"You're seeing Brody again this weekend?"

Nina describes the *Matrix* marathon she agreed to.

"Wow, you guys are seeing a lot of each other. Are you sleeping together?"

She snorts. "Sleeping, yes. And I mean actually sleeping and nothing more."

"Really? Weird. So are you dating or not dating him?"

"We're not putting a label on it," Nina says, using Brody's words to describe it. "But you could say we've become friends."

"I wonder how they'll both handle hearing that each of them might be a daddy."

Nina groans. "I don't know, but obviously we're going to find out."

Nina decides to tell Noel first. She texts to let him know she needs to meet with him. He responds right away.

What's this about?

I need to see you in person.

Why?

Nina rolls her eyes. And then figures to heck with it. Why not tell him in a text? It's not like he deserves better.

I'm pregnant.

There's a long pause, and she can only imagine the look on his face right now. She hopes it's one of shock and extreme discomfort.

Are you making this up?

She scoffs loudly. Why would she make something like this up?

I can send you a picture of the test result if you like.

So you're pregnant, and you're suggesting it's mine?

What a jerk. She can barely control her temper.

That is exactly what I'm suggesting.

I can't talk right not. I'm in a meeting, but I'll come to your place tonight.

Nina doesn't want him here but then realizes this is not a conversation to be had in public.

Fine.

I'll be there at seven.

By the time seven rolls around, Nina is nervous, but holding it together. She's been texting with Suzy all afternoon. The fact is, this is very likely Noel's baby. The timing is spot-on.

At ten after seven, she gets a call from downstairs in the lobby. "Yes?"

"I'm here," Noel says, sounding pissed. "Elliot won't let me up. He says you told him I wasn't allowed."

"Let me speak to him."

Her doorman gets on the phone, and Nina tells him it's okay to let Noel up this one time, but that's all.

When her doorbell rings, she answers it right away. Noel looks angry. "Seriously, Nina? You told your doorman I'm not allowed in the building?"

She doesn't bother responding. It's already hard enough seeing him again. Harder than she thought it would be. His wavy brown hair is a little longer and looks windblown from being outside. She hates his guts, but a part of her still remembers how much she loved him.

He follows her into the living room and glances around her apartment. His eyes stop on the pregnancy books she bought recently that she left on the coffee table.

Noel's gaze softens when he notices the books, and then when he looks at her, for a moment, they actually *see* each other.

"How far along are you?" he asks quietly.

"Six weeks."

"And how are you feeling?"

"Nauseous, hungry, and like I have to pee every ten minutes."

He nods and sits down on the couch. "That sounds like the same thing Claudia went through with all three of ours."

Nina sits down on the couch too, careful not to sit anywhere near him. She pretends to pick imaginary hair off the fitted white knit dress she's wearing and then crosses her legs. She chose it because it's flattering on her. Her hair is long and straight, the way he always liked it. Not that she wants to attract Noel, but it wouldn't hurt for him to see what he gave up.

He leans back on the cushions and runs a hand down his face. He looks tired. The lines on his face seem deeper. "So this child is mine."

"I actually don't know."

That gets his attention. "What do you mean?"

"Just what I said. It might be yours. It might not."

He seems shocked. Which is surprising, since he was ready to deny paternity only a few hours ago. But then Nina understands. Despite everything that happened, Noel's ego won't allow him to believe that Nina might have slept with another man so soon after they broke up. He'd prefer to believe she was at home every night crying her eyes out over him.

"Were you *cheating* on me with someone?" he asks, outraged.

"I'm not the cheater. *You* are."

"Then how is this possibly someone else's baby? Six weeks ago, you and I were still together. Hell, we had sex a couple days before we broke up."

She rolls her eyes. "Yes, how could I forget? Our last night together where you needed 'closure,'" she says with air quotes, "but conveniently forgot to tell me you were already having sex with Emily. You know, I had to get tested for STDs. Thank you for that bit of humiliation."

He doesn't reply. Instead, he loosens his tie, and the movement is so familiar. She wants to look away but can't make herself. He's still wearing his wool coat over his suit. She used to enjoy watching him remove the trappings from the office when he came here. The ritual of it, one by one. The coat, the tie, then rolling up his shirt sleeves.

He turns and glares at her. "Who's baby is it? What kind of game are you playing here?"

"I'm not playing any kind of game. I was with another man the day after we broke up, so there's a possibility this child could be his."

"You slept with some random stranger the very next *day*? I don't even know what to say to that."

Nina's temper flares. "You don't have to say anything. The fact is, it's none of your business. You're not really trying to take the high road here, are you?"

"Who is he? Do you even know how to contact him? Was it a one-night stand?"

She sighs to herself. "Yes, I know how to contact him. You actually spoke to him on Saturday."

Noel's eyes widen. "*That* guy?" He seems agitated. He jumps up from the couch and starts pacing the room. "That presumptuous prick? I thought that was a joke. I didn't take it seriously. I figured it couldn't possibly be real."

But Nina can tell he's lying. He knew it wasn't a joke, and he didn't like the way Brody shut him down.

"What the hell's going on between you and that guy? Who the hell is he?"

"None of your business."

He stops pacing and stares at her. "It damn well is my business." But then his face changes to one of concern. "I was afraid this might happen, that you might go off the deep end. I know how hard this whole thing with Emily has been on you. More than anything, I wish I could have spared you any pain over it." He shakes his head. "I never thought it would push you to start sleeping with strange men though."

"I'm not sleeping with strange men, and even if I were, it has nothing to do with you."

"You know I still care about you, Nina. I'll always love you."

"*Stop* saying that! You don't love me, all right? If you did, you never would have treated me like yesterday's garbage."

He comes back over to the couch and takes a seat again. "Jesus, I had no idea you'd be driven to this. Please tell me you're in therapy."

I wish I had another stapler to throw at him.

She forces herself to push down her anger. Instead, she sits up straight and pretends she's back at work, at a meeting, addressing all her department heads.

"Here's what is going to happen." She speaks to him in a clipped tone. "*I'm* going to make an appointment for the paternity test with a clinic, and *you're* going to go there and give them a DNA sample. *If* you're this child's father, then we'll work out whatever arrangements will be necessary regarding child support and future visitation. Understand?"

Noel studies her. "I'll be getting my lawyer involved. And if your clinic's test shows I'm the father, I may want a second test to be absolutely certain. *If* I'm the father, I'll pay child support, but I may or may not want to be a part of the child's life. I'll have to think further upon that."

Nina tries to hide her emotions, her hurt, that he could be so cold about a baby who might be his. She recognizes that he's gone into CEO mode though and is using his negotiator's voice on her.

"You do whatever you have to do, Noel. I wouldn't expect anything less from you."

After Noel leaves, Nina's so upset she lies awake all night furious at him. So his kids with Claudia deserve all his love and attention? But not *this* child?

A fierce protectiveness comes over her. She's never been pregnant before, never even wanted to be pregnant, but now that she is, no one is going to mess with her baby. Not if she has anything to say about it. And if they try, they're going to wish they hadn't.

She hasn't called her parents yet, but she's ready to face Brody and whatever his reaction will be to the pregnancy as she drives over there on Saturday with the guitar she bought him sitting next to her in the passenger seat.

It's almost dark out, and the streets are slick with rain when she pulls up into the short driveway in front of his house and parks next to his black truck. Outside, it's cold and smells like wet grass and damp pavement as she carries the guitar up his porch steps.

"Hey, Nina banana," he says, opening the door before she rings the bell. "Whoa, what's that?"

"I got you a gift."

His brows shoot up as she enters the house. "You bought that for me?"

She can't help smiling at his stunned expression. He's even more handsome than the last time she saw him. As always, he's just wearing jeans and a T-shirt, but they sure look good on him. "It's a guitar."

He chuckles. "Yeah, I figured as much. Either a guitar or a machine gun."

She takes off her coat and boots, and then they head into the living room, where she lays the guitar on the coffee table. "I didn't think you'd buy a guitar for yourself, so I got one for you."

"Damn, seriously?" He studies the case. "I don't know if I can accept this. I mean, it's kind of a lot."

"Think of it as a thank-you gift for taking care of me that night when I was passed out."

He shakes his head. "I don't need a thank-you gift for that."

"Please accept it. Otherwise, you'll hurt my feelings."

Brody raises a brow, but then his eyes go back to the case, and he seems uncertain. A smile tugs as this mouth though, and Nina suspects he doesn't get a lot of gifts.

"Open it."

He sits down on the couch and reaches over, unsnapping the

fasteners, then lifting the lid to reveal the shiny wood guitar inside. "Huh, will you look at that."

"There are a lot of beginner lessons available on YouTube," she offers helpfully as she sits beside him. "I checked. You'll only need to spend ten minutes a day on it, which isn't that much, so I don't think it'll be a huge drain on your time. And then just think, you'll get to learn something you've always wanted to."

He continues to stare at the guitar. When he finally looks at her, his expression reminds her of a kid on his birthday. "Thanks, Nina. This is really thoughtful."

She's happy to see him so pleased. "You're welcome."

He lifts the guitar out of its case and positions it on his leg. She watches him strum it a few times.

"I made sure it was in tune before I left the store."

"It sounds nice."

Nina nods in agreement. "It does."

"YouTube lessons, huh?" He glances over at her with that little smile. "Aren't you just full of surprises."

Her stomach plunges at his words, because obviously she has another surprise for him, except she's not sure he's going to be happy about this one.

"So." She takes a deep breath. "There's something I need to speak with you about."

He flashes her a grin as he strums the guitar a few more times and pushes down on some of the strings on the fretboard. "I hope you're not going to try and talk your way out of watching *The Matrix*, because that's not happening." There's a teasing note in his voice. "Even though you're trying to butter me up."

"I'm not buttering you up!" She laughs.

"Sure you're not."

"Actually, I need to talk to you about something serious."

He glances up at her from the guitar with concern. "What is it?"

She licks her lips. "Do you think I could have some tea first?" She knows she's chickening out, but she doesn't want to spring this on Brody. He's been so nice to her.

"Sure." He puts the guitar back in its case. "I'll make you some tea."

They both get up and head into the kitchen. Nina notices there are a bunch of snacks on the kitchen counter—bags of chips, cookies, licorice vines, and some grapes.

"I bought provisions for our movie marathon," he says with a grin when he sees her eyeing them. "We'll need to keep our strength up for six hours of *The Matrix*."

"Six hours of science fiction." She rolls her eyes. "I don't know how you talked me into this."

Brody smirks as he puts a mug for her in his Keurig, like he usually does. He doesn't make himself anything, just grabs a bottle of water from the fridge. She asks him how his week has been and how things went with Trevor.

He shakes his head. "He was supposed to come by and pick up his tools Monday, but he never showed at all this week." He adds a tea bag to the mug of hot water and then hands it to her. "I never heard from Aunt Jeanie—his mom—either. I'm starting to get worried. I tried texting him a few times, even rode by his apartment, but nothing."

"He's probably just angry with you. He sounds young and immature."

Brody nods. "He's only twenty-two. I'm thinking I might swing by his place again tomorrow."

The two of them move back into his living room and sit on the couch. She curls her legs beneath her and sips her tea. Glancing around Brody's modest home, she has to admit she's gotten quite comfortable here. If she weren't so nervous about what she has to tell him, she'd probably feel cozy.

"So what's going on?" he asks, cracking open the bottle of water and then taking a swig. "Is it something to do with your ex?"

"Sort of. Maybe. Actually, I'm not sure how to say this, so I'm just going to come right out with it."

He waits patiently.

Nina puts her tea on the table and then faces him again. She takes a steadying breath.

Here it goes.

"I'm pregnant."

CHAPTER TWELVE

Life & The Art of Automobile Maintenance
By Brody Austin

"Your vehicle is a complicated and intricate piece of machinery. Be sure to find a mechanic you trust."

Brody feels a strange detachment from his body. Like he's sitting here talking to Nina, but he's not sitting here. Like maybe aliens have sucked his brains out.

"Pregnant?" He stares at her. And then he asks what all guys ask when a woman they've had sex with tells them she's pregnant. "Is it mine?"

Nina smiles, but it doesn't have any humor. "I honestly don't know whose it is. It could either be yours or Noel's."

Brody sinks back into the couch and blinks a few times, trying to wrap his head around it. *The aliens must be using my brains for soup.* "Damn, I'm not sure what to say."

"I know it's a shock. Believe me, I was shocked too."

"There are tests... I mean, I know there are tests to figure out whose baby it is, right?"

She nods. "There are paternity tests. I'll be able to take one in a couple weeks. You'll need to submit a DNA sample."

"Okay, I can do that. No problem." He tries to breathe, but it's like he's sucking air from a tailpipe.

The two of them study each other.

"So how are *you* doing with all this?" he asks, and then he remembers the way she complained about being nauseous recently. "I guess that explains why you weren't feeling so hot before."

She nods. "It's not just the nausea. I've been feeling strange in general. I'm super hungry, and I have to pee all the time. Apparently I'm six weeks pregnant."

"Six weeks," he murmurs, and then his eyes go to her abdomen. Suddenly, he's struck with the enormity of what's happening.

Holy shit. Nina's pregnant, and it might be my baby. My child. "Damn, this is intense."

"I know." She puts a hand over her middle. "Definitely intense."

"So where do we go from here?"

She smiles. "That's up to you, Brody. Do you still want to spend time with me like before, or is this too much for you? I'll understand either way. I don't expect you to be a part of all this. I know I'm on my own."

He takes in her words, still processing this whole thing. "Kiera once thought she was pregnant. It happened a few years ago, except it turned out to be a false alarm." He remembers all the stages he went through when it happened. First shock and then fear, but then finally a kind of accepting calm.

"This isn't a false alarm. My doctor confirmed it."

He nods. "I wasn't suggesting that. I was just thinking out loud, I guess." He takes another swig of water. There's nervous energy dancing through him, but he's aware that calm is out there. It's like he's lost in a small boat at sea but senses there's land in the distance. "So when is the baby due?"

"June 10th."

His brows go up. "Right before summer starts. That's a month after my birthday."

Nina's watching him. Her blue eyes seem huge, and he senses her vulnerability. She's probably wondering if he's going to kick her to the curb. He knows there are guys like that, but he's not one of them.

"I have to be honest. This is a lot for me to take in," he says. "But I still want to spend time with you. If this baby is mine, then there's a lot of stuff we'll have to figure out."

She nods. "I know. And I know it's a lot to take in."

"Have you told Noel yet?"

"I told him a couple days ago."

"What did he say?"

She rolls her eyes. "Let's just say it wasn't a pleasant conversation. He told me if it's his, he's not sure if he wants to be a part of the child's life."

"Seriously?" Brody sits up straight, realizing what's at stake here. "Okay, well, I've got to be clear, then. If this baby is mine, I absolutely want to be a part of its life."

"I appreciate that." She smiles. "We'll figure it all out. Luckily, I'm not giving birth tomorrow."

"So when's your next doctor's appointment?"

"In a couple weeks. I have to go in for an ultrasound."

He nods. "All right. I want to go with you."

"You do?" She seems surprised.

"Sure I do." He's still nervous as hell about all this, but he's never been one to run away from his responsibilities. "If this kid is mine, then I want to be a part of everything."

"By then, we might actually know who the father is. What if it's not yours?"

"That's true." He shrugs. "Either way, I'll still go with you to the ultrasound. You'll still need the support."

She smiles. "Wow, you're a surprise, Brody. You're really one of the good ones, aren't you?"

He shrugs off her compliment because he knows he's done plenty of things in life that aren't good.

Nina picks up her tea again and takes a sip. There's a sniffle, and he sees her eyes are filling with tears. He moves closer to her on the couch. "Hey, come here. You okay?"

She puts her tea down and scoots closer. He slips his arm around her.

"I'm fine," she says. "I'm just kind of emotional these days."

"That's understandable. But before we go further, I do have to clear up one thing."

"What's that?"

"I hope you don't think you're getting out of watching *The Matrix* just because you're pregnant."

Nina laughs, wiping her cheeks.

"Because pregnancy isn't enough to get you out of this six-hour science fiction extravaganza you agreed to."

She punches him lightly on the arm. "And here I thought it would work. You've thwarted my plan."

He grins. "Hell, you'll need to do better than that. Maybe set the house on fire next time."

She laughs some more. "I'll keep that in mind."

Brody glances down at the black leather couch. "If you want, we can pull this out. It turns into a sofa bed. Kiera and I used to use it for watching TV sometimes."

"Okay," she says. "That sounds more comfortable."

They both get up. He closes the guitar case, putting it aside before moving the coffee table back. Nina grabs the cushions off the couch. When he pulls the bed out, he discovers there aren't any sheets on it. "I think I have some in the hall closet."

When he comes back with the sheets, Nina is standing by the

back patio doors, looking outside. "Do you have an abandoned garden out there?"

He nods. "Yeah, I grew vegetables for a while. I lost interest though."

"Really? Why?"

He rolls his eyes, embarrassed that so many things circle back to Kiera leaving him. Nina is definitely the only person he's ever shared so much of this with. "You know why."

Nina tilts her head. "She really did a number on you, didn't she?"

He doesn't bother to reply since it's so obvious.

She comes over to help him put sheets on the bed. "I wish I could say I didn't understand it so well, but I do. I think the hardest part of telling Noel about my pregnancy was seeing him again."

Brody takes part of the fitted sheet and spreads it on the bed. He glances over at her. "That was rough, huh?"

She nods. "He looks and sounds the same, except it turns out I've been deluding myself about the kind of man I thought he was all these years."

They both tuck in the corners. "At least you don't have yourself to blame. I mean, you did the best you could. With Kiera and me, I'm the one who messed things up."

"I've been thinking about that. At the time, you were just being honest with her, right?"

He fluffs the top sheet out over the bed. "Yes, but that turned out to be a mistake. I didn't want anything to change, but then everything changed anyway."

She grabs the comforter from the chair and shakes it out over the bed. "What if she appeared here tomorrow? Would you marry her now?"

Brody sucks in his breath at the thought. What would he do if Kiera came to him? "Yeah, I would."

"At least you've learned from your mistake."

He grins. "Of course, I might be having a baby with you. *You're* probably the one I should be asking to marry."

She shakes her head. "Forget it. I'm too old for you."

"Give me a break." He scoffs. "That's bullshit and you know it."

"Eight years, Brody. That's a lot."

He stands his ground now, watching her smooth down the bedding. "It's not a lot. Hell, men marry women that much younger all the time, and nobody says a damn thing."

"I agree it's a double standard, and it's stupid. But it's still there."

"It's just made-up nonsense. I've spent my whole life dealing with that shit, so I recognize it when I see it."

"How old is Kiera?" she asks with curiosity.

"A couple years younger than me."

Nina smiles at him. "See, even you were with a younger woman."

He shrugs. "Two years. It felt like we were the same age."

"But you and I are *not*." She motions toward the sofa bed. "Do you have any pillows we can use?"

"The ones in my bedroom." He leaves to go get them. When he comes back, Nina is lying flat on the mattress, studying the ceiling.

He tosses the pillows down and then lies beside her, propping his head up. Gently, he places the other hand over her flat abdomen. "You sure don't look pregnant yet."

Her eyes meet his. Those sky eyes. Different than what he's used to.

"I know. I wonder when I'll start showing."

He grins. "I'm looking forward to that part."

"To seeing me get fat?"

"You could use a little meat on your bones," he teases. "You remind me of a bird. That's what I thought when you first came on to me that morning."

"Really?" Her expression says she's not sure if she likes the comparison.

He nods. "A lost bird."

She snorts. "Wow, how flattering."

"When I was a kid, I used to have a thing about bringing home stray animals. Just about drove my mom crazy."

"Is that how you see me? Like I'm some kind of stray who you've adopted?"

He chuckles. "Yeah, except I think we're both strays who have adopted each other."

Nina's expression softens at that. "It's true, isn't it? We have." She reaches up and strokes his jaw. "Are you going to grow your goatee back?"

"I haven't decided yet. What do you think?"

She studies his face, the two of them gazing at each other. There's something inside him that's moved by her, that wants more. More of her independence, her optimism, the way she's become the first woman he's been able to relax with in a long time. More of everything. Even her insecurities and bossiness appeal somehow. He's been pulled into her orbit like a passing star.

"I think you look good either way," she says. "You're so handsome it's ridiculous."

He rolls his eyes. "That's nice of you to say." But then he grins at her. "You're not so bad yourself."

"Thank you."

He slides his hand over and squeezes her hip. "So, are we ready for some kick-ass *Matrix* action yet?"

Nina groans and throws an arm over her eyes. "Somebody save me."

"Wow, I finally get the whole 'blue pill, red pill' metaphor," Nina says, shoving a handful of popcorn into her mouth. They've just gone past the part in the film where Morpheus offers Neo a choice between the two. She can't believe how gripping this movie is. Either her tastes have changed, or she didn't know what she was missing.

"Damn, woman, this came out ages ago. You're like twenty years behind the times. It's weird you never wanted to see it."

"I never knew it was this good."

Brody smirks.

"Stop smirking. You were right. I admit it. Now hand me those cookies."

He hands her the package of Oreos. She can't believe she's eating all this stuff—buttered popcorn, chips, and cookies. It's not like her at all. She's spent so many years being careful, always avoiding anything fattening, always trying to stay thin. Apparently, that's gone out the window.

"It's highly unusual that I'm eating all this," she admits as she separates the cookies and nibbles off the cream. "I never eat food like this. Ever."

"Really?" He's chewing on a licorice vine. "You're kind of tightly wound, huh?"

"I suppose I am. I've always been an overachiever."

"Might be time to loosen up a little."

"I don't think so, especially now that I'll be a single mother. I need to be tougher than ever."

"Being tough and being tightly wound aren't the same. You can't control everything. Though I'd bet you'd like to." He takes another bite of licorice.

"I'm not sure if I agree with that distinction."

Brody rolls his eyes. "Of course you don't."

"Let's get back to the movie. I'm missing stuff with all your jabbering."

He laughs but quiets down, and they get engrossed in the movie again. At one point, they use the couch cushions as a headboard, and she sits pressed right next to him.

When the film is over, she realizes she can't wait to watch the next one. "I was worried that there were three movies, but now I'm glad." She turns to him. "I have to say, you really did look like him with your Halloween costume. Except you're not pale like he is."

He chuckles. "True. I'm definitely no pale face."

She smiles at his joke but then thinks about it. "I guess you could say I'm one. Supposedly we have family that's been in the States since the colonies."

His eyebrows go up. "Guess we're sort of on opposite sides then."

"Looks that way."

"Of course, my mom's family is Norwegian," he says.

"Really? So you're part Scandinavian too?" Nina finds herself particularly interested in his heritage, since this baby might be his after all.

He nods. "You wouldn't know it to look at me, but yeah. My great-grandparents came over from Norway."

"Hmm, I think I do see it. You're kind of big and muscular like a Viking. Actually, I think you have an impressive look about you, especially with your dark hair and eyes. You're very striking."

Brody chuckles and reaches for another licorice vine. "Thanks. Just don't call me exotic. I hate that."

"Is that so terrible?"

He snorts. "Are you kidding? Makes me feel like an animal in the damn zoo. Would you like to be called *exotic*?"

Nina considers this. "No, I wouldn't. You're right." She watches him chewing on the vine. "You know, black licorice is really popular in Scandinavian countries."

His brows rise. "No shit?"

"They have lots of different kinds. There are even gourmet shops where that's all they sell."

"Damn, I need to go to Scandinavia. I always feel like I'm the only person in the world who likes this stuff."

"Maybe you inherited a taste for it."

He chuckles. "Maybe so. How about that!"

She reaches for another cookie. "You know, I get pigeonholed too, especially for being blonde."

"Do you?" He touches a strand of her hair. "You're naturally blonde, aren't you?"

"I am. And people have commented on it my whole life." She

sighs. "Blonde jokes are the worst. I've had men make the rudest comments to me. You wouldn't believe."

"I believe it, and I agree that sucks." He considers her. "I imagine you get a lot of attention too. People kissing your ass."

She laughs. "Kissing my ass because I'm blonde?"

"A pretty blonde woman." He nods, still chewing on his licorice. "I bet you get what you want."

Nina considers this. In some ways, it's true, though it's not quite like it was when she was younger. "I also have to fight to prove I'm tough and capable. In the corporate world, looking the way I do, people often think I'm dumb or soft."

He snorts. "Trust me, I'm sure that notion vanishes after they spend two minutes with you."

Nina laughs and then smiles with satisfaction. "It certainly does."

His phone starts buzzing from his side of the sofa bed.

Brody picks it up. "It's Trevor," he says, taking the call and putting the phone to his ear. "Where the hell have you been? I've been calling and texting you all week."

Nina watches Brody and can tell right away something's wrong.

"Where are you now?" he asks, sitting up straight, his brows furrowed. He nods. "And you're sure you're okay?"

She watches him with concern.

"All right, I'll come pick you up. Tell me where to meet you." Brody listens some more. "I'll be there in a half hour or so." He puts the phone down.

"Is everything okay?" she asks.

"I need to go downtown and pick up my cousin."

She sits up and closes the bags of cookies and popcorn they were eating. "I'll come with you."

He gets up off the sofa bed. "No, just stay here and relax. You're pregnant. You don't want to be downtown with all the weekend craziness."

Nina laughs. "Brody, I *live* downtown."

"Shit. That's right." He chuckles and scratches his head. "You do, don't you? Except I'm picking him up in Pioneer Square. You don't want to go there."

She stands. "I was just there for lunch last week," she says in a dry tone. "I think I can handle it."

"You don't have to come with me if you don't want to, Nina."

"I *want* to."

He sighs. "All right, fine. But I've got to warn you about my cousin. He's kind of... mouthy."

They take Brody's black truck, and Nina reflects on the last time she was in it. Right after she woke up from her drunken episode. In some ways it seems like a long time ago, though it wasn't that long ago at all.

"So what happened to your cousin that we have to go pick him up?"

Brody shakes his head. "I'm not even sure. He said he was in a bar fight and that the cops came, and he ran off."

"And he's okay? He wasn't hurt?"

"He says he's fine. None of that makes any sense though. I can't picture Trevor fighting anyone. He's as skinny as a stick."

Since it's Saturday night, there's a lot of traffic downtown. Brody's a good driver though and easily maneuvers through it. They pass her building, and then pretty soon they're in Pioneer Square.

"Where's he meeting you?" she asks.

"The north side of Occidental Square by the Comedy Underground." Brody glances out her window as they slowly drive by it. "You remember what he looks like?"

She nods. "I think so. I don't see him anywhere though."

"I'm going to circle the block again. Hopefully I won't have to park." He goes around and drives past the south end of Occidental Square. "Wait, there he is!"

"You see him?"

Since there are no parking spaces and the traffic is lined up everywhere, Brody pulls to the right lane near the curb. Somebody behind them honks, but he ignores it. "Can you roll down your window?" he asks.

Nina rolls it down and sits back as he yells over to his cousin, but there's no response.

"I don't think he hears you."

"All right, give me a sec."

He quickly gets out of the truck and dashes over to where Trevor is standing next to a tree, wearing a hoodie with his hands in his pockets. Nina watches as the two of them jog back over.

Brody gets in the driver's side, followed by Trevor sliding into the back seat. Both of them bring in the damp smell of the city.

"What the hell are you doing at the south end of Occidental Square when you told me to meet you at the north end?" Brody asks Trevor as he puts the truck in gear and pulls out into traffic again.

"I said meet me by the Comedy Underground," Trevor says. "That's right where I was standing."

"No, you weren't. The Comedy Underground is on the *north* side. I don't know what you were standing next to, but that tree wasn't it."

Trevor laughs. "No way, cuz. You got it backward."

Brody rolls his eyes and glances over at Nina.

She turns to Trevor in the back seat. He's got his hood down now and is sitting right behind Brody. "Brody's right," Nina says. "The Comedy Underground is on the north end of the square."

Trevor's eyes grow wide, and his mouth drops open when he sees her face. "Holy shit, it's loco lady! What are *you* doing here?"

She stares at him with confusion. "Excuse me, what did you just call me?"

"Damn, cuz, are you and her really having a *thang?* Tell me it ain't so."

Nina turns to Brody. "Did he just call me loco lady?"

"Shut the hell up, Trevor," Brody growls. He glances over at Nina. "I'll explain it to you later."

Trevor starts hooting and laughing in the back seat. "I can't believe it's true. So you and loco lady are together as a couple, like for real? This is too much, dude."

"How about you explain it to me *now*," Nina says to Brody, getting irritated. "Why does he keep calling me that?"

"Because his mouth is bigger than his brain," Brody grumbles. He glances at her. "It's just a dumb nickname Chavez gave you that first day you came into the garage when you were acting so crazy."

Nina's mouth drops open.

"Nobody calls you that anymore," Brody says. "I put a stop to it."

"Did *you* ever call me that?" she demands to know.

"Of course not."

Trevor's voice comes rising out of the back seat like the hauntings of a ghost. "*I* think you did, cuz. Pretty sure you called this nice lady that nickname at least once."

Brody is staring forward as they wait at the light to get onto the freeway. Nina glares at him. "I can't believe you called me something like that. Do you give all your customers rude nicknames?"

He shakes his head. "Look, I'm sorry. I didn't make up the nickname, okay? But I'm the one who put a stop to it."

Nina turns away and doesn't speak.

"Don't be mad at him," Trevor says to her. "It's true. He did tell us to stop calling you that."

They drive onto the interstate, heading north.

Everybody's silent until Trevor leans forward toward Nina. "So, how old are you?"

CHAPTER THIRTEEN

"Life & The Art of Automobile Maintenance
By Brody Austin

"Don't forget. Your car's engine needs lubrication to keep it running smoothly."

"Forty," Nina says, glancing back at Trevor. "I'm forty years old."

Brody's hands tighten on the steering wheel. He wishes he had an ejector seat in back so he could send his cousin flying into the stratosphere. Parachute optional.

"Daaammn," Trevor says, leaning back. "You're really forty? That's pretty old."

"Knock that shit off," Brody growls at him.

"What's the problem? I'm just asking a question."

"You're being rude."

"It doesn't matter," Nina says to Brody. "Let him ask. I don't care."

"Well, I do," Brody replies. "Trust me, you can't let him get away with this shit or he'll never stop."

"How old are *you*, cuz?" Trevor asks with a smirk.

"None of your damn business."

"Aw, come on. Tell me. Is it top secret now or something?"

Nina turns her head toward the back seat. "Brody is thirty-two."

"Really? I didn't know that." Trevor starts cracking up. "Hell, you're old too!"

Brody tries not to let him get under his skin. "So what happened tonight? Why am I picking you up?"

He senses Trevor bouncing in his seat. "You wouldn't believe it, cuz. I was in this bar when a fight broke out right in front of me and my friends. Some dude poured his beer over some other dude's head, and then the second dude punched the first one. Next thing I knew, there were chairs flying. People yelling. It was crazy. That's when the cops came, and we all ran."

"So where are your friends now?"

"I don't know. We got split up."

"How did you get downtown in the first place?" Brody asks warily.

"On the bus."

"You couldn't just text each other or take the bus back home?"

Brody sees him shaking his head in the rearview mirror. "My phone was running out of juice, so I called you instead. I didn't know what else to do."

"Don't you have money for bus fare?"

"What does it matter? You got a problem picking me up?"

Brody glances over at Nina, who meets his eyes. At least she's not angry anymore. If anything, she seems amused by Trevor.

"I don't have a problem picking you up, but you shouldn't spend all your money like that," Brody says. "You weren't even thinking about how to get home?"

Trevor shrugs. "I knew I'd figure something out."

Brody turns on the wipers since it's starting to rain. His truck's clock says it's almost eleven at night.

"Put some tunes on, cuz," Trevor suggests. "Let's hear some jams."

Brody figures anything that will shut him up is probably a good idea, so he turns on the radio. It's set for his favorite alternative rock station.

"What the hell is *this*?" Trevor complains. "This sounds like boomer music. You gotta change it. Let's hear some real jams."

"This isn't boomer music," Brody says as Muse's "Supermassive Black Hole" comes on. It's one of his favorites. "This is a great song."

"Yeah, for boomers."

"That's absurd. I'm not a boomer. I'm only thirty-two!"

Trevor snorts. "Dude, anyone over thirty is basically a boomer. And this lame-ass music just proves it."

Brody rolls his eyes. He hears laughter and, when he glances over, sees Nina in the passenger seat cracking up. "I'm glad you find this so amusing."

She just shakes her head, still laughing.

They come up on the exit he needs for Trevor's apartment, and Brody gets off the freeway.

"Where are we going?" Trevor asks.

"What do you mean? I'm taking you home."

"Ah, about that. I kind of wish you hadn't taken that exit. Can't we just go to your house?"

Brody tries to see his cousin's face in the rearview mirror but only sees the top of his head. "Why?"

"Because I'd rather go there. It'll give me a chance to check out your sweet Zephyr again."

At least Trevor's smart enough to grasp the beauty of a car like that. "It's late," Brody says. "You can come up another time. I'm taking you home."

"I don't mind that it's late. Not at all. Come on, cuz, can't we go to your house?"

Brody gets a bad feeling in his gut. He takes an immediate right turn into the parking lot of a grocery store and parks in one of the spots. He lowers the volume on the radio, then turns around to face his cousin.

Trevor's eyeing the grocery store with interest. "Are we stopping to get food? Because I am kind of hungry. But let's get some burgers at a drive-thru instead.

"What the hell is going on here?" Brody demands. "Why don't you want to go home?" He senses Nina watching him. He can only imagine what she thinks of all this.

Trevor faces him but then looks away again. "Well, it's kind of a funny story, but Kevin kicked me out."

"*What?* Why would he do that?" Kevin is Trevor's roommate.

His cousin shifts around uncomfortably in the back seat. "Because he's pissed at me. We got into a fight."

Brody studies him. "A fight over what?"

Trevor rants about some video game and how Kevin was cheating. "I didn't give him any rent money, so he changed the locks on the door, and now I can't get in."

Brody tries not to get angry. His face grows warm, and he takes a deep breath. "That was stupid. You still have to pay rent, even if you're pissed at him."

"Screw that. I'm not paying him a cent. That money's gone. I spent it."

"You spent *all* your rent money?"

Nina is watching Trevor too. "What did you spend it on?" she asks.

Trevor shrugs. "Going out with my friends. Video games. Burgers and Chinese food. It seemed like it wasn't enough money to live on anyway."

"Not enough to live on?" Brody scoffs. Since he was the one paying Trevor's wages, he knows exactly what he made. "You made more than enough money to live on." He's always believed in paying his employees well, and they all make above an average mechanic's salary, even the ones just starting out like Trevor.

Brody turns back toward the front, massaging his forehead again. He's going to rub a hole in it at this rate. He sighs audibly. "How much do you need to get square with your roommate?" He figures he'll just pay Trevor's rent for him.

"Well, you see, it's kind of a lot. I was short last month too."

Brody spins back toward him. "You haven't paid rent in *two* months?"

Trevor smiles sheepishly. "It sounds bad when you say it that way."

"When did he kick you out?"

"Tuesday."

"So you've been homeless since then?"

"I was staying with some friends, but that house is too crowded. I don't want to go back there again."

"What about your mom?"

Trevor shakes his head. "Please don't tell my mom. She'll want me to move home with her and Mitch." Mitch is Trevor's stepdad, and Brody knows the two of them don't get along.

"Maybe you should have thought of that before. You're obviously not managing yourself very well."

His cousin looks out the window. "I don't want to move back on the rez. Not right now. I want to live in the city like you do."

Brody studies Trevor. His gray hoodie and his expensive sneakers. His eyes are large and dark and remind Brody of a deer in the scope of someone's rifle. He turns back and then pulls out of the parking spot. "Fine, we'll go to my house."

The drive is mostly quiet, though he agrees to stop at Taco Bell and get Trevor some food. He has no idea the last time this kid ate. He and Nina both order something too.

He keeps glancing over at her. She smiles at him with sympathy.

At one point she reaches over and takes his hand, and he holds it until he has to shift gears.

When they finally get back to the house, it's midnight. His neighborhood is quiet. It's still raining when the three of them get out of the car and walk up the front steps.

First thing Trevor does when he gets inside is flop down on the sofa bed that's been pulled out. "Damn, cuz, it's like you knew I was coming. What were you guys doing with this?"

"We were watching *The Matrix*," Nina says.

"No shit? I love that movie. You should have invited me over." He tucks his arms behind his head and lies on the bed like he owns the place. "I'm glad that's *all* you were doing. Otherwise, we'd have to wash these sheets, if you know what I mean. I'm not sleeping on somebody's else funk."

Brody frowns. "Get up," he says, annoyed. "At least take your shoes off."

Meanwhile, Nina is laughing again, though she's trying to hide it.

Brody puts the bag of food down on the dining room table. Trevor kicks his shoes off by the front door and comes over. "Can't we watch TV while we eat?"

Brody glances over at Nina to see how she feels about it.

"Maybe I should go home," she says. "It's getting pretty late."

His stomach drops. He was hoping she'd stay over again—even if it's just sleeping like last time.

"Aw, don't go," Trevor says to her. "Let's watch the second *Matrix* movie. You at least got to help us eat all this Taco Bell."

Brody's surprised his cousin's being so encouraging, but he agrees with him.

Nina seems uncertain. "I don't know."

"You *have* to stay," Trevor says to Nina. "You're probably the only thing that's going to stop my cousin from smothering me with a pillow."

She laughs and glances at Brody. "That's probably true."

"No comment," he says in a dry voice.

"Look, I'll take the chair over here," Trevor says. "You two lovebirds can sit on the bed together. I don't mind at all."

Nina looks over at Brody. "What should I do?"

He figures he might as well be honest. "If my opinion matters, then I'd like you to stay over again tonight."

She grins. "Okay, I'll stay. Let's watch the second movie."

The second movie is great, except just past the halfway point, Nina is having trouble keeping her eyes open. She's on the sofa bed with Brody, using the cushions as a headboard again.

"Come here, you can lie with me," he says at one point, lifting his arm to allow her access to his body.

Nina curls up next to him and rests her head on his chest, yawning for the fifth time. She's tired a lot lately, but it's usually during the day. At night is when she has trouble sleeping, too busy thinking about everything. But it's cozy with Brody. It's even cozy with his mouthy cousin. Definitely better than being alone.

When the movie's finished, she gets up and grabs the large purse she left by the front door. This time she brought stuff she might need if she stayed over again.

"I'm going to get ready for bed," she tells them both.

Brody nods. "I'll be in there in a bit."

Trevor's smiling at her. "I can't believe you two are together. Now that I see it though, it makes sense."

"It does?" Nina looks at him with surprise.

Even Brody seems curious.

"Sure. You two are kind of alike, you know? But you're different too. You got that yin-yang thing going."

Nina tilts her head, not sure what to say to this.

"What the hell does that mean?" Brody asks. "That sounds like gibberish."

"I'm saying you got *chemistry*," Trevor says, slicing the air with his hand. "You know what I'm talking about? It's obvious with you two."

Nina and Brody look at each other, both of them smiling a little. Trevor's not wrong.

Brody turns to his cousin. "I can't decide if you sometimes say smart things accidentally or if you *are* smart."

"What do you mean? Of course I'm smart. You think I don't notice shit? I notice everything. Nothing gets past me."

Nina can't help laughing at Trevor's bluster. "All right, I'll leave you two for now. Good night."

She heads down the hall to Brody's bedroom. Once inside, she turns the bedside lamp on and notices the bed is made. She wonders if he always makes it or if he just made it for her. Brody seems to be strangely tidy about some things but a total slob about others.

Yawning again, she goes into the bathroom and changes into the pajama bottoms and tank top she brought to sleep in. When she's done in the bathroom, she slides under the cool sheets. They smell like clean laundry, and she figures he must have put freshly washed ones on the bed for her.

That was nice.

She can hear Brody and Trevor talking in the other room. There's something about their deep voices and the steady cadence that's soothing. Even though she loves her condo, being alone there so much lately has been wearing on her. She likes hearing voices in the other room and knowing she's not alone.

Nina falls asleep, and when she opens her eyes, it's because Brody is getting into bed beside her. The bedside lamp is still on. He's bare-chested like last time, and she can't help admiring him in the soft light.

"Sorry, I didn't mean to wake you."

"It's okay. I'm a light sleeper. Though lately it's been hard to sleep at all."

He rolls on his side to face her. "That sucks. Why can't you sleep?"

"I'll nap during the day, but then at night my mind starts spinning, thinking about everything."

He nods. "I know exactly what you mean. My mind always works overtime at night."

"I slept great when I was here last weekend though."

He chuckles. "Me too." Then his expression softens. "I'm glad you stayed again. I like having you here."

"Even though we're not having sex?"

"I like it even then."

"You know, you're taking this pregnancy news very well."

"I'm just hiding my panic very well."

She laughs, and he smiles at her.

"To be honest," Brody says, "I'm still trying to wrap my head around it. It's hard to believe I might be a dad."

She nods. "I know. It's a lot to take in. I never thought I'd be anyone's mother." She sighs. "I haven't told my parents yet. I know they're going to lose their minds."

"Will they help you when the baby comes?"

"Probably not, since they live in Portugal. They retired there. I have my sister though." Nina shakes her head, thinking it over. "I'm prepared to do this on my own. I don't expect anything from anyone, unless this is Noel's baby. Then I expect him to pay child support."

"You don't expect it from me?"

She squirms a little. "To be honest, I feel like it's my fault we didn't use a condom that morning when we were together." It's something she's felt guilty about ever since it happened. "I'm really sorry. It was reckless. Like I said before, I was still kind of drunk."

He shakes his head. "It's not your fault. I could have said something too. You're not the only one who forgot." He's studying her now. "If this child is mine, I'll gladly pay child support."

Nina nods. She's not surprised he feels this way. Not after what he said earlier about wanting to be a part of their baby's life. "Okay. That's good to know."

She hears footsteps in the hall outside their door. It sounds like

Trevor leaving the bathroom. "Your cousin's quite a character, isn't he?"

Brody snorts and rolls his eyes. "That's one way of putting it."

"I can tell he drives you crazy. He seems very young. I think he's still trying to figure things out."

"I know. I keep trying to remind myself that he's basically a kid." He shakes his head and gazes at the window blinds. "I don't think I was ever that young."

"Of course you were."

"Not like that. By his age, I'd figured out enough about the world that I knew the score."

She watches him, wondering what he's referring to, and gets the sense he's dealt with a lot of stuff in life that's hard for her to even imagine.

He takes a deep breath. "I know I need to be more patient with him. It's just that he digs these holes for himself. It's frustrating. He needs to smarten up."

"Eventually he will." Nina studies his face in the soft glow from the lamp. She has an urge to reach out and touch him but isn't sure if she should let herself.

"What is it?" he asks, noticing her expression.

She decides to be honest. "I want to touch you, but I don't want to lead you on again. I'm not sure if I'll get upset like last time."

He reaches for her hand and places it against his chest. His skin is warm and smooth. "You can touch me any time you want, Nina. I don't mind. We'll take it slow, and if you get upset, we'll stop."

"Could we just kiss, maybe?"

He smiles. "You can do that any time you want too."

Her eyes go to his mouth. His lips are even and nicely shaped. She moves closer, and he watches her with a thoughtful expression. She closes her eyes and presses her mouth against his.

Brody shifts position so he's flat on his back, gazing up at her. Nina moves closer. She drapes her upper body over him and kisses him some more. He tastes minty like toothpaste and must have just brushed his teeth.

She touches his jaw and neck as she continues to kiss him, their tongues sliding over each other, his mouth pliant and willing against hers. One of his arms wraps around her back, pulling her in close while the other hand holds the back of her neck, tangled in her hair.

At one point she draws away to catch her breath, and Brody lifts off the pillow and kisses her throat, licking and sucking her skin. She gasps with pleasure, the sensation sending sparks through her whole body.

"How are you doing, Nina banana?" he whispers in her ear.

"I'm fine," she manages to say, smiling a little at his silly nickname.

He pushes the hair off her face, and the two of them study each other. His eyes are so dark in the muted light, they're black. She has this odd sensation that Brody sees her. That even though they haven't known each other long, he sees her, and what's more, he accepts her in a way that Noel never did. While she and Noel were close, she's starting to realize that being with him was like a constant audition. She always had to prove herself, always had to show him she was good enough. It was exhausting.

She caresses Brody's face, then leans in and kisses him again, this time with more passion. Erotic tension builds between them. She slides her hand over his hard chest, then down his body under the covers until she finds his erection. She slips her fingers beneath the waistband of his boxers to where he's hot and hard.

He exhales sharply as she strokes his cock. He opens his mouth and lifts up to kiss her neck again, one hand at her nape while the other moves down to grip her ass. The heat between them grows until even the molecules in the air seem charged with energy.

"Can you take this off?" he asks, tugging on her tank top.

"Okay," she whispers. She sits up and pulls it over her head as Brody maneuvers under the covers and slips his boxers off.

Thankfully, she doesn't feel that same awful emotional pressure inside like she did last time, though she senses it's still there, hovering around the edges.

"Come here, lie on top of me," he says.

She does as he says, and it feels good to be skin to skin, except she still has her pajama bottoms on. "I don't think I can have actual sex," she tells him. "I'm not ready for that."

He nods and then swallows. "It's okay. Is there other stuff you'd be okay with?"

She smiles. "Definitely."

His mouth kicks up at the corner, and then he lifts up to kiss her again. They make out for a while, his hard-on rubbing against her as they move their bodies with each other.

"Is it all right if I touch you?" Brody asks. "Can I take off your pajama bottoms?"

Nina nods. Her whole body feels like there's a live current running through it. She's getting really turned on. Everything about him is so different than Noel, but instead of freaking her out like it did last time, she likes it.

Brody slips his hands beneath her pajamas, tugging them down. She finally helps by lifting off him. The covers drop away, and he pulls everything off. Her panties go with them, and while she hesitates on that at first, then she lets them.

"You sure you're okay with this?" Brody's watching her with concern.

She takes a deep breath. "I'm okay."

"You'd tell me otherwise, right?"

"I would." And to prove it, she reaches for him again. Soon the two of them are lost in a tangle of passion.

His fingers slip between her thighs, gently exploring as an excitement builds within her. The pressure is so good. Just right. And the way he's licking and sucking her nipples is just right too. She bites her lip, grabbing his shoulder and breathing hard, because she knows she's close.

Brody must sense it too. "That's right," he whispers in her ear. "Let it happen."

She pulls him in tight, and then she does what he says. She lets it happen. Her climax builds up and then overtakes her. She moans, and then Brody's mouth is on hers, swallowing the sound.

As she comes down, Brody seems more excited than ever. He reaches for her hand and wraps it firmly around his cock, shows her how he likes it. He's breathing hard against her neck. She strokes and squeezes him, and it's not long before his breathing quickens and his rigid flesh gets even hotter and harder. His whole body tightens until he groans softly, grabbing her ass, while warmth spreads over her hand.

"Jesus." He's still breathing hard. She hears him swallow as he pulls his face out from her neck. "Damn...."

"That's my second orgasm since Noel," she whispers. But then she regrets saying it. She regrets mentioning Noel's name in a moment so intimate with Brody. Luckily, he doesn't seem fazed.

"We should make sure you have a lot more of those." He grins.

Then something occurs to her. "Do you think Trevor heard us? I tried to be quiet."

He shrugs. "Whatever. Hopefully not. I'm pretty sure he sleeps like a rock."

"Okay, good." She sighs. She'd be embarrassed if he heard them, although there's nothing to be done about it now.

Brody lifts away from her. "Let me grab a towel. I'll be right back."

Nina lies there in the quiet bedroom. Light rain taps on the roof and window. For some reason, she's smiling to herself. Her life has veered wildly off course in a way she never could have imagined. She knows the road ahead is full of bumps, but right now, in this moment, she feels oddly happy.

CHAPTER FOURTEEN

> ### Life & The Art of Automobile Maintenance
> #### By Brody Austin
>
>
>
> *"It's best to let your car's engine cool down before working under the hood."*

"We should go get your car today," Brody says to Trevor. They're sitting at the dining room table eating stuffed French toast Nina was nice enough to make again. "Let's go pick it up from your apartment."

"Can I have a couple more pieces?" Trevor asks. "This is really good."

Nina comes out of the kitchen carrying a plate stacked high with food. "Here you go." She puts it in the middle of the table and then takes a seat herself.

"Thank you for making all this. Have you had anything to eat yet?" Brody asks her. He's drinking coffee from a travel mug so the smell doesn't bother her.

"Not yet." She reaches out and puts a couple pieces of French toast on her plate, then drizzles them with syrup. Nina smiles. "But now I am."

He turns back to Trevor. "So like I was saying, I think we should go pick up your car and all your stuff today."

"That's going to be a problem," Trevor says around a mouthful of food.

Brody sips his coffee and tries not to get exasperated already. Everything is as circular as an ouroboros with his cousin—the snake eating its own tail. "Why's that? And no twenty questions. Just tell me straight out."

"I think my car's intake manifold has a vacuum leak."

"Is it running rough?" Most cars have a throttle to regulate engine speed and air flow, which creates a vacuum in the intake manifold, but if too much air gets mixed in with the fuel, it can cause problems.

"Real rough. It started a few days ago. I was going to fix it, but I don't have my tools."

"Why the hell didn't you pick up your tools on Monday like I told you to?"

Trevor shrugs. "I had other plans that day. I figured I can get them any time."

"Is that so?" Brody shakes his head and then smiles. "Well, because you never showed up, I figured you didn't want them. I gave your tools to Anka."

Trevor's mouth falls open with shock. "What the *hell*? I need those tools!"

Brody shrugs. "Guess you should have thought of that before you no-showed. You were throwing away Anka's tools, so now she has a new set. I think that's fair."

"You can't do that! Those are *mine*!" Trevor looks apoplectic. "And I didn't throw her tools away. I hid them. The problem was I kept forgetting where I hid them."

Brody leans forward in his chair. "So you admit you were doing that shit."

Trevor nods and looks to the side. "Yeah, I admit it."

"I want you to come into the shop next week and apologize."

"Will you give me my job back if I do?"

"No, but I'll help you find another job, and I'll give you a decent reference."

"How the hell am I going to get a job without tools? I can't afford to buy a new set!"

Brody picks up his coffee and then can't resist grinning. "All right, I didn't give them away. I was just messing with you. They're in my garage here."

Trevor's eyes widen. "Really?" And then as the truth hits, he howls with laughter. He puts his hand on his chest. "Damn, cuz, you totally had me going. You just about gave me a heart attack!"

"I *could* have given them to Anka," Brody says. "Remember that. Hell, I probably should have. She's had to replace a bunch of her own because of your dumb bullshit. I'll be taking that out of your last paycheck."

Meanwhile, Trevor has started fanning himself with a paper napkin like he's Marie Antoinette. "I don't care what you do." He's smiling with relief. "I'm just happy you didn't give them away."

Brody glances over at Nina, who's watching this whole thing with amusement.

"Do mechanics have to buy their own tools?" she asks. "I always assumed the garage provided them."

"I provide some, but yeah, most mechanics have their own set."

They finish breakfast, and Nina announces that she's going to head home. Brody walks her out and then kisses her when they get to the car.

"I had fun last night," he says. "Sorry about all this stuff with my cousin."

"I had fun too." Nina smiles, and she looks pretty. Her hair's pulled back into some kind of messy bun thing that women do. "I like your cousin. I think he just needs a little guidance."

"A little?"

"Maybe a lot." She laughs, but then her laughter quiets, and she studies him with affection. It's been a long time since a woman looked at him like this, and it's doing something funny to his insides. She pulls him down to kiss her again, and her lips taste sweet. And then, as she's hugging him, she whispers in his ear, "You're definitely one of the good ones, Brody."

Brody takes Trevor down to his apartment to get his belongings and his car. It turns out his stuff is still there, but the roommate, Kevin, is holding it hostage until he gets his rent money. Brody's met him a couple times. He's the same age as Trevor and, as far as Brody can tell, is just about as irresponsible.

As soon as the apartment door opens, the two roommates get into a screaming match.

"*What the hell do you want?*" Kevin shouts. "I hope you didn't come for your stuff, because you're not getting your shit back until I get my money. In fact, I'm taking you to court! That's what happens when you mess with *me*."

"Oh, I'll mess with you," Trevor yells back, trying to act tough. "I'll mess with your whole damn family. I'll mess with you so bad even your dead grandma is going to wish you'd never met me!"

"My dead grandma is going to kick your sorry ass!"

"Jesus, just shut the hell up, *both* of you," Brody shouts over them in amazement. The last time he saw these two, they were best friends. Even now, they're like two little kids squabbling. "Nobody's taking anybody to court, and nobody's messing with anybody's dead grandma."

Kevin and Trevor are both still glaring at each other, but at least they stopped yelling and are listening to Brody.

"I'm going to pay whatever Trevor owes you for the rent," Brody tells Kevin.

"Good. But he can't live here anymore," Kevin says immediately. "I don't want him here."

"I wouldn't live here if you *paid* me, asshole," Trevor spits out.

Brody puts his hand up to silence them again. "I'm going to pay what Trevor owes you, and then we're going to move his stuff out today, and that's the end of it."

Kevin finally nods in agreement, and that's what they do. Brody writes him a check for the missing rent, and then the two of them pack all his stuff up and put it in the back of Brody's truck.

"I'll pay you back, cuz, I promise," Trevor says as they're almost done loading everything. "I really appreciate this. And I appreciate you letting me stay with you."

Brody nods. "Let's worry about getting your car up to my house next." It's pretty obvious Trevor is going to be staying with him for a while. At least until he gets another job. He could try sending Trevor back home to his mom but suspects he'd only leave again. And Brody doesn't want to see him get into any real trouble.

In truth, Nina's words have stayed with him. He wants to be that guy she says he is. One of the good ones.

After they get both vehicles back to the house, Brody listens to Trevor's car and then takes a look under the hood. "You're right. The intake manifold has a vacuum leak."

Trevor gives him a smug smile. "I told you so."

"Luckily, all your tools are in my garage, so I'm going to let you fix it."

Trevor nods but seems uncertain.

"What is it?"

"It might take me a while."

Brody shrugs. "Start on it today, and then work on it tomorrow too."

"I won't be able to apologize to Anka or start looking for a job until I fix it."

"Don't worry, I'm not kicking you out. You can stay as long as you need to get back on your feet."

"Damn, cuz." Trevor grins. "You're totally the man."

"I expect you to help out around here, and I also expect you to start looking for a job, understand?"

His cousin is still grinning. "I understand."

That night, after they bring Trevor's stuff inside, with most of it stacked in the dining room, Brody goes out to the garage to work on the Zephyr. Trevor's watching TV, but after a little while, Brody hears the kitchen door open.

"I was wondering where you disappeared to," Trevor says. "Do you mind if I eat some of those cookies in the kitchen?"

Brody shrugs. "Help yourself."

But instead of leaving, Trevor comes out into the garage and walks around the Zephyr. "This is one sweet beauty. What color are you going to paint her?"

"Jade green," Brody says. "That's the original color."

"Shouldn't you have already painted her?"

Brody nods, pleased that Trevor's been paying attention to how things are usually done at the shop. "Normally I would, but I decided to wait until she's drivable. I don't have the equipment for it here."

"I don't go in much for old cars, but even I got to admit these Lincolns are awesome. I still can't believe you found one."

"Me either," Brody agrees. "It was pure luck."

Trevor comes closer and wants to see what's under the hood, so Brody shows him the 125-horsepower engine and then how he's working on the transmission and the driveline.

They hang out in the garage for a while. Brody works on the car while Trevor mostly talks, passes him tools, and helps when he needs an extra pair of hands.

"So why the hell have you been giving Anka such a hard time?" Brody asks. "I'm curious."

Trevor shrugs. "I don't know."

"You must know. Are you really that threatened because she's a woman?"

His cousin sighs. "I guess I can you tell you this since I'm not working for you anymore. She keeps figuring shit out faster than me."

Brody glances over at him. "So that's it? You're jealous?"

"It makes me feel stupid. How come this girl knows more about cars than I do?"

Brody sighs to himself. He had a feeling this all stemmed from Trevor's bruised ego. "You do know that Anka's whole family are all mechanics, right?"

"They are?"

"Her dad, brother, and uncle all own a shop down in Olympia."

"Then why doesn't she just work there?"

"Because, like you, she wants to live in Seattle."

Trevor goes quiet at this. "I didn't know that."

"I guess they've been pressuring her to move back to Olympia, but she's been telling them no." Trevor doesn't say anything, but Brody can tell he's listening. "You know how hard that is, right? When your family doesn't want you to leave?" Initially, Aunt Jeanie didn't want Trevor leaving the rez. She only agreed to it because Brody said he'd hire him.

His cousin nods.

"And the reason Anka figures stuff out faster than you is because she's been doing it longer. She's got a lot more experience. Hell, she basically grew up in her dad's garage."

"Must be nice."

Brody looks at him. "Instead of being jealous of her, you should pay attention and learn from her. You're talented, Trevor, but you don't know everything."

"I know that."

"Do you get why it was so messed up the way you were treating her? She's trying to make a go of it here in the city, just like you are."

His cousin nods.

"I mean, are you jealous of *me*?"

He rolls his eyes. "Of course not. I want to be like you."

"And how do you think I got here? Was it by doing stupid shit like you've been doing?"

Trevor seems uncomfortable.

"I learned from other people. Hell, I'm still learning all the time. Cars are always changing. There's always something new."

He sighs. "All right, I get it. I'm an asshole."

"I don't think you're an asshole, but you're acting like one. And if you aren't careful, you're going to turn into one." Brody studies him. "You don't want to be an asshole, do you?"

"No." His cousin goes quiet again and seems embarrassed. "Do you really think I'm talented?"

"I do," Brody says. "There's a lot you're capable of. But remember, talent isn't enough. If you can't control yourself, swallow your ego, and learn from people, your talent becomes meaningless."

The next week, while Brody's replacing the transmission on a classic Porsche 911, his sister Summer stops by the garage. Her reddish-blonde hair is pulled up into a mess of curls, and her green eyes seem lively.

"I was just in the area and thought I'd check to see if you were free for lunch. We haven't had a chance to talk much since I've been back."

Brody stops what he's doing for a few seconds and wipes his hands. "Sure, can you wait ten minutes? I'm just about done here."

"Of course."

"You can hang out in my office. I'll be back there shortly."

She leaves, and Brody gets back to it.

The Porsche's owner is a regular customer who brings in all his family's cars. When he's done with the transmission, he drives the 911 out of the bay and moves it off to the side area where they park all finished vehicles.

He takes off his coveralls and washes his hands, scrubbing his nails, then goes to meet Summer. Except she's not in his office. Instead, she's in the break room talking to Jackson, the contractor he hired to replace Trevor.

The two of them are laughing over something, though Jackson looks guilty when he sees Brody.

"Ah, I should get back to work," he says in his Australian accent. "Really nice to meet you, Summer."

Jackson walks off, and Summer's eyes linger on him until he's out the door.

"So, where do you want to eat?" Brody asks her.

She turns to him with a smile. "When did you hire that hunky piece of eye candy from Down Under?"

"Jackson? He's a contractor who's filling in for Trevor until I can hire someone more permanent."

"You should just hire him. Isn't he working out?"

Brody shrugs. "He's been great. I'm not sure if he wants to be hired though."

"Why do you say that?"

He chuckles. "The better question is why are you so interested?"

Summer laughs and rolls her eyes. "I don't know. You're right. Where do you want to eat?"

He lists a few of the restaurants nearby that he enjoys. They wind up at a Thai place, which suits Brody just fine.

"What's happening with Trevor?" she asks after they order their food. "Have you heard anything since you fired him? I hope he's okay."

"He's living with me."

Summer's eyes grow wide. "You're kidding. How did that come about?"

Brody takes a sip of his non-dairy Thai iced coffee and then tells her the whole story. Picking up Trevor downtown on Saturday night, the missing rent money, the fiasco with the roommate, all of it.

"Wow. I'm glad you're letting him stay with you. I'd hate to think of the kind of trouble he could get himself into."

Brody nods. "That was my thought exactly."

The waitress brings over their meals and then comes back to refill their waters.

Summer eats her noodles with chopsticks. "So Nina was with you, huh? Are you two serious?"

Brody shrugs as he picks up his own chopsticks. "You know, I've heard they don't even use chopsticks in Thailand, so it's kind of funny that we use them here."

"Don't change the subject," his sister says with a smile. "And besides, that's not true. They use chopsticks in Thailand for eating noodles and other foods as well."

"Oh really?" He spoons peanut sauce over his rice. He remembers then that his sister's been to Thailand.

"How serious are you and Nina?"

"Did Mom send you here to ask me this?"

"Of course not. I'm just wondering since it sounds like you're spending a lot of time together. I mean, we just found out about her."

"We're not serious," he says. "Not really."

"She seems very different than Kiera."

He nods and then can't help chuckling. Nina and Kiera almost seem like opposites. Easygoing Kiera against the bossy, antagonistic Nina. "Yeah, definitely different."

"But you like her?"

"I do." He picks up his iced coffee again. "Why? You don't like her?"

"I don't really know her, but she seems all right. Blair seemed to like her a lot."

Brody nods. He could see Blair and Nina getting along and probably becoming friends.

"She's... ah... a bit older than you," Summer says, trying to choose her words carefully. "Mom says she's forty?"

He digs into his food. "That's true."

"I've never known you to go for an older woman."

He swallows a bite of pad Thai. "Why does everybody care how old she is? I don't get it."

Summer shrugs. "You're right. I guess it just seems unusual for you. You have to admit, you're a creature of habit."

Brody takes in her words and realizes they're true. He doesn't usually stray far from what he's used to. He grins a little. "I guess there's more to me than meets the eye."

"To be honest, I'm glad you've met someone, and I don't care how old she is. It's good that you're moving on from Kiera. Mom told me you've hardly dated at all since she left."

He doesn't reply and instead takes another bite of food. He's ready to change the subject when Summer does it for him.

"I just started my new job last week," she tells him with a smile. "So far, so good. I'm assisting with births for now before I start taking on clients of my own."

It occurs to Brody that Summer would know all about paternity tests and pregnancy, since that's what she does for a living. He wonders if he should tell her about Nina.

"If I wanted to talk to you about something, can you promise not to tell Mom and Dad?"

Summer frowns. "Sure... I guess. Actually, I don't know. Is it something that concerns them?"

"Not at all. It concerns me, but I don't want them to hear about it until there's something to tell. I just don't want them to worry."

She's still frowning. "Okay, now I'm worried. What's going on?"

He takes a deep breath. "Nina's pregnant."

Her brows shoot up to her hairline. "Wow... just wow." But then she grins. "So you're going to be a father, and I get to be an aunt?"

"Not exactly."

"What do you mean?"

He tells her the rest of it and how Nina's not sure about the paternity. "I'm wondering if you know much about this kind of thing. What's the deal with these paternity tests? Are they accurate?"

His sister nods. "Very accurate. You'll have your cheek swabbed for DNA, and Nina will have to give some blood. She doesn't even need both men. Just one of you would eliminate the other, but it's best to test both of you to be certain."

"I see." He considers all this. "It's been a lot for me to process."

"I can imagine." She takes a sip of water. "For what it's worth, I think you'd make a great dad."

"Really? Thanks."

"Of course, the baby might not be yours. It might be her ex-boyfriend's, right?"

"True."

"Then you'd be off the hook."

He nods. And while most of him would be relieved to hear the baby isn't his, there's another part of him, a small deeper part, that isn't quite sure.

After lunch with Summer, he goes back to the garage. He's in the back office putting Jackson's hours into the computer when he gets a text from Nina.

Did you look up any beginner guitar lessons last night?

He smiles. *No, I forgot.*

Forgot? Don't forget tonight. Only ten minutes a day, that's all it takes.

Okay, I'll do it when I get home.

Good. I'm looking forward to hearing some cool jams. As long as it's not boomer jams.

He laughs out loud. In an instant, he realizes he wants to see her, even though he just saw her a few days ago.

Where are you? He texts.

At home.

I'm going to call you.

Okay.

Her phone rings and is immediately picked up. "I can't believe you're answering a text with a phone call," she says. "You know only boomers do that."

He chuckles. "According to Trevor, I *am* a boomer."

"So how did everything go when you went down to his apartment on Sunday? Were you able to get all his stuff?"

"Yeah, but it was a fiasco." Brody tells her the whole story about Trevor and Kevin yelling at each other, and Nina cracks up.

"They sound like little kids."

"I know. I felt like the school principal. It was weird."

"Are you at work right now?"

He nods. "I had lunch with my sister, and I just got back. I'll be here until six." He hesitates but then continues. "Do you want to come over tonight? Or maybe go out and have dinner downtown somewhere?" Kiera hated going downtown, so he never even suggested it. If she had her way, they would have moved out of Seattle altogether. He has to admit it's nice that Nina isn't like that.

The line goes quiet, and he can tell he's surprised her. "It's not even the weekend."

"I know. Do you have other plans?"

"Well, I was thinking about egging Noel's house, but I guess I can postpone that."

Brody chuckles. "Maybe I should help you."

"Good idea. We can cover more square footage that way."

"Do you want to meet at my house at six thirty, or I could pick you up?"

"I'll come to you. It'll be easier." She pauses. "I might bring a few dozen eggs along just in case we get inspired."

CHAPTER FIFTEEN

"What is this place?" Nina asks.

The two of them had dinner at a romantic Italian restaurant downtown, and now Brody's driven them to West Seattle and parked the Cougar at what looks like a nature area.

"Hamilton Viewpoint Park. I haven't been here in ages, but it's always been one of my favorite views of the city at night."

Nina looks outside at the dark sky and the bright lights. The view is certainly stunning.

"Come here." Brody's smiling at her, looking as handsome as ever. His face is all cheekbones and strong jawline in the interior shadows of the car. "Scoot closer."

"Are you going to kiss me?" she asks flirtatiously.

"Yeah, I am."

She moves as close as she can with the panel between the two seats, and he leans in and kisses her. His lips are soft against hers. She reaches up to caress his face. "I think this is even better than egging Noel's house."

He grins. "I'm glad you think so."

Brody leans back in his seat and takes her hand. They both gaze out at the city lights that seem to be rising out of the water and sparkling in the distance like a mirage. "I used to come here as a kid. Thunder had a friend who lived in West Seattle, and we'd hang out here."

"Did you spend much time with Thunder when you were growing up?"

"One weekend a month, and then one month every summer."

"And he lives on the reservation?"

Brody nods. "Yeah. I guess he lived in the city for a while when he and my mom were together but then moved back after they split up."

"That must have been hard for you to be shuttled back and forth like that."

He shrugs. "The hardest part was feeling caught between two cultures. I was never sure where I fit in. I had a foot in each one."

"That would be difficult. I felt a little of that when I went away to college. My parents are financially comfortable, but suddenly I was around people who were wealthy."

"I bet you fit in just fine."

Nina doesn't say anything. It's true. Somehow, she did fit in just fine. She's discovering that Brody is quite perceptive. "What does Thunder do for a living?"

"He's a mechanic."

She turns to him with surprise. "Really? Just like you?"

He nods.

"Does he have his own shop too?"

"No, he works for a garage on the reservation." Brody's demeanor shifts, and she senses there's a lot more to the story, but he doesn't elaborate.

"Why do you call him Thunder instead of Dad?"

He snorts. "Because I didn't meet him until I was five years old."

"Really? Wow, that must have been confusing." She thinks about the baby growing inside her. If it's Noel's, she wonders if she might be dealing with the same thing.

"It was confusing at first, but luckily everyone in his family was happy to have me around. My grandma was thrilled. She was a great lady." He smiles. "You would have liked her. She was tough but also a lot of fun."

Nina enjoys hearing about his family. She likes the idea that the child she's carrying might have such a rich heritage.

"What about you?" Brody asks. "Did you grow up here?"

Nina nods. "Mostly on the Eastside."

"I'll bet your life was perfect. Big family Christmases every year and picnics all summer long."

She rolls her eyes. "Give me a break. Is anyone's life really that perfect?" She takes a deep breath. "My parents are good people, but they put a lot of pressure on me when I was growing up. I think my dad wanted sons instead of two daughters, so I always felt like I had to make up for it."

Brody strokes his thumb over hers. "I'm sorry to hear that."

She shrugs. "It's fine. I'm something of an overachiever anyway. My sister was the rebel in the family, but I've always been the dutiful daughter." She rolls her eyes. "Of course, now look at me. I guess I'm a late bloomer in the rebel department."

"Have you told them you're pregnant yet?"

Nina shakes her head. "They don't even know that I've broken up with Noel yet or that I've lost my job. I haven't quite worked up the courage to tell them."

"I take it they like him."

"They love him."

Brody nods, and she can tell what he's thinking. If Brody's her baby's father, they probably won't be as crazy about him.

"It turns out they were wrong to love Noel," Nina says. "Just like I was." She thinks about how quickly he threw her over for Emily. It's like those six years meant nothing to him. "Did your family like Kiera?"

"Yeah. Just like your parents, they loved her."

"Do they know why she left?"

"I haven't told anyone what happened." He glances down and then smiles without humor. "Probably because I know they'll judge me for it, and I won't come out looking too good."

They study each other in the dim interior of the car. Brody's eyes shine like onyx. In only a short time, they've become so close. Two strays who found each other.

"This might sound weird," she says softly, "but I want you to know that in all the craziness that's been happening to me, you've become my oasis."

He smiles and gazes at her, playing with her fingers. "I don't think I've ever been anyone's oasis before."

"I honestly don't know how I'd be dealing with all this if I didn't have you to talk to. Suzy can only take so much."

"What about friends? Don't you have girlfriends?"

"I used to. And I thought I had friends at work, but it seems like everyone's abandoned me." She gazes out at the city again. "It's my fault. I've never been very approachable, and I didn't do a good job of tending to the friendships I had."

"You can change that. Maybe try contacting some of them now."

"Maybe I will eventually, when things settle down." Though she wonders if things will ever settle down. It feels like this is her permanent state now. Chaos.

But Brody has become the calm in the middle of the storm.

He considers her for a long moment, then squeezes her hand. "Whatever this is between us, it's helping me too. It helps to talk about all this shit I've kept bottled up."

The two of them gaze at each other. And then Brody leans in to kiss her again. Nina caresses his face and then his neck. The kiss deepens, and she lets it. She wants it. She wants *him*. He tastes so good. Like the starry night outside, like the city lit up with possibilities, like the only man in the whole world who seems to accept her and understand her anymore.

They pull apart, and without a word, Brody starts the car's engine. There's an erotic energy pulsing between them as he drives back to his house. Thankfully Trevor isn't there, because as soon as they walk through the front door, they're all over each other.

"Damn," Brody breathes. "Do you want me as much as I want you?"

"God, yes." She kisses him in response.

They make it into the bedroom in record time, stripping off each other's clothes on the way. There isn't any doubt in Nina's mind that she's having sex with him tonight. No danger that any sadness from Noel will come up, no thoughts of Noel at all. He's been obliterated by Brody.

"You sure you're okay with this?" he asks when he's on top of her, his hard cock pressing against her.

Nina is half out of her mind with desire, arching her body into his.

"Just do me already."

He chuckles but then stops as soon as she grabs his ass, pushing him deep into her.

They both groan at how good it is. Over the top. Unlike anything.

And then there's only the two of them. Because it isn't just her past that's been obliterated but his too.

"That's *wonderful* news!" Nina's mom gushes into the phone. "You're pregnant! Does this mean you and Noel are finally making wedding plans?"

"Not exactly." Nina takes a deep breath. "Noel and I broke up." She's been avoiding talking to her parents for weeks now, but when her mom called early this morning, she knew it couldn't be put off any longer.

"What?" She can sense her mother's euphoria come to a screeching halt. "I don't understand."

Nina takes a deep breath and finally explains to her how Noel left her for his twenty-four-year-old intern.

"But why would he do that? It sounds like he's lost his mind."

"Yes, it does, doesn't it? In any case, we're no longer together."

She hears her mom calling for her dad and then explaining it all to him. The next thing she knows, her dad gets on the phone. "This is outrageous! If you're pregnant, then Noel needs to do the right thing!"

Nina almost smiles. She knows her dad means well, but she's not interested in a shotgun wedding with a man who broke her heart and can't be trusted. "It's more complicated than that. This baby might not be his."

There's silence on the other end of the line. She's clearly shocked her father. "Ah... what exactly are you saying? Were you cheating on Noel?"

"No, I wasn't." She takes a breath and prepares to shatter her parents' image of her as their perfect golden daughter. "I met someone else after we broke up."

"So fast?"

"It was just something that happened because I was upset." But then she regrets saying that. She doesn't want them to think Brody took advantage of her, which couldn't be further from the truth. "I mean, I wanted it to happen. We have a connection. Anyway... I'm going in for a paternity test next week."

She can hear her mom in the background asking, "What did she just say?"

Her dad tells her, "The baby might not be Noel's."

Then comes her mom's high-pitched *"What?"*

"You can put it on speakerphone," Nina says. "That might be easier." Unfortunately, neither of her parents is that great with technology.

"Do you need us to fly back to the States?" her dad asks. "Are you in trouble? Do you need anything?"

"I'm okay." She feels bad for the way she's obviously worrying them. And to think she hasn't even told them she was fired from her job. She decides to keep that to herself for now. "You don't need to fly back. I mean, when the baby is born, you'll obviously want to."

"I'm having trouble understanding all this," her dad says. "It doesn't sound like you, Nina."

She sighs. "I know. But I'm honestly okay. Suzy and Luke have both offered to help me. And Brody wants to help too."

"Who's Brody?"

"Brody is the other man who might be my baby's father."

"And what does this Brody do for a living?"

"He's a mechanic who owns his own business." She can already sense the disapproval from her father. The truth is her parents are snobs. Being a mechanic doesn't sound as impressive as a CEO, though from what Nina's seen of Brody, his standards and work ethic are certainly on par with Noel's. "He's a really good guy."

"Are you two serious?"

"No, I wouldn't say that. We've become close though." She can only imagine what they'd say if they found out he's eight years younger than she is. She changes the subject and injects a liveliness into her voice, though it sounds phony, like she's a running for political office and is trying to get their vote. "So how are things in Portugal? Still beautiful as ever? I'm sure the weather's been much better than here."

"Don't rush into anything with this Brody guy," her dad says in a serious tone. "Promise me that. I don't think you're making good decisions right now. We need to talk this through some more."

Anger flashes through her. Where's the outrage over what Noel did to her? Somehow, this is all sounding like they think she did something wrong. "I'll let you go for now. I should get some breakfast."

They finally hang up, and Nina resists the impulse to throw her phone at the wall.

Normally she'd call Suzy, but instead she calls Brody. They've been hanging out or talking on the phone practically every day since they slept together last week.

"What's up, Nina banana?" he says, answering her call immediately. She likes that he doesn't seem in the least bit surprised or put out that she's calling him at seven thirty on a Monday morning.

"I finally talked to my parents."

"Oh shit." His voice lowers. "What did they say?"

She describes the conversation, leaving out the parts where her parents were skeptical about him.

"They're probably in shock. Once they get used to the idea, I'm sure they'll mellow out."

"I feel like I'm disappointing them," she says. "But what did I do wrong, exactly? I didn't make Noel cheat on me. And I was using birth control that failed when I got pregnant."

"You didn't do anything wrong. Eventually they'll see that."

She shakes her head. Brody's being so generous about her parents, far more generous than they were being about him.

"So how's the guitar playing going?" she asks. "I hope you're still practicing."

"Good. You'll be pleased to know I'm practicing right now." He strums the guitar in the background.

"When do I get to hear you play?" Brody is apparently learning a song but has kept it a secret from her. "I can't wait to hear what you've learned. I'm so excited you're teaching yourself."

"Yeah, I'm making steady progress."

"How about you play for me tomorrow after the appointments?" Tomorrow was the day of her first ultrasound appointment, and then afterward they were going to the lab together for the paternity test. Brody took the afternoon off for it. "I'm looking forward to being serenaded."

"Hmm, I don't think so. Give me a few more days. I promise I'll be ready by Friday."

"Okay, I'm holding you to it. The Brody concert is going to be great. Do you think you'll windmill arm it like Pete Townshend?"

Brody snorts. "Hell yeah, and afterward I'm going to smash my guitar on the coffee table."

"Wow." Nina laughs. "That sounds really wild."

"In fact, you should probably wear a helmet and safety goggles in case there are splinters flying."

She flops back on the bed, still laughing.

"Maybe I'll drink a bottle of whisky and shoot some heroin beforehand too," he says, cracking himself up. "Just to get the vibe right."

"What are you going to wear for this concert?"

"That's a damn good question."

"Might I suggest a pair of a tight leather pants and a torn T-shirt?"

"Well, shit... I better go shopping tonight."

Nina tries to imagine him dressed like that and decides she'd definitely enjoy it. "Or you could just do the old sock on the dick like the Chili Peppers."

"Simple yet classic."

"Elegance never goes out of style."

By now, they're both laughing like a couple loons.

She's glad she called him. That conversation with her parents feels like it's a million miles away.

～

"Can you tell what sex it is yet?" Brody asks, staring in awe at the fuzzy black and white ultrasound image on the screen. It's hard to understand exactly what's going on there. It doesn't much look like a baby.

"Not yet," the technician explains. "But you'll probably be able to tell by your next appointment in a few weeks."

Brody glances over at Nina lying on her back on the exam table with her sister standing on the other side. Her stomach is bare with shiny goop smeared on it.

"Isn't there a blood test that will also tell the sex?" Suzy asks.

The technician nods. "There is. You'll need to speak with your doctor or midwife about getting it. That's usually done at ten weeks."

Nina's still watching the screen. "And everything looks good? No sign of anything wrong?"

"Everything looks great. You're eight weeks pregnant. I'll forward the images to your healthcare provider." She hands Nina a tissue to wipe the goop off her stomach.

"Can you email or text me one too?" Nina asks.

"No problem," the technician says.

"I'd also like a copy," Brody says. "If that's all right."

Nina looks up at him and then reaches for his hand. The two of them smile at each other. Brody feels strange but oddly excited. He's still in that boat lost at sea, but the calmness of land is almost in sight.

After they finish with the ultrasound, Suzy gives Nina a hug goodbye and waves at Brody as she leaves to go pick up her daughter from kindergarten.

Brody and Nina head over to the clinic for the paternity test. He discovers there isn't much to it. It's exactly what Summer told him—they swab the inside of his cheek, and Nina has to give a blood sample.

"How long until we get the results?" she asks the nurse.

"You should have them in about a week. You'll get an email with a link to the results online. They'll also be mailed to you."

Nina takes a deep breath and then smiles over at Brody, though she looks nervous. "Okay, thanks."

Once they're done with that, it's still early in the afternoon. They're sitting in his truck.

"So what now?" he asks her. "Do you want to get something to eat?"

She nods. "I suppose. I'm not really that hungry. How about we go to my favorite bakery? They have food, though I'll probably just have some herbal tea."

"I have a better idea," he says. "How about we go to *my* favorite bakery instead?"

She seems surprised. "You have a favorite bakery?"

"I do. Do you remember Blair? She's one of the owners."

"Really? I didn't know she was a baker."

"She bakes wedding cakes mostly, but she co-owns a bakery with her business partner, Natalie."

Nina shrugs and then yawns. "Sure, I'm up for it. Is it far? I have to pee again."

"Damn, woman, you just went."

"I know, but apparently this little girl is pushing on my bladder."

He grins. "So you think it's a girl, huh?"

"Of course."

"I'm not so sure I agree with you."

"You think it's a boy?"

He imagines himself with a son. It's hard to imagine himself with a baby at all, but a boy is easier to picture. "Yeah, I do."

She laughs. "Well, one of us will be right. Though I'm looking forward to saying 'I told you so.'"

He starts the truck, and they drive on the interstate until he takes the exit for the U-District.

Nina glances around with interest. "Where are we going? What's the name of Blair's bakery?"

"La Dolce Vita."

She squeals. "Are you serious? That's my favorite bakery too!"

He glances at her. "It is?"

"Blair owns La Dolce Vita? I had no idea. That place is amazing."

As he gets closer, he looks for street parking and lucks out for a change, finding a spot right across from the bakery. It was raining earlier, but the sun has come out, and Brody enjoys the way all the trees nearby still show bright fall colors.

"Is the smell of coffee going to bother you?" he asks when they get to the door. Someone is coming out, so he catches it and holds it open for Nina. "I didn't even think of that."

"Hopefully not," she says. "I haven't thrown up in a couple days." This has been the latest thing with her pregnancy—not just nausea but actually throwing up.

When they get inside, it's busy as usual. "How about you grab a table, and I'll get in line," Brody says. He asks her if she wants more than just tea. "Maybe you should have some food."

Nina thinks about it for a second. "I'll take a croissant."

She goes off to find a table. He glances around but doesn't see any sign of Blair or Natalie. Natalie and her whole family are all customers at the garage.

"Hey, Carlos," Brody says when he gets to the front. "How's it going?"

"Good. I haven't seen you around lately. How are things?"

They make brief small talk. Carlos is the head barista and another one of Brody's customers. He orders himself an almond milk latte and a croissant sandwich, then gets Blair orange spice tea and a plain croissant.

As he's waiting for his order, he spots Nina at a corner table near a window. She's facing his direction but looking outside at the people walking by on the sidewalk. For a long moment, he studies her, looks at her as a stranger would.

She's sitting up straight with her hands in her lap, wearing a white knit sweater that's elegant against her silky pale hair. There's something classy about her. And he likes it. Probably too much. He likes that this beautiful woman who looks like she belongs in the society pages is sitting there waiting for him.

What's more is he likes that he knows the real Nina. The goofball beneath that classy veneer. The one who laughs at all his dumb jokes, and who he recently discovered likes to lick the flavoring off potato chips before she eats them.

"That's disgusting," he informed her, but she'd only shrugged and smiled.

"It makes them last longer. This way I can savor them."

Once their order is ready, he grabs it and heads her way.

"Nice spot," he says, putting the tray of food down before he parks himself in the chair across from her.

She looks over, and maybe he's only imagining it, but her eyes light up when she sees him. "It's fun to people-watch, isn't it? I was delighted to find a window seat."

He doles out the food and then digs into his sandwich. Just as he's swallowing his first bite of food, Blair appears next to them.

"Carlos just told me you were out here. I thought I'd pop over and say hi."

"Hey, Blair. What's up?" he says, putting his sandwich down.

She smiles at him and then at Nina. "It's good to see you again. It's a shame we didn't get to hang out more at Summer's party."

Nina agrees and then compliments Blair on the bakery, telling her it's been her favorite for years. "I had no idea you were one of the owners! Even before you moved to the new location, I always recommended this place to everyone."

Blair grins. "Well, that's nice to hear. Thank you."

She asks them what the two of them are up to today, and there's a bit of an awkward silence. Nina looks at Brody in a panic, clearly not ready to share that she's pregnant.

Brody finally says he took the afternoon off work and that the two of them are running errands.

Blair nods and seems to accept this, though he suspects she knows something isn't quite right. "Well, we should get together soon.

You guys should come over to our place." She motions back toward the kitchen. "I need to get back to work, but I'll tell Nathan to set something up with you." She turns to Nina. "Nice seeing you again."

Once she's gone, Nina shakes her head in obvious distress. "Thank you for telling her that, about the errands. I froze. I didn't know what to say!"

"That's okay." He takes a sip from his latte. "It's kind of an unusual situation we're in."

"I'd better get used to it. Once I start showing, we'll have to explain to people what's really going on."

CHAPTER SIXTEEN

Nina is sitting on the couch in Brody's living room, watching with pride as he plays Johnny Cash's "I Walk the Line" on his guitar for her.

The strings are buzzing, and there's some clumsiness as he tries to change chords, but overall it sounds pretty good. When he's done, she claps with great enthusiasm.

"Encore! Encore!" she says, still clapping. "I need to hear more."

He chuckles. "I'm afraid that's the only song I know."

"And it was brilliant. I loved it."

"Really?" He seems bemused. "Did it actually sound good?"

"It sounded amazing. I can't believe you learned a song so quickly."

He shrugs, but she can tell he's pleased with himself. "It wasn't all that hard. You were right about the videos and practicing a little every day."

"What made you choose that song? Are you a Johnny Cash fan?"

"I guess so. I've always thought that was a pretty cool song. It turns out it's not that hard to play."

She nods. "I've always liked that song too." She gets her phone out. "Play it again. I'm going to look up the lyrics so we can sing it."

"Can you sing?" he asks with surprise.

"I sing okay. I *was* in high school choir, after all." She fluffs her hair out and jokingly acts like a diva.

She finds the lyrics on a website and then sets the phone against the back of the couch so they can both see it.

He plays the guitar again, and she sings along. They're both laughing and stumbling through it as Brody tries to change chords fast enough to match her voice. She motions for him to sing with her, and eventually he joins in.

The two of them are getting into it, singing loudly while Brody tries to keep up on the guitar, when suddenly Trevor is standing in front of them with a big grin on his face.

They stop singing, and the guitar goes silent. Or mostly silent. Brody accidentally knocks a string, and it twangs.

"Damn, you guys should take that shit on the road," Trevor says, still grinning. "I didn't know you were turning into Sonny and Cher."

"Ha ha," Brody says. "We're just messing around."

"I thought I heard you practicing, but you're always doing it in the bedroom, so I couldn't tell what song it was."

Brody seems embarrassed. "It's easier if I practice alone. I didn't want you to make fun of me playing Johnny Cash."

"What?" Trevor seems surprised. "I would never do that. Johnny Cash is totally badass."

"So how did the job interview go?" Brody asks, leaning down to put the guitar back in its case.

Trevor shrugs. "It was okay, I guess."

"Did they tell you when you'd hear back from them?"

"Early next week. They asked me why I left my last job, and I didn't know what to say, so I told them I was looking for new opportunities."

"Did you tell them I'm your cousin?"

"No."

Brody nods. "That's probably for the best, at least for now." He's been thinking about it and realizes he's going to have to fudge some of the details about why Trevor isn't working for him anymore.

"I wish you could just hire me back, cuz," Trevor says in a cajoling voice. "It sucks going to all these interviews. It seems like a waste of time when I could just work for you again."

Brody is ready to go into another lecture on personal responsibility and consequences for our actions when Nina asks Trevor what he'd like for dinner. She glances at Brody, and he knows what she's doing. *It's probably just as well.* Sometimes when he hears himself lecturing Trevor, he wonders if he's turning into a curmudgeon at the ripe old age of thirty-two.

"You're cooking dinner tonight?" Trevor's eyes light up. "I have to admit, you're a good cook, Nina."

Brody nods in agreement. So far, she's made fettuccini primavera with a red sauce, chili with cornbread, and baked chicken. Everything was delicious, though Trevor painstakingly picked out every vegetable from his fettuccini.

"What would you like to eat?" Nina asks again. "I was thinking about making lasagna with non-dairy cheese."

"Do we have the ingredients for that?" Brody asks.

"Probably not. I'll have to go to the store."

"Hell yeah!" Trevor grins. "I'd love some lasagna. Meat lasagna, I hope. Not too many veggies, right?"

Brody chuckles, thinking Trevor eats like a little kid. He turns to Nina. "You staying over tonight?" He tries to keep his voice casual, but he hopes she says yes. Too often she goes home, and even though he knows she has to, he likes having her here. The irony is he hasn't been to her place even once yet.

"I could stay over," she says mildly, looking up at him through her eyelashes. "I brought my things."

They're smiling at each other, and he senses the heat between them. This constant attraction. You'd think it would be lessening by now or burning itself out, but it only seems to be getting stronger. It turns out Nina is both passionate and bossy in bed.

"Do you want to take the Cougar to the store?" he asks her. "I'll even let you drive." He's so happy she's staying over that he's feeling magnanimous.

Her mouth falls opens. "Really? I'd love to drive. Are you sure about that?"

Meanwhile, Trevor's gawking at him. "What the hell, cuz? How come you never let *me* drive that car?"

"Because I don't want you wrapping it around a tree."

"I wouldn't do that!"

He doesn't bother to reply. His Cougar is a true muscle car. Fast, responsive, and loud—although he muffled it somewhat so his neighbors wouldn't get pissed. The last thing he needs is Trevor driving it.

Once they're in the car and headed toward the grocery store, Brody nervously watches Nina managing the wheel.

"It's okay," she says. "You can calm down. I'm a good driver."

Except he's not a good passenger. She takes a corner too hard, and he has to grip the seat. "Slow down. Take it easy."

"I thought this car was built for speed," she says, laughing and glancing over at him.

"Keep your eyes on the road."

"Wow, you're terrible at this, aren't you?"

By the time they reach the grocery store, he's a nervous wreck.

"I'm going to drive us home," he says gruffly. "Give me the keys."

"What's the problem?" she says, grabbing a grocery cart. "My driving is just fine."

"It's not you, it's me."

She rolls her eyes. "And you think *I'm* tightly wound. You need to learn how to calm down and let go."

"I'll be calm once I have my keys back."

She hands them over, and he puts them securely in his front pocket. He takes the cart from her and pushes it down the nearest aisle.

He can feel her eyes on him. "What?"

"So you have to drive the grocery cart too?"

Brody pauses and then chuckles. "Apparently I do. Do you want to drive—I mean push the cart?"

She shrugs. "Actually, I'm fine with you doing it. Let's go to the produce area. I'm going to try to sneak some vegetables into Trevor's meat lasagna."

"He eats like a little kid, doesn't he? Maybe I should buy him a can of ravioli." He chuckles. "Although, I like those too."

While they're both standing side by side in the pasta aisle, his phone buzzes. He takes it out to see who it is. The caller ID says Danica. He stares at it for a second, trying to place the name, then remembers.

Nina is standing next to him and sees the display. "Who's Danica?"

"No one," Brody says and slips his phone back into his front pocket. It's obvious from his demeanor that it's definitely not no one.

Now Nina is curious. "Is it a woman you're dating?" She's joking around. Really, who could he be dating? They spend practically all their time together.

He shrugs. "It's just one of Tori's fix ups."

"Really?" She has to admit she's surprised. "I thought you ignored all of those."

"I did."

"So Tori gave her your number? That's presumptuous."

"Not exactly. I gave it to her myself."

Her brows shoot up. "Oh." There's a queasy feeling in her stomach that she doesn't like. "And when was that?"

"I can't remember. A while back."

"She must be very attractive." He told her he ignored all the fix ups, so there had to be a reason he gave this one his number.

He shrugs again, but she's gotten to know Brody quite well and can tell she's hit the nail on the head.

"So you were planning to go out with her?"

"I told her I was busy with work, but she was kind of insistent, so I said I'd meet her for coffee."

Nina tries to ignore the jealousy stabbing through her whole body. She can barely see straight. "Well, maybe you should call her back."

He shakes his head but then grins a little. "Don't be absurd. When do I have time for coffee? I'm too busy being your boy toy, remember?"

She smiles. It's become a silly joke between them lately. "True. I do keep you on a short leash, don't I?"

He snorts. "You're telling me. Catering to all your kinky sexual demands is wearing me out. I might have to call for backup."

"What do you mean? I'm not kinky."

"I'll be the judge of that. Good thing my tongue muscles are strong."

"Oh my gosh! Keep your voice down." She glances around the store. Some lady a short distance away is watching them and appears to be laughing to herself.

"Like I said, this tongue of mine is definitely getting a workout."

"Shhh... be quiet!" She reaches up and tries to cover his mouth with her hand, laughing when he licks her palm. "Stop! You need to stop talking. And stop licking me!"

He holds her fingers back and gives her a sly grin. "You don't really mean that, do you?"

Nina rolls her eyes. "Jeez, I can't take you anywhere." Then she grabs his arm and drags him along so they can hopefully end this conversation.

As they finish getting the rest of the groceries, Brody seems lighthearted. They're joking around with each other, but something has begun to weigh on Nina. She keeps thinking about that phone call he got from Danica, who's probably an attractive and age-appropriate young woman.

Am I holding Brody back?

The thought is jarring. Shouldn't he be out there dating and moving on from Kiera? Finding someone he can build a life with? She cares for Brody deeply and would never want to stand in his way. They may be two strays who found each other, but she wonders if they're also using each other as a crutch.

She touches her abdomen. *Of course, this baby might be his, and then what?*

Later that night, when they're in bed together, Brody is lightly stroking her hair. Her eyes fall shut. She told him once that she liked her hair played with, so now he does it all the time. It's wonderful.

"What's wrong, Nina banana?" he asks. "You were quiet all through dinner. Are you having morning sickness again?"

"I'm fine." She knows she should tell Brody what she was thinking earlier, that she should be encouraging him to call Danica back, but she can't bring herself to form the words.

"Are you missing Noel?"

She opens her eyes and looks directly into his. Warm and brown. So familiar to her now. Brody's eyes have become this soothing place, a place where she's completely accepted, where she never has to prove her worth.

"No, I wasn't thinking about Noel." The truth is she's hardly thought of him at all in the past couple weeks. Sometimes a memory will come up and she'll get a pang, but then it goes away. "Do you still think about Kiera?"

He shrugs. "Occasionally. She's come up in my mind lately. Mostly because I've been thinking about expanding again, but then I remember how she was always against it."

"What are you talking about?"

"Opening a second garage."

Nina sits up. "You're planning to open a second location?"

"I'd like to. I've thought about it off and on for years, but Kiera always talked me out of it. She said it was too risky."

"I had no idea. Are you that busy at the garage?"

He snorts. "Definitely. I have a long waiting list of people who want us to work on their classic cars. I also have a lot of customers who drive up from the south end. That's where I was thinking of opening the second shop."

Nina stares at him, digesting this. "That's amazing."

"Do you think it's too risky? Am I being foolish, dreaming too big?"

"There's no such thing as dreaming too big," she says, repeating something her dad used to say. It was years ago when she was applying to all those Ivy League colleges.

Brody seems to consider her words. "It's a risk. I'd have to take out a loan. If the second location does poorly, I'd still be on the hook for the money."

"How closely have you looked at the numbers? Have you drawn up a business plan?"

"I have. It's a few years old now. I need to update it."

She squeezes his arm. "I think this sounds exciting. If the numbers look good, you shouldn't let fear hold you back."

He lies on the pillow and studies the ceiling. "Maybe I should consider it again. It's one of those ideas I could never completely let go of, you know?"

She nods. "There's probably a reason for that. Sometimes you have to follow your gut."

He smiles and looks at her. "Just like this thing between you and me."

"What do you mean?"

"I mean, I think there might be a reason for everything." He's still grinning at her. "I really like having you here."

"Thanks. I like being here."

He goes quiet for a moment. "I think you should move in."

She blinks at him in shock, too stunned to even speak.

Brody is watching her closely. "You look like you're going to throw up."

"I'm sorry. You've just taken me by surprise."

He sits up on his elbows. "Is it really that crazy of an idea? You're pregnant and probably shouldn't be living alone anyway."

She scoffs. "I take offense to that. I'm perfectly fine living alone."

"Not to mention you're here all the time. It would save you money since you're not working."

"I couldn't live here without paying. And what would I do with my condo?"

He shrugs. "Sell it. Or rent it out if you don't want to sell it."

Nina is still stunned. She can't believe Brody is suggesting this. Only moments ago, she was trying to force herself to encourage him to meet another woman for coffee. "Brody, I'm too old for you. We both know it."

He rolls his eyes. "Give me a break. Not this shit again."

"It's true."

He shoves himself up so he's sitting, obviously angry. "No, it's *not*. Hell, you're pregnant with my baby, but somehow I'm too young for you? What kind of stupid logic is that?"

"It might not be your baby, and then what?"

"Then we'll deal with that too."

She shakes her head. "I appreciate you asking me to move in, and I know your heart is in the right place, but I'm starting to think maybe we're relying on each other too much."

"What's that supposed to mean?"

"It means I think we've started using each other like a crutch. Instead of spending all your time with me, you need to get out there and meet a woman you can build a life with. In fact, you should call Danica back."

His expression turns stormy. "You *didn't* just say that."

"We've gotten so comfortable with each other, but we can't avoid real life forever."

Brody snorts. "Look around, Nina. This *is* real life. You're the one choosing to accept all of society's made-up bullshit. If the situation were reversed and I was the woman, you wouldn't care less."

Nina takes a deep breath. "I guess I'm a product of our society then. Why do you think everyone was making cougar jokes at that party? Why was your mom so concerned with my age? She doesn't want to see you stuck with someone as old as I am."

"Eight years. You're acting like we're decades apart."

"I'm forty. You're thirty-two. I would have been your high school babysitter."

He slowly shakes his head. "I've dealt with so much crap in my life. So much prejudice from ignorant assholes. And now I have to deal with this shit from you too."

"I'm not prejudiced! What are you taking about?"

"Apparently you're ageist."

She almost smiles. "That's not how ageism works. It's against people who are older."

"It's about holding someone's age against them, which is exactly what you're doing."

Nina huffs. "I don't hold it against you. I think we're both getting over having our hearts broken, and as a result, we're turning this relationship into something it's not."

Their eyes meet, and neither of them speaks for a long moment.

"This is *good* between us," Brody says, lowering his voice. "You know it is. And it's got nothing to do with anyone else."

She goes quiet. She doesn't know what to say. What's crazy is a part of her was tempted when he asked her to move in. She loves being with Brody. He's so patient and kind to her. She worries she's taking advantage of him though, standing in his way. Somehow, this whole relationship has gotten more serious than either of them intended.

What happened to just "hanging out?"

Nina glances toward the bedroom door. "I think maybe I should go home tonight. Let us both cool off."

"Fine," he says, and she can hear the frustration in his voice. "Whatever."

Running away. Brody's out in the garage, lying on his back, working on the Zephyr's brake lines. He hasn't spoken to Nina all weekend. They usually call or text every day, but it's been complete silence. *That's what she's doing. She's running away from this because she can't handle the truth.*

He decides to take a break and sits up, cracks open a bottle of water. Leaning against the car, he opens his phone and studies the pictures from the ultrasound again. He's been looking at them a lot lately. In fact, he can't seem to stop looking at them.

This might be my child.

It's heady and powerful stuff.

The garage door opens, and Brody quickly shoves his phone into his pocket.

Trevor comes over to him. "Hey, what's for dinner? Should I go pick up some burgers?"

Brody considers this and then shakes his head. The two of them have been eating fast food all weekend, and he's sick of it. "No, I'll make something to eat."

"Like what? Because I'm getting hungry."

He thinks it over. He's not much of a cook, but he has his usual standbys. "How does spaghetti sound?"

"That sounds good. With meatballs?"

Brody tries to remember what he has in the freezer. "Yeah, with meatballs."

"Okay." But Trevor doesn't leave, just stands there. "Where's Nina? How come she hasn't been around all weekend?"

"She's at home."

"Did you two have a fight?"

Brody screws the cap back on his water bottle but doesn't reply.

"Because I like Nina," Trevor continues. "She's cool. I hope you didn't mess things up with her."

"I didn't mess anything up. Mind your own business," Brody mutters.

"Sheesh, I'm just trying to help. You can talk to me. I know I'm younger than you, but I'm still your cousin."

Brody puts the water bottle down, then grabs all the tools he was using and stands up. He puts everything back on the cart and reaches for a clean rag. "I know you're trying to help. I appreciate it. Nina and I are working through some stuff. I can't talk about it right now. Maybe later, okay?"

Trevor nods. "All right, I get it. A lovers' quarrel, huh?"

"Sort of. I guess." He throws the rag down. "Come on, why don't you help me make dinner?"

They head into the kitchen, where Brody goes to the sink and soaps up his hands, scrubbing the grease off his cuticles with a nail brush. He tells Trevor to fill up a pot with water and then to get down the pasta and spaghetti sauce from the cupboard. After drying his hands, Brody takes the meatballs from the freezer and puts them in a skillet.

He'd surprised himself when he asked Nina to move in. It's something he's noticed he does when he's around her. Even thinking about opening a second garage location was surprising, since he hadn't contemplated it in a long while. He likes it though. He likes the person he is when he's with Nina. Someone who isn't afraid of change. Someone who's willing to take a chance on new things.

Of course, she doesn't see it that way. All she can see is their stupid age difference. He doesn't know how to penetrate this absurd notion she has that she's too old for him.

He and Trevor eat their spaghetti with meatballs in front of the television.

"You know, we still haven't seen the third *Matrix* movie with Nina yet," his cousin says. "You should tell her to come over this week and watch it with us. That way you guys can make up."

Brody swallows a bite of food. "Maybe. We'll see."

"You two aren't breaking up, are you?"

He turns to look at Trevor. "Why are you so concerned with my love life?"

"Because you're a lot happier when she's around. I mean, shit, you've barely said two words to me all weekend."

"Just eat your spaghetti," Brody grumbles. He knows he's being grouchy as hell. He doesn't like arguing with Nina, and he doesn't like all this uncertainty in his life either. Asking her to move in with him had felt right. He'd trusted his gut. And when is that ever a bad thing?

His bad mood doesn't go away, and when he gets to work on Monday, it seems like everything is going wrong. He's making dumb mistakes and has to call two customers to tell them he's running late with their cars. The final straw is when some guy he's never seen before comes in to pick up his BMW that Anka's been working on.

"Hey, chief, how's it going? Is my car ready?"

Brody bristles. He can't tell if the guy is being a racist prick calling him "chief" or if he's just a clueless idiot. "We're almost done with it. Just finishing the last shock. You can wait here if you want, or there's a few restaurants nearby. We'll text you."

"All right, chief, that sounds good. I guess I'll go grab a sandwich. Can you tell me if there's a diner around here?"

Brody directs him down the street to a diner about a block away.

"Thanks, chief. I'll be back."

"My name is Brody. *Not* chief."

"What's that?" The guy looks confused, and Brody sees he really is just a clueless idiot.

"Never mind. I'll let you know when your car is done."

Brody glares at him as he walks away. Then he gets a soda from the machine and goes into the back office. He takes a sip of sugar and caffeine, hoping it will help lighten his mood.

As he's sitting there, his phone buzzes, and he pulls it out from the front pocket of his coveralls. It's Nina on the caller ID. His heart jumps in his chest, and he hopes she's calling to make up.

"Hey, Nina banana," he says, relieved to talk to her.

"Hi, Brody. How are you?"

"All right, I guess." He pauses. "Actually, I'm having a crap day. I'm glad you called. I wanted to apologize about that weird fight we had. If you don't want to move in, I totally understand. I wasn't trying to pressure you or anything."

"It's okay. I know you weren't."

He lowers his voice. "I've missed you these past few days. I don't like fighting like this."

She sighs. "Me either. I've missed you too."

"You have?" He likes the sound of that. "Then what do you say to coming over tonight?"

"We need to talk." She hesitates. "Something's happened."

He puts his soda down at the serious tone of her voice. "What is it? Are you okay?"

"I'm fine, but... I just got the results back from the paternity test."

CHAPTER SEVENTEEN

Life & The Art of Automobile Maintenance
By Brody Austin

"If there's a problem with your car's supsension system, your ride will be noticeably bumpier."

"I'm too nervous to look. Can you do it for me?" Nina is staring at the website for the lab that did the paternity test. She got an email from them with a link to see the results right away. It also said they were sending out printed copies to both Noel and Brody.

Holding a glass of wine, Suzy comes over to stare down at the computer. "So, what are we hoping for here? Team Noel or Team Brody?"

Nina shakes her head. "I've been trying not to think like that. I don't want to feel disappointed either way."

"Puh-lease." Suzy rolls her eyes and takes a sip from her wine. "You know you're Team Brody. I'm Team Brody too."

Nina glances at Suzy's wineglass with envy. She hasn't touched a drop of alcohol since that night she passed out, hasn't even wanted a glass, but she's so nervous that she almost wishes she could have one. Instead, she takes a sip from her glass of pineapple juice. She's had a strong craving for all things pineapple lately.

She puts her computer down on the coffee table and stands up. "You have to look. Just click on the link. I can't do it."

Suzy sits down on the couch. She places her wine on the end table and then reaches for the laptop. "All right, I get that. I'd be nervous too. Most women already know who their baby daddy is."

"Gee, thanks."

"You know what I mean. You're in an unusual situation."

Nina paces around the living room. "Just check for me. I'm freaking out too much." She walks over to the window and gazes outside, trying to let the view calm her. There are a few sailboats out on the water, and she lingers on them, imagines herself out on one of them right now.

"Oh my God!" Suzy gives a mini-shriek.

Nina spins around as adrenaline spikes through her. "What is it?"

Her sister's staring at the computer screen with a strange look on her face. She glances up at Nina, then reaches for her wine and takes a large swallow.

Nina sprints across the room. "What does it say?"

"Are you sure you want me to tell you?"

She stops directly in front of her sister. "Yes, tell me." Although she has a feeling she already knows.

Suzy takes a deep breath. "It's Noel's."

"*What?*" Nina's stomach plunges. She immediately sits down next to Suzy and snatches the laptop away from her. She has to see this for herself.

Meanwhile, Suzy is watching her with sympathy and taking larger gulps from her glass. "I'm going to need more wine," she says, getting up. "Lots more. Don't worry, I'll be drinking enough for the two of us."

Nina is staring at the results, trying to ignore the disappointment thudding through her. She told herself it didn't matter either way. She'll love this child no matter what—which is the truth. But apparently deep down, she'd been hoping it was Brody's.

"Well, that's it." She takes a deep breath. "Now I know." She puts her hand over her abdomen and makes a vow to herself that she isn't going to let Noel be a jerk to this child. No matter what. She'll fight tooth and nail for that.

Suzy is in the kitchen filling up her glass. "I'm so sorry. I guess you're stuck with that jerk forever."

Nina puts the laptop back down on the coffee table. "How am I going to tell Brody?"

"Do you think he'll be relieved or disappointed? You guys seem to have grown close."

"I don't know." Though she suspects she does know. "He asked me to move in with him recently."

Suzy's eyes grow wide. "Holy shit. I didn't realize things had gotten that serious. That's kind of fast, isn't it?"

"He mostly doesn't want me living alone because I'm pregnant."

Her sister tilts her head. "That's sweet, actually. What did you say?"

Nina relays the whole story to her, and how they've had a falling out.

"I don't think you're too old for him. That's silly," Suzy says. "You're both adults. Eight years isn't that much."

"None of it matters anymore now, does it? I'm pregnant with Noel's baby. Brody's not going to stick around for that."

"What if he wants to anyway?"

Nina sighs heavily. "He's not going to want to. What guy wants to be with a woman who's pregnant with another man's baby?"

It's almost dark out when Nina parks her car in front of Brody's house. Her hands are shaking as she tries to calm herself. She's not sure why this is so hard. She needed to end it with him anyway. This is the perfect reason.

Except she's going to miss Brody.

She's going to miss everything about him.

She doesn't know how it's happened, but he's become her best friend.

When she walks up the front steps, the door opens, and he's already standing there. So handsome. Those cheekbones and broad shoulders. His black hair looks damp, like he's just taken a shower, and when she moves past him to go inside the house, she can smell his clean scent.

His expression seems stoic as they study each other in the warm glow of his home. Neither of them speaks.

"Do you want some tea?" he finally asks.

"No, thanks." She glances around the living room. "Where's Trevor?"

"Out with friends."

Nina's relieved. It's best if they talk alone. "I wanted to tell you the results in person."

Brody reaches for his coat—a thick brown corduroy jacket—and puts it on.

"What are you doing?"

"C'mon, let's get out of here."

"And go where?"

"For a drive."

"Now?"

"Yeah, now."

She follows him out to the Cougar and watches as he pulls the cover off. Brody loves going for a drive. She's never met anyone who drove for pleasure and relaxation as much as he did.

They don't talk as they head into the city. She doesn't ask where he's going or why, when he takes the exit toward Green Lake. They've done this routine a few times now, and Nina's discovered she likes being driven around by him. It's strangely soothing.

The radio is playing Mazzy Star's "Fade Into You" when she turns her head in the dark and watches his profile, the streetlights reflecting across his features.

"You already know what I came to tell you tonight, don't you?" she asks softly.

He glances down at the gearshift between them and then over at her for a moment. "I could see it on your face when I opened the door."

She licks her lips. "Should I say the words?"

He shrugs. "I guess so. Go ahead."

"The baby is Noel's."

Brody's face doesn't change. It's like he's wearing a mask. She's gotten to know him pretty well, but this is something she hasn't seen before."

"Are you going to say anything?"

"Not much to say, is there?"

"I suppose not. Are you relieved?"

Now his expression does change. His brows draw together. "No, I'm not relieved. To be honest, I was conflicted about the whole thing. I was in shock at first. I didn't know what I felt."

"And now?"

"I feel sort of numb."

"I'm sorry. I think I've put you through the emotional wringer. I came barging into your life, and now you have to deal with the aftermath."

Brody glances at her but doesn't reply. Instead, things are silent again, and he eventually drives down and parks on a street near Green Lake. It's nighttime and starting to rain. People are walking to some of the nearby restaurants.

He reaches over and takes her hand. "I've never wanted to live in a small town," Brody says. "I know a lot of people love them, but I prefer the city. Maybe it's from spending a lot of time on the rez when I was growing up, but small towns feel confining to me."

Nina listens, wondering where he's going with this. She enjoys his touch, even though she knows this will be the last time.

"Kiera always wanted to move to a small town. She thought it sounded idyllic. We made a compromise once that we'd live in the city while we were young, but then when we had a family, we'd find a small town to raise them in."

"That sounds reasonable."

He plays with her fingers. "Except I always hoped I could talk her out of moving. I didn't want to leave Seattle."

"Why are you telling me this?"

He shrugs. "I guess it's because I'm starting to realize things weren't as perfect between Kiera and me as I liked to pretend they were. We had our differences."

"Maybe so, but you'll find someone else. Someone who *is* perfect for you. It'll happen."

"There's no such thing as perfection."

"You'll still find someone."

"And what if I want *you*?" His voice is deep in the charged air of the car. The rain has picked up and is pounding on the roof. She tries to pull her hand away, but he doesn't let her. "What if I don't care whose baby you're pregnant with?"

She tugs at her hand again, and finally he releases it. "Brody, you don't know what you're saying. You don't want to be with a woman who's eight years older than you and is carrying another man's child. Trust me, your family is going to agree with me on this."

He leans back in the seat and closes his eyes, pinching the bridge of his nose. "So now I have to get over you too. That's what you're telling me."

Nina tries to breathe. She never meant for any of this to happen. "It won't be that hard. We haven't even known each other very long."

But as she says it, she knows it isn't true, knows it doesn't matter how long they've known each other. She already misses him, even though he's sitting here beside her.

It's a lot different than when Noel and I broke up, Nina realizes over the next couple weeks as she tries to keep busy with all her classes. In fact, she's added a new one—pregnancy yoga. She goes over to Suzy's for Thanksgiving dinner and only throws up once in the bathroom while she's there. Her morning sickness has come on full blast, though at least it's usually only once a day.

It's different because Noel and I had years of history, she decides. Noel was the man she thought she was going to spend the rest of her life with. Her one true soul mate. It makes sense why she was so devastated when he cheated on her, why she's still struggling with it even now.

It makes no sense why she's so upset over Brody.

We were never meant to be.

It's the truth, and yet it's been harder than she thought it would be not seeing him anymore.

"I don't know why I miss him so much," she tells Suzy over lunch after her pregnancy yoga class. They're having Mexican food instead of meeting at La Dolce Vita because Nina doesn't want to run into Blair. Which is a shame since she likes Blair. "We weren't putting a label on it. We were just hanging out. It was supposed to be casual."

"Friends with benefits," her sister says, raising a brow.

"Basically."

"I don't think it's that complicated." Suzy dips a tortilla chip into some salsa. "Brody is a great guy. That's why you miss him."

"He's so different from Noel. So much younger, and his tastes aren't as refined."

"You mean he's not a snob."

"He's down-to-earth, yet he's also ambitious." She tells her sister about how he wants to open a second garage. "He's competitive too.

You should see the way he goes on about this softball trophy he has to win every summer."

"For someone who ended it with Brody, you're spending an awful lot of time thinking about him."

Nina sighs. "I know. I need to stop."

"Have you heard anything from Noel about the baby?"

She nods and swallows a bite of enchilada. "Yes, he texted me. He said he got the DNA test, and that he was 'processing it'—whatever that means." She rolls her eyes.

"Have you found a lawyer?"

Nina smiles. "Oh yes." She tells Suzy that her lawyer is already putting together preliminary child support papers to send to Noel. "Let him process *that*."

"Good. I'm glad you're taking care of things. And you started seeing my midwife, Tula?"

"I had my first appointment with her a couple days ago."

"And how did it go?"

Nina describes it to Suzy, how they listened to the baby's heartbeat and then talked about what she's planning for the birth. Even though it's months away, and Nina isn't even showing yet, Tula encouraged her to start working on her birth plan.

The waiter comes by and brings them more water. Suzy murmurs a thank you before he walks away.

"Well, I'm going to be there to support you during the birth. Are you going to try for a water birth?" Her sister had Henry in the hospital but had a water birth with Grace.

"I don't know. I figure any way I can deliver a healthy baby is a win for me."

Suzy nods, taking a sip of her water. "I totally agree."

Nina already knows she wants to deliver at the birth center, but beyond that, she's not sure what to do for a birth plan. She was concerned about her age, but Tula said as long as her pregnancy remains low-risk, then it won't be a problem. If something changes, then she'll need to switch to a hospital. "It's a lot to figure out. I'm trying not to let myself get overwhelmed."

"You know you have me and Luke. We'll do anything to help. Have you told Mom and Dad any more about this?"

"I talked to them a few days ago. It wasn't a pleasant conversation. Dad still thinks Noel should marry me. It sounded like he was ready to force him at gunpoint."

Suzy nearly chokes with laughter. "I'm sorry. I know it's not funny. It's just that for years I was the one always getting in trouble."

"Well, now you're the good one, and I'm the bad one."

"What else did they say?"

"I finally told them I lost my job and that Noel's the one who fired me. That put them in a state of shock. I think they went catatonic."

Suzy's still chuckling. "I'm sure they'll get over it."

After lunch, Suzy heads off to pick up her kids from school, and Nina goes back home. There was one thing about her midwife's appointment that she didn't mention to her sister, and it's that she saw Summer there at the birth center. Apparently, she's a midwife. Brody had mentioned it a while back, but somehow she'd forgotten.

"Hi, Nina. I thought that was you."

Nina had finished her appointment with Tula and was in the lobby looking at some of the various lotions they sell when she realized someone was speaking to her. A pretty young woman with strawberry-blonde hair who she couldn't quite place.

"It's Summer. Brody's sister."

"Oh, yes! Of course, I'm sorry. The last time I saw you was at your Halloween party. You wore a costume with your hair up in a towel."

She laughed. "That's right, I was spa girl. How are you doing? Are you seeing one of the midwives here?" Summer's eyes fell to Nina's still-flat stomach.

"I am," she said. "I'm seeing Tula. She delivered my sister's daughter."

"That's wonderful. Tula is amazing."

"So you work here too?"

"I just started. I was in Oregon for a while before this."

"How nice," Nina said, feeling awkward. She glanced down at the container of lotion still in her hand.

"That cocoa butter is really great for stretch marks."

"Oh, I'm sure it is." She wondered how much Summer knew about her situation. It was obvious Brody told her she was pregnant.

"I'm sorry things didn't work out between you and my brother."

Nina nodded and met her eyes. "I guess it wasn't meant to be."

"I guess not."

She put the cocoa butter back on the shelf. "I should get going. It was nice seeing you again."

"You too. In fact, I'll probably see you around. I'm assisting with births for now until I start taking on clients of my own."

"Well, okay. Good to know." Nina started to walk away but then stopped and turned back. "How is he doing?"

Summer smiled. "Brody is doing... okay."

Nina took this in. "I really care for him."

"I know you do."

"It's why I broke up with him."

"I know that too."

Nina nodded and then left the birth center. She wanted to ask more questions but knew there wasn't any point. Hopefully things didn't get difficult seeing Summer there every time. What were the odds? But there was no way she was changing midwives.

She tried to put it out of her mind as she slipped behind the wheel of her car. It was just one more complication in what had become the mixed-up jigsaw puzzle of her life.

"Why don't you come up and see your auntie for Heritage Day?" Aunt Jeanie says to Brody on the phone. "You can ride up with Trevor. It's been way too long since we've seen you."

Heritage Day was his tribe's version of Thanksgiving. Some tribal members celebrated Thanksgiving, but many of them saw it as a holiday that glorified their ancestors' oppression.

"Sorry, I know. I promise I'll come up for Christmas. I just have too much going on here right now."

"I don't like these excuses. And what's this I hear that Trevor isn't working for you anymore?"

"He got hired at another garage." Brody knew he'd be hearing about this as soon as Trevor accepted the new job, so he was prepared. "We decided it would be good for him to work someplace where his cousin wasn't the boss and always looking over his shoulder." He chuckles and tries to make light of it.

"Hmm. I don't know about that. It seems to me it would be good working for you, but I guess you two know what's best."

"So, how is everybody else doing? How's Mitch?"

"He's fine."

Brody asks about a few more family members and is glad to hear everyone is doing well. "And Thunder?" he finally asks, wondering what she'll say. You could never tell what you were going to get with his father. Sometimes he was sober, working and living a normal life, but other times he'd go for weeks drunk and incoherent.

"Oh, you know. Thunder is... just being Thunder."

Brody nods to himself. It was code for "He's on a bender." Probably because of the holidays. His father never could handle the holidays that well.

He and his aunt chat a little more, but he's mostly trying to get off the phone so he can get back to work.

"I'll for sure see you at Christmas, right?" she says before they hang up. "You're not backing out of that."

"Yes, Auntie, I'll see you at Christmas."

He ends the call and checks the time before slipping the phone back into his front pocket. Trevor was driving up to the rez tomorrow and had tried to talk him into going, but he wasn't feeling that festive.

He's been doing his best to get over Nina, but his best isn't working.

How the hell did this happen? How did I wind up with two women weighing on my mind?

I should start writing country songs.

Except that only made him think of Nina and the guitar she still has him learning how to play.

Thanksgiving at his mom's house winds up being long and uncomfortable. Half of his extended family is there. Apparently everybody knows about the situation with Nina and her pregnancy. Summer told Tori—swearing her to secrecy. But Tori, of course, told Liam and Blair—swearing both of *them* to secrecy. Blair told Road. Road swears he didn't tell anyone, but somehow Aunt Lori heard about it, and now both his parents know too.

It was like a crazy game of telephone. By the time his mom approached him, it was as though Nina was pregnant with triplets, had run off to join the circus, and was in talks with producers to have her own reality show.

"I know you two were close," his mom says after dinner. They're both standing outside on the back patio while his mom vapes. Brody joined her to get away from all the babies inside. "But Nina was right to break it off."

"You shouldn't vape," he says. "That shit is bad for you."

"It's just occasionally." His mom blows out a stream of white smoke. "I think Nina was a rebound relationship after Kiera. You needed to have one of those, and now you've gotten it out of the way."

He stares out at his parents' familiar backyard. The fruit trees his dad planted when he was in high school that are still going strong.

"She's pregnant with another man's child, and she's quite a bit older than you," his mom continues. "The relationship is best left in the past."

He doesn't say anything.

"You're going to have to put it behind you. You know that, right?"

"I *know*." He can't quite hide the frustration in his voice.

"Then why are you so glum?" She blows out more white smoke. "You had a long face all through dinner."

"I'm fine."

He's not fine though.

There's a squeal of laughter from inside the house. Probably Road's daughter, Ava. That little girl is a pistol.

In the past, being around everyone's babies was uncomfortable because he didn't want to acknowledge that everything had changed, but now it makes him remember how close he came to being a father himself. He can't stop thinking about it. It's like some kind of switch in his brain has been flicked on.

"My mind's on other things. I'm considering opening a second location again."

Her brows go up. "You are? I thought you'd put that idea to rest."

"Apparently it woke up."

"Can you afford it?"

"With a loan from the bank I can."

His mom nods. She's a small business owner herself, but he's never heard her talk of expanding. "Just be careful. Don't get in over your head. You don't want to lose everything you've worked so hard to build."

They head back inside the house. He has a beer and makes conversation but only stays long enough to be polite. It's a relief when he can finally get the hell out of there.

Nothing's the same, he thinks, driving home in a funk. *Yet everything's the same.*

CHAPTER EIGHTEEN

> **Life & The Art of Automobile Maintenance**
> By Brody Austin
>
>
>
> "So many cars out there in the world.
> If only you had time to drive them all."

"Oh me too. I *totally* agree," Danica says, grinning at Brody. They're eating dinner out at an Italian restaurant downtown. Not the same romantic one he and Nina used to eat at but a different one he'd read about online.

He picks up his glass of red wine. He never used to drink wine, but Nina convinced him to try it once, and he discovered he liked it with Italian food.

After Thanksgiving, he wondered if maybe everyone was right.

Maybe Nina being pregnant with another guy's baby was a sign that he should move on. So he finally called Danica back. Instead of coffee, he asked her out on a proper date.

So far the main problem with the date was that Danica seemed to agree with every single thing he said. He was pretty sure if he said grass was purple and the sky was green, she'd completely agree.

"I just love classic cars," she continues after he told her that's what he specializes in. "They're just so... classic. So cool."

"Do you have a favorite car?"

"What's the car you just drove us here in called?"

"A 1969 Mercury Cougar XR7 convertible."

"That's my favorite."

He raises a brow. "Really? You're familiar with them?"

"No, not exactly. But I really like your car."

"Huh. Would you like to get some dessert?"

Danica gives him a seductive smile. "Oh, definitely. I *love* dessert." Her blue eyes linger on his.

He has to admit, she's not quite as attractive as he remembers. In fact, beyond the endless agreeability, there's something else that's off-putting about her.

They decide to share a rich fruit cobbler for dessert. They continue to make small talk, and as hard as he tries, Brody doesn't feel a single spark for Danica.

When he finally drives her home, he's surprised when she asks him if he'd like to come inside and see her apartment.

He hesitates. *Is there really any point in dragging this out further?*

"Oh come on, Brody. What have you got to lose?" Danica smiles at him. "I promise I'll make it worth your while."

He remembers how he's supposed to be moving on and figures what the hell? Does it really matter if their personalities aren't suited? At least one of them seems to think the evening was a success.

"Okay, sure." He parks the car, and they both get out. Brody follows her to a townhouse-styled apartment with a combination brick and wood exterior. "This is nice," he says.

"Thank you. I have a roommate, but they won't be bothering us." She gives him a seductive grin. "We have the place to ourselves."

Once they're inside, she offers him a beer. He says yes, mostly out of politeness. She disappears into the kitchen while he glances around her generic-looking apartment that smells mildly like cat piss. Once again, he questions what he's doing here. For some reason, his Spidey senses are tingling.

Danica brings him the beer and then pulls him over to the couch. "Come on, let's sit down together."

They sit next to each other, and he takes a sip of his beer while Danica smiles at him.

"You're not shy, are you, Brody?"

"Not particularly."

She scoots closer and then takes the bottle from his hand. She takes a sip herself and then places it on the coffee table. Then she turns back, and before he knows it, she's slid her arms around his neck and is kissing him.

He kisses her back, though he's not sure why. Her mouth feels hard and strange.

Finally, he breaks it off. "Look, I'm just going to go."

"Oh, don't do that. You're such a good kisser."

She lifts her leg and slides herself onto his lap. They kiss some more, but Brody isn't into it.

"I have to get up early tomorrow."

"No, *stay*. Pretty please?" Danica wraps her arms tightly around his neck and then, out of the blue, starts gyrating on his lap like she's giving him a lap dance. It's so weird that he's not even sure what to say.

Eventually she stops and grins at him. She reaches around for the beer on the coffee table and takes a drink. "Do you want some?"

Brody shakes his head, trying to figure out this odd situation.

Danica takes another swig, then gives him an eye smolder. "What do you say we take this into the bedroom?" She puts the bottle to her mouth again, except this time she starts licking and sucking on it like she's giving it a blow job. She's smiling at him, trying to look sexy as she runs her tongue up and down the length of it.

He watches this bizarre display with embarrassment. If she was joking around, it might be silly sexy, but the fact that she's going at it so intensely for real is making him cringe.

While she soaks the entire bottle with spit, Brody realizes he's made a huge mistake. He needs to get the hell out of here. *What was I thinking?*

Ding dong.

He jerks his head toward the front door, where someone's just rung the bell.

Meanwhile Danica's eyes are closed, still sucking on the beer bottle, convinced it's going to climax.

"Someone's at your door," Brody says, stating the obvious. "Don't you think you should answer it?"

"Just ignore him for now."

"Him?"

"That's my boyfriend."

"You have a boyfriend?" Brody's mouth falls open. He gets her off him and scrambles away. "Don't you think you should have mentioned that?"

Ding dong.

"Trust me. It's no big deal." She smiles again and then hops up from the couch, putting the wet beer bottle on the coffee table. "In fact, I'm going to let him in. I can't wait to see his face. He's going to be *sooo* jealous."

Brody jumps up. "Are you kidding me?" He searches around for an escape route and notices some patio doors. He doesn't want to get into a fight with some dude over a woman he has zero interest in. "I'm going out the back."

"No, don't go anywhere. Stay."

"Are you nuts?" But then something occurs to him. "Wait, are you afraid of him?"

She laughs. "Of course not. Don't be silly. This is all part of the game."

"What game?"

"The one where he finds me with another man and gets all jealous and horny."

Brody blinks at her in shock as reality dawns on him. "Is this some kind of sex game?"

The doorbell rings again, and the sound makes him jumpier than a virgin on prom night.

What kind of strange shit have I gotten myself mixed up in? Tori's going to get an earful about it, that's for sure.

Danica is smiling seductively. "I'm going to let Brendon in now. I think the three of us should get better acquainted. *Much* better acquainted, don't you think?"

Brody's standing there trying to decide if he should escape out the back or leave through the front when some tall, skinny guy with short blond hair comes inside with Danica. The guy grins at him and then kisses her.

"Look, sorry, but this isn't my scene," Brody says, awkwardly moving past them. He's hardly a prude, but no way is this happening.

He can hear them both trying to call him back right before he slams the front door shut, practically sprinting for his car.

It isn't until he's halfway home that his adrenaline wears off, and he bursts out laughing. *"Jesus,* what was *that?"* He pulls the car over, still laughing and trying to catch his breath. He wants to call someone, and the first person he thinks of is Nina. Nina, who's become his closest friend, and who he's not supposed to talk to anymore.

He glances at the time. It's ten at night.

Oh, what the hell.

She answers on the first ring. "Brody? Is... everything okay?"

"You're not going to believe what just happened to me."

"What?"

And he tells her the whole story. The uncomfortable date with Danica, going back to her apartment, then the boyfriend showing up as part of some crazy sex game.

Nina howls with laughter. "Oh no! Are you kidding? And you had no idea that's where the date was headed?"

"How the hell would I know *that*? It's not like she announced it up front." He chuckles some more and then shakes his head. "Isn't there an etiquette for threesomes? Aren't they supposed to ask you in advance?"

"I wouldn't know. I've never had one."

"Me either. Of course, in pornos they never ask people in advance."

She laughs. "I guess your life just turned into a porno."

"Great. Just what I've always wanted. Group sex with two unattractive strangers—one of them a dude."

She laughs some more. "I assumed Danica was really great-looking."

He snorts. "Hardly. Definitely not my type."

"So what is your type?"

"Someone not crazy or weird, for starters."

"Hmm, that probably excludes me."

"Hey, I make an exception for crazy, weird pregnant ladies, especially if they're overbearingly managerial." He can hear her laughing into the phone and gets a rush over how much he misses her. "So, what are you doing? Were you sleeping?"

"No, I was reading and watching television."

"Do you want some company?"

Nina goes quiet. "We're not supposed to see each other anymore."

"I know, but I miss you."

She doesn't say anything.

"Don't you miss me at all?" He wonders if this whole thing is one-sided, but he doesn't think so. "Tell me you do."

"I miss you a lot." Her voice is soft.

He likes hearing that. "I want to see you. Let me come over."

"We're supposed to be moving on with our lives."

"Yeah? Well, screw that."

"I don't know, Brody. It's probably a bad idea."

"Invite me over. Do you know I've never even been to your place?" She doesn't speak for a long moment, and his stomach knots with worry that she's going to turn him down. "I need to see you, Nina."

She takes a deep breath. "Do you remember how to get here?"

"Pretty sure I do."

"I'll let the doorman know I'm expecting you."

It's only been two weeks, but when Nina opens the door to him, it feels like it's been forever.

"Brody," she whispers just before he takes her in his arms.

The door closes behind him as he hoists her up so her legs are wrapped around his hips.

"Nina banana," he murmurs with a grin before walking with her until her back's pressed against the wall in her entryway.

He kisses her, and she tastes so good, like the woman he's supposed to be with. Everyone keeps telling him it's wrong, but this doesn't feel wrong.

They're already getting lost in each other when he pulls back.

"What is it?" she asks, catching her breath.

"Let me look at you. I've missed this face."

She laughs. "It hasn't been that long."

"Too long."

She sticks her nose in his neck. "You smell so good."

"What do I smell like?"

"You."

"Well, you taste good." He kisses her and then squeezes her ass. "And feel good too. Everything about you is just right."

"Oh shit, Brody." She strokes his jaw, wearing a thoughtful expression. "What are we doing?"

He grins a little. "I think it's obvious what we're doing."

"You know what I mean."

In response, he brings his mouth down to hers, ending the conversation. He doesn't like where it's headed. His hands slip beneath the little tank top she's wearing, caressing smooth skin. Her breasts are soft and malleable in his palms, the beaded nipples taut. More than anything, he wants to taste them, but the angle is too awkward. His cock's gotten so hard it's painful.

"Where's your bedroom?" he asks, pulling away from the wall. He starts walking with her still wrapped around him. In passing, he notices her apartment has an incredible view of the city lights, but all he really cares about is trying to find her bed.

She guides him down a hallway to an open door, where the view appears to continue. With relief, he lowers her onto the mattress, and the two of them go back to making out. He groans when she slides her fingers over the outside of his jeans, squeezing his erection.

"Let's get out of these clothes." He sits up and kneels.

Nina's wearing a pink top and stretchy black yoga pants, all of which he quickly helps her remove. She works on unfastening his belt buckle while he reaches behind himself and pulls his T-shirt off.

"Look at you," he murmurs once they're both naked. "Gorgeous and all mine."

She smiles at that, then reaches out for him, and he's sucked down into the rabbit hole. A tangle of lust and hot emotion, the two of them get lost in each other. He's licking and sucking her breasts while she moans and runs her hands through his hair. His mouth slides down her body.

Nina's panting as he kisses her thighs. "You're not supposed to be here," she says, gasping when he puts his mouth exactly where he knows she wants it. "We shouldn't be doing this. Oh *God*."

He pleasures her for a long while, enjoying himself, taking his time. He's always been a patient man, though the sounds she's making are about to drive him crazy.

When she hits her climax and starts pulling his hair, Brody gets the strongest sensation in his chest. It's exciting, but there's something else too. Tenderness. He wants to make her feel good, wants to be the source of her passion.

When she eventually pushes his head away, he sits up and gazes down at her, trying to control his arousal. He's not doing a good job though, and when Nina pulls him on top of her, he spreads her legs and takes her deep, groaning at the sensation. It's so good.

"You're perfect for me," he whispers with a shaky breath. "Don't you know that?"

Nina's eyes widen. Time seems suspended as they study each other in the tangle of bedsheets.

She strokes his jaw. "How did we get here?"

"All that matters is that we *are* here."

She nods. Their gazes lock on each other, and something so intimate passes between them. For a moment, Brody wants to escape it. It's too intense, this rush of emotion. He's never been a coward though, so he opens his heart and lets her in, realizing deep down that there's nothing to fear. That this is where real strength lies.

He begins to move his body, still buried within Nina. For a fleeting moment, he thinks about the child inside her and feels strangely connected to it, even though it's not his.

The thought flickers past like a breath of air and then is gone because Nina has started moving with him. She's grabbing his ass, drawing him in deeper. He follows her lead, and soon they're both lost to the sensual. To the animal. His heart beats like a drum as they give each other everything.

"Oh shit," he groans, right on the edge. "I'm so close."

"I know." Nina's voice sounds husky, and it's obvious she's there too.

Then they take that leap, jumping off the cliff together.

"That's some view of the city," Brody says afterward, stroking her hair while gazing out the window. "Unbelievable."

The two of them are lying in Nina's bed. She's still trying to get her mind around what just happened. She's never had sex like that.

Not even with Noel. She felt so close to Brody. It was otherworldly. She's wrapped around his firm body, her head resting on his chest.

"When you told me your condo had a great view, I figured maybe you could see the Space Needle or something."

She laughs. "I can't see the Space Needle at all."

"It's no wonder you didn't want to move in with me."

"That's not why I didn't want to move in." She lifts her head up to look at him. "It had nothing to do with my view."

"If you say so."

The two of them gaze at each other. "I just wasn't ready for that. It was too much."

He nods in understanding. "I know."

She puts her head back down and hugs him close. The truth is she's glad Brody called her tonight, glad his date was a disaster, even glad he hasn't found someone new since they've been apart. *I want him.* Even if it means she's selfish. She can't seem to help herself.

"So how are you feeling these days?" he asks. "How's your pregnancy going?"

"I've started throwing up every day, but besides that, everything is going fine."

He slides his hand down her arm. "I'm glad to hear that. You don't appear to be showing much yet. Your boobs are bigger though."

"They are, aren't they?" She laughs and props her head up. "I've never had big boobs before. It's sort of fascinating."

"They look great, though they looked great before too."

She smiles. "That's the right thing to say. Though I wonder what you'll say when I'm big and pregnant." The words slip out before she can stop them. The implication that he'll still be here with her when she's further along.

He reaches for her hand. "I'll still say you look great."

Her eyes roam his handsome face. Nothing's changed. He's still too young for her. She's still pregnant with another man's baby. Yet somehow it feels like things have changed.

"What?" he asks. "You've got a funny look."

"Why did you call me tonight?"

"You know why, Nina. I'm not giving up on you."

She nods. "People are going to talk."

"Let them. I don't care. I've been miserable without you."

Her heart warms hearing this, even though it shouldn't. "Me too." She leans in and kisses him. It's with affection, but like a match to kindling, the flame catches, and before she knows it, they're getting into it again.

She holds his head as the kiss deepens, their tongues tangling with each other. Nina pulls back and smiles at him. And then she does what he did for her earlier. She kisses her way down his body until she reaches his very erect cock.

Brody's watching her through half-lidded eyes as she licks all around the head and then takes him into her mouth. As she sucks on him and licks some more, his whole body starts to shake, except it's not with passion but laughter.

She looks up at him in surprise. "Is something funny?"

"Damn, I'm sorry, but I can't get it out of my head." The back of his hand rests on his forehead as he continues to laugh.

"Get what out of your head?"

He shares some more about his date earlier and how this woman, Danica, was giving a blow job to a beer bottle.

"A beer bottle? Are you kidding?"

"I wish I was. The whole bottle was soaked with her spit. It was gross."

"And this is what you're thinking about when I'm going down on you?"

"I'm trying not to." His brown eyes search hers with amusement. "Shit, Nina, I think I'm traumatized."

She laughs and caresses the happy trail on his stomach. "What can I do to help? Should I avoid giving you blow jobs for a while?"

"Now, let's not be hasty." The corner of his mouth kicks up. "I'm pretty sure I can work through this."

"You think so?" She strokes his erection again, which is as hard as ever.

He lets out a shaky breath. "I'll be fine," he says, watching her as she takes him in her mouth again. "As long as your doorbell doesn't ring."

The next morning, she wakes up early and watches Brody in bed sleeping beside her. He's on his stomach and facing her, his arms tucked under the pillow, highlighting his tribal armband tattoo. She never shut the drapes yesterday, so the early morning sun is shining on his face. He's so handsome.

How did this incredible man come into my life?

And in a strange roundabout way, she has Noel to thank. If he hadn't cheated on her with Emily, she would never have met Brody.

She thinks about where she'd be right now if she were still with Noel. It's Saturday, so they'd be getting dressed to go out for breakfast at one of the cafes nearby. Usually his kids or Claudia would call him with some mundane crisis or another. She used to feel guilty for her resentment of those phone calls. The way they disrupted their limited time alone together. In fact, she was convinced Claudia did it on purpose.

"Hey there, Nina banana," Brody says, blinking his eyes open and giving her a purely masculine grin.

"Hey there, yourself."

His grin grows wider. And then, before she knows what's happening, he rolls her over so she's underneath him as she shrieks with laughter.

"What are you doing to me?" She can feel his morning wood pressing against her.

"I'm ravishing you, woman."

"After last night? My God, you're insatiable."

He chuckles. "*I'm* insatiable? You practically put me in a wheelchair."

She laughs. It isn't far from the truth. They basically had sex all night, with Brody stopping three times to ask her if it was okay to be doing it this much while she was pregnant. She told him what every book she's read about it said—that it was fine.

They ravish each other again and then take a shower together. Afterward, Brody stands in the kitchen with wet hair eating a banana and looking around her condo with obvious amazement. "This place must have cost you a fortune."

Nina shrugs and tries to make light of it. "It's only a two bedroom. I got lucky with the timing. Noel knew someone at the bank, and I managed to get a very attractive rate." She glances over at him and regrets bringing up Noel. She needs to stop doing that.

Brody's watching her. "Did Noel help you buy it?"

She shakes her head. "He helped me find it though."

"I'm surprised he didn't want to live here with you."

"He's got his own house in Medina."

Brody nods but is studying her. She knows how smart he is and that he's probably already guessed how much time Noel spent here.

After she finishes getting dressed, she finds Brody sitting on the couch, scrolling through his phone. "Would you like to go to a car show with me today?"

"A car show?"

"Yeah, there's a classic car show down in Tacoma. I told the sponsors I'd drop by. A number of my customers are showing their cars there."

"So it's a work thing?"

He shrugs. "Basically, but it's a lot of fun too. Lots of great cars to see."

She comes over to him. "I don't know. That sounds boring."

"*Boring?*" He laughs and reaches out, pulling her onto his lap. "You get to spend the day with *me*."

Nina wraps her arms around his neck, inhaling his clean scent.

She rolls her eyes. "Okay, I *guess* I could go."

Brody smiles at her, obviously pleased. "Good. I think you'll be surprised at how much fun it is."

They take the Cougar and get coffee and herbal tea at Starbucks before stopping at the shop to grab some business cards for him to hand out at the show.

It's about an hour drive down to Tacoma. When they arrive, Nina can see all the classic cars lined up on the street. Kind of impressive. They find parking a couple blocks away.

"Why didn't you enter your Cougar in the show?" Nina asks once they get out and are walking around. "It would fit in perfectly."

He shrugs. "I just wasn't in the mood. I've entered it in lots of shows in the past. Once the Zephyr is ready, I'll start entering that for sure. Trust me, that car's going to get a lot of attention."

"Is it a contest? Do people vote for the best one or something?"

"Sometimes, but not usually. It's mostly just classic car enthusiasts coming together. It's great for business. I've gotten plenty of customers over the years from car shows."

It's a brisk December day, and there are Christmas decorations up in the city. The two of them walk around hand in hand, checking out all the cars. Nina has to admit some of them are pretty amazing. And it's fun seeing Brody in his element. He seems to know a lot of people, and it's obvious they all consider him an expert and are hanging on his every word.

She used to love watching Noel when he was addressing their shareholders. The way he commanded a room. The way everyone treated him with such deference. Seeing Brody surrounded by all these men asking questions and wanting his opinion ironically reminds her of those meetings.

"Oh my God, Nina? Is that you?"

No, it can't be.

Nina turns with dread and, to her dismay, discovers the last person on earth she would have expected to see here.

Noel's ex-wife, Claudia.

CHAPTER NINETEEN

> ### Life & The Art of Automobile Maintenance
> #### By Brody Austin
>
>
>
> *"Your decision on what kind of car you choose to drive should be yours alone."*

Will I ever be able to escape this woman? I could go live in a bomb shelter in Antarctica, and she'd still find me.

"Nina, it *is* you!"

"Hello, Claudia. How are you?"

"I'm wonderful, of course." She turns to the short, balding, middle-aged man standing next to her. "This is Michael. I can't remember if you two have met before. He's a heart surgeon."

"Hello, Michael. It's nice to see you again." Nina's met him numerous times, and each time Claudia has reminded her that he's a heart surgeon.

"What are you doing here?" Claudia seems confused. Her eyes roam the length of her, focusing on her stomach.

"I'm here looking at classic cars just like you," Nina says with irritation. She's already feeling like a frump standing next to the glamorous Claudia, who, of course, looks ready for the runway. Her dark hair is pulled back into a high ponytail that emphasizes her cheekbones. Her shiny gold hoops glitter and catch the sunlight, matching her multiple gold necklaces. The shearling jacket she's wearing is the height of fashion, and her dark skinny jeans are tucked into a pair of designer boots that probably cost as much as Nina's mortgage.

"*Alone?* That seems odd." But then Claudia smiles at her with sympathy. "I'm glad you're getting out and doing things. I know it's been difficult for you."

Nina tries not to scowl. "I'm not here alone." She glances around. *Where the heck is Brody?* Finally, she sees him talking to a couple guys standing in front of an old-fashioned hot rod.

"Well, I'm glad to hear that. How *are* you?" Claudia asks breezily and doesn't bother waiting for an answer. "Things at the gallery have been *so* busy lately. You wouldn't believe." She starts talking about various artists who Nina's never heard of and all the glamorous shows her gallery is putting on in the coming months. Nina feels a headache starting.

"Hey, I just found out there's a Zephyr here," Brody says, coming up next to her. "It's not a coupe, but we should go take a look at it."

"Oh, sure." Nina glances across at Claudia, who has stopped talking and is staring at him.

Brody eyes her with confusion and then glances at Nina.

"This is Claudia," Nina says. "Noel's ex-wife."

His brows shoot up, and he puts his hand out. "I'm Brody. Nina's boyfriend. It's nice to meet you."

Claudia takes his hand and seems shocked but recovers quickly. She gives him a flirtatious smile. "It's very nice to meet you, Brody."

Boyfriend. Nina digests this. She's never heard Brody refer to himself as her boyfriend before but has to admit she likes it.

"This is Michael," Claudia says, introducing him with smugness in her voice. "He's a heart surgeon."

Brody shakes his hand as well. "It's good to meet you."

"Are you Brody Austin, by chance?" Michael asks.

"I am."

Michael grins. "This is fortuitous. I was hoping to run into you here today."

"You *were?*" Claudia glances at Michael with widened eyes.

Michael tells Brody about a classic Mercedes he bought and has been wanting to restore. "I understand you're the man to talk to. I emailed you a few weeks ago."

"I think I remember that." Brody strokes his jaw. "Remind me some more about your car."

Michael describes the Mercedes he bought at an auction and how he's been wanting to bring it back to its former glory. The two men get into a discussion. To Nina's amusement, Claudia can't seem to take her eyes off Brody. She's pretending to understand what the guys are talking about, making little comments, all the while trying to catch his attention. Except Brody barely glances at her.

Finally, Claudia seems to give up and turns to Nina. "I understand you're pregnant with Noel's baby," she says loud enough for anyone within shouting distance to hear. Her eyes slide over to Brody, clearly hoping for a reaction.

"He already knows," Nina says. "And he doesn't care."

"Really? How forward thinking. Of course, he does appear to be quite a bit younger than you."

"That's true."

"I prefer older men myself, men who are more distinguished and worldly." Claudia fiddles with one of her gold chains, all the while eyeing Brody like he's the last ice cream sundae before the diet starts.

Nina laughs to herself. She can't help it. She's been jealous of Claudia for years, and now it appears the tables have turned.

"I guess you're dating a younger man to get back at Noel. Is that it?"

Nina tilts her head. "That reminds me. How is Emily doing? Have you two become best friends yet?"

Claudia sucks in her breath. "I don't know why you didn't listen to me, Nina. If you had, you'd be back with Noel, and Emily would be a distant memory for both of us. Now we're stuck with her."

Nina shrugs. "I'm not stuck with her. She's already a distant memory for me."

Thankfully, the two men wrap up their conversation. "So I'll bring it by next week and you'll take a look at it?" Michael says to Brody.

"Sure, that's fine. We're scheduled out pretty far, but I can give you some guidance, at least."

Claudia links her arm with Michael's. "Darling, I think we should get going. I've still got that *thing* later."

Michael glances at her with confusion but then nods. "Oh, sure. We should head out."

"Good luck with the baby," Claudia says to Nina, though she's looking at Brody. "I hope the birth goes smoothly. Let me know if you want my trainer's number to help you lose all that weight you'll be putting on soon."

Nina scowls at Claudia's back as she walks off. She remembers how Noel once told her that Claudia hired a photographer for each one of their children's home births. She has three thick photo albums filled with artsy black-and-white pictures of herself from every angle while laboring and giving birth.

"So that's Noel's ex-wife," Brody says. "Was it my imagination, or was she staring at me?"

Nina smiles and takes his hand. "I think she's jealous of my boy toy."

Brody laughs and then leans down to give her a kiss. "Apparently I'm a hot commodity."

"We need to have a talk about your friend Danica," Brody says, sitting at Tori's kitchen table. He's over at her and Liam's new house in north Seattle, which is all decorated for Christmas. It's Saturday afternoon, and he's meeting Liam and Road here so they can go to the batting cages. It's been a week since his bizarre date.

"Did you finally go out with her?" Tori asks, distracted. She's holding her baby on her hip while pulling out various items from the fridge. Her four dogs are all lined up, waiting in anticipation for some kind of meal. "Here." She walks over to Brody. "Can you hold Oliver for a second? I need to get the dogs fed."

Before he knows it, Tori's dumped this four-month-old baby in his arms. Brody smiles uncomfortably at the little boy, who smells like shampoo. Oliver's brows are knit, suspiciously studying Brody as he chews on a teething ring.

"You seem to be enjoying that," Brody says to him. "Does it taste good?"

Oliver's brows slam together even further, but then, to Brody's surprise, he reaches out and grabs his nose.

"Hey," Brody says with a laugh. He grins as Oliver giggles and tries to grab his hair. This time he succeeds and gets a good fistful. "Whoa, that's quite a grip you got there, buddy." He tries to get his hair back. "I think I'm going to have to wear a ponytail around you next time."

Liam appears in the kitchen and comes over to take the baby from him. "It's his thing lately," he says, picking up his son. "He likes to grab everyone's hair. I think he wants all of us to be as bald as he is." He rubs his hand over the kid's curly blond fuzz.

Brody studies the baby, who, he has to admit, is pretty cute. He's not feeling as uncomfortable around him as he has in the past.

By now Tori's given all her dogs their lunch, and she's come back over to the table. "Would you guys like some iced tea while you're waiting for Road?"

"I'd love some, *rubia*." Liam bends down to give her a quick kiss, holding the baby on his hip.

She pours them each a glass of tea and hands the first one to Brody. "So tell me more about what happened with Danica. I was hoping you two would hit it off."

Brody snorts. "I went out with her, but I can't say we hit it off."

"What do you mean? You guys didn't get along?"

Brody leans back in his chair and studies his cousin. "How well do you know her exactly?"

Tori shrugs. "She brings her cats to the animal hospital, so I mostly know her from that. Why?"

"She's kind of... strange."

"What do you mean by strange?"

"Well, for starters, she has a boyfriend."

Tori's eyes grow wide. "She *does*? Well, she certainly never told me that! I'm so sorry. I never would have set you up with her."

Brody takes a sip of his iced tea and leans forward in his chair. "It gets worse."

"What do you mean?"

Brody tells them the story. The only thing he leaves out is the thing with the beer bottle. When he gets to the part where the doorbell rings and the boyfriend's on the other side, Liam is shaking his head with laughter.

"Apparently they were into some kind of weird sex game," Brody says. "They wanted *me* to participate."

Tori's mouth drops open and she glances at her baby. "Maybe I should cover Oliver's ears."

Liam is still chuckling with amazement. "So what did you do?"

"What do you think I did? I got my ass out of there."

"That's crazy," Tori says, shaking her head. "Danica always seemed so nice. I can't believe she'd spring that on you. I'm really sorry."

"Well, at least I got a funny story out of the whole thing."

Tori studies him, chewing her bottom lip. "Does this mean I can't set you up with anyone else? Because I volunteer with this woman at the animal shelter who—"

Brody puts his hand up to stop her from saying another word. "No more fixing me up. I've started seeing Nina again."

"You have?" Tori glances at Liam. "Isn't she pregnant?"

"She is. So what?"

"Nothing. You're right. I'm glad for you two. In fact, we'll have to get together so we can finally meet her."

But Brody can tell there's something more. He's not sure if he wants to hear her opinion. He's tired of everyone having a say about his love life. Especially after what he had to endure with Danica.

It isn't until later, at the batting cages with Liam and Road, that the subject comes up again. Liam is up to bat, and Brody and Road are standing outside the cage.

"So you and Nina, huh?"

Brody glances at Road and then looks in at Liam, who must have told him. Sometimes he feels like he's living in a soap opera. "I guess news travels fast."

"Hey, if you're happy, that's cool. I know Blair likes her. But you got to admit it's an unusual situation. How long have you two known each other?"

"A few months."

"That's not long. "

Brody's fingers tighten on the fencing around the cage in annoyance.

When Road takes his turn at bat, he gets to hear the same earful from Liam. "We just don't want her taking advantage of you. What happens when the baby's father comes back into the picture? Then what?"

"Look, I know you're in the FBI, so it's in your job description to be suspicious. But you don't know anything about this."

Liam studies him like he wants to say more but thankfully doesn't.

Frankly, Brody's having a hard time not getting insulted. Since when has he ever given anyone shit about their love life? He's always been supportive. Even when everyone freaked out about Tori dating an FBI agent, he never said a word against Liam. In fact, he's the one who finally got Road to calm down over the whole thing.

Later the next day, Nina's over at his place. They went out and got a Christmas tree earlier, and now the two of them are searching through his junk room for the box of ornaments.

"What is all this stuff?" she asks, referring to the furniture and other items crowding the room. She holds up a painting of a vase of flowers. "Is this yours?"

"It's from when Kiera lived here."

"Why didn't she take it with her?"

He lifts a bulletin board and stack of placemats out of the way and finally sees the box of ornaments. "I don't know. Some of it's stuff she didn't want, and the rest we bought together."

Nina glances around. "You should get rid of it. Donate it all to charity."

He tries to wiggle out the box labeled "Christmas" without knocking everything else over. "I suppose."

"It would probably be cathartic."

Finally, Brody gets the Christmas box out and then glances around the room at all the physical remnants of his relationship with Kiera. It's like a fossil record. The bones from their time together.

"Then you'd have use of the room," Nina continues. "You could set it up for Trevor so he doesn't have to keep sleeping on the sofa bed."

After bringing the box out into the living room, Brody realizes Nina is right. It's time to clean out that junk room. Trevor's been staying here to save money, and giving him his own room would be the decent thing to do.

And maybe it's time I quit hanging on to all that stuff from Kiera.

While they're decorating the tree, Trevor comes home, and he's brought Anka with him. She smiles and says hello to him and Nina.

"Hey, Anka. I don't think you two have met yet," Brody says, introducing Nina.

"It's nice to meet you." Nina says with a smile. Brody had already updated her on the situation. After he forced Trevor to give Anka a formal apology at the garage, Trevor apparently called her on his own and asked if he could take her out to lunch as a second apology. Since then, to Brody's surprise, the two of them have become friends.

"Damn, cuz, you finally got a tree. Now it feels like Christmas around here." Trevor goes over and gives Nina a hug. "I'm so glad you're back. And congratulations on having a baby."

"Thank you, Trevor."

"I've been trying to get Brody to put up a tree since last month, but he wouldn't do it. Talk about a Scrooge."

"I'm not a Scrooge," Brody says, grouchily, hanging up a Santa ornament that his mom gave him years ago.

"Not anymore." Trevor says. "Nina has un-Scrooged you."

The women both laugh while Brody raises a brow. "I'm not even sure how to respond to that." He glances over at Anka. "So what are you two up to tonight?"

"Trevor invited me over to watch Christmas movies," she says. "I hope that's okay."

Brody nods. "Of course it's okay." He knows Anka doesn't have a lot of friends in Seattle. He's glad she's become friends with his cousin—especially after the rocky start they had. In truth, he's proud of Trevor for turning it around. He always knew there was a good heart in there somewhere.

"Yeah, we were going to watch *Die Hard*," Trevor says. "And maybe *First Blood*. Do you guys want to watch them with us?"

Brody shrugs and looks over at Nina. "I'm cool with that. How about you?"

"*Die Hard* and *First Blood*?" She makes a face. "Those don't sound like Christmas movies."

Brody chuckles. "They are actually. My family watches them every year."

"Really?" She considers this and then finally shrugs. "All right, fine. I'm not sure if I've even seen either of those."

The three of them gawk at her. "You've *never* seen them?" Anka asks in amazement.

"I've heard of them. I always assumed they were guy movies."

Anka nods. "I guess they kind of are. I always watched them with my dad and brothers."

Meanwhile, Trevor appears to be inspecting the tree. He tilts his head. "You guys need more ornaments on the top over there. It's not balanced."

"Since when are you such a Christmas fanatic?" Brody asks Trevor.

"What do you mean? Since always."

Brody thinks back to when Trevor was a kid. Of course, he was mouthy even then. It's true that Aunt Jeanie usually decorates her house nicely for the holidays.

After they finish with the tree, Brody orders a couple pizzas. A cheese-less one with extra meat for him and Trevor to share, and one with cheese for Nina and Anka.

Eventually, they settle in to watch *Die Hard*. Brody's on the couch with Nina right beside him. She has one leg casually thrown over his. Anka is sitting in the recliner.

"Damn, I'm so glad you two are a couple again," Trevor says with a grin from his position over on the love seat. "You guys belong together."

Brody and Nina glance at each other.

"That's nice of you to say," Nina tells Trevor.

His cousin shrugs before taking a bite of pizza and looking back at the screen. "It's the truth."

Brody sighs and takes it all in. The Christmas tree all colorful and lit up, the friendship between Trevor and Anka, and then finally Nina, who's somehow made his life feel complete.

It's ironic that this cousin who aggravates him half the time is the only one in his family who seems to understand anything.

"Is everything okay?" Nina asks later when they're lying in bed. "You've been kind of off since you came back from batting with Road and Liam yesterday. Did something happen?"

"It's nothing," Brody says.

But Nina suspects it's not nothing. "You can tell me. Were they giving you a hard time about me?"

"I don't know why everyone has to discuss and analyze every damn situation. Why can't they just let things be?"

"They're your family, and they care about you."

"Are Suzy and your parents giving you shit about me?"

Nina props her head up. "Suzy likes you." She slides her hand down his muscular forearm. "My parents... well, I haven't told them much about you."

His eyes go to hers. "And why is that?"

"Because I haven't really been talking to them lately." Her parents called twice last week, but she hasn't called them back yet. "It's too frustrating. They want a reality that doesn't exist anymore."

"I get that. But you have to talk to them sometime."

Nina thinks about how supportive Brody has been since they started seeing each other again. He truly doesn't seem bothered that she's carrying Noel's baby. "Are you sure you know what you're doing, Brody? What you're getting into here with me?" A part of her still worries that she's standing in the way of him finding someone else. Someone more suitable.

He grins. "I'm your boyfriend. Aren't pregnant women allowed to have boyfriends?"

She doesn't reply. She knows he's trying to lighten the mood. Instead, she wonders what happens when her baby arrives. Will he still be her boyfriend? But she doesn't want to ask him. She doesn't want to push him into a corner, into making promises to her he might not be able to keep.

"Hey," he says. "Look at me, Nina."

Her eyes go to his face.

"I'm a grown man. I make my own decisions. You don't have to worry about me, okay?"

She nods. "I know. But I want you to know that it's also okay if, down the road, you decide this whole thing is too much for you to handle. I'll completely understand."

There's a frown on his face, but he doesn't get a chance to respond, because as soon as she stops talking, a powerful wave of nausea comes over her. She jolts to a sitting position and covers her mouth. "Oh no, I think I'm going to throw up."

Nina jumps off the bed and runs into the bathroom, barely making it to the toilet in time to barf up the pizza she ate. She squeezes her eyes shut, trying not to look at it so she doesn't keep throwing up.

Finally, she takes some deep breaths and flushes everything down. She goes to the sink and rinses her mouth out with water, then brushes her teeth.

Brody's standing in the doorway. "You okay?"

She nods still brushing. "I'm fine now."

"Damn, what set you off?"

She shrugs. It's usually a smell that gets her started, but sometimes it's nothing. "I haven't thrown up all day. I guess it was time."

"Can I get you anything?"

"A glass of water would be good."

He leaves the room, and she goes to sit on the bed again. She should probably bring over some of her natural electrolyte drinks to keep in his fridge. It's something her midwife recommended to help replenish herself.

When Brody brings the water, she thanks him and takes a long swallow before putting it on the nightstand.

"Better?" he asks.

"Much better. Thank you." She yawns. "Wow, I'm really tired."

"Come here, lie down. I'll play with your hair."

Nina lies on her side, facing away from him. She brings her knees up and relaxes as he brushes his fingers through her scalp and hair. It's so calming. Her mind drifts back to what she told him earlier, just before she threw up, how she'll completely understand if all this becomes too much for him to handle. Except as her eyes fall shut, a hidden thought rises to the surface, lingering, forcing her to accept the truth.

And the truth is she hopes Brody *never* decides this is too much for him to handle.

CHAPTER TWENTY

"Trevor says you have a girlfriend. Why don't you bring her up with you for Christmas?" Aunt Jeanie says to Brody on the phone. "You can bring her to the powwow."

"I thought that happened a couple weeks ago."

"They had to postpone it. There was a plumbing leak at the community center, so they rescheduled it for the twenty-third."

Brody takes a seat behind the desk in his office at work and opens a water bottle. "I appreciate the offer, Auntie, but I'm sure Nina has plans."

"Trevor says she's pregnant."

He takes a drink of his water. Of course Trevor told his mom everything. "That's true, she is."

"And the baby's not yours?"

"No, it's not."

"Where's the father?"

"He's not in the picture."

"And why is that?"

Brody doesn't want to get into a discussion about Nina's ex. In the past, he couldn't care less about Noel, but lately he's noticed an irrational jealousy whenever his name comes up. "He cheated on her and left her for someone else."

There's silence on the other end of the line. "Well, that poor girl. It can't be easy for her. Pregnant and all alone like that."

Brody smiles to himself. Aunt Jeanie has always had a good heart. Apparently Trevor didn't tell his mom that Nina is forty years old and tough as nails, that she's already got a lawyer going after Noel for child support. "She has family. She's not alone."

"And she has you too. Is that right?"

"That's right."

His aunt sighs. "Okay, well, at least we'll finally get to see you. If you back out of Christmas, I'll be coming down to stay with you and Trevor for a full month. Just keep that in mind."

She hangs up, and Brody chuckles. Since his grandma died, Aunt Jeanie has definitely taken over the role of family matriarch.

He gets up and heads back out to the shop floor to discover his sister is there talking to Jackson.

"Hey, I didn't know you were coming by today," Brody says to Summer.

She's laughing at something Jackson said, and it's pretty obvious the two are flirting with each other. Brody likes Jackson, but flirting with Summer isn't earning him any points. He's seen how the guy operates—turning on the charm for women, while that Australian accent seems to make them all swoon. It's fine for the garage's customers but not for his sister.

"I was just in the neighborhood," Summer says, still smiling. "I figured I'd say hello."

Brody studies her. There's no way she was just in the neighborhood. Tori must have told her he's together again with Nina. Which is fine, he realizes. Because that saves him the hassle of having to tell everyone himself.

Jackson grins at Summer. "Well, if you'd like to go together, you know where to find me. I think you'll like the food." He turns to Brody, who's staring at him, and grins. "No worries, mate. I'm getting back to it."

After Jackson goes back to work, Brody raises an eyebrow at Summer.

"What?" she says. "He told me about this Moroccan place in Ballard. I've always loved Moroccan food."

"Just be aware that he's a flirt," Brody says. "He charms the pants off every female who comes in here."

"I don't care about that. Look at him. He's gorgeous."

Brody shrugs. "All right, it's your life. Have fun."

"Oh, I *will*," she says and then laughs out loud. "All kinds."

"I think I'm going to need earplugs for the rest of this conversation," he says, glancing up at the ceiling.

Since he doesn't have time for lunch, he and Summer go sit in the break room together. "So, why did you really come by? I hope it's not to give me shit about Nina."

"No, of course not." Though she has a guilty look on her face. "It's sort of about Nina. I'm not sure if she's told you, but I'm one of the midwives at the birth center she's going to."

He nods. "Yeah, she told me."

"Oh, okay. Good. I believe she'll be coming in soon."

"I know. It's her three-month appointment. I'm going with her."

Summer's brows go up. "You are? Well, that's great. I'll probably see you there then."

They talk a little more, and then his sister leaves. It was a strange short conversation, and he's not even sure why she dropped by. Unless, of course, it was simply to chat up Jackson again.

He hasn't seen Nina since Sunday, but she texts and asks if he wants to come to her place tonight. Apparently she has a craving for Chinese food, so he picks some up on the way over. He also stops at Whole Foods and gets her a container of pineapple since she's constantly hungry for that too.

"You know, your cravings aren't that weird," he says, placing the bags of food on her dining room table. "Where's the pickles and ice cream? Where's the sardines and whipped cream? I was looking forward to seeing some really crazy shit. So far I'm disappointed."

Nina laughs. "I guess you're right. Though this pineapple obsession is weird. I've never liked pineapple this much."

"Are there any foods you normally love but can't stand right now?"

She nods. "Peanut butter."

"Really? Peanut butter sounds gross to you?"

"Very gross."

"Interesting."

She pulls the chopsticks out of the bag and then the rest of the small containers. "You're eyeing me like I'm a specimen for your school science project."

He ignores the food and comes closer to her, slipping his arms around her waist. "I'm definitely eyeing you. I don't know about the science part." He kisses her, then runs a hand down to her ass and gives it a squeeze. "Maybe we should eat dinner later."

They kiss some more, and while Brody always turns her on, Nina keeps looking over his shoulder at the food on the table.

"What is it?" he asks.

"My craving for Chinese food is currently stronger than my lust for you."

He sighs. "All right, I get it. I'm standing between a pregnant woman and her next meal."

She kisses him again and strokes his jaw. "Sorry, but you kind of are."

They hang out together, eat, and talk. Nina tells him how she heard from Davis, her former assistant, recently.

"Really?" Brody digs into his food with chopsticks. "I didn't know you were still in touch with anyone from your old work."

Nina pours soy sauce over her rice. She's been seriously craving salt lately. "Davis and I still email occasionally. It sounds like there might be a scandal brewing with Noel."

"A scandal?"

"Over him and Emily. I guess he never disclosed his relationship with her to Human Resources. The word is they finally found out about it." Nina admits to having feelings of schadenfreude over this but doesn't want to get too gleeful. "Also, this arrived yesterday." She reaches over and picks up a large envelope from a basket where she keeps her mail. "It's the invitation to Rochelle and Guy's wedding."

He eyes it quizzically. "I'd forgotten all about that wedding. Do you still want to go?"

After the invitation arrived yesterday, Nina stared at it while pondering the same question. But in the end, she decided she has nothing to feel embarrassed about. So what if she was fired for throwing a stapler at Noel? He's the one who wronged her in the first place.

"Yes, we're going," she says with determination. She's going to that wedding, and she's holding her head up high.

"All right. I'll have to get my suit pressed."

"Something else happened today," Nina says with a grin, scooping up some chow mein noodles. "I made a friend at pregnancy yoga. She's in her forties like me, and she's also having her first baby."

"Really? That's great."

She swallows a bite of food. "We'd been talking in class the past couple weeks, and then today we went out for smoothies afterward. Her name's Piper. And you're not going to believe this, but she's the owner of Suds & Honey!"

"What's that?"

"It's an organic soap and skin care company. They've got a few stores in Seattle, and now they're thinking about moving into the Portland area."

Brody chuckles. "It figures you'd make friends with someone like that."

"She seems great. And it just so happens that I love their products."

"Did you tell her you've been taking a soap-making class yourself?"

Nina smiles. "I did. I told her I had an interest."

"Maybe you can sell her some of your soap."

She laughs and rolls her eyes. "Very funny." Her recent Christmas tree soap looked like lumpy red-and-green-speckled potatoes. "I was thinking more of sending them my résumé."

Brody turns to her. "Now that's interesting. It's the first time I've heard you mention going back to work."

"I know. I've been skating around it, but my savings aren't going to last forever. It occurred to me after talking to her that I don't have to work for a big company like Tolland again. I could work someplace smaller." The notion has really gotten her excited. She loves the idea of being part of a growing company.

"Did you tell Piper this?"

"I did. She told me to send her my résumé and that she'd look at it."

The whole conversation with Piper had been fun and enlightening. It felt great to make a new friend. It also felt great talking to another woman her age going through the same thing—although Piper is married, so it's not quite the same.

As a result, Nina's been walking on air all afternoon. For the first time, she's envisioning her future with a sense of adventure and not just a sense of duty.

After dinner, Brody says he needs to answer some emails and then he's going to take a shower, so Nina figures she'll get started on her résumé. Except all the files she needs are on the desktop computer in her office. A room she hasn't entered in months. Ugh. She's been actively avoiding it since Davis and that temp brought all her stuff from Tolland.

She opens the door. The air smells stale. It's so crowded she has to squeeze through a narrow path to get to the desk with her computer.

A few minutes after she's seated, Brody pops his head in the door before his shower. His mouth drops open when he sees all the boxes and furniture piled up everywhere. "And you gave *me* a hard time for my junk room." He looks around in amazement. "Hell, yours is even worse than mine."

"This isn't a junk room. It's my office," Nina says with indignation as she boots up her computer.

"It looks like a garage sale exploded in here."

"Go take your shower," she says with amusement.

Once he's gone, she spends some time searching for her old résumés. She's in a cheery mood.

Her phone buzzes on the desk beside her, and she figures it's Suzy, but her stomach drops when she sees Noel on the caller ID. She wants to ignore it but knows it'll only gnaw at her.

"What do you want?"

"Is that how you greet people these days?" Noel's familiar voice comes across the line.

"Why are you calling me?" Her cheery mood has evaporated, and it's all his fault.

"Claudia told me she saw you at an auto show in Tacoma recently."

"So that's why you're calling me?" Nina wonders if Claudia mentioned she was there with Brody. *I hope so.*

"She said you were there with some guy, and that he's younger than you. Is that the same one you were seeing before?"

Nina smiles. *Bingo.*

"Claudia also said you were showing with your pregnancy."

"Really?" Nina glances down at her mostly flat stomach. She's still been able to fit into her normal jeans.

"It got me thinking about you. How is everything? How is your pregnancy going?"

She clicks open a folder that shows her last résumé from four years ago. She used to update them every year but then got lazy and complacent when her boyfriend was also her boss. "Why do you care, Noel? You've made it very clear you want nothing to do with me or this baby."

He goes quiet. "I've been rethinking that lately."

"What do you mean?"

"I think I might want to be a part of this child's life after all."

She rolls her eyes. "You *think* you *might*. Gee, that sounds definite."

"It's a lot for me to adjust to, okay? I thought I was nearly done raising my children, and then you spring this on me."

"Spring this on you? I didn't get pregnant by myself."

"But you were on birth control. How the hell did this even happen?"

"It failed, obviously."

She hears him take a deep breath. "Look, I didn't call to argue. I called to see if you're okay and if you need anything."

"Then I'll keep it simple. I don't want or need anything from you except child support once this baby is born."

"Stop being so hostile, Nina. I know you don't believe me, but I still care about you."

Her hand tightens on the phone. "Speaking of caring about me, how's Emily doing?"

Noel pauses. "I don't want to talk about Emily. That's not why I called. I called to talk about you."

Nina smiles to herself. *Is that tension in his voice?* Maybe what Davis told her was true, and Noel really is in hot water. "Well, then, let me put your mind at ease. I'm doing fine. In fact, I'm getting my résumé together. A job opportunity has come up." She kicks herself for saying anything to him.

"Oh really? Where's the job?"

"I'd rather not say."

"All right, I understand. If you need me to be a reference or write you a letter, let me know, and I'll give you one."

Nina sits up straighter at this. "You will?" As much as she hates to admit it, she could use his recommendation. "Even after firing me?"

He chuckles. "We both know there were extenuating circumstances. I don't see that as a problem recommending you. You've always done excellent work, Nina."

"Thank you. I appreciate that."

"No problem."

After they hang up, she stares at the phone for a long moment and then puts it back down on her desk. She takes a deep breath. While she may be over Noel, she still remembers the pull he had on her.

"Who was that?" Brody asks, standing in the doorway. He's shirtless with jeans on and his wet hair combed back.

"Nobody."

He studies her. "Nobody?"

"It was Noel."

"Oh." He leans against the doorframe, crossing his muscular arms, looking sexy as always. Her own personal bad boy. "What did *he* want?"

"Claudia told him she saw me at that auto show." Nina doesn't know why she's being evasive, but she's started to feel strange talking about Noel with him.

"And that's it?"

"I guess he wanted to see how I was doing with my pregnancy."

"What did you tell him?"

"That I'm fine."

Brody remains still, studying her. She gets up from her desk and weaves her way through the obstacle course toward him. He doesn't say anything, and when she's right in front of him, she slips her arms around his neck.

He stops leaning against the frame and slides his arms around her too. Nina rests her head against his shoulder and closes her eyes as they hold each other. He smells clean, like the oatmeal soap in her shower, and feels solid against her. Brody always feels solid. And in more ways than one.

"What are you doing for Christmas?" he asks, his voice rumbling low against her ear.

She lifts her head to look up at him. "I'm going to Suzy and Luke's. What else would I be doing?"

"Do you want to come and stay with me at my aunt's house on the rez?"

Nina's eyes widen. She hadn't expected this, and a sense of elation runs through her. "I'd love to."

"Yeah? It's for a few days. Trevor and I are headed up on the twenty-second."

"But don't you have to ask her about it? You can't just invite me to stay at her house during Christmas."

"She already invited you."

"Really?" Nina takes this in. "That's very nice of her. I gather she knows about me."

Brody chuckles. "Trevor told her. Who else?"

Nina wonders what he said. At least she has a good relationship with Trevor.

"There's a powwow on the twenty-third," he continues. "I haven't been to one in a while. You'll like it."

"Am I allowed to go to something like that?"

"Of course. Anybody can go. You don't have to be a tribal member."

"Really?" To Nina, the term "powwow" has always evoked images of something exclusive.

"There's lots of food and tribal dancers," Brody continues. "Since it's during the holidays, there'll be toys and stuff for the kids. It's pretty cool."

She gathers his damp hair into a ponytail. "That sounds great."

Nina tries to pull him close to hug him again, but something in her office appears to have caught his attention.

"What is it?"

His mouth opens. "Jesus, am I reading that correctly? You went to Yale *and* Harvard?" He motions toward the college diplomas on the wall.

She turns and nods. "I did my undergrad at Yale and then got my MBA from Harvard."

He blinks at her with astonishment. "And you never thought to mention that?"

She shrugs uncomfortably. "I told you I went to Yale."

"But not Harvard too. Damn. That's crazy. I had no idea." Then he gets a strange expression on his face. "So did Noel go to both Yale and Harvard?"

"Just Yale. He was there five years before me."

"You guys have a lot of stuff in common." His brown eyes meet hers, and she senses a strange kind of distance.

She steps closer to him and slips her arms around his neck again. "What does it matter where I went to college?"

He's quiet. She knows he has an associate's degree from a local community college. He got it after he went to trade school to be a certified mechanic. "Because that's prestigious as hell. I can't believe you never told me." He considers her. "Does it bother you that I'm not more educated?"

"You're incredibly talented, Brody. And you're obviously one of the best mechanics in the city. I heard people at that auto show calling you a genius."

He doesn't say anything.

"Where's this coming from?"

He shrugs and sighs. "I don't know."

"I think you're amazing. I could never do what you do. Most people couldn't."

"I suppose that's true."

She's never seen Brody insecure like this. "Is something else bothering you?"

He shakes his head. "It's nothing." He pulls her close this time and kisses her. "Let's forget about it," he whispers, sliding his hand down her back and then to her ass. "Come on, Nina banana. Let's go to bed so I can rock your world."

"You already rock my world."

He grins at that. "Then we *do* have something in common."

CHAPTER TWENTY-ONE

"It's very nice to meet you," Jeanie says to Nina. They've come inside the house after driving up from Seattle in Brody's truck. It was a long enough drive that they had to make two rest stops so Nina could use the bathroom.

"Same here," Nina says with a smile. Jeanie is a pretty woman, full-figured, and obviously not much older than Nina. Her shoulder-length hair is pulled up into a clip. Nina can already tell by Jeanie's expression that she isn't at all what the woman expected. Although by now, Nina has gotten used to this reaction from people.

"Trevor speaks highly of you."

Nina looks over at Trevor, who's already flopped on the couch with his big size thirteen sneakers hanging over the armrest. There's a black-and-white dog that he's laughing with and petting as it jumps all over him. "That's nice to hear."

"My husband, Mitch, is at work, but he'll be here for dinner tonight."

The television flicks on, and Trevor starts flipping through the channels while still petting the dog.

"It's so good to see *this* one," Jeanie says, grinning up at Brody. She's already hugged him twice. "You know it's been over a year, right? That's too long."

"You're right, Auntie." Brody nods in agreement. "I should have come up much sooner."

Trevor has stopped channel surfing at some auto racing. The volume seems to grow louder.

"Are you hungry or thirsty?" Jeanie asks. "I can get you a snack or —" She looks over at Trevor and the blaring television. "Will you turn that down? I can barely hear myself think."

Trevor glances at them. "Sorry." The volume drops to a lower level.

"These kids today." Jeanie rolls her eyes and then smiles at Nina. "Though I understand you'll be learning about that soon enough."

Nina opens her mouth and realizes she shouldn't be surprised that everyone knows she's pregnant.

Jeanie is still smiling, but Nina senses that she's being observed too. If she had to guess, the jury is still out on whether she'll win this woman's approval.

"Okay, then." Jeanie claps her hands together. "Let me show you where you two will be staying."

Brody, Nina, and the dog—Pumpkin—follow her down a long hallway to the other side of the modest rambler.

"This used to be a sunroom," Jeanie explains to her as they enter a room that appears to be a later addition to the house, "but we turned it into a guest bedroom and office. As a result, it can get chilly in here at night, but hopefully the space heater should keep you warm enough. If not, let me know, and I can give you some extra blankets."

Nina bends down to pet the dog, who puts her paws on her thigh.

"Get down, Pumpkin," Jeanie says. "Don't jump on Nina."

"It's okay," she says. "I don't mind." She glances around the room. "This is really cozy." There are three large windows looking out at the woods surrounding the house. Besides the bed and the two nightstands, there's a desk with a computer in the corner. Some beaded native medallions hang on one wood-paneled wall along with some other pieces of tribal art. There's also a painting with a colorful background against an elaborate red totem pole bird. "I really like that painting."

Jeanie nods. "My first husband did that—Trevor's dad. It's the only one of his that I have left."

Nina takes this in. Brody told her that Trevor didn't get along with his stepdad but never mentioned what happened to his real one.

"I'm going to go check on dinner. I have a roast in the oven," Jeanie says. "I'll let you two get settled in. Come on, Pumpkin."

She leaves, and the dog follows her.

Nina looks up at Brody. It's hard to put it into words exactly, but somehow seeing him here with his father's family has already given her a better understanding of him.

"Your aunt seems nice," Nina says, slipping her arms around his waist. "I can tell she's protective of you. She looks so young. How old is she?"

He hugs her back. "Mid-forties. She's about ten years younger than my dad."

"I don't think I'm what she expected at all."

Brody chuckles. "Probably not."

Nina looks up at him. "She's basically my age." *Or Noel's*, she thinks but thankfully doesn't say that out loud.

"She got married and had Trevor pretty young."

"What happened to his dad?"

"He died when Trevor was only a few years old."

"That's sad to hear." She glances over at the painting. "And he was an artist?"

"Yeah, he was. I remember him a little. He was a cool guy."

"What happened to him?"

Brody hesitates. "I'll tell you, but don't bring it up with anyone. He was killed in a bar fight."

Nina's eyes widen. "That's horrible." She tries to digest it, imagining how difficult it must have been for Jeanie.

"Our whole family was wrecked. It's not something we talk about."

"I understand. I won't mention it."

He takes a deep breath. "I should go out and get our bags from the truck."

"Do you want me to help?"

"Nah, I got it. I'll be right back."

When he leaves, Nina sits down on the bed and gazes out the window at the trees. From what she could tell driving here, the house sits on a decent amount of land and is surrounded by woods. She hates to admit it, but she feels out of place and hopes coming here wasn't a mistake.

Nina goes out to see if Jeanie needs any help in the kitchen. She notices all the holiday decorations and the Christmas tree in the living room. Everything is clean and cozy. She gets the impression that Jeanie runs a tight ship.

"Can I help with dinner?" Nina asks.

Jeanie shakes her head. "I have it under control. Just relax while you're staying here."

Nina tries to make small talk, and while Jeanie is nice and always polite, Nina definitely senses a distance.

After bringing the bags in, Brody finds them in the kitchen. They hang out with Jeanie as she prepares a salad. Trevor's still watching television in the living room while eating a bag of chips with Pumpkin beside him.

"Why don't you two go for a walk?" Jeanie suggests to Brody and Nina. "It's a long drive to get here. It might feel good to stretch your legs. You should probably take the bear spray with you. Mitch thinks he saw one the other night, though it might have been a raccoon."

"Bear spray?" Nina's eyes widen. "Do you guys have bears out here?"

"It's late in the season, but we still get them occasionally. The spray is just a precaution."

"Don't worry." Brody smiles. "I've only seen bears here during the summer months. Most of them are hibernating now."

Nina and Brody put their coats and boots back on and head outside for a walk. It's late afternoon, and the air smells clean with a hint of wood smoke. Right away, Nina is glad to be out and moving around. Jeanie was right. It feels good to stretch her legs, and she's enjoying the cold air. She and Brody hold hands as they walk through the woods, following an obvious trail.

"Is all of this land Jeanie and Mitch's?" Nina asks.

"They have a few acres. The rest is up against a protected forest."

The two of them walk mostly in silence, but it's companionable. Eventually they get to a clearing near a small lake.

"What is this?"

"Angel Lake. I used to come here fishing with Thunder when I was a kid. It's one of my favorite places. I sometimes come here to sit and think."

The sky is stone gray above them while all the deciduous trees nearby are bare. Even though it's brisk and wintery, there's something beautiful about the austere landscape.

They walk out near the water's edge, and Brody pulls her in close. They're both so well-padded with clothes that Nina laughs a little. When he bends down to kiss her, her laughter trails off. He tastes delicious. His breath warms her whole body.

"Thank you for inviting me here," she whispers. "I like meeting your family and learning more about you."

"I'm glad you came." He pauses and glances out at the lake. "The last woman I brought to visit my family was Kiera, and that was like five years ago."

Nina strokes his cheek, which is a little rough from where he's been letting his goatee grow back. "They must think we're serious about each other then."

Brody nods and smiles at her. "Serious enough."

Once they get back to the house, there's a silver truck parked out front that wasn't there before.

"It's looks like Uncle Mitch is home." Brody nods toward the truck.

It's warm and inviting inside the house. Pumpkin rushes up to greet them while both she and Brody bend down to pet the excited dog. Dinner smells delicious. Nina hasn't thrown up in two days, and she has her fingers crossed, praying her morning sickness is tapering off.

Mitch turns out to be a gregarious type. He's tall, stout, and mostly bald on top, with long dark hair pulled into a ponytail. On the way back from their walk, Brody told her that Mitch had been one of his dad's best friends when they were growing up, and she can see he's a bit older than Jeanie.

Dinner conversation is lively as Mitch tells them all a funny story that happened at his work with the tribe's planning department. Trevor gets sullen though after being told to turn the television off.

"But I'm watching it," Trevor complains.

"Not while we're eating dinner. You know the house rules," Mitch says.

There's a moment of awkward silence before Trevor gets up and turns off the TV. He comes back to the table but doesn't say much after that.

Nina thinks about how difficult it is being a parent. Even when kids are grown, parenting still continues.

After dinner Nina, Brody, and Trevor help clean up. Brody and Trevor start joking around, flicking each other with a dish towel.

"Hey, you got me," Brody says, grinning at Trevor. "I better up my game."

Trevor laughs as he gets flicked on his lower back. As a result, he grabs a second dish towel and flicks them both at Brody.

Meanwhile, Jeanie is sitting at the kitchen table, smiling and watching the whole thing. "You look like you're doing a chicken dance," she tells Trevor. Pumpkin is sitting next to her, watching intently with her tongue hanging out.

Nina joins in with the two guys for a while and manages to flick Brody's butt.

He grins. "Nina banana, you're paying for that one!" He goes after her as she yells with laughter.

It's fun, but she finally goes over and joins Jeanie. "I'm not as good at it as they are," she says.

"It looked like you were holding your own."

Pumpkin comes over to her, and Nina pets her again, telling her what a good dog she is.

"She likes you," Jeanie says. "Do you have any pets?"

Nina shakes her head and thinks about how she's always wanted a pet, then gets an odd pang as she remembers Sherlock—the dog she and Noel were supposed to have someday. "No, but I'd like to get one. Maybe after the baby arrives."

Jeanie is watching her. "If you don't mind my asking, where is your baby's father?"

Nina doesn't say anything for a few seconds, debating how much to tell her. She briefly explains how Noel isn't involved and has misgivings about ever being involved.

"And what happens between you and Brody after your baby is born? How is he going to be involved?"

Nina considers this. It's a fair question. "To be honest, we haven't figured things out that far."

"A baby changes everything." Jeanie glances over at Brody and Trevor, still goofing around. "You'll see. The child becomes your life."

Nina nods, still trying to imagine all the changes that are coming. She senses Jeanie studying her.

"I can tell Brody really cares for you. He wouldn't have brought you here if he didn't."

"I care for him too. It's why I broke up with him after we got the results back from the paternity test."

This seems to surprise Jeanie. "And what happened then?"

Nina turns to watch Brody as he's laughing with Trevor. So handsome. And so good to her. It dawns on her that Brody has been better for her than Noel ever was. She shrugs and smiles at Jeanie. "We couldn't seem to stay away from each other. It's ironic because we were just hanging out before that, trying to get over other people."

She nods. "You two have fallen in love."

Nina's eyes widen. Has she fallen in love with Brody? She glances at him again, and her pulse jumps with that familiar sense of pleasure.

"Just be careful with his heart," Jeanie says. "That's all I ask. My nephew is one of the most decent men I know. He'll always try to do the right thing. Even if it's to his own detriment."

The powwow the next day turns out to be a lot of fun. Having never been around much Native American culture, Nina does her best to absorb it all. She notices she's not the only outsider, but from what she can tell, most everyone appears to be a tribal member or at least married to one.

"You've never had fry bread?" Trevor gawks at her. "*Never?*"

She shakes her head and laughs at his comical expression. "I've never even heard of it."

"Damn, that's crazy."

Brody grins. "You're in for a treat, Nina banana. You should try an Indian taco first. Those are my favorite."

Nina agrees, and Brody asks for two tacos from the women set up behind a food prep area. Both of them seem to know him and ask how he's doing as they make the tacos, all the while eyeing Nina with curiosity.

"Thank you, Aunties," he says when the tacos are done.

He hands one of them to her. She takes a bite and nearly groans aloud. "This is so good!"

"I told you." He opens his mouth to take a large bite.

"Are those women your aunts too?" she asks, glancing back at them. There's a crowd of people lined up for the tacos.

Brody shakes his head as he chews. "Auntie and Uncle are terms of respect we use with our elders."

"Yeah, you wouldn't want to insult them even accidentally," Trevor informs her. "Trust me on that."

After they finish eating, Brody holds her hand as they walk around. Trevor notices some of his friends and takes off to join them. People who know Brody stop and hug him, or shake hands while he introduces her to them as his girlfriend. Everybody seems curious and friendly while they chat and catch up on their lives. Nina mostly listens and smiles politely. Eventually they wind up with Jeanie and Mitch and a few more friends and relatives standing on the other side of a large auditorium. A number of young boys wearing colorful outfits are gathering in a circle in the center.

"Are the boys dressed up in costumes for dancing?" Nina asks.

"Those aren't costumes," Brody explains. "It's regalia. They reflect personality and culture. Some of those have been in people's families for generations."

"You should have seen Brody when he was that age," Mitch tells her with a wink. "He was out there dancing too."

"You were?" Nina turns to him. "I'll bet you looked amazing."

"He was good," Jeanie says, nodding. "He did both grass and

fancy. I'll have to dig out some pictures. My mom kept them all in an album."

Nina smiles. "I'd love to see that."

Brody laughs and rolls his eyes. "That was ages ago. I was just a kid."

They watch the boys dance fancy, and then the girls dance in a style called jingle. Native music blasts through the speakers as some people are clapping and cheering them on. Afterward, Nina and Brody wander around outside again to check out some more of the vendors and the various art displays. There are drummers and, of course, there's more food to try.

Brody holds her hand the whole time, pointing out things and answering her questions. He seems relaxed, enjoying himself. They keep catching each other's eye, and every time, Nina feels this sense of excitement and elation. She wonders if he feels it too.

A few times, he bends down and sneaks in a kiss. "You're glowing," he whispers. "Did you know that?"

"So are you."

He laughs. "Maybe I am."

She keeps thinking about what Jeanie said, that she and Brody have fallen in love. Is it true?

Later that night, when the powwow is over and they're back at the house lying in the guest bedroom, the two of them are giggling and being silly. Brody keeps lightly biting her ankles as she squirms away, trying not to shriek with laughter. "You have to stop! I don't want to kick you accidentally."

He pulls her ankle up and bends down to bite her again.

"Aaaah, it's too much." She giggles crazily. "It tickles."

"Jesus, you're making a racket. The whole house is going to wake up."

"Then stop biting me!"

"Why are you so damn ticklish?" He grins and then slides a hand down her leg. "I just can't resist all this smooth skin. I want to sink my teeth into you."

She tries to catch her breath as he bends over her in the glow from the bedside lamp.

"How about if I kiss you instead?" he murmurs and touches his soft lips to her calf.

She quiets at that, watching his handsome face. The way his dark hair falls silky against her skin.

"You're beautiful, Brody."

He turns and meets her gaze. "Thanks." He smiles. "You're not so bad either."

"Thanks."

His eyes are still on her as he caresses her leg, but there's something serious in them. "I think you're beautiful too, Nina. Sometimes I wish I could call off work and stare at you all day."

"You do?" Her breath trembles. No one's ever said anything like this to her before. Not even Noel.

He nods, still caressing her leg. "This is going to sound weird, but I'm glad you got drunk and passed out in my garage."

"Oh no, don't remind me. I'm still embarrassed about how I treated you that day." She shakes her head.

He smiles. "I admit, it was a terrible beginning, but I'm still glad because we wouldn't have met otherwise."

She reaches out and strokes his jaw. "I'm glad too."

Brody moves closer, so he's lying on top of her, and brings his mouth down to hers. She wraps her arms around his neck, and all she can think is that he's so perfect. Just right. Everything about him.

As his kiss deepens, she worries about where they are.

"We can't have sex in here," she whispers. "I don't want your aunt and uncle to know."

"They won't know," he whispers back. "But you have to be quiet."

"Me? What about you?"

He chuckles. "You're right. We both have to be quiet. At least we've had plenty of practice."

She laughs at that. They've had to be quiet at his house with Trevor sleeping on the sofa bed.

Nina's gaze goes to all the native art on the walls and the painting where that red bird now looks like it's staring at her. "Can you turn the light off?"

He reaches over and flicks the lamp switch, plunging them into darkness. And then he's back with her, surrounding her with his delicious scent and his powerful body. It's like being pulled into a vortex of pleasure.

They're lost in it. An avalanche of sensuality. Except there's a tiny part of her that's holding back. The part that thinks maybe their time together is fleeting. That eventually he's going to move on.

"I want you so much," he whispers as he moves inside her, and it's like he's sensing her fear. "That's not going to change."

"I want you to stay," she admits.

"I know. I'm here, Nina."

The room is dark, and all she can see is the barest outline of his face. But it doesn't matter, because his scent and his body have become so familiar to her. She'd know him anywhere.

They sink deeper into passion, and when she climaxes, he muffles the sound with his mouth over hers. He's breathing hard, and she loves the intimacy of this. Brody's always so giving, but this is the part she loves best. The part where he's not giving anymore, where he's not gentle because he can't be. Where he's selfish and losing control.

Finally, he groans, and Nina holds him tight. Feels his climax with him, and then is surprised by another one of her own.

"Damn." He's breathing hard afterward. "Did you come a second time?"

"I did." She tries to catch her breath. She's had multiple orgasms with him before, but it's always when he's going down on her. Never from intercourse. "Maybe it's all these hormones raging through me."

"Maybe so."

He moves off her, but instead of falling asleep like usual, Brody strokes her body, his hand gliding over her breasts, her hip, and then down to her stomach. "You're starting to show," he whispers. "It's just a little, but I can tell."

It's true. She's been noticing it lately too, that her stomach is more rounded.

He's still caressing her, and her eyes drift shut. She thinks about the powwow earlier and how it was an experience she's never had before. "I want to see those pictures of you dancing," she says softly. "The ones Jeanie said your grandma had in albums."

"Sure, if you want."

"Why did you ever stop dancing?" They saw men dancers later and women too. "You could still do it as an adult."

"Well, for one thing, I had a crazy growth spurt when I was thirteen and outgrew all my regalia overnight."

She turns to face him. "Is that really why?"

"I guess." He shrugs. "I don't know. When I was a kid, I wanted to be part of the tribe so bad, but as a teenager I began to feel more disconnected."

"A foot in both worlds." She remembers what he told her when they were at that park in West Seattle.

"Yeah, basically. It's not easy being half of something. I read once how some tribes call it being 'lost in the woods.' I thought that was a good description."

"It's obvious your family here loves you and cares about you though."

"I know, and I love them too. They're incredible people. I'm lucky to have them. But you have to remember, I didn't live here full-time growing up. Not everyone on the rez accepted me, and some people still don't." Brody takes a deep breath. "Then sometimes, back home, I'd get shit from kids at school, or I'd look at pictures of my mom's family, and it felt like I didn't fit in anywhere."

She takes his hand. "That can't be easy."

"It's taught me some things. And it's why I know bullshit when I see it." His eyes meet hers in the dark. "What's *real* is what matters. You can't live your life trying to fit other people's expectations or you'll drive yourself crazy."

She knows he's talking about all the hang-ups she has with their age difference. "You're right. I shouldn't care what anyone thinks when they see us together."

"People are always going to talk. Let them. You're not living your life for them."

"Wow, you're so wise." She lightly pushes his shoulder. "What are you? Some kind of Buddha or a shaman?"

"Hardly." He chuckles. "Shit, I'd never be able to handle celibacy."

"That's for sure." Brody has a strong and healthy libido. "You'd be in big trouble there."

He laughs some more, but there's something deeper in it she recognizes. Soon he's moved closer, and a spark lights within her when he kisses her again. His body's pressed against hers, and she can feel his hard-on.

"I think you're already losing your war with celibacy," she whispers.

"Around you, I'd never fight that war in the first place."

CHAPTER TWENTY-TWO

Life & The Art of Automobile Maintenance
By Brody Austin

"Not everything about your new vehicle will be written in the manual."

Nina's never spent the holidays with any other family but her own. She's grateful that Jeanie and Mitch make her feel welcome, and she's been trying her best to be a good houseguest and help with everything, though Jeanie keeps telling her to relax.

On Christmas morning, she's not sure what to expect, but it turns out it's a very social time, and lots of Brody's family members drop by —all of them bringing food. Everyone is friendly, and no one seems surprised to see Nina there. She figures word must have gotten around.

"Oh hell yeah," Trevor says with a grin when she asks him about it. "Everybody knows about the white lady Brody brought home for Christmas. They're all curious to meet you."

Nina's currently parked on the couch with Trevor and Pumpkin as dozens of relatives come through. She stands up and shakes people's hands and then sits back down. Trevor gets hugged and squeezed by all the relatives, and it's obvious they view him with great affection.

Brody's still socializing with everyone in the kitchen. Nina was in there for a while too but decided to come out here and join Trevor.

She keeps wondering when Thunder is going to show up. Brody told her he planned to see his father on Christmas Day, so she figures he'll be arriving any minute.

"Have you heard when Thunder is coming today?" she asks.

Trevor gives her a strange look. "I wouldn't hold my breath on that one."

"Why is that?"

Trevor shakes his head. "I'm not even going there. You'll have to talk to my cousin."

Nina isn't sure what to make of this. No one seems to mention Thunder. Later, when the daylong festivities have died down and they're alone taking a breather in the bedroom, she asks Brody why his father never showed up.

"Shit. What time is it?"

She picks up her phone and tells him it's almost five. Nina notices some texts from Suzy with cute pictures of Henry and Grace dressed in matching Christmas pajamas. She spoke to her parents early this morning but did her best to keep the conversation short.

"Dammit." Brody stands up. "I have to get going."

"You're going to see him now? Can I come with? I'd like to meet him."

Brody heads toward the bedroom door. "It's not a good idea, Nina."

"What do you mean?" she asks with surprise. "Why not?"

She follows him down the long hallway to the main part of the house. He heads to the door, grabs his boots, and then goes to sit in one of the kitchen chairs. The house smells like coffee and a mixture of all the food people have brought.

Jeanie and Mitch are in the kitchen along with another couple who are friends of Jeanie's.

They're all watching Brody as he tightens the laces on his boots. "I'm going to get Thunder and take him home," he tells everyone.

"He's at Hawk's," Mitch says.

"Yeah, I know. Rodney told me."

Nina doesn't understand what's happening. "What's Hawk's?" she asks, though no one answers her.

"Let me go with you," Nina says to Brody, sensing this is something serious. "I want to help."

"It's best if you stay here." Brody ties his second boot. "Trust me. There's not much you can do." He pushes his pants legs down and stands up.

Mitch puts his coffee mug on the counter. "I'm coming with you. It's Christmas. You shouldn't have to deal with this alone."

No one else is saying much, but Jeanie pulls Mitch to her and kisses him. "Make sure your phone is turned on."

Brody goes to grab his coat from the rack by the door and stands there with a grim expression, waiting as Mitch gets his shoes on.

Nina comes over. She's feeling desperate. Brody's probably right, and she probably shouldn't come along, but she's stubborn.

"Please let me help. Whatever this is." She takes his hand. "You always support me so much. Let me support you."

Brody turns to her, and his face is so distant, it's like she's looking at a stranger. He pulls his hand away. "I'm protecting you, Nina. There are some things in my life you're better off not knowing about."

"I *do* want to know. I want to know everything."

Their eyes meet, and he seems to be searching hers. She can sense Jeanie and the others watching them.

"This is what's *real*, right?" she asks him. "No bullshit. That's what you said."

He's still studying her, but Nina can tell she's hit the mark. Finally he nods. "All right. You can come with us."

Mitch's head whips up. "I don't think that's a good idea."

"Let her see everything."

He shrugs. "It's your funeral."

Nina quickly throws her boots and coat on before Brody can change his mind. She glances over and sees Trevor and Pumpkin watching from the couch. Trevor's expression is grim too, but he nods at her, and his encouragement bolsters her, reinforces that she's doing the right thing.

They take Brody's truck. Nina sits in the back this time and gives Mitch the passenger seat. She doesn't ask any more questions. It's cold out, and even though Brody has the heater blasting, it's still taking a while to warm up. She watches the scenery passing by. They leave the woods and then drive through a small town, past the community center where they had the powwow a couple days ago, and then soon leave all that behind too.

It's almost dark when they finally pull up to a bar with a beat-up sign on it that says "Hawk's." It's right across the street from a run-down motel.

Glancing around, Nina realizes they're not on the reservation anymore. It's some nearby town, and whatever part this is, it's not a good one. She sees women who look like prostitutes standing in front of the motel. There's a diner lit up nearby that seems busy with a number of large semis parked.

The three of them get out of the truck. The air is freezing enough that it steals Nina's breath. She tucks her scarf closer to her neck.

"Hawk's only closes once a year," Brody tells her in a flat voice. "On Christmas Day at six o'clock."

Neon beer sign are displayed against the bar's blackout windows.

There was a half-hearted attempt to string up Christmas lights in front, though they look more depressing than cheery.

Nina has to admit she's nervous, wondering what to expect.

The bar is mostly empty when they go inside. It smells like beer, sweat, and cheap cologne. But mostly it smells like desperation. She's never seen a place so dreary. There's a jukebox, but it's not playing music. A couple biker guys are playing pool, and they look up, studying the three of them as they walk past.

There are a few more people sitting on barstools. One guy is in the corner with his head down.

"Good evening, Shelly," Mitch says to the woman standing behind the bar. "Merry Christmas."

She nods and then smiles when she sees Brody. "I haven't seen you in a while, stranger."

"Hey, Shelly."

"I've already cut your dad off," she says. "We're closing in twenty minutes."

"Yeah, I know. That's why we're here."

Nina watches as Brody goes over to the guy with his head down. She assumed he was asleep, but he jerks up as soon as Brody touches his shoulder.

"What the hell are *you* doing here?" the guy snarls at him. "Get away from me."

"It's Christmas," Brody says. "Come on, Thunder, we're taking you home."

Thunder glares at him, then at Mitch. His eyes pass over her too. He frowns. His hair is long, well past his shoulders, and mixed with gray. Right away Nina sees the resemblance to Brody. Thunder's eyes are bloodshot, and his skin is puffy and blotched, but she suspects he was once handsome.

She stays out of the way as Brody and Mitch try to get him off the barstool.

"They're closing," Mitch tells him. "It's Christmas Day. Come on, it's time to go home."

"Screw that!"

It takes about ten minutes of constant cajoling before they somehow convince him to leave. Nina follows, walking uncomfortably past the guys playing pool who are staring at her in a predatory way.

When they get to the truck, Brody and Mitch manage to get Thunder into the passenger seat, while Mitch climbs in the back with her. Brody starts up the engine. It's night out, and Nina has no idea where they're headed, though she assumes it's back to the reservation.

On the drive, Thunder careens back and forth between babbling nonsense and hurling insults. Brody doesn't say much, but when he speaks, it's in a quiet tone, obviously meant to try and calm his father. It saddens Nina to hear how practiced he is with it.

Eventually they head down a long driveway in the woods and pull up in front of a ramshackle house that has a carport attached. There are a few cars lined up in various states of disrepair. On closer inspection, she realizes the house is actually a double-wide. There's a tarp on the roof and a rickety chain-link fence in front.

Brody and Mitch get Thunder out of the truck. He's cursing at them loudly, his voice carrying into the night. When he notices Nina, he yells insults at her too. Startled, she takes a step back.

"That's *enough*," Brody snaps at him. "No more of that, old man. Leave her alone, or you'll be sleeping in the woods tonight."

"You think I care? Screw you and your damn whore!"

Brody's expression hardens, and for a second, it looks like he's going to lose his temper. But then he manages to dial it back.

He glances over at her, his voice tight, "Sorry for this."

"It's okay, Brody."

Meanwhile, Mitch is shaking his head. "Damn, Thunder. Why do you got to put us through this shit? You think we like it?"

For some reason, Thunder finds this hilarious and cackles with laughter. The two men take advantage of his laughing to get him up the steps and into the house.

Nina glances around outside. The sky is mostly clear, and she can see stars above the clouds. She wonders how close the nearest neighbors are and if they can hear all the yelling.

Once inside the house, she's accosted by a sour, rotten odor. She holds her scarf in front of her nose. Brody and Mitch are dragging Thunder into the back bedroom. There's more shouting, all of it coming from Thunder. She can hear Brody and Mitch trying to speak calmly to him.

Nina stands alone in the messy living room. It looks like a tornado has swept through, like it hasn't been cleaned in ages. There are papers and books scattered on the floor. Empty beer cans, liquor bottles, and old fast-food containers piled so high around a beat-up recliner that it's like the walls of a castle.

She doesn't understand how anyone can live like this.

Brody comes out of the bedroom and stalks past her into the small kitchen.

"Shit. I forgot to bring water bottles." He searches through the cupboards and opens the fridge. Finally, he grabs a dirty glass near the sink, squirts some dish soap in it, and quickly washes it.

Nina watches him fill it up with cold tap water. He glances at her. "Listen, you're not going to want to stay for the rest of it. It gets even uglier. I'm going to have Mitch call Jeanie to come pick you up."

"No, don't do that."

But he's already headed back to the bedroom with the water. She immediately hears more yelling and complaining from Thunder.

She stands there with her hands in her coat pockets. Staring at the overflowing trash can, a feeling of unreality settles over her.

Mitch appears from the back. "Hey, Nina, I'm going to call Jeanie to come get you, okay? This is going to take a while before we can leave."

She knows Brody told him to do that. For a moment she's tempted to follow their advice, to get the heck out of here. "Don't call her. I'm staying."

His brows go up, and it looks like he's ready to argue when there's a loud crash and more yelling from the bedroom. "Shit!" He rushes back.

Nina decides the overflowing trash in the kitchen is probably where the worst smell is coming from. She finds some garbage bags under the sink along with a few meager cleaning supplies. Then, getting on her knees, she picks up all the trash off the floor and puts the overflowing garbage into it as well. She takes the whole thing outside. Afterward, she puts in a clean bag to line the empty container.

Next she goes to the sink that's filled with dirty dishes. There's a half bottle of dish soap, so she pushes her coat sleeves up and starts washing the dishes.

Thunder's still shouting at Mitch and Brody from the bedroom. He sounds like someone possessed. For being so drunk, he certainly has a lot of energy. She ignores it though.

Once she's finished with the dishes, she goes through and empties all the spoiled food from the fridge, then wipes down the counters. Unfortunately, her pregnancy disgust meter gets triggered a couple times, and she has to throw up into the sink, washing it down the garbage disposal—which thankfully works fine. A few times, she's forced to stick her head out the front door to stop her nausea, sucking in the cold night air before getting back to work.

Once she's done with the kitchen, she starts on the living room. At least the shouting appears to have finally stopped. At one point, she hears what sounds like someone retching repeatedly. Later, she hears water running in another part of the house.

She fills two more garbage bags with fast-food containers. As she gathers and stacks up all the loose papers and books—most of them mechanic-related—she finds a framed photo under the coffee table.

It's a picture of Brody with Thunder. She even recognizes the location as Angel Lake, where they went on their walk the other day. It's an old photo. Brody's just a kid of maybe eight or nine with shoulder-length black hair. So cute. She can see she was right about Thunder too. He was handsome when he was younger. She studies the way Brody is giving an impish smile for the camera and can't help smiling herself.

She discovers lots more photos hanging on the walls. Mostly of Brody growing up. School pictures, and then pictures of him and Thunder working on various cars together over the years. There's another picture of them fishing at the lake. Whatever the situation is with this guy's alcohol addiction, it's obvious to Nina that he loves his son very much.

By the time she's done cleaning the kitchen, living room, and the small dining area, the bedroom has gone quiet. Mitch and Brody finally emerge, though Brody looks shocked to see her.

"You're still *here?*" He glances at Mitch. "I thought you said Jeanie came to pick her up!"

"I didn't say that. She told me she didn't want to go."

Nina wipes her hands on her jeans. "That's right. I decided to stay."

"Why the hell would you do that?" Brody is obviously upset. He rubs his forehead. "Jesus, you should have left hours ago. You've been waiting this whole time?"

Mitch looks around the house. "Damn, check this place out. I don't know if I've ever seen it this clean before."

Brody's brows shoot up as he notices the kitchen and then glances around the living room. "Holy shit, Nina. Did you do all this?"

"I just made myself useful, that's all."

Mitch is quietly studying her.

"I couldn't find the vacuum cleaner. And I just put the bags of trash outside. There's no garbage can anywhere."

Brody's wearing a funny smile. "Thunder usually takes his trash to the dump. Or burns what he can."

"Well, that explains it." She pauses. "How is he doing?"

"Finally asleep. I had to force him to take a shower."

She nods, and that's when she notices his clothes are soaking wet. Brody must have had to literally get in the shower with him. She can see how tired he is. He looks worn out.

The ride back is mostly silent. Mitch insists she sit in front this time, and Nina doesn't bother to argue.

Once they're back at the house, they both need to take a shower, but she tells Brody to go first and get out of those wet clothes.

Nina sits on the love seat in the living room with Pumpkin resting her head on Nina's leg. *I'm definitely getting a dog*, she thinks as she pets Pumpkin's soft fur. *And a cat too.* She wants her baby to grow up with all the animals she never had.

"Mitch told me what you did for my brother. That was nice of you."

Nina shrugs as Jeanie takes a seat on the couch. "It was no big deal. Besides, I didn't do it for your brother." She cleaned that house for Brody. She figured if it eased his burden even the tiniest amount, it was worth it.

Jeanie nods. "I know. But thank you anyway. I'm sorry you had to see Thunder like that." She takes a deep breath. "You'll have to come visit again and hopefully meet him sober next time."

Nina glances over in surprise that she's being invited again. "How often is he like that?"

Jeanie shakes her head. "Too often these days. You might not believe this, but when he's not drinking, my brother is a good man."

Nina nods. Oddly, she does believe it. After seeing all the photos Thunder has of his son everywhere, it clearly shows another side to him. She continues to pet the dog's silky fur. "What kind of dog is Pumpkin?"

"Oh, she's just a mutt." Jeanie smiles. "She's a stray. We found her in our pumpkin patch one morning. She looked so lonely and lost that we kept her."

"Really?"

"She was unexpected, and at first we weren't sure about her, but she turned out to be a good surprise."

∼

Brody is lying in bed, studying the wood ceiling, when Nina comes in from her shower. She's wearing a camisole and silky white pajama bottoms.

He's not even sure what to say to her after everything she witnessed today. *Some Christmas it must have been for her—cleaning some old drunk guy's house.* He still can't believe she did it. If he's honest though, he's glad she did. It was kind of her. And it means there's one less boulder pressing on him.

"I'm surprised you're still awake," she says, climbing into bed. "You looked so worn out earlier."

"Come here." He holds his arm out, and she slides closer to him, bringing the scent of the coconut body lotion she's been using lately. Her hair feels damp as she lays it against his shoulder.

He closes his eyes, enjoying her softness and warmth. Enjoying everything about her. Nina drove recklessly into his heart and then somewhere along the way took it over.

"Thank you for bringing me with you today," she says, stroking his jaw. "I know that was difficult for you."

"Jesus, Nina. You shouldn't be thanking me." He thanked her earlier for what she did, but he could tell she didn't want his gratitude either. He understood completely. They were alike in that way.

She doesn't say anything more and continues playing with the goatee he's growing back. Both of them are quiet, listening to light rain dripping off the roof outside.

"You saw my darkest secret today," he says in a low voice. "No one knows about the situation with Thunder except my family." And even there he's been selective. "Even Kiera doesn't know."

"You never told Kiera about your father's drinking?"

"I told her he drank, but she never saw it. She met him once, but I made sure he was sober." Because hearing about something and seeing it with your own eyes were two very different things.

Nina turns on her stomach to face him. "What's Thunder like when he's sober?"

"A completely different person. He's kindhearted and has a dry sense of humor." Brody takes a deep breath. "Jeanie thinks he's possessed by a demon when he drinks. And I know it sounds crazy, but sometimes I think it's true."

"That must have been really hard when you were a kid."

"It wasn't easy, but I had my grandma. She'd check on me and take me to her house if he started up. Jeanie always helped too."

"I'm surprised your mom still allowed you to stay with him."

He smirks without humor. "She didn't know."

"Are you kidding?"

"I didn't tell her because I didn't want to stop coming here. Despite everything, he's still my father."

She nods. "It's probably why they split up when you were a baby."

"Probably. I think for a while he must have completely stopped drinking, and that's why she finally allowed me to start seeing him again."

"I'm so sorry you've had to deal with this your whole life."

He shrugs. "Things weren't as bad when I was a kid. It only happened occasionally, and I could handle it." But then he stops talking because he knows that's bullshit. "Okay, that's not true. The truth is, it scared the hell out of me when I was a kid." He rubs his forehead. "It doesn't scare me anymore. Now I just hate it. It's why I haven't been up here in over a year."

She considers this. "What does Thunder do for money? I mean, how does he get by? I know you said he was a mechanic, but I can't imagine him working."

"When he's sober, he does work. It's for this guy named Al who has a garage on the rez. He lets him come and go as he pleases."

"Really? Why would any employer put up with that?"

Brody snorts. "Because Thunder is a wizard with cars or anything mechanical. Seriously. You think I'm good at what I do? Well, I got it from him."

"I guess that explains all those pictures I saw in his house. The two of you working on cars together over the years."

"Yeah, we had some good times." He goes quiet remembering it but then shakes his head, still embarrassed by everything she saw and heard. "It doesn't change the fact that he's a mess. I'll bet you're glad now that I'm not your baby's father."

"What?" Nina sits up at this and stares at him. "What are you talking about?"

"You saw who I'm related to."

"That's absurd. You think I care about that?" She studies him. "Most families have alcoholics in them. My grandfather was an alcoholic, and my uncle too, except he's in recovery."

Brody's brows go up. He has to admit he's surprised, though he'd bet money it's nothing as severe as what she witnessed tonight.

"You don't have the corner market on it," she continues. "Trust me." She's still watching him. "Is that really how you feel about kids?"

"Sometimes." He stares up at the ceiling again. "Sometimes I wonder if I should have any at all."

"Well, then, let me tell you *my* darkest secret." Nina leans closer. "When I found out you weren't this baby's father, I was upset."

His brows knit together. "You were?"

"Don't get me wrong. I love this child no matter what, but I wanted it to be yours. I didn't even realize how badly I wanted it until I was faced with the truth. What kind of mother does that make me?"

"You never told me that."

"How could I? How could I tell anyone? Suzy made jokes about Team Brody or Team Noel, but I had to be neutral."

"That doesn't make you a bad mother." He's silent for a long moment. "I wanted your baby to be mine too," he says, admitting it out loud for the first time. "Despite everything I just said. I guess that makes me selfish."

"No, it doesn't."

The two of them study each other.

He reaches for her hand. "For what it's worth, I think you're going to be a great mother. Seriously, Nina."

"I hope so. This little girl deserves the best life I can give her."

"You mean that little *boy* deserves the best life *both of us* can give him."

Her blue eyes widen, and he can tell he's surprised her. "We've never talked about what happens after this baby is born. Are you sure you want to be a part of its life?"

"I'm sure. I'm sure, because I want to be part of *your* life." He's still gazing at her. "I love you, Nina." He can't believe he feels this way and that he's fallen so hard for her, but he has.

She bites her lip and then smiles. Her pretty sky eyes are shining. "I love you too."

CHAPTER TWENTY-THREE

> **Life & The Art of Automobile Maintenance**
> By Brody Austin
>
>
>
> *"A transmission doesn't require much maintenance but can be very expensive to replace."*

"What do you think of Astrid, or Elsa?" Nina asks Brody. "I like Kirstin a lot too."

They're on one of the walking trails near Brody's house. It's been almost two months since Christmas, and being in her fifth month now, Nina is showing enough that she's switched to wearing maternity clothes. She had an ultrasound done last month, and while, thankfully, everything looked great with the baby, it was inconclusive as far as gender. She could always have a blood test done but has decided to wait until the baby is born.

"You're always so focused on girl names," Brody says. "We need more boy names."

"I suppose you're right." She goes quiet and then perks up. "I know. What about Basil? I've always liked that name."

"Basil? Yeah, that's a great name."

She gets excited. "Do you really think so?"

"Sure, if you want him to get his ass kicked every single day."

She rolls her eyes. "It's not *that* bad."

Brody snorts. "Trust me, before he starts kindergarten, little Basil's going to need to learn kung fu, or better yet, Krav Maga."

"What the heck is that?"

"It's a type of combat fighting they use in the Israeli military."

She laughs and smacks his shoulder. "That's silly. Basil is a perfectly nice name."

"What about Jesse or Wyatt? I like both of those."

"Those sound like gunslinger names."

"Yeah, but they're tough. No one's going to mess with a Jesse or a Wyatt."

A cyclist speeds past them on the trail, and they step over to the right. It's Saturday, and this has become their thing lately. Walk a mile and a half on the trail, stop at the juice bar up ahead, and then walk back.

"How about Jake?" Brody asks. "That's a good solid name."

"Hmm." Nina thinks it over. "You know what? I like that. It sounds like someone who's handsome and smart."

"A James Bond type or a private eye."

She nods. "Let's add that to the list." They started a list on their phones recently of all the baby names they both approve of. "What about Ashley?"

"That's a girl's name."

"Not always. Sometimes boys have it."

He gives her a look. "Give me a break. You really want this kid to take a beating, don't you?"

"No, I don't!"

"Maybe you should name him Matilda."

She laughs. "Actually, I like Matilda."

"Yeah, for a girl. Not a boy."

Nina sighs. "I don't know. Maybe you're right. Maybe if it's a boy, I'll just call him Bullet. Would that make you happy?"

"Hell yeah." Brody chuckles. "Now we're talking."

"People will be terrified of him."

"We'll probably have to make sure he doesn't wind up in prison."

Nina laughs some more and shakes her head. She wonders what Noel would think if she named this baby something wild like that. She hasn't heard from him since December, when he called to say he might want to be part of this child's life. Apparently he's changed his mind, which is fine by her.

When they get to the juice place, Brody orders them both smoothies. Nina has her usual pineapple banana, and Brody has strawberry coconut. They take a seat at a table near the window.

"I almost forgot. I signed us up for birth classes," she says. "They start next month. Are you still sure you want to go with me?"

"Of course. How else am I going to learn all those labor breathing techniques?"

She smiles and then glances outside. The trees are still bare. It's near the end of February, and she's looking forward to spring.

"How's it going with the new job?" he asks. "Any more excitement?"

Nina started working at Suds & Honey three weeks ago. She's been made head of marketing, except there isn't much of a marketing department, so she's been tasked with creating one. It should be daunting, but instead it's been invigorating. She loves it.

"Well, I hired two new people last week. And I might poach Davis, my old admin from Tolland."

Brody sucks on his straw. "Damn, you've been busy."

"I know. And we're moving into our new offices in Fremont next week, so it's going to be even crazier for a while."

"You sound like you're enjoying it though."

She smiles. "I am. I love this company's products. It's going to be a lot of fun marketing it and growing its brand. I just found out we're opening a store in Portland next year."

"Do you guys hire ad agencies, or how does that work?"

She swirls the straw around in her smoothie. "We'll probably hire out for certain campaigns, but we plan to handle most of our branding and packaging in house. I think that'll give us more flexibility. I had a meeting with Piper about it, and we both agreed."

"You really know your stuff, don't you?"

Nina shrugs. "It's what I do." She had to take a small pay cut to work for Suds & Honey, but she doesn't care. Her job is already a hundred times more satisfying.

Once they finish their smoothies and are walking back, Nina reminds Brody about the wedding next Saturday.

"Seriously? So we're still going to that?" He sounds like a little kid who's been told he has to eat broccoli.

"That was our original agreement, remember?" she teases. "I went to Summer's party, and you come to this wedding with me."

"Except you agreed to *three* family parties. Not just the one. I got gypped."

"Doesn't Christmas count? So that's two. I'll go to more family parties if you want."

He doesn't say anything. He's been dragging his feet about this wedding, and she has no idea why. Whenever she asks him, he evades her questions.

"What kind of suit do you own?" she asks. "I don't think I've ever seen one hanging in your closet."

"That's because it was hanging in my junk room's closet." Brody finally cleaned out his junk room and gave it to Trevor as a bedroom. Trevor's still living with Brody to save money. He's also still hanging out with Anka, so much so that Brody and Nina suspect something romantic might be going on.

"What does this suit look like exactly?" she asks. "Maybe I should see it before you take it to get pressed."

He glances at her. "What? You don't trust me?"

"It's not that. It's going to be a formal wedding though, so you'll want to look appropriate. What color is it."

"Blue."

"Dark blue?"

Brody tilts his head. "Nah, more like the color of bubble gum. It's got these two stripes that run down the front made of rhinestones. Trust me, it's kickass."

Nina's mouth falls open. But then she gives a snort of laughter. "Wow, you almost had me."

He smirks. "Speaking of kickass, maybe I should wear my *Matrix* costume. I'll bet it would make the whole thing a hell of a lot more fun."

Nina tries to picture that. It probably would make it more fun. "What does your suit actually look like?"

"Black and boring. Trust me, it's fine. I wore it to Tori's wedding."

"Do you have a tie that doesn't have cars or baseballs on it?"

"Sure, of course. What do you take me for? My tie is respectable and only has rainbow glitter and unicorns."

Brody is dreading this wedding. He's got a bad feeling about it. And not just because it's going to be full of people from her former workplace, or that he's going to have to deal with Noel face-to-face—though that's not helping.

The truth is, he likes to pretend that asshole doesn't exit. Because all Brody wants to do is be with Nina and little baby Bullet once he arrives. He's cool with that. He's ecstatic about it.

Of course, the problem is Noel *does* exit.

As the day of the wedding draws closer, he wishes he could get out of it. His Spidey senses are going haywire. He even considers faking an illness or some other emergency so he and Nina can skip it, but he knows he could never do that to her.

In the end, he goes because it's what she wants.

"You look really pretty," Brody says when he arrives to pick her up at her condo. She's wearing a long fitted blue gown with sleeves that come off her shoulders and a chain of pearls around her neck. "Elegant."

"Do you think it highlights my baby bump too much?" she asks, turning to the side.

He rests his hand on her back and then slides the other one over her rounded stomach. "I think you look just right. Sexy, actually."

She laughs with disbelief. "Sexy? Really?"

"Yeah. Sexy."

"I don't think it's possible to look sexy while being pregnant."

He draws her closer and kisses her neck, inhaling the scent of her jasmine perfume. "And that's where you're wrong, Nina banana. Trust me, a lot of guys think pregnant women are sexy."

"Uh-oh." She gives him a look. "This isn't some kind of weird fetish, is it?"

He laughs. "A fetish? I don't think so. There's something cool about it. I just think you look beautiful."

She moves closer and puts her arms around his neck. "What am I going to do with you, Brody? You're so perfect."

"Just remember that the next time I get engine grease on your clothes."

She smiles. "I'll try to." Her eyes roam over him. "Speaking of sexy, you look handsome in this suit. Totally hot, actually."

He smirks. "Better than you thought, huh?"

"I honestly didn't know what to expect." She fingers the material on his jacket. "But this is really nice. Is it from a designer?"

He shrugs. "Probably. It cost a fortune. Blair's the one who helped me pick it out."

"She did?"

"Guess I should have mentioned that before."

"Definitely," she says with a laugh. She goes over and grabs a white shawl and her purse. Just before they leave, she primps in the mirror by the front door.

He stands there, and as he's watching her apply a layer of pink gloss to her lips, he has this sudden urge to have her. To pull that dress up and take her right there against the wall. There's something about seeing Nina dressed so elegantly that makes him want to rough her up a little. He shifts his body position, trying to stop the blood flow to his cock.

She glances at him with a pointed expression. "We can't."

"I didn't say anything."

"It's the way you're looking at me."

He grins. "So you know this look, huh?"

She laughs a little and puts her tube of lip gloss away. "I know it well."

They leave the condo, and on the way down in the elevator, Nina announces she wants to take her Audi to the wedding instead of the Cougar.

"The Audi? Why would we do that?"

"It's just that the Cougar is so loud and flashy. Don't get me wrong, I love that car, but I think the Audi is better for this occasion."

He plays with the car keys in his pocket. Her announcing that she wants to take the Audi is making his bad feeling about this whole thing increase. He's tempted to argue with her but can't think of a good reason.

It gets even worse when they arrive at her car, and she insists on driving. "I don't know why you never let me drive," she says. "I'm a perfectly good driver."

"I know that. It's got nothing to do with it."

"Is this some kind of macho thing, then? Is that why you always want to drive?"

He rolls his eyes. "Just give me the keys. Hell, it's bad enough we're not taking the Cougar."

"No, forget it. I'm driving. It's my car. And besides, I'm pregnant."

"What's that got to do with anything?"

"It means I'm going to do whatever makes me the most comfortable."

He stands there ready to argue some more but then asks himself, *Is this really the hill you want to die on today?* "All right, fine. Whatever. You drive."

Brody sits on the passenger side. He's already claustrophobic and crowded as he adjusts the seat to fit his legs. He doesn't know why they've started arguing, but it doesn't bode well. In fact, his Spidey senses are currently at DEFCON One.

Once they arrive at the church, he sees what they're dealing with. Everything is foreign-made and high-end. Mercedes, BMW, Lexus, and even a couple Jaguars.

So this is why Nina didn't want to take the Cougar.

He glances at her but doesn't say anything.

They're running late and are seated only a few minutes before the ceremony begins. Despite the cold outside, the church is stuffy. The smell of perfume and cologne is overpowering, and he can't wait until this day is over.

The ceremony drags on until finally they announce the happy couple, and everyone streams outside. Nina runs into a few people she knows and introduces him as her boyfriend. He can see the surprise on their faces. He's guessing they weren't expecting some Native American dude.

They head off to the reception, which is being held at a swanky hotel downtown. Nina still insists on driving, but he doesn't say a word.

Once they hand the car keys off to the valet and make their way inside, Brody has to admit, this isn't like any wedding reception he's ever been to. It's more like something you see in the movies. The swankiness is dialed up to eleven. The band is playing rockabilly, something he enjoys, at least. A waiter guides them to their table, which they share with several people Nina knows from work.

Another waiter comes by and fills their glasses with champagne.

Nina asks for a glass of pineapple juice instead. He's tempted to ask for a beer but instead drinks ice water, since he dislikes champagne.

Lots of people are coming over to say hello to Nina, exclaiming about her pregnancy, and at least she seems to be enjoying herself. He's glad for that. Glancing around, he hasn't seen any sign of Noel. Even though he's only seen pictures of him online, Brody is pretty sure he'd recognize him.

"Brody, it's good to see you again."

He looks up, surprised to see a familiar face. It's Michael, the heart surgeon. "Hey, it's good to see you too."

Nina, who's talking to someone, smiles and gives Michael a wave.

"So how's your Mercedes roadster doing?" Brody asks, taking a sip from his water glass. Michael brought the car into the garage last month. It's a 1962 Mercedes-Benz 190 SL.

"Good, though I could definitely still use your help."

Brody listens as Michael tells him about how he's been struggling to get some of the parts he needs. When he brought the car in, Brody told him he'd love to work on it but that he has a long list of waiting customers.

As Michael talks, Claudia comes over. Unfortunately, he remembers her too. She's staring at him in the same weird way as the last time he saw her.

"Hello, Brody." Claudia puts her hand out so he's forced to take it. "I see you're still with Nina." She glances to the side at Nina, who appears to be ignoring Claudia, not that Brody can blame her.

Michael asks him a question about the car's four-speed transmission, which Brody answers. The whole time, Claudia continues to stare.

What the hell is this woman's problem?

Finally she turns and talks to a few more people who have stopped by their table.

"What do you say we go over to the bar and get a normal drink?" Michael asks him. He motions at his glass. "I can see you're not much for champagne either."

"Sure," Brody says. "That sounds good." He tells Nina, who nods and then smiles with relief. She's already asked him three times if he was having fun. And all three times he lied and said yes.

The bar is outside the main ballroom. A number of people are standing around or sitting in chairs set up for the wedding guests.

Michael orders a scotch on the rocks, and Brody asks the bartender to list his bottled beers.

"I'll take the California IPA," he finally says. "No glass."

"So, what can I do to get you guys to work on my car?" Michael asks after they take a seat. "Should I offer you more money?"

Brody chuckles. "Well, if you're patient, I can put you at the top of the list when we open our second location."

"You're opening a second location?"

He nods. "That's the plan." He and Nina drove down to SoDo and even as far as Renton, looking at a few contenders last month.

Michael takes a sip of scotch. "Are you taking on investors?"

Brody shakes his head. "I plan to get a bank loan."

"Well, let me know if you change your mind."

They sit and shoot the breeze for a while, talking about cars. He discovers Michael is a collector, so Brody tells him about the 1941 Zephyr coupe he's been working on for fun.

"Damn, those are beautiful cars. I can't believe you found one. Are you planning to sell it?"

Brody laughs at the hopeful note in his voice. "Hell no. I'm keeping it for myself."

Eventually, Nina and Claudia come out to find the two of them.

"There you boys are," Claudia says, sounding playful and like she's had a few drinks. She sits on the arm of Michael's chair, smiling at Brody, though he ignores her.

He gets up and tells Michael it was good talking to him, then goes back inside the ballroom with Nina. The band has switched to R&B, and when he hears "At Last" by Etta James, he grins and holds his hand out. "Come on, let's dance."

"I love this song," she says as they join all the other couples.

"Me too," he agrees. "It's one of my favorites."

They smile at each other, and she looks so radiant that he bends down to kiss her. "You *are* my love," he whispers.

"You'e mine too," she says as they gaze at each other.

He kisses her again, his heart filled with tenderness. *This will be our song forever.*

They're so lost in each other that at first he doesn't notice there's some guy standing next to him, tapping his shoulder.

"Excuse me. I'd like to cut in."

Brody turns his head. "What?" He stares in confusion at some tanned middle-aged dude who's telling him he wants to dance with Nina. It takes Brody a second to realize who it is—Noel. "Forget it. Go find your own dance partner."

"Nina, I'd like this dance," Noel says, ignoring him.

"Did you hear me?" Brody knows he needs to stay calm, but there's a warning bell clanging deep inside of him.

"Yes, I heard you," Noel says dismissively. "But I wasn't asking you, I was asking Nina."

"Well, she's already with someone."

"Why don't you let her answer for herself?"

Both men turn to Nina, who's shaking her head. "Just go away, Noel. I don't want to dance with you."

"You don't mean that." He smiles. "For old time's sake."

"Are you deaf?" Brody asks. "The question has been asked and answered."

Unfortunately, people are starting to stare at the three of them arguing. Nina glances around, noticing it too.

Noel puts his hand toward her. "C'mon. One dance with the father of your child?"

Brody would like nothing better than to lay this sonofabitch out flat on his ass. He's actually thinking about it when Nina places her hand on his arm. "I don't want to cause a scene. I'm going to dance with him."

"You *are?*"

Nina nods. "I'll be fine. It's just one dance."

Brody blinks at this, but he takes a step back. There's not much else he can do. The band is already starting a different song, another slow one. Billie Holiday's "The Very Thought of You."

He leaves the dance floor and isn't even sure where to go. He glances back and watches how Noel steps in and takes his place. Brody has a disturbing thought that he's seeing the future. But that's crazy.

He leaves and heads for the restroom, figuring he needs to calm down. Except he doesn't know where the restroom is. Instead, he notices a private alcove with a leather couch and a palm tree. No one's there, so he decides to sit and take a breather.

He leans his head back on the couch and closes his eyes, massaging his forehead.

The band is still playing "The Very of Thought You," another song he's always liked, except at the moment he hates it. It's romantic. Too romantic for something Nina should be dancing to with Noel.

He had a bad feeling about coming here, and now he knows why.

As he's thinking all this, he realizes he isn't alone anymore. He opens his eyes and sits up. To his dismay, Claudia is standing in front of him.

"Hey there, handsome." She smiles and seems drunk.

He doesn't reply.

Claudia plops down beside him, and he's ready to get up when she starts talking. "I saw Noel with Nina out there dancing together. I'm not surprised he wants her back."

Brody knows he should leave, that he shouldn't listen to a damn thing this woman has to say. "What the hell are you talking about?"

"It's obvious, isn't it? Especially now that he's gotten rid of Emily. Thank *God*."

There's a sinking feeling in his stomach. "Noel broke up with Emily?"

Claudia nods. "That's why he came stag tonight. He knows how badly he screwed up with Nina, and he's going to try and win her back."

"Nina will never go back to him."

She smirks. "Of course she will." Claudia moves in even closer, sliding her fingers down the front of his suit. "God, you're hot. Where did Nina find you?"

He pushes her hand away. "This is bullshit. I don't know why I'm listening to you."

"It's not bullshit. She'll take him back because he's the father of her child. Trust me, that's how women are programmed."

"No way." Except she's speaking to his deepest fear. "He cheated on her."

"That doesn't matter. But guess what? I know something that will make you feel a *whole* lot better."

And before Brody knows what's happening, Claudia has climbed on top of him and is straddling his lap.

"What the hell? Get off me!"

"I've seen you watching me, Brody. Don't deny it. We have chemistry."

"You're crazy. I'm not interested in you." He wants to shove her off, but the only way is to dump her on the floor.

"Nina and I have already shared one man," she says in a husky voice, her breath reeking of alcohol. "I don't see why we can't share another."

"Get the hell off of me, Claudia." He's got his hand on her backside, trying to lift her up, but she's surprisingly strong. Her thighs are locked around his hips, and she's grabbed hold of the couch somehow.

And that's when he hears a loud gasp.

With dread, he looks around this linebacker's shoulders to discover Nina standing there.

Great. Just great.

Claudia turns and laughs. "Oh, hello, Nina. I hope you don't mind. I figured now that you're done with him, I'll have a turn."

CHAPTER TWENTY-FOUR

> ### Life & The Art of Automobile Maintenance
> #### By Brody Austin
>
>
>
> *"A malfunction in your car's electrical system can affect many of its components."*

That's it.

Brody shoves Claudia off. He doesn't want to hurt her, but at this point, he's desperate. She sprawls onto the floor.

"I guess you like it rough, huh?" she says, laughing and obviously drunk.

Nina is standing there in apparent shock as Brody tries to get to her.

"Don't go!" Claudia lunges for him and grabs his leg. "You know you want me!"

"Jesus Christ." He tries to pull himself free. He's never experienced anything like this in his entire life. "Let go of me, you freak."

Finally, he yanks his leg away from this woman's bear-trap hands. Nina's staring at Claudia with a pissed off expression, but when her eyes shift to him, she's still pissed off.

"It's not what it looked like," he says. "She forced herself on me."

"Did she?"

"Yes, she did." He glances back at Claudia, who's pulled herself up from the floor and is sitting on the couch now. "I think she's wasted. We should probably find Michael so he can take her home."

Nina is studying him. "Why were you out here alone with her to begin with?"

"I came out here after you decided to dance with Noel." He's trying not to sound angry. "I wanted some peace and quiet, and then she showed up."

She glances over at Claudia, who's lying on the couch. "You're right, we should find Michael or Noel to take care of her."

"Forget Noel. I've had enough of that asshole."

Nina sucks in her breath. "You know, you totally overreacted. It was just one dance. You looked like you were ready to punch him. I was trying to avoid a scene."

Brody stares at her with amazement. "So you chose to *dance* with him? You should have just told him to got to hell."

She rolls her eyes. "We're at a wedding in front of all my former work colleagues. I'm not going to start cursing at people."

"Good to see you have your priorities, then."

"It's not like that." She sighs. "Let's just go back inside."

They head back into the ballroom, and he searches around for Michael. When he finds him, he tells him Claudia has had a few too many and needs his help. Brody doesn't tell him anything else that happened.

Afterward, he goes to join Nina at their table. Somehow they make it through dinner, though he doesn't have much of an appetite. It isn't long after that Nina announces she's tired and wants to leave.

"Sounds good to me."

They wait out front for the valet to bring them their car. When it arrives, she heads toward the passenger side. "You can drive," she tells him. "I don't care."

He knows it's meant to be a peace offering, so he's trying not to stay angry. Light rain falls as he pulls out onto the street. Brody seldom drives her car, so he messes around with the lever, trying to figure out the wiper settings.

"Why was your hand on her ass?"

"What?" he asks, clicking through to set it for low.

"Your hand was on Claudia's ass when I went out there and found you two together."

He glances over at her. "Are you kidding? My hand wasn't on her ass for pleasure, if that's what you're implying. I was trying to get her off me."

"By grabbing her ass?"

He rolls his eyes. "Look, you can believe me or not."

Nina is quiet the rest of the ride back to her place.

After he drives into the underground garage and parks, he wonders what happens next.

"I think I'm just going upstairs alone tonight," she says, turning to him. "I'm tired, and I want to get some sleep."

He shakes his head. "I knew that wedding was going to be a disaster."

"What do you mean?"

"I had a bad feeling about it."

"Then why didn't you say something?"

He stares through the car's windshield out at the cement wall in front of them. There's no way he's going to admit that he's jealous of Noel. "Would you have agreed to stay home if I had?"

She doesn't reply.

"That's what I thought."

"Let's just call it a night, Brody."

They don't speak all week. Nina's obviously angry at him, but Brody is pissed too. Every time he thinks about her dancing in Noel's arms, he feels like punching something. Not to mention that ridiculous scene with Claudia. Did Nina really think he'd cheat on her?

It's no wonder Noel and Claudia were once married.

The two of them are poison.

"Uh-oh," Trevor says when Friday rolls around and Brody's studying the menu to have Chinese food delivered. "What's going on? Are you and Nina having a fight?"

"It's fine. We've been in each other's face so much lately that we're taking a break."

Trevor looks skeptical, but Brody isn't much in the mood to talk about his love life.

"You want to come to the movies with me and Anka? It's the new *Star Wars*. Though we've already seen it once."

"Nah, that's okay." He doesn't want to be a third wheel on their date. "You guys go have fun."

"You sure? Or we could stay here and hang out and watch Netflix. I'll have to ask Anka, but I don't think she'd mind."

Brody smiles to himself and realizes Trevor's come a long way. His new job is going well, he's saving money, and he even paid back the rent check Brody wrote Kevin. On top of all that, he's got a great girlfriend.

"So how are things with you and Anka? It's obviously gotten romantic."

Travis grins but seems kind of embarrassed. "Yeah, Anka's cool. I can't believe I was such an asshole when I first met her."

"She's forgiven you, huh?"

He nods. "I had to grovel, but it was worth it. It turns out it's awesome being with a girl who knows about cars. She's teaching me stuff all the time." Trevor grins. "We've always got things to talk about."

"I'm glad for you two. And don't worry about me tonight. I'm going to work on the Zephyr."

After Trevor leaves, Brody thinks about what an awful week it's been without Nina. To make matters worse, Jackson asked him if he could get Summer's number yesterday, putting him in an awkward position.

"You want to date my sister?" Brody asked. He had nothing against Jackson. He was a good mechanic, and in fact, Brody was thinking about asking him if he'd like to stay on permanently. The problem was Jackson had a female fan club, or at least that's the way it seemed to Brody. "Why?"

He laughed. "What do you mean, why? Because I like her."

"As far as I can tell, you've got more women than you can handle."

Jackson smirked a little and glanced to the side. Besides that Australian accent, he had a James Dean vibe going. "None of them are quite like Summer."

Brody considered that as he crossed his arms. "I'll tell you what. How about I pass your number on to her, and she can decide for herself what she wants to do with it."

"That works for me."

And so Brody gave Summer Jackson's number, along with a stern warning. She sounded so delighted about the number though that he suspects she didn't hear a damn word of the warning.

He stares at the Chinese food menu. The problem with ordering Chinese food is it's making him think of Nina and all her cravings. He smiles to himself. Her latest obsession has been eating hot sauce on everything. Literally. He watched her eat a chocolate chip cookie with hot sauce. It was so funny he took a picture with his phone. "Damn, I'm finally getting my money's worth here," he'd joked.

Instead of Chinese food, he makes himself a peanut butter sandwich. He's been working on the Zephyr a lot this week. The brown leather saddle seats for the car's interior arrived, and he and Trevor have been installing them together.

He turns the radio on in the garage and tries to work on the car but keeps brooding over Nina. Finally, he figures to hell with it. He's going to go see her.

After a quick shower, he throws on some clean clothes—jeans, a black T-shirt, and a flannel shirt over that. He puts on his lined corduroy jacket and heads out the door.

He knows he should probably call first, but he's learned that sometimes in life, the best thing you can do is show up.

On the way there, he stops at the grocery store and picks up some fresh pineapple, a bottle of Nina's favorite hot sauce, potato chips, licorice, chocolate chip cookies, and a tub of snickerdoodle coconut milk ice cream.

He says hello to Jason, one of the doormen in the lobby of her building. Brody's been here enough that he's gotten to know them all pretty well.

"Is she expecting you?" Jason asks.

Brody holds up the bag of goodies. "I thought I'd surprise her with some of her favorite pregnancy cravings."

Jason chuckles and lets him go up.

Once Brody gets to her door, he's glad he decided on this. Despite the terrible fight they had, he misses Nina.

He knocks and waits.

When her door finally opens, she seems startled to see him.

He holds up the bag of food. "Just thought I'd drop by and see what little Bullet is craving tonight."

She smiles, resting her hand on her belly. There's a sparkle in her eyes. "You mean little Elsa, don't you?"

The two of them gaze at each other, and it's like all the hurt and bad feelings from their fight seem stupid and inconsequential.

"I'm sorry," he says. "I acted like an ass. It was just one dance. I made too much of it."

She sighs. "I'm sorry too. I never should have danced with him in the first place, and I definitely shouldn't have doubted you over Claudia."

"Can we make up now? I've been missing you something fierce."

Nina smiles, then pulls him inside, and all is right with his world again.

Nina is so happy to see Brody. It's like a miracle he came tonight. She's been in a horrible place all week, and it was all made worse because Noel started calling her.

Apparently, he broke up with Emily and has now decided he wants to win Nina back. Not that she wants anything to do with him.

"I love it that you had your lawyer send me preliminary papers for child support," he said to her on the phone a few days ago.

"You do?" She was busy at work and really didn't have time for this.

"I'd forgotten how sharp your teeth can be, Nina." He chuckles. "It's one of the things I missed about you."

It figures. It's one of the things she doesn't miss about herself. She doesn't have to have sharp teeth around Brody. He likes her when she's soft and silly, not trying to impress anyone.

"Don't call me anymore," she says and hangs up on him.

There's some sharp teeth for you, asshole.

He doesn't call. Instead he texts her, sending questions about her new job. And not just any questions. Intelligent and thoughtful ones that show he's done his homework and has researched Suds & Honey. She doesn't answer, of course. But she remembers all too well the hold he once had on her.

That's why seeing Brody's handsome face at her door is like a soothing balm. She must have been out of her mind dancing with Noel that night. And that whole thing with Claudia? What a joke. She'd seen with her own eyes the way Claudia couldn't take her eyes off Brody.

After Nina pulls him inside, she wraps her arms around his neck. He smells like the rain outside. Like the shampoo from his shower. Like her man. The one she's fallen head over heels in love with.

Brody pulls her in tight, and his mouth crashes against hers. While she's moaning, something falls to the floor. It's the bag of groceries he brought.

Their hands are all over each other, the two of them going at it like a couple of maniacs. She's tearing his coat off, and he's pulling her tank top up. They're still in the entryway, but she doesn't care. He backs her against the wall, and his brown eyes are hot on hers, though there's a little smile on his face when he turns her around so she's facing the wall.

"This is how it's going to be, Nina banana," he whispers in her ear.

His hands slide down her hips, and her eyes close. Desire floods her veins, shutting off everything. The world. All she cares about is this moment.

Brody yanks her panties and pajama bottoms off together. And then he's right there again, fully clothed against her back, caging her in. He's breathing hard, but so is she, both of them trembling. There's the sound of his belt buckle and then his jeans zipper. He pushes his thigh between her legs to widen her stance.

"Tell me you missed me," he says, his voice rough in her ear, his hands lightly stroking her breasts that have gotten so sensitive these past months. "That you *need* me." His cock presses hard at her center.

"I missed you," she says, then swallows, gasping as he enters her, but then pulls out again.

"What else?" He breathes. "Tell me the rest. Convince me."

She moans a little, moving her hips to press backward into him. "I *need* you."

"That's right," he growls. "You do." And then he pushes into her all the way, thick and long. Nina gasps, dizzy, as desire rushes through every limb.

Brody isn't in a hurry though. He takes her slow and hard, both of them panting and groaning with every stroke. She pushes her ass against him, her hands pressed against the wall. They're making so much noise, she hopes none of her neighbors are walking by.

He slips his fingers between her thighs, circling her clit, and Nina reaches down to grab his wrist, holding him there.

When she comes, it's a storm overtaking her. Thunder and lightning. She's out of her mind, gasping his name and begging him not to stop.

Brody's control breaks. "Oh *shit*," he groans. He moves faster and harder until the storm overtakes him too, so they're caught in this hurricane together.

"Wow," she says afterward, sagging against the wall. She slides her hand over her belly. "I think my orgasms are stronger now."

Brody is still pressed against her back, basically holding her up. "I guess there have to be some perks to being pregnant." He's still catching his breath. "Or maybe it's that you're with the right man."

She smiles over her shoulder at him. "That must be true."

He kisses the top of her shoulder and then turns her around in his arms. "Tell me you love me."

She strokes his jaw. "I love you."

"I love you too."

They gaze at each other, and she wonders how she ever got this lucky. It seems like her whole life has been nothing but a series of wrong men. Even the one she thought was right turned out to be wrong.

"What are you thinking about?" he asks.

"Just how good you are for me. I hope I'm good for you."

He strokes her cheek and then her neck. "Of course you are."

"You're so good that you even brought me snacks," she says with a smile, gesturing to the bag of groceries on the floor.

"Shit!" Brody steps back and quickly pulls his pants up. "There's ice cream in there."

"There is?" She laughs and struggles a little to bend down and get her pajamas. "Well, it's probably melted now."

"Here, let me get that for you." Brody reaches down for her

pajama bottoms and panties. Then he kneels and patiently helps her get dressed while she holds on to his shoulder for balance.

"What kind of ice cream is it?"

"Snickerdoodle with coconut milk."

"Oh *no*, that's your favorite."

He shrugs. "It's probably fine. Or I'll just get another one tomorrow."

Nina gazes down at the top of his shiny black hair, and happiness flows through her, lighting her up inside. She's so relieved Brody is here, and their terrible fight is over.

While he deals with the bag of groceries, she goes into the bathroom to pee and clean up, changing into a pair of fresh panties.

They spend the rest of the evening in bed, hanging out, watching a movie, and being cozy together.

He tells her about his week at the garage and how Jackson asked for Summer's number.

"Wow, really?" Nina feeds him a spoonful of the snickerdoodle ice cream, which turned out wasn't too melted. She's gotten to know Summer a bit more since she's usually there when they go in for her midwife appointments. "I wonder if she's going to call him."

He snorts. "I warned her what he's like, and that he's basically a player."

"He's really cute though."

Brody chuckles and gives her a glance. "Oh? Is that right? Well, I know you like them young, but I think Jackson might be a little too young even for you, Nina."

She laughs and smacks his arm. "That's not what I meant."

"Sure it isn't."

She rolls her eyes and eats a spoonful of ice cream. "Actually, how old is Jackson?"

"Wouldn't you like to know."

"That's it," she teases, holding the container to the side. "You're not getting any more of this. I hope you're happy with yourself."

"And here I was thinking I'd be your only boy toy." He scoffs with mock injury and crosses his arms. "Little did I know you'd be throwing me over for a younger model with an Australian accent."

She leans in and kisses his lips. "Don't worry, you can be my boy toy forever."

He raises a brow. "Do you promise?"

"With all my heart."

"All right." He grins. "Now give me some more of that ice cream before you eat it all."

They talk some more. He asks how her week went, and she tells him things have been busy at work since they've started moving into the new location in Fremont.

"Anything else going on?"

She thinks about Noel calling and texting her, and she wants to tell Brody, but she worries he'll freak out. She doesn't want to risk another fight right now. "Not really. Except I missed you."

He reaches for her hand. "Me too."

Later, when they've turned the lights out and Nina is drifting off to sleep, she hears Brody say something.

"You know I'd never cheat on you, right?"

Her eyes open, staring into the shadows of her bedroom. "I know."

"Because that shit with Claudia was crazy. She's got issues."

She turns around to face him. It's dark, and she can just barely make out his features. "Believe me, I get it. I had to put up with her for years."

"Noel betrayed you, but I'm not like that. Those two are lost or something."

Nina moves closer and slides her arms around his neck. "They are."

"I couldn't live that way." He shakes his head. "I don't know how they can even look at themselves in the mirror every morning."

She's caressing the back of his neck, and that's when she suddenly feels a flutter in her belly. "Oh, wow."

He pulls back. "What is it?"

"The baby just moved! It's kicking me." She grabs his hand and places it against her stomach. Sure enough, there's another flutter. "Did you feel that?"

"Holy shit. Yeah, I did."

"That's the first time I've ever felt it move," she whispers in awe.

Brody still has his hand against her stomach when it flutters again. "Damn, I think our little Bullet is going to be an ass kicker."

Her eyes fill with happy tears. "I never thought I'd be pregnant. Never. This whole experience has been so powerful."

"It's been pretty amazing from the cheap seats too."

"Thank you for being a part of this." She leans in to kiss him, then strokes his jaw. "I don't know what I'd do if you weren't here to share this with me."

She senses him smiling in the dark. "Come here, Nina banana." He kisses her again, and then he lies down and holds his arm out so she can snuggle against him. "I'm glad I'm here too."

CHAPTER TWENTY-FIVE

> ### Life & The Art of Automobile Maintenance
> #### By Brody Austin
>
>
>
> *"There are certain diagnostic tests a mechanic might run to search for problems with your vehicle."*

"You were right about Emily," Noel says. "She was too young for me. I never thought I was susceptible to a midlife crisis, but apparently I was wrong about that."

Noel has been texting and calling Nina every week for the past month. She's ignored them all, and the only reason she answered her phone this time was because he texted asking her to pick up, saying it was urgent.

"You know Claudia and I married young," he continues. I never really sowed any wild oats, but I'm done with that now."

"You said there was something urgent?" Nina asks, irritated.

"I can't believe I finally met the love of my life, and I screwed it up so badly."

She rolls her eyes. "Oh, I don't know. Emily might take you back."

He sighs. "You know damn well I'm not talking about Emily."

"Why did you call me, Noel? None of this sounds urgent."

"I'll get to that. First, tell me how you're doing. How is the pregnancy going? You're in your sixth month now, right?"

Nina has to admit she's surprised he knows that. He must be paying closer attention than she thought.

She rubs a hand over her growing bump. "Yes, that's right." She and Brody started taking birth classes a few weeks ago.

"And is everything okay with you and the baby?"

"I'm fine. The baby's been getting active lately." She hesitates sharing this, even though he is the father. In her mind, she's started to think of Noel more as a sperm donor.

"That's great. So you're feeling movement. When will you find out the sex?"

"When she's born."

"So you're waiting for the birth." He chuckles. "Well, that should be exciting. You know, Claudia and I did that with our youngest."

"Yes, I know." Unfortunately, she knows all about his and Claudia's marriage and their kids' births.

"Of course you do." He goes quiet. "Can I ask you something, Nina?"

She sighs, staring at the computer screen in front of her at work. "Will it be quick? Because I have a meeting to get to, and you still haven't told me what's so urgent."

"How long are we going to play this charade?"

"Charade?"

"Yes, how long do I have to grovel before you finally take me back? I've told you how sorry I am. I know I made a huge mistake, but it was just *one* mistake."

"One mistake? You can't be serious."

"It's not like I had numerous affairs. I never cheated on you before that, and I never will again. Yes, I made a terrible mistake, but the truth is I still love you, Nina."

She goes silent.

"And now we're having a child," he continues. "Don't you think this kid deserves both of its parents together? A real family? Just imagine it, how good it could be."

She feels a wave of nausea listening to him. She closes her eyes and takes slow breaths. It all sounds so reasonable. But Noel is good at spinning the truth, good at making a bunch of crap sound reasonable.

"I'm not in love with you anymore."

"You can't be serious about this boyfriend," he goes on as if she hadn't spoken. "What is he, a mechanic? Claudia says he made a pass at her at the wedding reception."

Nina tries to stay calm. Brody's right. These people are lost. "Claudia is a liar, but then you already know that because you were married to her." She takes another deep breath. "I want you to stop calling me, Noel. Stop texting me. Stop pretending this is urgent. I'm not putting on a charade."

"At least let me see you in person. I *miss* you, Nina. Give me the chance to make this right. Don't we owe it to each other and to our child to fix this?"

"There's nothing to fix. I want nothing more to do with you. Just leave me alone." She hangs up the phone. Then she closes her eyes, rubs her belly, and reminds herself that she's tough. "Don't worry, Elsa. I'm going to do everything I can to surround you with love."

Nina does her best to put Noel out of her mind as she goes to meetings all afternoon. In tandem with moving to a new location, she's still setting up her marketing team. Happily, Davis will be joining them soon.

It's Friday, and she and Brody have plans to meet his cousins and their spouses at a Mexican restaurant in Wallingford. Obviously she's met Blair and Road, but she's never met Tori and Liam, though she's heard a lot about them.

Nina has to admit she's nervous. These people are close to Brody. Road and Liam are two of his best friends. If they don't like her, it's going to make everything so much harder.

Since they're both coming from work, she and Brody are taking their own cars. Unfortunately, she's already running late and texts him from her office to let him know she'll be there soon. Luckily it's not far to drive. She grabs the two bags of products she put together for Blair and Tori and heads out the door.

It's spring finally, and the air smells green from all the deciduous trees near the building's entrance. As she heads toward the parking garage, checking her phone, someone approaches on her left.

"Nina."

She turns and is dismayed to discover it's Noel. "What are you doing here? Are you stalking me?"

"I wanted to see you in person. Can't we go someplace quiet and talk?" He's wearing a dark blue suit with his Burberry raincoat, and it looks like he came from work.

"I don't want to talk to you. Leave me alone." She walks away, but he follows.

"Just give me ten minutes. That's all I ask."

"Look, I have somewhere to be, and I'm already running late."

"Then agree to meet me another time."

She shakes her head. "I've got nothing to say to you. It's over between us."

"Just so you know, I'm planning to pursue joint custody when this baby is born."

"*What?*" She abruptly stops as ice water floods her veins. "What the hell are you talking about?"

"Just what I said." He motions at her stomach. "This child is mine too. I have legal rights."

A protective fury like she's never experienced takes hold of her. "What the *hell*, Noel? It was only a few months ago that you were telling me you wanted nothing to do this with this baby!"

"Look, calm down. I'm not trying to upset you. Just meet with me so we can talk, okay?"

"You're threatening to take away my child, and you want me to calm down?"

He smiles. "Come on, Nina. It's *me*. Noel. I'm not some stranger. I'm sorry I'm upsetting you. Maybe I'm not stating all this very well. I'm a good father, and you know that."

She doesn't say anything because it's true. Throughout the time she's know him, he's always put his kids first. She's seen him skip important client meetings if they interfered with something he'd already promised one of his children.

"How does breakfast tomorrow morning at Roberto's sound?"

Roberto's is a cozy cafe near her condo where they used to eat breakfast regularly when they were together.

"All right, fine," she hears herself say. "I'll meet you there at nine."

Then she walks off, her stomach churning. *Did I really just agree to meet Noel?* But she doesn't know what else to do. If he's really considering joint custody when this baby is born, then she needs to talk him out of it.

"It looks like Nina's running a little late," Brody says as he reads her text. He's sitting at a table in a Mexican restaurant with Road, Blair, Tori, and Liam. It's taken a while to get this dinner set up, since everyone had babysitters and work schedules to maneuver around.

"I'm looking forward to finally meeting her," Tori says, dipping a chip into a bowl of salsa. "I feel like I've heard so much about her. It's weird that we haven't met yet."

Brody grins. "You'll like her. Nina is cool."

"How far along is she now in her pregnancy?" Blair asks.

"Six months, almost seven. She has her seven-month midwife appointment next week."

Everyone nods, and he notices how they all gently sidestep the fact that this baby isn't his, yet he's obviously very much involved. Brody can't explain it, but he's grown an attachment to little Bullet or Elsa. He doubts any of them would understand it. He's not sure if he even understands it himself.

Road tells them all about his trip to London. He's a travel blogger and attended a conference there recently. He describes how hard it was being away from Ava for the first time. "I was gone almost two weeks. I worried she'd forget who I was."

Blair smiles. "We did FaceTime almost every day. She definitely didn't forget you."

As they continue to talk about various things, Brody finally sees Nina making her way toward the table. Her blonde hair is shiny and long, and she's wearing a classy blue knit dress with black boots. Her baby bump is really noticeable now. She's carrying her purse and what appears to be a couple of gift bags.

She looks as pretty as always, though as she gets closer, he can tell something's wrong.

"Hi," she says when she arrives at the table. "I'm so sorry I'm late."

Brody stands up and gives her a kiss. "Hey, Nina banana."

She smiles at him, and he can definitely see she's upset about something but is trying to hide it.

They both sit down, with Nina taking the empty chair next to his.

Brody introduces Tori and Liam. Nina smiles and tells them both how it's nice to meet them.

The women ask about her new job, since Brody told them about it earlier.

"Oh, the job is great," Nina says. "And that reminds me, I brought you both some gift bags." She reaches under the table to pull out two gold-and-white bags with the Suds & Honey logo on them, handing one to each of the women. "I thought you might like to try some of our products."

"Samples?" Blair asks.

"They're mostly full-sized, though I threw in some samples too. If there's anything you like in particular, let me know, and I can get them for you at a discount."

Brody laughs watching Tori and Blair squeal with delight as they pull out all kinds of soap, lotions, creams, and potions. He glances at Nina, who's smiling. He has to hand it to her. This was smart.

"Oh my *God*, smell that," Tori says to Liam, sticking a container under his nose.

He takes a whiff. "Smells good."

"Is that the lemon coconut butter? I love that," Nina says. "I've been using it on my belly to help with stretch marks."

Blair is rubbing some kind of lotion on her arms. "Oh wow, this is great. My skin gets so dry from being around ovens all day. I've been meaning to try this brand. Everybody's been raving about it."

"Well, that's great to hear. I'm head of marketing, and word of mouth is king, or at least *queen*," she says with a laugh. She looks over at Road and Liam. "I threw a couple of our products for men in there too. There's some shaving cream and some non-girly skin moisturizer."

"Oh, I see it." Blair pulls out a tube of shaving cream and hands it to Road. Brody recognizes it since he's started using it himself. His whole bathroom has been taken over by Suds & Honey.

"That's good stuff," he says, rubbing his jaw. "Really helps with ingrown hairs."

Road and Liam join in with the sniffing and inspecting of the various products, and the energy at the table is lively. At some point, the waiter comes by, so they all grab their menus to order.

Even though Nina is smiling and talkative, Brody can tell something's not quite right. She told him before tonight that she was nervous about meeting everyone, so he hopes that's all it is.

As the dinner progresses, he's happy to see that Nina fits in well. The conversation flows smoothly. And since Blair and Tori recently had babies, there's lots for them to talk about with Nina.

At one point, the women all go to the bathroom together, which Brody figures is a good sign.

"She's great," Liam says with a nod, sipping his ice water. "Now that I see you guys together, I get it."

Road pops a tortilla chip in his mouth. "Nina definitely seems cool."

Brody nods. "We're different, but it really works."

The women come back from the bathroom and take their seats. Everyone's debating whether or not to get dessert when Nina's phone pings. She glances at the display and her face changes.

"What is it?" Brody asks. "Everything okay?"

"It's Suzy. She says I need to call her and that it's a 'code red.'" Nina glances around the table. "I'm so sorry, but that's my sister. I'm going to have to see what's going on. A code red usually means there's something up with our parents."

"Of course," Blair says, and everyone nods in agreement. "Go call her."

Nina puts her napkin down and gets up, touching Brody's shoulder as she leaves. "I'll be back in a few minutes."

As soon as she's gone, Blair and Tori are all over him.

"We *love* her!" Tori says. "I was so worried over nothing!"

"You were worried?" Brody asks.

"She's fantastic," Blair says in agreement. "We really like her. She's smart and funny, and she seems down-to-earth."

"And I can tell you guys are good together." Tori nods. "I'm so happy."

"Well, I'm glad to hear that," Brody says.

"So now we have to ask you something." Blair gives him a sly smile. "It's this thing we have called the Bandito Test." She glances at Tori. "Though in this case I guess it's the *Bandita* Test instead."

Tori seems to consider this. "Hmm, I believe you're right. That makes sense, since this is from the guy's point of view."

Meanwhile, Liam is shaking his head with amusement. "I can't believe you guys are still doing this."

Road chuckles, eating more chips and salsa. "This should be interesting."

"What's a Bandito or a Bandita Test?" Brody asks, bewildered.

Blair leans forward. "It's something we came up with years ago to help us distinguish the right guy from all the losers out there."

Then she explains, "If you were kidnapped by a group of dangerous banditas, would Nina rescue you, even if it meant she might be killed in the attempt?"

"Would Nina rescue me?" he asks, trying to get this straight. "Even if she could be killed?"

"Of course, she wouldn't be pregnant in this scenario," Tori clarifies.

Brody strokes his jaw, trying to imagine the scene Blair and Tori have laid out. "Now what do these banditas look like exactly?"

Road and Liam laugh.

"What's that got to do with anything?" Blair asks.

Brody shrugs. "I don't know. If they're hot, I might not want to be rescued. At least not for a while. What are they wearing?"

"They're not hot!" Tori says. "They're evil, and they're going to cut you into little pieces."

He leans back in his chair. "For some reason I can only picture hot banditas. They're all wearing tight leather clothes and serving me ice-cold Mexican beer."

By now Road and Liam are full on cracking up.

"I don't think you're taking this seriously," Blair says. She frowns at Road. "Stop laughing. You're just encouraging him."

Brody grins. He can't help himself.

"Come on," Tori says. "Pretend this is for real. Would Nina rescue you, or would she be cowardly and leave you to whatever terrible and excruciating fate awaits you with the banditas?"

He takes a sip from his beer and puts it down, then forces a straight face. "Okay, that's easy to answer. Nina would rescue me."

"She would?" Tori says with an excited note in her voice.

"You're sure?" Blair asks.

"Positive. You don't know Nina that well, but trust me, she's tough. She'd figure out a way to get me out of there."

Tori and Blair glance at each other, both of them grinning.

"Well, congratulations," Blair says. "Nina has passed the Bandita Test."

Tori nods. "We give you two our full blessing."

Later that night, when Brody is staying over at Nina's place, he tells her about the test from Tori and Blair.

"Bandita Test?"

He nods and then explains the whole thing to her.

"Of course I'd rescue you," she says. "You poor thing. I'm not going to let you suffer at the hands of a bunch of hot banditas who are forcing you to drink your favorite Mexican beer."

He grins. "Maybe I should start calling you Nina bandita."

She laughs. "Please don't."

"I could find you some tight leather maternity clothes, and you can serve me an ice-cold Tecate. What do you say?"

She rolls her eyes and then kicks him with her foot. They're sitting on the living room couch facing each other with the full view of the city shining through her floor-to-ceiling windows.

"So now you're supposed to take the test too," he says. "You have to ask yourself whether I'd rescue *you* if you were kidnapped by a group of banditos."

Nina smiles. "I don't have to even think about it. I *know* you'd rescue me."

He nods with approval. "Hell yeah, I would."

The two of them grin at each other.

"That was fun tonight," Nina says. She's lying back on the couch, sliding her hand over her belly. "Everyone was really great. I'm so glad I got to meet Tori and Liam finally."

"They said the same thing about you."

"Really? That's nice."

Brody smirks. "And I noticed that bribing them with fancy soaps and lotions isn't beneath you."

She laughs and pretends to act innocent. "I don't know what you're talking about. I was just giving them some products to try. I figured it would be a good icebreaker."

"You figured right. It was ingenious." He's watching her. "What happened with Suzy's phone call anyway? Was everything okay?"

"It's fine." Nina closes her eyes, then opens them to stare up at the ceiling. "Except my parents are flying out from Portugal in two weeks. They're talking about moving back to Seattle."

"I can't say I blame them. They have two, soon to be three, grandchildren here."

She sighs. "That's true, and I know they want to help, but you don't know how overbearing they can be."

"Hopefully it'll be all right. I'm actually looking forward to meeting them."

"You are?" Her brows rise. "Why?"

"Because I want to know you better, and I think meeting your parents will give me the full picture."

She laughs and puts her head back again. "I hope you're right, and they don't just wind up insulting you. Unfortunately, they're still hung up on Noel." As soon as the words leave her mouth, her expression changes, like a shadow passing over her face.

"Hey, what is it?" he asks with concern.

She shakes her head. "Nothing." She tries to smile. "I think I'm just tired. It's been a long day. I should probably go to bed soon."

He strokes her leg. "You can talk to me about anything. You know that, right? I mean, you've seen what I've been dealing with. No one outside my family knows how bad it gets with Thunder." It occurs to him that because Nina knows, it makes her feel like family.

She meets his eyes, and for a moment, he gets the sense that she wants to tell him something.

"What?"

But then she shakes her head. "It's nothing." She glances toward the windows. "I have a breakfast meeting tomorrow morning, so I'm going to have to kick you out of here early."

"On a Saturday?" He picks up her foot and massages it. "I hope you're not working too much."

She groans with pleasure. "That feels so good. You have no idea."

He grins. "Yeah?"

Nina closes her eyes and appears to sink back into the couch. "Please don't ever stop."

He chuckles as he finishes one foot and moves on to the next one with her moaning the whole time. Her eyes slide open, and she lies there watching him. "You're so good to me, Brody. And so good *for* me."

He shrugs. "It goes both ways." He thinks about how encouraging she's been with him opening a second location for Seattle Motor Works. She treats it like a reality and not a dangerous pipe dream. She even found him a lawyer who specializes in small businesses to look over all the paperwork when he applies for the loan so he doesn't miss anything.

After he finishes massaging her second foot, she's smiling at him drowsily. "I can barely keep my eyes open."

He yawns and nods in agreement. All that socializing, while fun, kind of wore him out. He gets up from the couch and holds his hand out to her. "Come on, Nina bandita. Let's go to bed."

The next morning, Brody wakes up at seven. He never bothers to set an alarm on his phone since he typically wakes up at the same time, no matter what. When he glances over, Nina is still asleep.

He doesn't wake her though, just throws on his clothes from yesterday and goes into the kitchen to make himself coffee. He peels a banana and eats it while standing in the living room staring out at the view. It's hypnotic. There's something about being surrounded by high-rises while watching boats on the water that's hard to resist.

As he's standing there, he hears a little pinging sound and notices it's Nina's phone. Apparently she left it on the coffee table all night. He glances down, wondering if the message has to do with her work meeting this morning.

Except his eyes catch on the sender and his blood runs cold. It says *Noel*.

Brody blinks at it. *What the hell?*

He grabs her phone off the coffee table. He can't open it, but he doesn't have to, because Nina's texts scroll on her lock screen.

I wanted to let you know that I'll be a few minutes late for breakfast. How about we meet at 9:45 instead? I'm looking forward to seeing you again.

He stares at the message from Noel in disbelief. *This can't be right.* His heart hammers in his chest. But then he tells himself to calm down. There has to be a reasonable explanation.

Brody takes a deep breath and goes into the bedroom, bringing the phone with him. Nina's still asleep.

He sits next to her on the bed. "Nina," he says, sliding his hand down her arm. "Wake up, I need to talk to you."

She blinks her eyes open. "Brody?" She turns to glance at the window. "What time is it?"

He holds up her phone. "You left this on the coffee table last night."

"I did?"

He studies her face. "Noel texted you this morning about meeting him for breakfast." He tries to keep the accusation out of his voice. "You want to tell me what the hell is going on?"

CHAPTER TWENTY-SIX

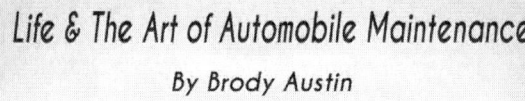

By Brody Austin

"Problems with your vehicle may arise when you least expect it. Try to remain calm."

"Oh no." Nina sits up in bed. Just a moment ago, she'd been in a deep sleep, but now it feels like someone threw a bucket of ice water over her. "It's not what you think."

Brody's face looks like he's wearing a mask. She can see he's upset, but that he's trying to control himself. "Then how about you explain it to me."

She rubs the sleep from her eyes and sits up fully. "Noel showed up at my work last night when I was leaving. He told me he plans to pursue shared custody once the baby is born."

"He wants custody? I thought he didn't give a shit about this baby."

"Well, apparently he's changed his mind." She shakes her head. "Or he's just saying that. But that's why I agreed to meet with him. I need to talk him out of it. I'm not letting him take my baby!"

Brody nods, but she can see the gears in his mind turning. "Why didn't you tell me about this last night?"

"Why do you think? Because I knew it would upset you."

"I'm upset because you kept this from me." He studies her. "So that's why you seemed off when you showed up for dinner last night. It makes sense."

"I told him I'd meet him for breakfast. I didn't know what else to do."

"You're not meeting him for breakfast." He scoffs. "No way is that happening."

"I have to go. If I don't meet him, he's just going to keep hounding me."

"Hounding you? What do you mean?"

She sighs and then leans back against the pillows. Her mouth tastes metallic from dread. What a terrible miscalculation on her part. She realizes now that she should have told Brody what was happening all along. "There's more I haven't told you."

"Like what?"

"Noel's been calling and texting me since the wedding."

Brody's mouth drops open. "He has? And you never thought to mention this?"

"I was hoping he'd get tired of it and stop. I mean, I want nothing to do with him."

"So you've been talking and texting with him this whole time? Seriously?"

"I've mostly been ignoring him. Except, well...."

"What?"

She licks her lips. "This is going to sound bad. Please don't get upset, but he wrote a letter of recommendation for me before I got hired at Suds & Honey."

"I don't believe this." He bends over and rubs his hands over his face. "Jesus. I can't believe you've been keeping all this from me."

"I'm sorry, Brody. I know I should have told you." She moves closer to him and slides her hand down his back. "After that big fight we had, I didn't want to have another one."

He shrugs her hand away. "Don't touch me."

"I want nothing to do with Noel. You *know* that."

"Do I?" He turns to looks at her. "This is really messed-up, Nina."

"Like I said, I'm sorry I didn't tell you about all this. I thought I was doing the right thing. But it's not my fault that he keeps contacting me."

"What exactly does he want?"

"What do you think? He wants me to come back."

"Are you thinking about going back to him?"

"No! Of course not."

"Then why hide it?"

"I just told you why, because I didn't want you to freak out. Exactly like you're doing now."

Brody stands abruptly and goes over to the window. He stares outside at the buildings across from them for a long moment. "I don't know if I believe you."

"Are you serious? You know what he put me through. I'd never go back to him."

He turns to her. "I also know you were deeply in love with him, and now you're pregnant with his baby. That's got to mean something to you."

"It doesn't. I'm not in love with him anymore." She gets up and goes to him. "You were still deeply in love with Kiera when I met you, remember?"

His brown eyes gaze into hers, and she can see he's hurt and conflicted. "I need some time to figure this shit out. I can't be around you right now."

"What? Don't go, Brody. Let's talk this out. I realize I made a mistake, but that's all it was."

But he's not listening to her. Instead, she follows him out to the living room, where she smells coffee. Glancing over at the kitchen, she sees his mug in the Keurig.

Brody goes to the front door and grabs his boots, shoving his feet into them without bothering to tie the laces. Then he grabs his coat from the rack.

"Please don't leave like this," she says. "Let's talk."

"I need to clear my head. I have to get out of here."

And then he's gone.

Tears burn her eyes, but she ignores them. Nina goes into the kitchen and dumps his coffee down the drain. She knows she screwed up, that she shouldn't have kept this from him. If the situation were reversed, she'd be upset too. But why run out like that?

She glances at the clock on the wall. It's eight thirty. She debates whether she should still meet Noel. The problem is she knows how tenacious he can be. Brody might not believe her, but if she stands Noel up, it'll just make things worse.

After taking a quick shower, she throws on some black maternity leggings and a long maroon hoodie. She's trying not to worry about the fight with Brody, but of course, it's all she can think about.

By the time she heads downstairs, it's nine forty-five, so she's already late when she arrives at Roberto's. She hasn't been here since she and Noel broke up, and one whiff of that familiar mélange of butter and sausage brings it all back. All the cozy breakfasts they used to share.

Noel has already gotten a table next to the window. One of their preferred spots. He smiles when he sees her, looking handsome wearing a zippered athletic shirt with long sleeves, his sunglasses on his head. A distinguished, middle-aged rich guy who keeps in shape.

"Nina, I'm glad you made it."

She takes the chair across from him but doesn't say anything.

"I just got here myself." He pulls the sunglasses off his head and exchanges them for some reading glasses before picking up his menu.

She picks up hers, though she's not exactly hungry, still too upset over her fight with Brody.

"Their menu hasn't changed at all," he says. "And they still have your favorite orange French toast." He looks at her over the rims of his reading glasses. "Or maybe you're craving something else this morning."

By the time the waitress comes over, Nina still hasn't said one word to Noel. He orders himself his usual eggs, sausage, and pancakes combination, along with a cappuccino.

Nina knows she has to eat, so she gets a bowl of oatmeal with fruit and a glass of orange juice.

"That's all you're having? That's not much food. You should be eating more than that."

"I'm not really hungry."

The waitress leaves, and the two of them sit in silence.

Nina takes a sip from her water.

"Would you like a bottle of Evian?" he asks. "I noticed they still have it on the menu."

She glances down at her perfectly good glass of water. It's been ages since she made a fuss about drinking expensive water, since she put on airs like that, and she realizes she only ever did it because it pleased Noel.

She doesn't reply.

He sighs. "What is this? You're just going to sit here and not talk to me the whole time?"

"You forced me into this."

He leans forward. "Come on, Nina. At least look at me."

She turns her head from watching the street traffic and meets his eyes. They're the same hazel shade she remembers. They haven't changed at all.

But I have. I've changed.

Nina thinks about how Brody always tells her that what's *real* matters. That you have to ignore the rest of it, ignore all the bullshit, because it's too easy to drown in it.

She takes a deep breath. "You know what, Noel? I'm not doing this. I've given you so many moments of my life. Some of them wonderful, and I'm glad for them, because they've made me who I am today. But you're not getting a single moment more from me."

"You don't mean that. I know you still love me, Nina." He gives her a knowing smile and puts his hand across the table toward her. "You're my golden girl."

Nina realizes there's a kind of freedom in tossing out the bullshit. "I don't love you anymore. And if you continue to harass me, you'll find out just how much I don't, because I'll take a restraining order out against you. Good luck explaining that to a judge when you try to get joint custody."

He's stares at her with a stunned expression, but she sees the truth as it works its way through to him. He leans back in his chair, the light in his eyes shuttered. "You really *don't* love me anymore, do you?"

"I don't. I've moved on, and you should do the same." She reaches around for her purse and stands up.

"What about our baby?"

She smiles and places a hand on her belly. "This little girl is going to be just fine. If you want to be a part of her life, then we'll figure that out. But you and I are done forever."

And with that, she walks away from Noel, out of Roberto's, and into the better life she knows she deserves.

"You really said all that to him?" Suzy's eyes are dancing with joy. She claps her hands. "I wish I could have been there to see it."

"It was pretty great," Nina admits. They're having a quick lunch at one of the artsy cafes near her work. "I finally realized that in a weird way, I was still under his spell, that he was still manipulating me."

"So what are you going to do about Brody?" Suzy asks, taking a sip from her latte.

"Go talk to him." It's been three days since their fight, and she had hoped to hear something from him by now. "I'm going to drop by there tonight."

"He seems so invested in you and this baby. I don't think he'd break up with you."

"I hope you're right."

After work that day, Nina doesn't bother to go home first. Instead, she stops at the grocery store to pick up some Tecate beer before driving to Brody's house. It's after seven, and she sees his black truck parked in the driveway.

She knocks, and Trevor opens the door, grinning when he sees her. "I'm sure glad you're here, Nina. Shit has been weird lately."

She steps inside, and they give each other a quick hug. "Is Brody around?"

"Yeah, he's in the garage working on the Lincoln. I don't know what's going on, but he's grouchy as hell. He hasn't said two words to me all week."

It pains Nina to hear this. She's noticed Brody can be quite taciturn when he's hurt or angry. "I'm going to go talk to him."

Trevor nods. "Good luck."

Nina brings the bag of beer with her and opens the kitchen door that leads to the garage. Right away she's surrounded by the smell of motor oil. The radio's playing Walk the Moon's "Kamikaze."

Brody's there, wearing jeans and a T-shirt, bent at the waist as he works under the hood of the Zephyr.

"Wow," she says. "This car is really coming along."

His head jerks up. "Nina?"

She smiles. "Hi."

He doesn't say anything for a moment. "What are you doing here?"

"I brought you a surprise." She holds up the bag. "It's that Mexican beer you like. I know I'm not an actual bandita, but I figured I'd try to fulfill at least part of the fantasy."

He glances at the bag. "Thanks. You can go ahead and put it in the fridge over there."

Nina takes the bag over to the small fridge Brody keeps in the garage that's stocked with soda, beer, and water bottles. She tucks in the six-pack of Tecate. "Can I offer you one?"

He considers it. "Sure, I'll have one."

It feels like a triumph as she brings him the bottle. "You should have seen the look the checker gave me when I bought these. It's like she thought I was planning to drink them myself. I'm surprised she didn't call the police."

He chuckles. "I'd come bail you out of jail."

"Would you?"

He meets her eyes. "I would."

She takes a step closer to him, resting one hand on the car. "I'm really sorry, Brody. I know I made a huge mistake."

He nods, then turns back toward the engine and is quiet for a long moment. "So what happened Saturday after I left?"

She knows he's asking whether she met with Noel. "I decided to meet with him."

He flashes her a look, and she can see on his face that it's not what he wants to hear.

She holds her hand up. "Please let me explain." Then she tells him what happened and how it was a cathartic experience, and how she realized Noel was still manipulating her.

Brody takes another sip of his beer, but it's like he's barely paying attention. He puts the bottle down on the tool cart. "Good for you."

"Noel finally understands. He's not going to keep harassing me. I told him if he did, I'd get a restraining order."

"I'm glad. Does he still want joint custody?"

"I don't know." Nina tells him everything that was said. "Obviously I can't stop him, but I doubt he's going to want to share custody." It's a hunch she has, but she doubts Noel is going to want to take care of a baby on his own.

Brody goes back to working on the car, and Nina stands there helpless, not knowing what to do.

"Should I leave?" she asks. "Is that what you want?"

He remains still then, staring at the engine. Seconds tick past, and she wonders if he's going to respond. Finally, he looks at her. "No, it's not what I want."

"Really?"

Brody stands up and reaches for a cloth to wipe his fingers. "I don't like feeling like I can't trust you."

"You can trust me."

He sighs and tosses the cloth back on the cart. "Come on, let's go inside the house."

They hang out for a while and watch TV with Trevor, who keeps giving them quick worried looks. She brought an overnight bag in case she was staying, and Brody was nice enough to go out to her car and get it. When they go to bed, they even have sex. It's good like always, and as a result, she relaxes, thinks maybe he's finally moving past being hurt and angry with her.

"I have my appointment with the midwife on Friday," she says afterward, feeling drowsy. "It's every two weeks now. Do you still want to come with me?"

Brody's lying on his side next to her with his head propped up. The only light in the room is the glow from the lamp on his nightstand.

"Of course," he says. He runs his hand gently over her belly, which has gotten quite large. "I want to make sure everything is good with you and little Bullet here."

Just as he says it, her belly moves. She laughs. "Oh wow, did you feel that?"

He grins. "I did. I guess he heard me."

Nina gazes up into Brody's face. So handsome and so kind to her.

She strokes his jaw. "I promise I'll never keep a secret from you like that again. Ever."

He nods but doesn't say anything more.

They go to sleep, and the next couple days seem fine on the surface. She texts him a few times during the day, and he always responds, but Nina still senses a distance in him. When they meet with the midwife for her eight-month appointment, he's as supportive as always. Summer is there and hugs them both hello. After peeing in a cup, Nina finally joins everyone in one of the birth center's gorgeous bedrooms.

"I'm really getting this pregnancy waddle down, aren't I?" she jokes as she climbs onto the bed. They listen to her baby's heartbeat with the fetal Doppler.

"I'll never get over how fast that is," Brody says. "It like he's running a race."

Tula tells them everything sounds good and, after gently feeling around Nina's belly, says she suspects the baby will probably weigh around seven to eight pounds when it's born.

"Oh, wow." Nina rubs a hand over her stomach. "So I'll be pushing out an eight-pound watermelon." In truth, she's a little nervous about the birth. At least she's been to both of Suzy's, so she has some idea what to expect.

Summer smiles and takes her hand. "Don't worry, Nina. Your body knows what to do."

Nina nods. She's grown quite fond of Summer over the past few months. She has a calm and capable presence about her and has already agreed to come to the birth.

After the appointment, Nina stands outside with Brody in the parking lot, since they came in separate vehicles.

"Do you want to come over tonight?" he asks. "Or we could go out to dinner and a movie."

Nina considers this. "To be honest, I think I'd rather stay in. I don't know if my back can take sitting in a movie theater for two hours."

Brody nods.

She studies him. "Is everything okay?"

"Sure, it's fine."

"Except I feel like it's not fine. Like you're holding me at arm's length." She wants to reach for his hand, but he's even standing too far away. "I know you're still upset. All I can do is promise that I'll never keep anything like that from you again."

He takes a deep breath. "Stop promising me that you won't do it again. It's not helping." Brody gazes across the street. "I grew up with a parent who was an alcoholic. Do you know how many times Thunder promised me he'd stop drinking?"

Nina's mouth drops open. "But this isn't anything like that."

"I have to be able to trust you. I don't like knowing that any time you want, you can pull the rug out from under me."

A knot of worry develops in her stomach. She licks her lips, afraid to ask the question that's on her mind. "Do you want out, Brody? Is that it? Is this too much for you?"

"That's not what I said."

She takes a deep breath. "Okay."

He massages his forehead. "Let's just drop this whole thing. Come over tonight, and we'll put it behind us."

Brody heads back to work in his truck. He knows he's being distant with Nina. Finding out that she was talking to the father of her baby behind his back has really done a number on his head.

It's made him realize the precarious position he's in. How vulnerable he is. If Nina decides to go back to Noel, there isn't a damn thing he could do about it. It's like he's finally starting to understand the thing that everyone was trying to warn him about in the first place.

This pregnancy isn't just happening to Nina. It's happening to him too. All the midwife appointments and birthing classes he's gone to. Before all this, he had a hard time ever picturing himself as a father. But somehow, over the course of these past months, he's begun to see the three of them—himself, Nina, and little Bullet—as a family.

It felt like his whole world was crashing when she told him she was in contact with Noel. It scared the shit out of him.

When he gets to the garage, he notices something unusual going on. Everyone's gathered around Anka, and they're all looking at something she's holding in her arms.

"Hey, what's happening?" he asks, walking up to the group.

Jackson turns to him. "Anka just found a kitten in the engine compartment of that Honda."

Brody's brows go up. "No shit. Alive?"

"Yeah," Jackson says. "Amazing, huh?"

"Damn, that doesn't happen every day." This isn't the first time he's seen an animal that's been hiding in an engine or its undercarriage, but sadly, they don't usually survive.

Anka is petting the little gray tabby. "He's a cutie, isn't he? I wish I could keep him, but I'm not allowed to have pets."

"Has anybody contacted the car's owner?" Brody asks.

"I called him," Chavez says. "He told me it's not his cat and that he didn't even know it was there."

"How long was the drive to get here?"

Chavez grins. "Ten miles, if you can believe it."

"Seriously? That little guy had quite a ride."

Anka's still holding the cat. "What are we going to do with him? Can one of you guys take him home?" Brody watches as the kitten tries to climb up her arm.

"My dogs would go insane if I brought this cat home," Chavez says.

Jackson scratches his head. "Yeah, I wish I could, but I'm not allowed to have pets either."

Everyone turns to look at Brody.

"What?" he says and then chuckles. "Uh-oh, did I just get a cat?"

Anka laughs. "Yes, you did."

She hands the squirming kitten over to him. He lifts the cat up and looks into his face. "Hey there, buddy, I guess you and I are going to be friends."

"What are you going to call him?" Chavez asks.

"I don't know." Brody holds the cat in his arms, petting him as he tries to climb onto his shoulder. "He obviously had one hell of a ride to get here. Maybe Rocket?"

Anka helps him find a box for the kitten, and he puts in a little dish of water. He figures he'll pick up some food and litter on the way home tonight.

Everyone goes back to work, but they're all in there constantly checking on Rocket. Brody puts one of his hoodies in the box so the cat has something soft to sleep on.

By the time he's ready to go home, everybody's checked on the cat at least ten times.

"He's getting so much attention," Brody jokes. " I might have to call him Rock Star instead."

When Brody finally makes it to the house, Trevor is home from work and has already heard about the cat from Anka.

"Let me see him, cuz." He peers down into the box. "Aw, damn, he's cute. Anka said you named him Rocket?"

Brody nods. "I thought it appropriate."

While Trevor pets and plays with the kitten, Brody goes ahead and sets up a litter box in the hallway and then dishes of food and water in the kitchen. He shows the cat where everything is and hopes he understands.

He got a couple cat toys at the store too and is playing with the kitten when the doorbell rings. "That must be Nina," he says, handing the toy over to Trevor. "She's not going to believe the story behind this cat."

There's a grin on his face when he goes to open the front door since he's looking forward to Nina's reaction to the kitten. Except when he opens it, it isn't Nina who's standing there.

It's Kiera.

CHAPTER TWENTY-SEVEN

Life & The Art of Automobile Maintenance
By Brody Austin

"Engine failure are two words that no car owner ever wants to hear."

Brody is stunned. For a second, it feels like he's hallucinating. "Kiera?"

She smiles. "Hi, Brody. I hope it's okay that I dropped by like this."

"Ah, sure." He stares at her, trying to process the fact that she's standing on his porch after not seeing her for two years. "You've just caught me by surprise is all. What are you doing here?"

"Visiting family mostly. Can I come inside?"

"Oh sure, sorry. Come on in." He steps out of the way to let her into the house. She walks past him, and he recognizes the beach-scented perfume she's always worn.

Trevor looks up in surprise from playing with the cat. "Wow, Kiera? Holy shit."

She laughs. "Hi, Trevor. It's good to see you. And who do you have there?"

"It's Brody's new cat."

She turns to him. "You got a cat? I don't believe it."

Then he remembers how she always wanted to get a cat or a dog when they lived together, but he didn't. He can't even remember what his reasons were anymore.

"Well, he sort of drove into my life." He explains how Anka found the cat hiding in the engine compartment of a car at work and that it survived a ten-mile drive.

Kiera sits down on the couch to pet him. "Wow, lucky kitty."

"Brody named him Rocket," Trevor says.

"That's a cute name."

Trevor keeps glancing up at Brody and then back at Kiera. He seems comically concerned.

"So how are things going?" Brody asks her. "How's your family?"

She tells him they're fine and describes what her various family members are up to. As she talks, he keeps staring at her. She looks different, yet the same. Her hair's longer than it was, and the color seems a darker blonde. Kiera was always curvaceous, and she appears to have slimmed down some. She's still attractive—that hasn't changed.

There's a strong sense of familiarity with her. Like a comfortable baseball mitt that you forgot about and recently found in your closet again. *Maybe not the most flattering comparison.* But her voice and mannerisms are coming back to him.

"What brings you here tonight?" he asks, knowing her well enough to know she wouldn't drop by for no reason.

"There's something I wanted to talk to you about." She glances at Trevor, who immediately gets the hint.

"Right! Well, I'm going to go in my room and play video games with friends on Discord." He gets up. "Nice to see you again, Kiera."

He gives Brody a worried look and heads off to his room. Brody glances over at Rocket, who's climbed on top of some couch cushions and has fallen asleep.

"His room?" Kiera asks after Trevor's gone.

"Yeah, he's been living here for a while, saving money for his own place."

"I'm surprised you're okay with that."

"Why wouldn't I be?"

She looks around the house. "I don't know. I just can't picture you taking on a roommate. You were so territorial about having your own space."

"Was I?" He tries to remember what she's talking about. "Well, I wasn't *that* territorial. Obviously you lived here for two years."

She grins. "That's true."

Brody remembers that smile. Those dimples. "So what's up?" He sits down on the other end of the couch from her. "Everything okay?"

"I heard you're involved with someone," she says, her voice light. "That she's a bit older than you?"

He nods, wondering where she heard that from. Probably his mom telling her mom, if he had to guess.

She looks around the house some more. "It's weird. Everything's the same but different somehow. I can't tell exactly what's changed though."

"What about you?" he asks. "You must be making lots of wedding plans."

She runs a hand over her jeans. "Not exactly. Scott and I have decided to call off the wedding."

This surprises him. "You have? I'm sorry to hear that."

"Are you?"

"Sure, of course. I always wanted you to be happy, Kiera. You know that."

She smiles. "Thanks, Brody. I do know."

"So what are your plans now?"

"I'm not entirely sure. We broke up, but Scott hasn't moved out yet. I've started looking for a job out here again."

His eyes widen. "I had no idea you were moving back."

She nods and meets his gaze. "I am. Or I'd like to. I've taken a month's leave from work right now to figure it out."

Brody takes this in and tries to decide how he feels about it. If this were nine months ago, he would have been elated.

"How serious are you about this woman you're seeing?" Kiera asks. "I understand she's pregnant by another guy?"

"That's true."

She licks her lips, and he can see she's nervous. There's a funny feeling developing in the pit of his stomach. "I was wondering if maybe we could spend some time together while I'm here. I've missed you."

He blinks, unsure what to say. It's weird because he fantasized this exact scenario in his head a thousand times after she left. Now that he's actually living it though, it's different than he thought it would be.

As he's absorbing this, the doorbell rings. His pulse jumps because he knows who it is.

Brody gets up off the couch to answer it. He feels Kiera's eyes on him. When he gets there and opens the door, of course, it's Nina.

"Sorry I'm running kind of late," she says, coming into the house carrying a grocery bag. "I got hung up at work, and then I stopped at the store to get hot sauce and more snickerdoodle ice cream. You'll be pleased to hear that I'm planning to eat them together tonight." She laughs but then stops when she notices someone sitting on the couch. "Oh, you have company?"

Brody nods. "This is Kiera."

He watches as Nina's eyes widen and flash over to the couch

again. "Hello," she says, a strained note in her voice. "It's nice to meet you. I'm Nina."

Kiera doesn't get up. "It's nice to meet you too."

"So you're out here visiting from Arizona?"

"Actually, I was just telling Brody that I'm moving back to Seattle. I was engaged, but that's been called off."

The two women study each other from across the room, and something seems to pass between them.

Brody has the oddest sensation that he's a passenger on a train just before it leaves the station. He glances over at Kiera and knows he can still get off this train if he wants. There's still time.

But when he turns back to Nina, something has shifted in her eyes. The two of them gaze at each other, and for a long moment, neither of them speaks.

Finally, she smiles softly. "I guess I'll be going then. I'm sure you two have a lot to catch up on."

Nina turns and leaves.

Brody stands there and doesn't do anything, doesn't say anything, frozen in place.

What the hell is wrong with me?

He shakes himself out of his stupor and chases after Nina.

She's almost to her car when he catches up with her.

"Nina. Stop."

She turns. "It's okay, Brody. I get it. Don't feel bad."

"What do you get?" He's not even sure if he gets it himself. "What are you talking about?"

"Kiera is back. You're going to get everything you ever wanted. I understand."

"And what about us?" He's breathing hard. His chest feels so tight that for a moment, he wonders if he's having a heart attack. "You, me, and little Bullet? You're saying that's over?"

"It is." She takes a deep breath. "I think we both always knew this wasn't going to last forever."

He tries to swallow, but his throat is closing up. "Look, I know I was pissed off recently, but I never said I wanted out."

"I know you didn't. You're a good man, and I know you're trying to do the right thing. So I'm going to do the right thing too. I'm letting you go."

"Are you serious, Nina? You're ending this? I thought we loved each other."

"I think we were both caught up in the intensity of everything. That's all."

He stares at her.

"We were never going to put a label on it in the first place, remember?" she says. "You don't owe me anything. We've been on this amazing ride together. But now it's time for you to go and live the life you were always meant to."

She walks over, opens her car door, and gets inside.

Don't go. The words are on the tip of tongue, but he doesn't say them, only watches as she drives off.

The train has left the station, and there's no going back.

Nina doesn't cry until she gets home. And even then she doesn't go overboard because she knows she has to stay strong, to be tough for this little girl growing inside her.

She keeps thinking about what Jeanie said when she was staying with his family on the reservation. That Brody would do the right thing, even if it was to his own detriment.

And I'm not going to allow that.

"It's over," she says to her sister on the phone. Her eyes fill with tears despite all her pep talks to herself about how tough she is.

"Over? What's over?" But then Suzy gasps. "Not *Brody*! You guys broke up?"

Nina nods and tries to catch her breath. "We did."

"I can't believe it. Over that business with Noel? Wow, I guess Brody's not who I thought he was if he'd break up with you over that."

"That's not it. I broke up with him."

"Why would you do that?"

Nina tells her how she went over to his house and Kiera was there. "You should have seen her, Suzy. She's gorgeous and young. Just perfect for him in every way."

"So she wants him back?"

"She didn't say it outright, but it was obvious. She even told me her engagement was called off and that she was moving back to Seattle."

"But how do you know he wants to go back with her?"

"Because he was crazy in love with her when I met him. He once told me letting Kiera go was the biggest mistake of his life."

Suzy seems skeptical. "But you guys are so good together. This just feels wrong."

"It's not wrong. It's the right thing to do." Her breath shakes. "But I sure will miss him." Nina starts to cry. She can't help it.

"I want you to come stay with us," Suzy says. "No arguments. I don't think you should be alone right now, especially since you're so far along."

For once, Nina agrees. It's probably best if she's not alone right now. "All right, I'll come over. Do you need to talk to Luke about it first?"

"Don't worry, he's fine with it. You're family."

Nina nods. Her brother-in-law is a great guy. Suzy lucked out when she met him.

After they get off the phone, Nina goes into the bedroom and digs her small suitcase out from under the bed. She's so hugely pregnant now that it's an athletic endeavor.

She hoists it on the bed and fills it with clothes and other items she'll need. When she goes into the bathroom to get more of her things, she notices the Suds & Honey shaving cream Brody's been using, along with all the other products she's had him try.

"I've never had such smooth skin or smelled so pretty in my whole damn life," he joked.

Nina knows she should toss it all in the garbage but somehow can't quite make herself do it yet.

Once she finishes packing, she grabs a jacket and makes her way down to the lobby, rolling her suitcase behind her. Jason is the doorman on duty tonight, so she asks him if he'd be nice enough to load her suitcase into her car when she drives it out front.

"You're not having that baby yet, are you?" he asks.

She smiles and places a hand on her belly. "Not yet. I'm just going to visit my sister for a little while."

Suzy lives in Magnolia, so it won't be too far for Nina to get to work on Monday.

As soon as she parks her Audi in their driveway, Suzy comes out to greet her.

"I'm so glad you're staying here." She gives her a hug. "Grace and Henry are going to be delighted too."

"Oh no, I didn't get them anything," Nina says with concern. She always likes to bring a little treat or a small toy when she sees her niece and nephew.

"Don't worry about that. Just come inside."

Luke comes out as well and hugs her. "Hi, Nina." He gives her a sympathetic smile. "Can I get your bag for you?"

Nina knows they're just being kind, but somehow all this sympathy is making her feel worse.

Eventually she's in their guest bedroom, unpacking her suitcase.

Suzy pops her head in. "Can I get you anything? Do you want some herbal tea?"

"I'm fine. But stop being so nice to me. Both of you. It's getting on my nerves."

Her sister comes over and sits on the bed. "Geez, fine. I won't be nice. Should I make you do the dishes? Actually, there's a load of laundry you can fold to earn your room and board."

"Well, you can be nicer than *that*."

"The master bathroom could use a good scrubbing. The kid's bathroom too. I'll make you a list so you can get started right away."

Nina throws one of her shearling slippers at her.

Suzy laughs. "Hey, that hurt."

"No, it didn't."

Suzy tosses the shoe aside. "Just so you know, I bought some breakup food, but I'm not sure if I'm going to share it with you anymore."

Nina glances over at her. "What did you get?"

"Ice cream, potato chips, and a pineapple upside-down cake."

"Do you have hot sauce?"

Suzy considers this. "I think there's some in the fridge. I'll have to check."

Nina smiles and reaches for her purse. "Never mind." She pulls out a bottle of her favorite brand, the *only* brand that satisfies her craving. "I brought my own."

Her niece and nephew are in bed, but Suzy lets her peek in on them before they head downstairs. Both of them are sleeping.

"They look like little angels," Nina says.

"I know," her sister agrees. "I could stare at them all night."

After that, they go down and join Luke where he's sitting in the living room, studying his laptop. Suzy asks him if he wants to join them in their breakup food bonanza.

"Sure," he says. "Bring it on."

The three of them wind up hanging out for the next couple hours, eating ice cream, cake, and chips, all of which Nina sprinkles generously with hot sauce.

"Well," Luke says, pushing his glasses up his nose. "I've heard about this craving of yours, but I haven't actually seen it in real life."

"I can't believe it's not giving you heartburn." Suzy watches in amazement as Nina puts more hot sauce on her pineapple upside-down cake. "Especially since you're so far into your pregnancy."

Nina shrugs. "I haven't had heartburn at all." She's relieved too, because then she'd have to give up her beloved hot sauce.

Unfortunately, all of this is reminding her of Brody and his continuous delight with her strange cravings. If he were here, he'd be taking pictures for sure.

"How's the nursery coming along?" Suzy asks. "Is it finished yet?"

Nina nods. Brody helped her clear all the junk out of her office so they could set it up as a nursery. She moved her normal desk and computer to the dining room. "It's nearly finished. The crib arrived a few days ago, and Brody just needs to build it." She stops talking as she realizes what she's saying.

"Luke can help," Suzy says quickly. "Or you and I can figure it out. Don't worry, we'll get it done."

"I don't mind at all," Luke says. "I'd be happy to build the crib for you."

Nina tries to smile, but the reality of Brody being out of her life is crashing over her like a tsunami. "Thanks," she manages to say. She swallows and tries not to break down crying in front of them. "I'd appreciate that."

Suzy and Luke are both studying her with sympathy again.

They thankfully change the subject. Luke talks about his job at Boeing, and then Suzy, who used to work as an accountant for a big firm, but now does it freelance and part-time, tells them about a new client who's a famous local musician.

Eventually, Nina yawns and tells them she's going to bed. Except once she's lying in bed, it's not easy to fall asleep. She keeps picturing Kiera at Brody's house. The way she looked sitting on that couch. Beautiful, perfect, and *not* almost nine months pregnant.

There's no way Brody isn't going to want her over me.

Even if he won't admit it.

She wonders how long it'll be before she gets over him, before she looks back on this time in her life like it was some kind of distant memory. A wonderful dream that she eventually woke up from. It only took her a few months to get over Noel, but that's because she had Brody to help her.

There won't be anyone to help her get over Brody.

But she also knows she'll have a new baby to care for and a great job, and somehow, life will go on.

As she tries to sleep, her mind won't quit. It wanders back to the holidays and staying on the reservation. She remembers the photo albums Jeanie pulled out for her with pictures of Brody dancing in his regalia as a kid. And then the ones of him at Thunder's house. Even though some of it was dark and unexpected, she's so glad Brody invited her into his life. That he let her see everything.

Nina spends the weekend hanging out and playing board games with Henry and Grace, relaxing with Suzy and Luke, and trying to tend to her broken heart.

Because even if the relationship with Brody wasn't meant to last forever, while they were in it, Nina can't deny that it felt just like the real thing.

CHAPTER TWENTY-EIGHT

Life & The Art of Automobile Maintenance

By Brody Austin

"Some high-maintenance vehicles are worth the price while others may not be. You have to evaluate the cost."

Brody notices it doesn't take long for him and Kiera to fall into the same old groove. It's weird, because it's only been a couple weeks and already they're hanging out at the same restaurants and shopping at the same stores.

"What do you think?" she asks him, holding up a blue tablecloth. "It's great, isn't it?"

"Sure," he says, glancing around. He'd forgotten how much time Kiera liked to spend shopping.

"You don't sound very excited about it."

"It's a tablecloth. How excited am I supposed to get?"

"I can't believe you forgot to get your mom a birthday present." She shakes her head. "Talk about last minute."

"I know." He feels like garbage already and wishes Kiera would quit rubbing it in. If Summer hadn't called to remind him, he would have forgotten about the dinner tonight altogether. Brody doesn't know what's wrong with him lately. He can't seem to focus.

"Do you think we should get it? Does she like using tablecloths?"

"I don't know."

"Well, you must have some idea." She's still holding it up. "Maybe we should get a different color."

"I'm sure it's fine." His eyes wander across the aisle and then stop on the baby stuff. He stares at it.

"I guess we'll just get the blue one then." Kiera glances at him. "I think she likes blue, right?"

He nods but is still staring at all the diapers, baby clothes, and nursery furniture. *Shit.* He sucks in his breath. *Who's going to build the crib for little Bullet's nursery?*

But then Brody reminds himself that it's not his problem anymore. Nina made sure of that when she dumped him.

He knows he's supposed to feel relieved that Kiera's back in his life, relieved that he's no longer tangled up with a woman who's having another guy's kid, but that's not how he feels.

Relief doesn't describe it.

Mostly he's pissed off.

Though sometimes—like now, when he sees all the baby stuff, or he thinks about Nina and some of her quirky habits—there's a strange tightness in his chest. His throat wants to close up, and he has to keep swallowing to make it go away.

The rest of the time, he's left fighting this anger. At least he's been good at hiding it from everyone. Going to work every day. And now going to his parents' tonight.

He hasn't told anyone in his family or at the shop about the breakup, but they all seem to have figured it out. At least no one's talking to him about it, which is a relief. Though he hasn't spoken to Tori or Blair yet, so who knows what they'd have to say?

Once they get back to the house, Kiera puts the tablecloth in a gift bag for his mom and fixes it up with a nice bow. He knows he should be thanking her more.

Instead, he sits on the floor and plays with Rocket, his new best friend, remembering all the strays he used to bring home as a kid. He still wishes Nina had a chance to meet this crazy cat. He already knows she'd be researching the best cat toys and food for him, probably trying to find a class for cat owners. He chuckles to himself, picturing it.

Kiera comes over and sits next to him on the floor. She's been throwing out a lot of hints lately about staying over. They've kissed a few times but haven't slept together yet. He hasn't wanted to, and the only reason for that is because he feels like he's cheating on Nina. Like that makes any sense at all.

Just one more reason to be pissed off.

"Do you want something to eat?" she asks. "It's still a couple hours before we go over to your mom's."

"Sure."

"There's pita bread and hummus, or I could make sandwiches."

"Hummus is fine." He starts to get up. "I'll get it."

"No, I've got it. Let me do it."

She gets up and goes into the kitchen, treating it like it's her own. It irritates him. This isn't her house anymore, and he wishes she'd quit acting like it was.

He decides to give Rocket a few cat treats and goes to get the bag from under the sink.

"You really like that cat, don't you?" Kiera says.

"Sure, what's not to like? He's great."

"I still can't believe you finally got a pet. You were always so against it. I guess this is the new improved Brody."

"I suppose." Rocket's already rubbing against his legs, meowing.

He knows all about the bag of treats. Brody sprinkles some onto a small dish for him.

They sit at the dining room table and eat while Brody checks his phone. There's an email from the bank where he's getting the business loan for his second location.

"Don't go on your phone, Brody. Talk to me," Kiera says.

"I have to take care of this. It's from the bank about the loan."

"Oh." She doesn't say anything more, just tears off some pita to dip into the hummus.

He types his response and cc's his lawyer. The bank's asking for underwriting paperwork that he's certain has already been sent.

"I'm surprised you're actually going through with that whole thing. Can you really afford it?" Kiera asks. "A second location seems so risky."

He puts his phone down. "I know you were always against me doing this, but I think expanding is a smart move."

She seems skeptical. "It's just that so many small businesses fail. You've been one of the lucky ones to be so successful. Why risk it?"

"Because I don't want to live my life from a place of fear," he says with more force than he intends.

Her brows go up. "Sorry. I guess I hit a nerve."

For a moment, he remembers how excited Nina was about him expanding. All the locations they scouted together. If anything, she saw him opening a second garage as a natural next step.

Eventually they head over to his parents' house. He hasn't seen his mom in a couple months, though they text and call fairly regularly. He already knows she's thrilled that Kiera's back since she invited her to this family-only birthday dinner.

"Happy birthday," Brody says to his mom when they arrive, giving her a hug.

"Thanks, honey. And who do we have here?" she says with a laugh when she sees Kiera.

"Happy birthday, Lisa. It's great to see you."

"It's been much too long," his mom says, hugging her. "Thanks for coming. And I understand you're moving back?"

Kiera nods. "I've started looking for a job. I'm staying at my parents' house until I find something."

Brody goes to the fridge to get himself a beer as Kiera and his mom continue to catch up with each other. He wanders over to the back and sees Summer outside talking to his dad, who's cooking on the grill.

He goes outside to join them.

"Hey, Brody," his dad says, and Brody gives him a hug too. "We were just talking about the baseball game next Sunday. You're coming with us, right?"

"Yeah, definitely." His dad always buys season tickets, and it was their thing when he was growing up. Brody bonded over baseball with his dad and then over cars with Thunder.

His dad motions to Summer. "Your sister says she's going to bring her new boyfriend."

"New boyfriend?" Brody turns to her. "Let me guess—Jackson."

"One and the same."

"Does he know he's your new boyfriend?"

Summer laughs. "Of course he does. What are you implying?"

"Nothing."

"Oh, how's your kitty doing? Jackson told me all about him."

Brody nods. "Great. His name's Rocket. And judging by the way he practically flies around the house, it fits him pretty well."

The three of them chat while their dad grills up steaks and burgers. When he leaves to go check on their mom, he hands Brody the spatula, and Summer practically jumps on him.

"What the heck happened between you and Nina?"

Brody flips the burgers one at a time and then the steaks. "We broke up." He tightens his jaw. "Actually, she dumped me."

"She did? I couldn't believe it when she told me you guys weren't together anymore. I thought you were so close."

He glances at her. "How is Nina doing? And don't say you can't tell me because of some patient confidentiality bullshit. Just tell me."

"She's doing fine. I can tell you that much. She's getting really close." His sister laughs a little. "Also, her parents are in town. They came with her to her last appointment."

"Really? How did that go?"

"They're nice enough. Kind of intense in a country club sort of way. Her dad tried to tip me twenty bucks after the appointment." She chuckles. "Maybe I should have accepted it."

Brody nods. "I know they kind of drive her crazy a little. How did she seem otherwise, besides the pregnancy? Does she seem okay?"

Summer is studying him. "Maybe you should call and ask her that yourself."

He's quiet for a moment. It's not like he hasn't thought of calling her. "What for?" he finally says, feeling pissed off again. "I know when I'm not wanted."

His sister glances over at the house. "So now you're back with Kiera? Is that what you want?"

He turns back to the grill and grumbles, "It's what everyone seems to think I want."

Summer studies him in a funny way, and it looks like she's ready to ask more questions, but Kiera steps outside on the patio to join them.

"Look at you," she says to him. "I've never seen you grill anything. Is this more of the new and improved Brody?"

"What are you talking about? I've grilled meat before."

"Not that I remember. You wouldn't even go near a stove, much less a grill."

Brody tries to think back to when they lived together. It was true Kiera did most of the cooking, but he's pretty sure he cooked sometimes. "You make me sound like I was an asshole."

"Not at all, but you were fixed in your ways. Stubborn and hated anything to do with change."

Summer laughs. "He's still kind of like that."

"That's not true." He thinks of all the changes he's gone through this past year but realizes there's no point in bringing that up.

When the food's finally done, the five of them sit outside at the table to eat dinner. His sister Autumn calls from New York, where she's still touring with her boyfriend's band, and they all pass his mom's phone around to talk to her.

After dinner, they sing "Happy Birthday," and then Kiera helps pass out ice cream and cake to everyone.

Brody watches her and knows he should be appreciating her more. The way she always fits in so easily with his family.

Nina's right. He's getting everything he ever wanted, isn't he? Shouldn't he be happy? The woman he once thought was the love of his life is finally back in his life.

So why am I not happy?

Later, Brody and his mom are alone for a few minutes outside. Summer and Kiera are chatting in the kitchen with his dad.

"I'm so glad you're together with Kiera again," she says, smiling at him. She's vaping—"Just one for my birthday," she told him. "I always had a feeling you two would wind up together in the end."

Brody takes a sip of his beer but doesn't reply.

"Don't get me wrong, I had nothing against Nina." She blows out a stream of smoke. "But she just wasn't right for you. That whole situation was wrong."

"Why?"

"What do you mean?"

"Why was the situation wrong?"

"You know why. Come on, Brody. Do I really have to say it? She's pregnant with another man's baby."

He glances around their backyard, the one he played catch in with his dad when he was growing up. "So what? I'd be helping to raise another man's child. Is that so wrong?" He motions his head toward the kitchen. "Isn't that what Dad did for me?"

His mother stares at him. She seems at a loss for words. "That was different. I wasn't pregnant when I met your dad."

He rolls his eyes. "Give me a break. I was two when you guys got married."

"Nina is also quite a bit older than you."

"You think I care about that?" He knows he's being rough on his mom—and on her birthday, no less—but he's fed up with people telling him what's supposed to make him happy. "Because I don't. I couldn't care less."

Her eyes widen. "I had no idea you felt so strongly about this."

"Yeah, well, no one seems to be asking me how I feel about anything these days."

"Oh my goodness, Nina! What are you doing?"

Nina glances up at her mom from where she's currently scrubbing the kitchen floor on her hands and knees. "Is that a trick question?"

"You're going to hurt yourself. You're nine months pregnant."

"Yes, thank you. I know how pregnant I am," she says, still scrubbing. Her belly is hugely in the way, and she's using potholders as kneepads to save them from the hard surface.

"Why don't you just use a mop?" her mother asks. "Wouldn't that be easier?"

"Probably." Except she doesn't think a mop cleans the kitchen floor as well as doing it by hand. She's become obsessed the past week with getting her condo clean and organized. She even organized underneath the bathroom sink, a place so dark and freaky she hadn't cleaned it in years.

Nina knows she's nesting. She's read about it in all her pregnancy books, and Suzy says she went through the same thing. It's what women do when they're getting close to having their babies.

Which is a good thing, because damn, is she ready to have this baby. She's never been so uncomfortable in her entire life. It's like she's walking around with a giant bowling ball strapped to her body twenty-four hours a day. She's so huge it's hard to do anything. Just getting up has become an ordeal. And that's not good, because she has to get up at least three times a night to pee.

Her mother steps past her, trying to get to the fridge.

"Just give me a minute, I'm almost done here," Nina says.

"Well, I need to pull the chicken out from the freezer. We have to eat at six so your dad can take his pills."

"I know." She sighs. Her parents have been staying with her since they arrived from Portugal, sleeping on the sofa bed in her living room. Normally they'd stay in a hotel, but because she's nine months pregnant, they thought it best to stay with her.

And that's where the dichotomy comes in. Because on the one hand, Nina's very grateful to have them here, but on the other, they're driving her crazy.

Her condo is too small for this many adults to be living in such close quarters. The only other option was for the three of them to stay with Suzy, but her house wasn't that big either.

Besides, Nina is having all these urges to scrub the shelves in her kitchen cabinets and dust the baseboards in her bedroom.

The nursery, at least, is all set up. Her parents wound up helping her put together the crib, or mostly her dad did it. Suzy threw her a baby shower a week ago and invited all her new friends from work, and a few of her old friends too. Nina likes to go into the nursery these days and touch all the little onesies and soft baby blankets.

"Do you think you'll be working tomorrow?" her mom asks.

"Yes, I do."

"I think you should go on maternity leave. I don't know why you're waiting."

Nina tries not to roll her eyes. This is the first part of the same discussion they have every single day. And every day Nina explains that, unless she goes into labor first, she's still working. Her official maternity leave doesn't start until next Monday. The irony is that she'll be working from home this last week. Her dad helped move her desk into the bedroom so she can shut the door when she needs to video conference.

"I'm perfectly capable of working," Nina says. "And the longer I can put it off, the more time I'll have with Elsa."

Her mom shakes her head. "I can't believe Noel turned out to be such an idiot. He should have been the one taking care of you right now."

And there's the second part of the discussion they have every day. "Well, Noel is no longer in my life. And good riddance to that."

"And what about this other man you were involved with. Brody? Where is he?"

This makes Nina pause. She sits back on her feet, surveying her clean kitchen floor. She tries not to think about Brody. "He's no longer in my life either."

"You're burning through men like kindling these days, aren't you?"

Nina glances up at her mom, who's smiling. "Did you just make a joke?"

"Yes, I did, sweetheart."

Nina grins. "I guess I'm burning through them fast because I'm so hot." She tries to strike a glamorous pose with her huge belly, and they both laugh.

Her mom shakes her head. "I remember when I was that pregnant with you. It was so uncomfortable that I worried it was never going to end."

Nina nods. "'That about sums it up."

The three of them have dinner at six like they do every night, and then her parents usually watch TV until bed. Sometimes Nina joins them for a little while, but usually she goes into her bedroom to read or surf the web. Sometimes she'll watch a movie on her iPad. What she tries not to do is think about Brody and how much she misses him. Because she misses him deeply. Brody has been part of this journey from the very beginning. All of it. And he never once let her down.

Just the thought of him makes her heart ache so much that it's almost unbearable.

Since her midwife appointments are every week now, at the last one, she finally broke down and asked Summer how he's doing.

"He's okay. I just saw him at my mom's birthday dinner recently."

"I take it he's with Kiera now?"

Summer nodded. "Between you and me, I don't know how long that's going to last."

"What do you mean?"

Summer shrugged. "It's just a sense I get."

Nina doesn't believe a word of it. She figures Summer was trying to spare her feelings. If she had to guess, Brody and Kiera picked up right where they left off. It hurts, but at the same she wants him to be happy more than anything.

In the morning, Nina gets up to take a shower, and then later, while she's in the kitchen pouring herself a bowl of cereal, her whole belly tightens. It doesn't hurt, but it's definitely something new and noticeable.

She immediately stops what she's doing and holds her stomach.

"What is it?" her dad asks, looking up from his phone. He's at the table where he's eating breakfast.

"I think I'm having Braxton Hicks."

"Braxton who?"

"It's a type of contraction."

"Contraction? Are you in labor?" He jumps up from the chair. "Well, that's it then! Let me get the car. You have a bag packed, right?" He yells for her mother, who runs out of the bathroom with soap on her face.

"What is it? My God, is the kitchen on fire?"

"She's having contractions. We need to get moving *now*."

Meanwhile, Nina is waving her arms like a traffic cop trying to stop him. She tells him it's not a big deal and that her midwife told her all about Braxton Hicks. "They're just false labor, that's all. They happen sometimes during the third trimester."

"Why would you think it's false labor?" her dad demands to know. "I've never heard of such a thing."

Her mom rolls her eyes. "Of course you have. You just don't remember."

"Maybe you should call someone anyway," her dad says. "Or we should take you to the hospital to be sure."

Nina slides a hand over her belly. "Let's just wait and see if I have any more. Braxton Hicks happen randomly. Real labor isn't random."

"I'm going to go rinse this soap off my face." Her mom turns and heads back to the bathroom. "Next time don't yell for me unless it's a real emergency."

Her dad sits back down at the table, though he seems as alert as a pointer dog. Nina has to admit it's sweet that he's so ready to take action.

She heads into the bedroom to start her first workday at home. Since she's head of marketing, her job involves numerous meetings, so she knows she'll be spending a good part of her day videoconferencing. As a result, she had a talk with her parents about it.

"Just pretend I'm at the office," Nina said. "Don't come into the bedroom for any reason, understand?"

They both agreed, acting annoyed that she was so vehement. "Of course we understand," they said. "What do you take us for?"

About two hours into her day, and twenty minutes into a meeting with her team about the summer campaign, her mom sticks her head in the door.

"Do you have any pickles? I can't find them, and your dad usually has pickles on his sandwich for lunch."

"I'm in a *meeting*," Nina says with annoyance. "Remember? I told you not to disturb me?"

"Okay, I get it. Just tell me if you have pickles or not."

"They're in the fridge on the second shelf. Now please don't come in here again."

Her mom leaves, and Nina apologizes to everyone on the video call. They all smile and say not to worry about it.

Five minutes later, her mom sticks her head in once more. "I found the pickles, but I don't see the mustard. I hope you have mustard, because I don't want to run to the store."

"Mom, as I just told you, I *can't* talk right now."

"Oh, sorry." She backs out the door. "I know you're busy. But do you have mustard?"

Nina grits her teeth. "I don't know."

An hour later, while she's in a meeting with two of the artists going over some new package designs, her dad opens the bedroom door. "Where's your wrench? I'm going to fix that drip in your bathroom sink."

She shakes her head, waving him away.

"I couldn't find a toolbox," he continues, like she isn't frantically waving at him to leave. "But you must have a wrench somewhere."

"Not now," she says, trying to keep her cool. "Let's discuss it later."

"Well, I don't think you should wait. Water going down the drain is like money going down the drain."

Nina smiles at her colleagues on-screen. "Please excuse me for a moment." She hoists herself out of her chair and goes to the door, walking outside with her dad. She asks him to follow her into the living room where her mom is and tells them both that they *have* to stop coming into the bedroom.

"What's the big deal?" he says. "You're just talking to someone on your computer. What's that called?" He turns to ask his wife instead of asking his daughter, who's standing right in front of him.

"I think it's called FaceOff? I'm not sure."

Nina tries not to roll her eyes. "I'm *working*. That's what you both need to comprehend. Am I going to have to go into the office this week because you two won't leave me alone?"

"Calm down," he says. "It's fine. We'll leave you alone."

She heads back to her bedroom, and Nina can hear both her parents talking about how pregnancy has made her hysterical.

"It's just all those hormones," her mom is saying. "They mess with you. Now, do you still want a sandwich for lunch?"

Brody still hasn't slept with Kiera, and he can tell it's bothering her. She keeps pressing herself against him, trying to get a reaction.

"I think you should invite me over tonight," she says in a sexy voice. They're standing in his kitchen together. It's been a week since his mom's birthday.

"I have to get up early. I'm having breakfast with my dad and Summer before we go to the game later tomorrow."

"So what? Don't you find me attractive anymore?"

He sighs. "Of course I do. I'm just going through something right now."

Kiera studies him. "It's about that woman you were involved with, isn't it? That's why you won't sleep with me."

He doesn't know what to say to this. He doesn't want to hurt Kiera's feelings, but he's not in a good headspace. And he has a strong sense that sleeping with her will only make it worse.

"Come on, Brody." She moves closer and slips her arms around his neck. "I've missed you all this time. Didn't you miss me a little?"

"Sure I did."

She pulls him down to kiss her, and he's surrounded by her beach-scented perfume. Except he doesn't want to smell the beach. He wishes he was smelling jasmine.

Abruptly, he pulls away.

"This isn't like you," she says, clearly irritated. "You've always been such a horndog, and now you won't even touch me."

It's true. His libido has taken a nosedive. It's just that emotionally he's not feeling any of this.

They study each other.

The front door opens, and he can hear Trevor and Anka coming inside the house.

"Hey, cuz," Trevor says when he sees them in the kitchen. "Do you mind if Anka and I play video games on the TV?"

"Go ahead." He glances at Kiera, who still seems irritated.

He wishes he could tell her to go home. He'd like to work on the Zephyr, but that's been the other problem lately. Kiera never seems to leave. She's always here. He's starting to wonder if maybe she's upset about breaking up with her fiancé and just wants the distraction of all this.

"Should we order pizza?" she asks everyone.

Brody shrugs. "I guess. I don't really care."

Surprisingly Trevor doesn't seem interested either. "Nah, we just ate," he tells her. "I'm not hungry."

Trevor meets his eyes but then looks away. He and Anka go into the living room. Brody gets the feeling that somehow he's let Trevor down, though he's not sure how exactly.

There's a meow, and Rocket rubs against his leg. He picks the cat up and lets him climb onto his shoulders, petting him.

"That cat is getting more affection from you than I am," Kiera says.

"What's that?" Brody glances at her.

"Nothing," she mutters.

Eventually he goes into his bedroom and picks up his guitar while Kiera makes herself something to eat. He's been learning how to play "Wonderwall" by Oasis. He was learning it as a surprise for Nina since it's one of her favorite songs. He's not sure why he's continuing to learn it, except that he's getting pretty good at it.

"That sounds great," Kiera says, coming into his room. She sits on the bed with what looks like a ham and cheese sandwich. He does a double take. She must have brought that cheese over and put it in his fridge herself. "I can't believe you started playing guitar."

He shrugs. "It's just something I've always wanted to learn."

"More of the new improved Brody."

"Stop saying that."

She takes a bite of her sandwich. "It's true though, isn't it? All these improvements. Though obviously you're still as grouchy as ever."

He remembers the way Nina always told him he was so good for her. It's like he was a different person when he was with her. Someone kinder, more fun, and less grouchy.

His phone buzzes on his nightstand, and when he reaches over to pick it up, he's surprised to see it's Summer calling.

"Hey, what's up?" He lays his guitar on the bed.

"Listen, I don't know if I should be doing this, but I'm going to do it anyway."

His brows crease with concern. "Do what?"

She hesitates. "Nina is in labor."

"She is?" He stands abruptly as his pulse skyrockets. "How long? Is she okay?"

"A few hours now. We're at the birth center. She's doing okay. She's fine, but I think...." Summer takes a deep breath. "I think you need to come."

CHAPTER TWENTY-NINE

Life & The Art of Automobile Maintenance
By Brody Austin

"Sometimes if you're lucky, you'll come across a car that is so amazing it changes your life."

Nina is in the kitchen after dinner. She's still hungry and is standing there eating cucumber slices with hot sauce when she feels a delicate pop between her legs and a gush of warm liquid.

She's wearing a sundress, and when she looks down and sees the puddle on the floor, she nearly drops the bottle of hot sauce. Her parents are on the couch watching Netflix.

"I believe my water just broke."

Her mom glances over. "What's that?"

Nina repeats herself.

Her mom gets up from the couch. "Your water broke?"

Her dad seems enthralled by the television but glances up. "What's going on?"

"Nina's water broke."

By now, her mom has come into the kitchen and is standing next to her. Her dad gets up to join them. "What does that mean? Do we go in now?" He sounds anxious. "Are you in labor?"

Nina strokes her giant baby bump. "I'm not feeling any contractions. I better call the midwife."

She goes into the bathroom to stuff a pad in some clean underwear and then gets her phone from the bedroom. She brings it into the kitchen and calls Tula to tell her what's happening.

"Are you having contractions?" Tula asks.

"No." She senses her parents watching her. Her dad has gone into pointer dog mode again.

"Well, then, get some rest. First babies usually take a while, so try and relax. Sleep if you can. You'll need your energy. Once you start feeling any contractions, let me know." She also explains that if she doesn't go into labor within twenty-four hours, then she'll have to give birth at the hospital.

Nina tells her parents what Tula said.

"We're not going to the birth center now?" her mom asks, looking up from where she's cleaning the spot on the kitchen floor where Nina's water broke.

"I think we should go in," her dad insists. "It doesn't seem right to do nothing."

Nina pours herself a glass of water from the fridge. "I'm not even having contractions yet. I'm going to do what Tula says and see if I can nap."

She lies down in bed and tries to rest. It's not easy though. Excitement and anxiety are coursing through her, making her a bundle of nervous energy. *My baby's coming.* She had her last day of work yesterday, so the timing is ironic.

Amazingly, she does nap a little, but then she wakes up when her whole belly area and lower back have tightened in a vise grip. It's brief and then goes away. She drifts into sleep some more, and then about fifteen minutes later, it happens again, the last one more intense and uncomfortable.

She immediately calls Tula and explains that she's definitely having contractions now.

"Okay, that's terrific. You're in labor, Nina. Meet me at the birth center. I'll call Summer and let her know too."

Nina goes out to tell her parents, who immediately turn off the TV and get up when they see her.

"Everything okay?" her dad asks.

Nina tries to smile, though she's nervous about what's happening to her. She remembers all the birthing classes, and if she's honest, she wishes she had Brody here. "I'm fine, but you'll be happy to know it's finally time to go."

Her mom calls Suzy to meet them at the birth center while Nina gets her birthing bag and slips on some flip-flops. Everything around her seems surreal.

The car ride there is surreal too. Nina sits in the front seat while her dad drives her Audi. Her mom is in back. The two of them are bickering over the route to take to get to the birth center while Nina has another contraction and does her best to breathe through it.

As they pull up, her parents continue to argue over where to park.

"You can't park there," her mom says. "Didn't you see the sign?"

"That sign is only for weekdays."

"We don't want the car towed. How are we going to get home?"

"It's *fine*," Nina says, irritated. "Just park anywhere. Let's go inside."

It's almost nine at night. Thankfully, Tula and Summer are already there waiting.

"Nina, how are you?" Summer gives her a hug. "I'm so happy you're in labor." She says hello to Nina's parents.

They head into the birthing room, and Nina sets her bag down and pulls out some of the snacks and drinks she brought. She chats with the midwives and then breathes her way through another contraction. Suzy and Luke arrive soon afterward, and she's glad to see them.

Suzy gives her a hug. "You've got this. I'm here for you, whatever you need."

"Thank you so much for coming."

As she continues to labor and has more contractions, she feels adrift. There's a growing sense of being out of control. She walks around the birth center with Suzy, and when each contraction comes on, her sister holds her hand. But Nina has a hard time centering herself and is on the edge of panic. Her parents are constantly asking her how she's doing, and she knows they mean well, but she wants to tell them to leave. She needs more privacy and peace. But how can she tell them to go without hurting their feelings?

Most of all, she wants Brody.

"How are you, Nina?" Summer asks while Tula listens to the baby's heartbeat. "You seem like you're fighting this, but don't fight it."

"I can't center myself. I'm having trouble staying focused."

Summer nods and studies her with compassion. "What would help?"

But Nina doesn't want to tell her because she has no right to do that.

Summer seems to understand anyway. "My brother?"

Nina glances away and doesn't reply. How can she admit to that? And then it doesn't matter because another contraction has come on, and she tries to get through it without sliding into fear.

There's a roomful of people here to support her, yet somehow she feels alone.

"You're going to her, aren't you?" Kiera says in a flat voice after Brody hangs up the phone and tells her Nina's in labor.

"I am."

She studies him. "For good?"

"Yeah." He grabs his wallet from the nightstand. "I'm sorry, Kiera. For good."

He realizes he wants off this train and never should have gotten on it in the first place.

She sighs and glances around his bedroom. "I don't know why it doesn't work between us anymore. It's not like it used to be, is it?"

"I guess we're not the same people."

He strides out of the bedroom to the front door and quickly puts on his sneakers.

All this time, he thought the reason he didn't marry Kiera was because he was afraid of change.

But he's changed more in this past year than ever.

Maybe he and Kiera were once right for each other, but that time is over, because you can't go back to the person you used to be. You can only move forward. And besides, Brody doesn't want to go back. He's different when he's with Nina. And more importantly, he likes who he is when he's with her.

Trevor jumps up and comes over to him. "Nina's in labor?"

Brody nods. "My sister called." He grabs his car keys and then pats his pockets to make sure he has his wallet and phone.

"You're going to her now?" Trevor looks worried. "Is Nina okay?"

"Summer said she's fine but that I should be there."

Trevor nods. "I think you should too. She's going to need you." He glances at Kiera, who's coming out from the bedroom, and lowers his voice. "You belong with her, cuz. For real."

Brody nods and grips Trevor's shoulder. "I know."

He drives down to the birth center like he's in the final lap of a NASCAR race, constantly checking his rearview mirror for cops.

When he arrives, it's late, after midnight. There are a few cars parked nearby, and the lights are on inside. He sees Nina's Audi and Summer's Toyota.

The front door is locked, but as he's ready to text his sister, she opens it for him.

"I saw your truck pull up," she says. "I'm glad you came. We need the birthing energy to change for Nina."

He nods and follows her inside. The place is empty until he gets to one of the very nice bedrooms in back where everyone seems to be crowded. There's an older couple sitting in some chairs who are obviously Nina's parents. Luke, Suzy's husband, is there. And then finally he sees Nina too. She's standing off to the side of the room with Suzy beside her. Her eyes are closed, and she's breathing hard.

"Who are you?" Nina's father asks when he sees him.

But Brody is focused on Nina. He immediately goes to her side. Suzy seems surprised to see him but then smiles with what looks like relief.

Nina's eyes are still closed, and he realizes she's breathing through a contraction. He takes her hand. They practiced these in their birthing classes, though he suspects practicing something like this and actually experiencing it are miles apart.

Her eyes fly open at his touch, and when he sees the fear and panic in them, it's like a blow to the gut. He never should have left her.

"Brody?" she says in quiet disbelief. "You're here?"

He nods. "I'm here, Nina banana."

"Thank God." She closes her eyes again and squeezes his hand. He knows she's scared, and that this is hard, but they're going to get through it together.

When Nina's contraction is over and her breathing returns to normal, she seems to drink him in. "Summer called you, didn't she?"

"She did."

She smiles. "Thank you for coming."

"You should know that I'm here for good this time. I love you, Nina. And I won't let you push me away ever again."

Her eyes fill with tears. "I love you too. I thought I was doing the right thing, but I was wrong. I was lost without you."

They gaze at each other, and then she's in his arms. He's surrounded by the scent of jasmine, and everything is the way it should be.

When they pull apart, he realizes the whole room is watching them.

"Is that Brody?" Nina's mom asks.

"Yes, Mom," Nina says to her, laughing and wiping her eyes. She's holding his hand again. "This is Brody."

Brody nods to both her parents and says it's nice to meet them.

The midwives seem pleased that he's here, and Summer is beaming.

Despite all the good vibes, the next nine hours turn out to be the longest and most intense of Brody's life. As Nina's labor progresses, he does everything he can to support her. Including asking Luke to take her parents out of there, which they reluctantly agree to. Nina loves them, but he can tell she's having a hard time with them here and that she needs more privacy. More quiet. He's changing the energy, just like Summer said.

Finally, it's just him, Suzy, the midwives, and Nina.

"Thank you," Nina says once her parents and Luke have left. "I'm not sure if I could have done that myself."

"I know. That's why I did it."

Between her contractions, they catch up on their lives. He tells her about the business loan that's currently going through underwriting and then all about Rocket, showing her pictures of the cat on his phone.

"I haven't had a cat since I was a kid," he says. "It's pretty cool."

"He's so cute." Nina admires the photos. "I can't wait to meet him. What a little survivor. He's a stray just like the two of us were."

Brody leans down to kiss her because it's true.

Suzy's mostly hanging out with the midwives, who are in and out of the birthing room, which is nice because it gives them time alone. He's relieved not to see the fear and panic in Nina's eyes that was there earlier. And when they have to stop talking because she has a contraction, Brody rubs her back, patiently helping her.

Eventually the contractions became more intense, more painful, and closer together, so Nina gets in the birthing tub. Brody takes his shirt off and stays beside her, wishing he'd brought some swim trunks.

They check the baby's heartbeat regularly. When Nina feels the urge to push, she stays in the water for a while longer but then decides she's too uncomfortable and gets out.

The midwives set up something called a birthing stool. She sits on it and starts to push with each contraction, with everyone encouraging her.

It goes on for a long time, and Brody understands why they call all of this labor, because from what he can tell, it's damn hard work.

"You're doing great," Tula keeps telling her. "Almost there."

Summer and Suzy are the cheerleading section, telling her how she's getting closer and will be meeting baby Elsa soon.

Nina is obviously exhausted but still hanging in there as Brody rubs her shoulders and tells her she's amazing.

After about two hours of pushing, she says she feels a burning sensation.

"That's because your baby is crowning," Tula and Summer both tell her.

There's more pushing, and Nina's vocalizations are getting loud, so loud that Brody is sweating and trying to stay calm. It's hard seeing Nina in so much pain.

And then, before he knows it, there's a new little person in the room.

He can barely believe it. Nina's holding the baby while the midwives do their thing, and then there's a cry of sound from that first breath.

Brody's eyes tear up with relief and joy. Their lives have changed forever.

"Congratulations," Tula says. "You guys have a handsome little boy."

"What?" Nina laughs. "I have a boy? Are you kidding?"

Brody chuckles. "I always knew I was right."

Suzy grins. "Well, I don't think you should name him Elsa, but that's just my opinion."

"Is Bullet still on the table?" Brody jokes as they're all admiring the newborn.

Nina leans against him and has another contraction for the afterbirth. Once that's finished, Brody takes the baby in his arms as everyone helps guide Nina so she can rest in bed.

He looks into the sweetest face ever. "Hey there, little Bullet."

"We're *not* naming him Bullet," Nina says from over on the bed. "Don't even think about it."

"How about a family nickname?"

She smiles. "Maybe."

Suzy comes over to him, admiring the baby. "He's beautiful. It's hard to believe we were all once this small and helpless, isn't it?"

Brody brings little Bullet back over to Nina so the midwives can show her how to nurse him. He goes over to the window and draws back the curtain. Daylight washes over him as he takes in the mundane scene outside with parked cars, trees, and pedestrians. Except everything looks different, brand-new, and he knows he'll never be the same again. This night has changed him.

Eventually he goes over to check on Nina and the baby, gazing down at them both. He remembers how he once felt lost at sea, hoping for the calm of land in the distance. Well, he's finally found that land, and it's right in front of him.

Nina glances up and smiles. "What do you think of Jake? That was one of the names we both liked."

He sits down next to her on the bed and nods. "It's a good one. No one's going to mess with a Jake."

"Then Jake it is," she says, softly stroking the baby's cheek.

Brody takes in the sight of the two of them, and he's never been so at peace. He's run the gamut of human emotions in the last twelve hours, and he should be worn out. But when he gazes at Nina and his new family, all he feels is love.

EPILOGUE

I t's a summer day when Brody asks Nina to marry him. Their son, Jake, is a year old. He's a great little kid, always curious and quick with a smile, and, to Brody's delight, is obsessed with cars.

They've come up to the rez for the weekend and are staying with Aunt Jeanie and Uncle Mitch, who are babysitting, while Brody takes Nina for a walk.

He purposefully bought her here to Angel Lake, one of his

favorite places. If he's going to ask Nina to be his wife, this is where he wants it to happen.

"What are you doing?" Nina asks when Brody gets down on one knee.

He fumbles with the ring box, which is stuck in his pocket, and he can't seem to remove it. "I'm proposing to you if I can get this ring out of my pocket."

She's wearing a bemused expression. "What are you really doing?"

Finally he manages to retrieve it, and when Nina sees the box, her eyes widen. "Oh wow, you *are* serious."

He grins at her. "Of course I am. Why do you think I brought you here?"

She glances around at the lake and the peaceful surroundings. Amazingly, they have it all to themselves. "I didn't know," she murmurs.

"I'm going to do this the right way, Nina banana. Are you ready?"

"Okay." She straightens her shoulders and grins. "I'm ready." And when she gazes at him with those sky eyes, he feels blessed in every way.

"Nina Ellis, will you marry me?" He opens the ring box.

She nods. "Yes, I will, Brody Austin. I would love to marry you."

He chuckles. "Good." Instead of standing up, he pulls her down onto the grass and rolls her on top of him.

"Hey!" She squeals with laughter. "What's happening? This isn't the proper way!"

He smirks. "Who said anything about being proper?"

They study each other in the afternoon sunshine. His whole life is surrounded by sunshine these days. Brody slides his hand down her back and then cups her ass. "Kiss me, my future wife. Looks like I'm definitely putting a label on this relationship."

She laughs but then quiets down and kisses him. "That was a pretty great proposal," she says.

"I'm pleased you think so."

"Now let me see that ring. What happened to it?"

He turns his head. "It's over here somewhere. I put it on the grass." He sees the box a couple feet away and reaches for it.

They both sit up beside each other, and he opens the box and hands it to her.

"Oooh, that's gorgeous. I love it."

Brody's glad. He didn't know a damn thing about buying an engagement ring. It's not a huge stone, but it's not tiny either. "Suzy helped me pick it out. She said you wouldn't like anything too ostentatious."

Nina nods. "She's right."

"Shall I put it on your finger?"

"Okay."

Brody pulls the platinum engagement ring out of the box and slips it onto Nina's finger. She holds her hand out, admiring it.

"It's perfect," she says with a smile before turning to kiss him softly. "Just like you."

Nina had a feeling Brody was going to propose. Not by the lake today, but she sensed there was something in the air. He was asking too many what-if questions about weddings and honeymoons, trying to act nonchalant while asking her, "What if we got married? Where would you picture it happening?" Or "What if we had a honeymoon? Where would you want to go?"

They walk back to Jeanie and Mitch's house holding hands, and she's amazed at her life. Two years ago, when she was still with Noel, if someone had told her this is what it would look like today, she never would have believed them.

All the hang-ups she used to have about Brody being younger than her seem silly and inconsequential now. Because in the end, it's who we love that matters. The everyday is what's real, and she's been so blessed because every day is filled with the people she loves.

Thunder comes over for dinner at Jeanie and Mitch's that evening. Introductions are made, and Nina shakes his hand for the first time. She's glad to see he looks so much better and healthier than the last time she saw him.

"I brought a present for Jake," he says with a grin, holding a box wrapped in brightly colored kid's paper. "Brody told me he likes cars, so I figured he'd enjoy one of these too."

They sit on the floor and help Jake tear the paper off. Inside is a toy truck, which he immediately starts pushing around.

"Thank you." Nina smiles up at Thunder. "What a thoughtful gift."

It's pretty clear Thunder has no memory of ever meeting her on Christmas Day last year, and she's glad for that. Because Brody was right. His father is a completely different person when he's sober.

Over dinner, they announce their engagement, and everyone congratulates them. Brody describes to his family what it's been like opening the second location for Seattle Motor Works, and while there's been a lot involved, so far the shop is doing well.

She can tell Thunder is really proud of Brody. They all are.

Trevor didn't come with them on this trip, but he's doing great too. He moved out of the house and has gotten his own apartment. He's still dating Anka and has even gone down to Olympia to stay with her family a few times. Nina's not sure what their long-term plans are, but for now they're happy. The two of them drop by all the time, and Brody and Nina are always delighted to see them.

After dinner, Nina gives Jake a bath and then puts him to bed in the travel crib Brody set up last night. Jake started walking recently, so that's been a new adventure all its own.

"How's he doing?" Brody comes up beside her.

"Good. I think all this activity and fresh air up here has worn him out. It didn't take much to get him down."

He nods and gazes at their sleeping son.

In the past year, Brody has proven to be a great dad. And Nina knows there's no one else she'd rather be co-parenting with.

She's only heard from Noel once. It was right after the birth, when he texted her from Malaysia. Apparently he quit his job at Tolland and has decided to go "find himself." He at least had his lawyer set up monthly child support payments.

It's obvious now that Noel doesn't intend to be a part of Jake's life, and that's okay, but in her mind Nina hasn't closed that door completely. She knows most children want to meet their biological parents. Brody agrees, since he's been through it himself, and they decided if Noel wants to have contact with Jake in the future, they won't discourage it.

"I showed Thunder pictures of the Zephyr," Brody tells her later when they're in bed talking quietly. "I might drive it up here or have him come down to Seattle to see it. I don't know how long the current sobriety is going to last."

She takes his hand. "I know. And I'm sure he'll enjoy seeing that car." Nina has also fallen in love with the Zephyr. Brody finished it, and a few times now they've gotten her parents to babysit so they could go out for dinner and then cruise around town. She felt like a movie star. Brody even let her drive and managed not to freak out too much. Nina's decided cars aren't quite as boring as she thought.

Her parents officially moved back from Portugal last fall and bought a house near Green Lake in Seattle. They're close enough to see all their grandkids regularly and are enjoying doing some remodeling on the new place.

Brody's parents are also doing well. Nina's gotten to know them better and has noticed that Lisa seems a lot friendlier toward her these days. And even though Jake isn't her biological grandchild, both she and Kurt treat him like he is.

Right after Jake was born, Nina moved in with Brody and has been there ever since. She kept her condo with its gorgeous view though and has turned it into an Airbnb. It's been a great arrangement, since she didn't want to sell it, and the three of them still get to use it for the occasional weekend getaway.

They've also let Summer stay there a few times. She's still at the birth center working as a midwife and has started taking on her own clients now. She's still seeing Jackson, though there's been a plot twist, because an ex-boyfriend she once had strong feelings for has come back into her life.

Speaking of exes, Brody heard from his mom that Kiera moved to Arizona and was back together with her fiancé. The two are once again planning to get married. Apparently they worked through their problems.

Nina is no longer obsessed with hot sauce. In fact, she hasn't used hot sauce on anything even once since she gave birth. Brody says he misses those crazy food days.

Besides Rocket, she and Brody have also adopted a dog. They got him from the animal shelter where Tori volunteers. He's an older mixed breed dog named Watson, with a gentle way about him, and as soon as Nina heard his name, she knew it was destiny. They worried Rocket wouldn't like it, but surprisingly the two of them have become friends.

"I noticed you brought your guitar," Nina says to Brody. "Does that mean you're going to play for everyone while we're here?"

"I just might." He smiles. "I've been learning some Neil Young songs for Aunt Jeanie. He's one of her favorite musicians."

"Darn it," Nina says. "I should have brought my bagpipes. I could try playing a duet with you." She started taking lessons recently. It's a little weird because she isn't Scottish, but who cares?

Brody grows evasive. "Ah, yeah. Sure, maybe next time."

"I tried to play my bagpipes for Suzy and my parents last week, but all three of them had some kind of sudden emergency and left. Isn't that weird?"

He doesn't reply.

"It's almost like they didn't want to hear me play, but that can't be right."

Brody is suspiciously silent.

"You like my bagpipes, don't you?"

He shrugs. "What's not to like?"

"I played them for Piper, and she said it sounded like someone was being murdered."

Brody cracks up.

"Do you think that's true?"

"I'm sure you'll improve with time. The important thing is you're having fun."

Nina watches him closely. "Maybe I should play them for our wedding. That might be a nice surprise for everyone."

Brody chuckles. "It'll definitely be a surprise." He wraps his arms around her, drawing her in close. "Whatever you want to do is fine by me. As long as we're together, Nina banana, I know we'll be happy."

<u>The End</u>

AUTHOR'S NOTE

Thank you so much for reading Nina and Brody's story! I hope you enjoyed it. I loved writing about those two. They were so different, yet somehow they brought out the best in each other.

The sixth book in the Sweet Life in Seattle series will be Summer's story. In the meantime, you might like to read some of my other books. (See the next two pages.)

I love hearing from my readers. If you'd like to contact me, you can find me at my website andreasimonne.com or drop me an email at authorsimonne@gmail.com.

If you enjoyed this book, please consider telling a friend about it or leaving a review or rating. I'd appreciate it very much.

With so many book choices out there, thank you for choosing one of mine.

xo,
Andrea

SWEET LIFE IN SEATTLE SERIES

Don't miss book #6 in the Sweet Life in Seattle Series!

Find out what happens when, after tens years, Summer encounters the biker bad boy she was once in love with...

Order WILD KIND OF WONDERFUL today!

MORE BOOKS

Nina is a small side character in the first romance I ever published. A steamy standalone called FIRE DOWN BELOW.

Still single and just turned thirty-five, Kate finds herself engaged to one man, while obsessing about another...

Order FIRE DOWN BELOW today!

ABOUT LOVE SERIES

Read the first book in my About Love series!

Discover what happens when a billionaire agrees to help his awkward cousin win the girl of his dreams, but then accidentally falls in love with her himself...

Read TRUTH ABOUT MEN & DOGS today!

NEWSLETTER SIGN UP

Be the first to hear about new releases! Sign up for my newsletter and get a FREE gift!

Would you like a collection of recipes from the Sweet Life in Seattle series? Natalie and Blair have put together some of their favorites in LA DOLCE VITA FAVORITE RECIPES. (Includes Natalie's favorite chocolate chip cookie and Tiramisu recipes!)

I'm gifting FREE ebook copies to everyone who joins my mailing list.

If you're interested, please click or type the following link into your web browser: BookHip.com/NZSZBW

ALSO BY ANDREA SIMONNE

Sweet Life in Seattle series
Year of Living Blonde
Return of the Jerk
Some Like It Hotter
Object of My Addiction
Too Much Like Love
Wild Kind of Wonderful

About Love series
Truth About Men & Dogs
Truth About Cats & Spinsters
Truth About Nerds & Bees

Other
Fire Down Below

ABOUT THE AUTHOR

Andrea Simonne grew up as an army brat and discovered she had a talent for creating personas at each new school. The most memorable was a surfer chick named "Ace" who never touched a surfboard in her life but had an impressive collection of puka shell necklaces. Andrea still enjoys creating personas though now they occupy her books. She's an Amazon best seller in romantic comedy and contemporary romance, and author of the Sweet Life in Seattle series and About Love series. She currently makes her home in the Pacific Northwest with her husband and two sons.

She loves hearing from her readers. You can find her on the web at www.andreasimonne.com.

Email: authorsimonne@gmail.com.

Made in United States
Cleveland, OH
20 November 2024